FIRE FROM ASHES

HONOR & DUTY 4

SAM SCHALL

Copyright © 2018 by Amanda S. Green (writing as Sam Schall).

Hunter's Moon Press

Print ISBN: 978-1-949901-03-0

E-Book ISBN: 978-1-949901-04-7

Cover art: Spaceship Warp Celtic copyright © by Luca Oleastri.

If you enjoyed this novel, please visit Nocturnal-Lives.com for more titles.

❀ Created with Vellum

To those authors who believe in paying it forward and who have been there to help me along the way. You know who you are and you have my everlasting gratitude and love.

FIRE FROM ASHES

Fire burns dishonor.
Duty avenges betrayal

Fubar

1

Crocket's Landing
Tenasic System

"Incoming!"

Dirt and debris filled the air as another mortar round exploded mere yards from where they huddled behind what might euphemistically be called cover. Lieutenant Colonel Lucinda Ortega ignored the inventive cursing of some of her Marines. Instead, she ordered them to sound off. That blast had been a bit too close for comfort. Not that the others had been much better.

"Someone get me a location for that mortar!" she ordered as she flipped through her visors various filters, studying the area around them.

Damn it, this mission had gone to Hell in the proverbial hand basket almost from the moment they landed. At least they'd managed to clear the shuttle before a mortar hit it. Not that it meant much in the grand scheme of things. Her Marines might have made it off, but most of their equipment had still been onboard. Worse, they weren't going to get any support from topside until they managed to take down the controls for the defense platforms. Assuming they managed to find a way through the no man's land they found themselves in.

"Sorceress, we can't stay here much longer," Master Sergeant M. J. Anderson said as she moved to her CO's side.

Ortega nodded. "I know, Reaper." She blew out a breath. "Answer me this. The enemy's had us pinned down for more than two hours. Why haven't they moved in?"

Even as she asked, she knew one possible answer. By holding their troops back, they prevented the Fuerconese Marines from picking them off. This area might be a no man's land for the Marines, but it could quickly become one for the Callusian invaders as well. That might be why their commander continued to rely on his artillery. Still, it didn't make any sense. By continuing this line of attack, it gave the rest of the Warlords time to get into position to flank them.

Not that it mattered much if the enemy managed to zero in on them before then. If they did, it would be over for Alpha Company. There wasn't enough cover to hide behind. All it would take was a few good hits and there would be little for their fellow Warlords to find and return to the home system. Not that she had any intention of allowing that to happen.

"Wish I knew, Sorceress." Anderson's concern, as well as more than a little curiosity, about the enemy's tactics was clear. "Orders?"

"Tell the heavies to be ready to move on my signal. If we have a drone left, I want it up. We need eyes on them yesterday."

The master sergeant nodded and moved off, crouching low to the ground. As she did, Ortega closed her eyes, thinking hard.

Damn it!

Praying she wasn't about to make a fatal mistake, Ortega carefully shifted positions. She dropped to her belly and inched toward the edge of the barricade. Barricade! What a laugh. For the last ten minutes, she had crouched behind a pile of rubble, part of what had once been a single-story building. As she did, she reached over her shoulder for her sniper rifle. For not the first time, she thanked whoever decided Marine armor should default to black unless its camo capabilities were activated. With the twin suns of the planet below the horizon, that meant the enemy would have to be checking with infrared to be able to see her.

Unfortunately, that also meant she couldn't see anything without using her own filters. Even then, her field of vision was limited. Even so, a little was better than nothing.

For several long moments, she ignored Adamson's demands that she get back under cover. Instead, she scanned the area. A slight smile touched her lips as she caught sight of an enemy foolish enough to show himself. With a precision that would have impressed her Academy instructors, she carefully squeezed the trigger and watched as he fell to the ground a few seconds later. Then she continued her scan, looking for something, anything that would help them break out of this trap they'd found themselves in.

"Sorceress, if you don't get your ass behind cover, I'm going to drag you back," Adamson growled over a private channel. "We can't risk you, damn it."

Ortega didn't respond. Adamson was right. The Warlords lost their previous CO in an ambush a few months earlier. Even though Paul Pawlak hadn't been with them for long, Ortega knew from personal experience that he'd been the kind of CO who quickly earned a division's loyalty. His death, as well as the deaths of those with him, had rocked the battalion. When she and Adamson arrived to take command, they'd found Marines hurting and in need of a commanding officer who could not only lead them but who could gain their trust and respect. She'd worked hard to be that CO. She'd be damned if she did anything to set them back now.

Besides, she'd seen what she needed to. Safely back behind her barricade of rubble, she sat up. One part of her brain listened as her company commanders reported in. Some called for medics. Others called for fresh battery packs or ammo. Others reported on enemy troop movement. Not that there was much along that line to report. It seemed each of the companies faced a situation similar to her own.

And it made no sense.

Somehow, she had to figure out a way to break her company free and quickly, before it was too late.

"Wraith, Sorceress," she commed. "Report."

"Sorceress, Wraith. Enemy dug in at two. No change in status."

She produced her datapad and pulled up the drop zone map. For several long moments, she studied it. Nothing about the map matched what they'd dropped into except the geography. Troop placements weren't where they were supposed to be. Defenses the enemy shouldn't have had time to build were in place. Someone had fucked up and badly. If she lived through this, she'd make it her personal mission to find out who and make them pay. Every Marine she lost, every one of her Marines injured, would be avenged.

Risking not only her master sergeant's ire but an enemy projectile, she once again looked around the edge of her cover. Filters flipped from one to another as she scanned the area. Instinct and training. That's what she had to rely on. Her own and as well as that of the rest of the battalion. They might not be the Devil Dogs but, by God, they were almost as good. They would not let the enemy win. Not here and not now.

Ooh-rah!

"Reaper, I want Tusker and Bird here on the double. Falcon and Eagle are to get ready to soar," she ordered as she ducked back behind the pile of rubble.

"Roger that," the master sergeant replied before relaying her orders. A moment later, Ortega heard the soft *beep* that signaled Anderson had once again switched to a private channel. "Sorceress, would you mind telling me what you have going on in that warped mind of yours?"

Despite the seriousness of their situation, Ortega chuckled softly. "I might enlighten you if you get over here ASAP." She ended the comm and closed her eyes, hoping she wasn't about to make the biggest mistake of her career.

Less than five minutes later, the heavy weapons specialist and comms specialist she had sent for slid to a halt in front of her. Adamson came next, followed closely by several others. Ortega nodded once, not at all surprised the master sergeant had added Captain Ross Halverson, her exec, or Sergeant Tariq Benton, the next senior non-com in the company. Without speaking, Ortega motioned for them to gather round. As they did, she active her data pad once again. A 3-D map of the area appeared above it. She entered a few corrections and waited as the image adapted to the changes. As it did, she sat back on her heels.

"We'll have time later to discuss what went wrong." She shook her head before any of the others could say anything. "For now, our ships are getting pounded. They don't have a chance if we can't get the defense platforms off-line."

"You have a plan?" Adamson asked, her tone indicating she knew the answer and also knew she wasn't going to like it.

"I do." She tapped in a command and the map focused in on their position. "The enemy has held here." She highlighted the area. "For the last half hour. They're showing no indication of moving. It might be the dark. It might be they are waiting for reinforcements. Whatever it is, we aren't going to sit here waiting for them to make a move."

"What do you have in mind?" Halverson asked.

She tapped in a command and the map image adjusted to show a wider area. "A fire team is going to move out and take the high ground here." A red dot indicated the target zone. "That will give Tusker a clear shot at the enemy location. Bird will paint the targets for him. Once the team opens fire, I want the rest of the company pressing forward. We have to break out of this mess now."

For a moment, no one said anything. Then Anderson glanced up, her expression hard. "Sorceress, you aren't planning on taking this little walk with Bird and Tusker, are you?"

"Can you name a better sniper in the company to go along?"

She knew the answer and knew Anderson wouldn't like it. But they had both served under not only Pawlak but Ashlyn Shaw. That taught them a CO did whatever she had to in order to get her people home safely while still fulfilling her mission. Not that it would prevent Anderson from giving her an earful later.

"Tag and Zen will go as well," Anderson said, her expression warning Ortega not to object. "Your plan?"

For the next ten minutes, Ortega laid it out, listening to their comments and amending the plan on the fly. She knew this was their best chance of success. If they failed, she would have no choice but to contact the taskforce commander and tell him to withdraw from the system, stranding the Marines dirtside. That was one call she had no intention of making. This had to work. If it did, not only would they finally be able to move against the groundside controls for the defense platforms, but they could call in air support once the platforms were down.

"Sorceress, you need to stay here," Halverson said once she finished the briefing. "I'll go in your place."

For a moment, Ortega said nothing. She saw the worry in the captain's eyes and understood. He'd been with Pawlak on that last mission. Pawlak had chosen to lead the charge against an enemy encampment, not realizing they had reinforcements hidden nearby. Pawlak and every Marine with him had perished. When she rendezvoused with the taskforce to take command of the battalion, Admiral Wu, Fourth Fleet's commanding officer, warned that her XO blamed himself for not stopping Pawlak. That guilt shone through once again and she had to put a stop to it.

"Snapper, I have to go and you know it. I'm sorry, but you're not a sniper and that's what we need on the fire team." She laid her hand on his shoulder, hoping she found the right words to not only reassure him but get through his guilt. If she couldn't trust him to take command if she fell, she might as well signal their surrender now. "You know our Marines. More importantly, they know you. If something does happen to me, I need you to take command and make sure those platforms come down. But I promise, nothing's going to happen. That's why we're going up high. I want to rain our vengeance down on these bastards. I want to make them pay for Hammer and the others. That means I need you and the rest of the company to give us cover until we're in position. You can and will do this, Marine."

"Ooh-rah, Sorceress."

"Ooh-rah, Snapper." She pounded her fist lightly against his chest and gave a jerk of her head to dismiss him. "Stick close to him, Reaper," she added over the private channel.

"I will." Adamson paused and motioned the others to give them some space. "I swear to God, Luce, if anything happens to you, I'll kill you. Then I'll contact Angel, tell her what happened and watch as she figures out a way to resurrect you just so she can then beat you senseless." Her eyes flashed, and Ortega chuckled softly.

"You just take care of the company for me, MJ." She glanced around and then gave her friend's hand a quick squeeze. "If I don't make it back, find out what the hell happened. Our intel shouldn't have been this wrong. It couldn't have been. Not without someone purposefully feeding us wrong information."

Anderson said nothing. Instead, she nodded once. That was enough to let Ortega know the master sergeant agreed with her, at least when it came to the reasons behind their current situation. More than that, she could trust Anderson to do as she asked.

"Just remember, you have one duty right now, ma'am. That is to come back to the battalion. It can't take losing a second CO so soon and I sure as hell don't want to be the one to tell Angel something happened to you." With that, Anderson promised to make sure everything would be ready by the time she moved out.

Alone, Ortega closed her eyes and offered up a quick prayer. She didn't like her plan any more than Adamson did. But what choice did she have? She had a duty to save as many of her Marines as possible. More importantly, she had a duty to take down the defense platform controls. That would help save the taskforce ships and that, in turn, would help drive the enemy off-planet. Honor and duty demanded she do whatever it took to fulfill her orders and complete her mission.

She glanced around, watching as her orders were quickly relayed to the rest of the company. Soon those orders would go out over the battlenet to the rest of the division. Hopefully the diversion she and the rest of the fire time caused would be enough to help the others break free as well. There was one thing left for her to do.

Three minutes later, she ended the recording and input the order to send it should anything happen to her. Before making the drop dirtside, she'd dictated a message for her family. In some ways, this one was more difficult. But she wanted to make sure someone she trusted to look into the breakdown in their intel knew what happened. She had no doubt Ashlyn Shaw would do everything possible to get answers – just as she had almost five years before when Shaw and others had been brought up on charges following a mission that now looked too much like her own current mission.

"Ready?" she asked the four who would accompany her?

They now crouched behind a makeshift barricade of rubble, shuttle debris and other things best left unnamed. Each of them carried more weapons than the regs required. She had no doubt they, like her, had added to their usual loads. Good. They couldn't risk running out of ammo or losing comms to the rest of the company. Now all they had to worry about was getting to the target safely.

They nodded.

"We'll move out one by one. I know I don't have to say it but make yourselves small, stick to the shadows and use what cover you can."

"Tag, you have lead," Adamson said from where she knelt next to Ortega. "Zen, you are on Sorceress. Stick to her and make sure she makes it to the target. Tusker, you bring up the rear."

"Roger that, Reaper," the heavy weapons specialist replied.

"Then let's do this." Ortega reached over her left shoulder and pulled her battle rifle. She checked its load and watched as the others followed suit. Then she turned her attention back to Adamson. "If there is any change in the enemy's status, comm me. Otherwise, you have my orders."

"Understood, Sorceress." Adamson nodded to each member of the fire team. "First round once we've got liberty is on me. Good hunting."

Slowly, carefully, they moved out. Keeping low, Ortega waited until Tag signaled the all clear. The moment he did, she raced across a clearing that suddenly seemed much larger than it had moments before. As she did, she swept the area, her rifle at the ready. Then she slid to a stop in the shadows of the narrow alley running between two of the very few buildings still standing. She gave a quick nod to Zen as the private slid to a halt at her side.

A tap on her shoulder came at the same time Tag's voice over the fireteam's 'net. "Movement," he said softly before reading off the coordinates.

Ortega switched her battle rifle for her sniper rifle. As she did, she dropped to one knee. With Zen at her shoulder, she focused on the coordinates Tag called out. Her implants kicked in, slowing her pulse and breathing. Eyesight sharpened, and the sights of the rifle synced with her ocular implant.

There!

One corner of her mouth twisted up in a parody of a smile. She waited, wanting to be sure of her target. The battle-hardened veteran in her knew she should take the shot before they were spotted. But she had to be sure. There was a chance, small though it might be, that the figure wasn't one of the enemy. All she needed was for it to step into the light.

Come on, take another step this way. Give me a better look at you.

"Now, Sorceress!" Zen said softly.

Sniper rifle snugged against her shoulder, Ortega gently squeezed the trigger. She watched through the scope as the projectile severed the soldier's spine at the base of his neck. He dropped where he stood. Ortega waited, scanning the area for any indication the Callusian foot soldier hadn't been alone.

"Tag, Bird, you've got retrieval. We'll cover."

Zen and Tusker moved to take up positions that left Ortega between and slightly behind them. As they did, Tag and Bird slowly picked their way across what might once have been a small park or greenway. Ortega watched through her rifle's scope, scanning the area. The last thing she wanted was for more of the enemy to come upon them and catch them unaware.

"Sorceress, Bird. We're in place."

"Roger that, Bird. Strip out his weapons and anything else you can carry. Leave ID if he has any but make note of it. Then hide the body. Let's not get sloppy now."

The comms specialist acknowledged the order. As she watched him doing as she said, Tusker on look-out, Ortega listened to reports coming in over the battlenet. Rear Admiral Kieran O'Malley, commanding officer of Taskforce Liberator, wanted a status update. Unfortunately, she didn't have one for him. Even if she did, she couldn't risk the enemy intercepting their comms. At least Halverson, possibly with input from Adamson, knew how to respond. All she had to do was make sure the fireteam got into position before the enemy discovered what they were up to.

Five minutes later, they were on the move again. Tag and Bird returned to their positions in the formation. Zen now carried what they had confiscated from the dead Callusian. Later, assuming there was a later, Ortega would examine what they found. For now, however, it had to wait. They still had a great deal of territory to cover and she wanted it done before the sun came up. Once that happened, they'd be caught in the middle of a no man's land. That had to be avoided at all costs. So much depended on them getting to their destination before the enemy knew what they planned.

For more than an hour, the fireteam crept further and further away from the rest of the company. Not that it stopped the reports from coming in or muted the sounds of battle. The battlenet saw to that. Ortega listened in, occasionally clarifying an order or making a suggestion on a private channel to Halverson and Adamson. Even as she did, she reminded herself she needed to focus on the task at hand. Halverson and Adamson were more than capable of keeping the rest of the company safe, at least as long as the enemy didn't try to overrun their position. The best thing she, and the rest of the fireteam, could do was reach their goal. Fortunately, they were almost there.

Tag dropped to one knee and lifted his left fist, signaling everyone to stop. Ortega repeated the signal. She waited until the others dropped to a knee. They turned outward, weapons ready, watching all approaches. Trusting them to warn her if anyone – or anything –

approached, Ortega silently moved to where Tag knelt, his attention focused on the area directly in front of them.

"There's your target, Sorceress." He nodded to several buildings approximately one hundred yards from where they knelt. "Optimum position is the first building."

She studied the buildings, doing her best not to let her emotions show. They waited at the edge of what had once been a thriving commercial center. Most of it was now a smoldering pile of rubble. In the time since the Callusians invaded the system, they had followed their normal order of battle. After either destroying or taking over military installations, they moved on to planetary infrastructure. Because the system had done its best to hold out, the invaders had taken to bombarding the capital in an attempt to force a surrender. The government had gone underground. Most of the survivors in the capital had fled. Those who hadn't had been killed or captured by the invaders. But the survivors had continued the fight, keeping the enemy focused on the capital instead of the rest of the planet.

Not that it helped them just then. The building Ortega targeted as the best location to begin their part of the op looked as if it might not remain standing if it took another artillery hit. Hell, she wasn't sure it would remain standing once they started making their way to the rooftop. Unfortunately, the other building looked to be in even worse condition and none of the remaining buildings in the area would give the vantage point she wanted or needed.

"Bird, let Snapper know we are about to move into position. We're going dark until we have."

Trusting the comms specialist to do as instructed, she scanned the area between them and the building. There was too much open space and too little cover. Their best bet in case the enemy had eyes on the area was to make a run for it and cross the open area as quickly as possible.

"Tag, you have point again. Same order of advancement as before," she said as Bird ended the transmission to Halverson. "Keep an eye out but hit the building without stopping. That's an order.

Once inside, find us a way to the roof. We move, and we move quickly. Questions?"

"You keep between us, Sorceress," Bird told her. The others nodded in agreement.

"Let's move out."

Tag took another moment to scan the area in front of them. He gave a quick thumbs up. Then he shouldered his rifle and rose to a crouch. Ortega watched as he took off, moving quickly in a zigzag across the open area. She waited, knowing at any moment a shot could ring out. The fact they hadn't spotted the enemy nearby didn't mean there wasn't a sniper in position keeping watch. Or a drone. Until they were all inside, she couldn't relax.

One by one, they raced across the clearing. By the time Tusker slid to a halt inside the building, Ortega had the others looking for the quickest route to the roof. Now they were in for the long slog. With the power out, they had no choice but to climb. The only question was whether they could use the stairs all the way or if they would have to improvise. Either way, it was going to take time and, as tempting as it was to simply race upstairs, they had to go carefully. They had to make sure they weren't walking into an ambush along the way.

"Zen, you have point. Bird, you get the rear. If we run into trouble, let Snapper know and extract. Zen, give Bird the goods." She watched as Zen handed over the items taken from the fallen Callusian soldier. "Let's get it done."

After what seemed like hours, Ortega watched as Zen and Tag forced open the door leading to the roof. While the rest of them waited, weapons aimed either at the doorway or down the stairs, Tag cleared the roof. When he signaled the all clear, Ortega was the first out the door. Instantly, she dropped to her stomach. As she did, she cursed softly. The damage up here was worse than what they'd encountered on the slow climb up. The roof was pitted from mortar fire. The parapet around the roof, the architectural feature she hoped would make it harder for the enemy to spot them, was missing. In fact, much of the roof and wall on that side of the building was gone.

"Bird, Tusker, you're with me. Zen, Tag, hang back."

She slid her battle rifle into place across her back. Then she slowly, carefully crawled across the roof. Her breath caught and her pulse pounded as the surface seemed to groan under her weight. Instantly, she signaled the others back. If the rooftop was going to give way, better it be under just one of them. At least that's what she told herself.

Inch by inch, she crossed what was left of the roof. Over some debris and then down, sliding feet first, to the next level where the roof collapsed. She might have her doubts about the stability of the building, but she approved of this location. Unlike the partial roof above, this floor offered at least a modicum of cover from anyone who might look her way from ground level.

Crouched next to what had once been a window, Ortega scanned the area below. Then she lifted her sniper rifle. Once again, she scanned the area. She felt a moment's relief to see the enemy had yet to change position. She didn't understand why, but she wasn't going to complain. At least this way she didn't have to recalculate for their strike or change locations. Hopefully, their luck would hold a little bit longer.

As the others took up positions, Ortega continued to watch the enemy. Between the building where they perched, readying to signal the rest of the company to move, and the enemy's location was a dead zone. How different it looked now than it had a mere month ago. Then it had been alive and prosperous. Even this late at night, people would have been coming and going from the entertainment sectors. Others would have been working the night shift or preparing to head in for the morning. Then the Callusians invaded. Now much of the city lay in ruins. How many had died in the last month? Ortega didn't know and knew she couldn't focus on that, not yet. Just as she couldn't think about all those who had died throughout the system as the Callusians ran through it. All she could do was make sure they recaptured the remaining defense systems, taking them off-line so the taskforce could finally close in on the enemy ships and deal with them.

"How long, Tusker?" she asked as she lined up her shot.

"Two minutes."

She nodded. She marked her first shot, then her second and third. By the time she managed those, she knew the enemy camp would be alive and moving. Everything after that would have to be done on the fly. But it would be enough. It had to be.

"Reaper, Sorceress."

"Go for Reaper."

"Get ready."

That was it. She didn't dare say more in case the enemy somehow managed to intercept the signal. But it would be enough. She and Anderson had been through too many battles not to understand one another. Anderson would relay the message to Halverston and then she'd get the company ready. Now it was up to her and the rest of the fire team.

"On my second shot, Tusker. Bird, light his target."

Ortega said a silent prayer. Then she opened her eyes and once again focused on her first target. *Inhale. Exhale. Let the heart slow*. As she did, she felt more than saw the others preparing to take their own shots. She flicked through her HUD's filters, verifying her data. Then, just before squeezing the trigger, she sent confirmation to Anderson. The battle was about to turn — she hoped.

A split-second later, her target's chest exploded. Even before his knees buckled, she shifted her sites to the second target and then the third. By the time she zeroed in on a fourth, Tusker began his assault. A grim smile touched Ortega's lips as she watched the enemy camp turn into a mass of turmoil.

"Reaper, move in! I say again, move in!"

Immediately, hell rained down on the enemy position as heavy weapons from the rest of the company came to life. She continued to carefully select her targets, picking them off one by one. At the same time, reports came in over the battlenet as not only Alpha Company, but the rest of the battalion as well, began a fresh push against the enemy.

"Movement at two o'clock," Bird reported. At the same time, he painted the new target for Tusker, ready in case Ortega gave the order to open fire.

Ortega glanced to her right. She fired off three quick shots, hitting two targets. Three others broke for cover. She cursed and began scanning for them. They couldn't be allowed to break out.

"Tag, Zen, new positions. Don't let anyone get past us."

"Sorceress, Reaper."

"Go, Reaper." She sighted another target and fired.

"Moving to forward position. Sending you reinforcements once in place." The sounds of weapon fire almost drowned out Adamson's words.

"Secure the target first. I repeat. Secure all targets."

For a moment, Adamson said nothing. "Watch yourself, Sorceress."

"Always," she replied and switched channels to let Admiral O'Malley know their status.

———

J. W. Campbell, flagship
Taskforce Liberator
Tenasic System

"REPORT!"

Rear Admiral Kieran O'Malley clung to the arms of his command chair as the *Campbell* rocked under another wave of enemy fire. This time, however, he had the satisfaction of knowing the ships under his command were no longer at a disadvantage. Somehow – and, at the moment, he didn't care how – the Marines on the surface had finally managed to break through. They might not have taken command of the defense platform controls yet, but the distraction they created worked in the taskforce's favor. At least he hoped so. If not. . ..

He wouldn't think about that.

"Admiral, message coming in from. Colonel Ortega."

Relief he didn't dare show filled O'Malley as he turned to the comms officer. The young lieutenant had held up well during the battle, as had all the bridge crew. If they made it through this – and, by God, he'd do everything possible to make sure they did –he would be recommending each of them for commendations. They had done themselves, the Navy and Fuercon proud.

"Put it on my screen."

He glanced at the screen and waited as it changed from the ship's insignia to Ortega's image. The woman's armor looked as if she'd been caught, and buried, under a ton of debris. He saw where enemy fire had hit and, hopefully, been deflected. Exhaustion lined Ortega's face. Her eyes looked bruised. A cut along the left side of her jaw had bled freely before someone treated it. He needed only to look at her, and the other Marines he could see in the pick-up, to know it had not been an easy fight.

"Sir, we now hold the groundside defenses. We should have control of the orbital defense platforms shortly. Your orders?"

"Continue according to plan, Sorceress. Bring the platforms down. If your Marines can reprogram them to work for us, do so. Otherwise, do whatever you have to and shut them down." He paused, listening as a report came in from one of the other ships in the taskforce. "Sooner is better than later."

Otherwise, he would lose even more ships.

"Understood, sir."

"Then get to it, Sorceress. Keep me informed. *Campbell* out."

O'Malley allowed himself a quick sigh of relief. It wasn't much, not in the grand scheme of things, but it was something. It was also more than they had a few minutes earlier. Now he needed to do everything possible to keep the enemy focused on his ships and not on the Marines dirtside.

"Comms, set up a link to ships' commanders," he said as he studied the holo plot in the center of the bridge.

The relief from a moment before dissipated when he did. The lights indicating the taskforce told a story no commanding officer ever wanted to hear. The enemy outnumbered them and had been slowly whittling away at their LACs and leading edges. If Ortega and her Marines didn't get the defense platforms down soon, the battle would be lost.

And he was damned if he'd not do everything possible to keep that from happening.

"Comms?"

"Ready for you, Admiral."

He nodded and leaned back. The forefinger of his right hand hovered over the button on the arm of his chair that would activate his pickup. He gave himself a moment to collect his thoughts. Then he pressed the button, watching as each commander's face appeared on his screen.

"New orders. On my command, initiate Attack Plan Barca. I repeat, on my command, initiate Attack Plan Barca."

He leaned back, his attention focused on the plot before him. One by one, each ship in the taskforce confirmed receipt of his orders. He waited, doing his best not to think about the men and women who would lose their lives if he made the wrong call. So much depended on the Warlords.

"Incoming message from Captain Osterhaus, sir," Comms reported.

O'Malley drew a deep breath and schooled his expression not to show his frustration. "Put it on my screen."

"Begging the Admiral's pardon, but I have to protest these orders," Osterhaus began without preamble.

O'Malley leaned back. This time, he didn't bother to hide his flash of irritation. From the beginning of this mission, Osterhaus had been a thorn in his side. At least he'd been warned. Both Miranda Tremayne and Richard Collins told him Osterhaus would question every order, especially if he felt it might put his ship at the forefront of the fighting. While the man wasn't exactly a coward, he wasn't one to risk himself if he could find a way around it.

"Captain Osterhaus, you have your orders and you will carry them out or I will relieve you of your command." He leaned forward, wondering if Osterhaus understood how lucky he was to be on another ship at the moment.

"Sir, the defense platforms will tear us to shreds!"

"The defense platforms will no longer be an issue, Captain. They have been dealt with." As if his statement had been the cue, the platforms opened fire on the enemy ships within range. "Comms, give the order. Attack Plan Barca now!" He turned his attention back to Osterhaus. "Captain, if you fail to carry out my orders, there will be hell to pay and none of your family connections will be able to save you." With that, he ended the comm and turned his attention back to the plot, praying as he did that he wasn't sending his people to their deaths.

"Comms, signal Sorceress with my thanks and tell her we have initiated Attack Plan Barca."

With luck, the tide of battle had turned, and they might actually live to talk about it one day. At least he hoped so.

———

Crocket's Landing
Tenasic System

"SORCERESS, WE HAVE MOVEMENT."

Her XO's voice held both exhaustion and concern. Not that she blamed him. They'd been dirtside almost twenty hours and most of that had been spent fighting for every inch of ground they'd gained. The fact they managed to take control of the groundside defense installations was a miracle in itself. If this battle ever ended, she wanted a long bath, food and an even longer sleep. Then she would start pouring over the intel gathered to find out why the enemy hadn't tried overrunning them. Of course, that might be exactly what they were about to try.

Damn them.

She pushed away from the wall where she'd been leaning, listening to reports from the techs as they nursed the defense comps until the reprogramming had been accepted. Now they needed to hold out until O'Malley could get them air support. But that wouldn't be any time soon. He needed to deal with the enemy ships attacking the taskforce. That meant she and the rest of the Warlords had to hold out. More than that, they had to hold the groundside defense installations. The taskforce would be decimated should the enemy manage to retake them.

"Heavy armor and artillery, you're with Snapper. Do not let them get a bead on the building. Bird, Falcon, Eagle, I want all our eyes in the sky active. If we don't hold this position, the taskforce is lost. Reaper, get snipers into position. Then get teams together to reinforce all entries. Stand ready. We will not let them retake this facility.

"Comms, message to the other company commanders. New orders. Groundside defense installations are to be held at all costs. I repeat, at all costs. If the enemy cannot be held off until reinforcements arrive, the installations are to be destroyed. Repeat. Installations to be destroyed before they are allowed to fall back into enemy hands."

"Roger that, Sorceress," Comms said and then repeated back her orders before passing them on.

"New message to the admiral. The enemy is making a push to retake our position. We will hold out as long as possible. If forced to withdraw, we will blow the installation. We will not let the defense platforms fall back into enemy hands. Add that I respectfully suggest he get the ships moving and deal with the bastards topside. We need air support ASAP, before we are overrun."

The building shook as enemy artillery began raining down on it. Ortega cursed softly. Before she could issue new orders, Adamson's voice came over the battlenet, sending reinforcements where needed. Bird's report came in next, assuring everyone the enemy's aim was as bad as ever. Ortega hoped that continued to be the case. The building had taken a beating from her own people before they managed to secure it. How much more it, not to mention the equipment inside, could take was a question she really didn't want to answer.

"Incoming!"

The XO's warning came a scant moment before the building seemed to rock on its foundations. The fight was on – again – and it was up to the Warlords to hold out as long as necessary to keep the defense platforms under their control. Failure meant not only their deaths but the deaths of everyone in the taskforce. The enemy wasn't known for taking captives, not often at any rate. Worse, if they failed, FleetCom wouldn't know how they'd been betrayed.

She'd be damned if she let the bastards who betrayed them win!

2

Fuerconese Defense HQ
New Kilrain, Fuercon

L t. Col. Ashlyn Shaw leaned back and studied her company commanders over the rim of her coffee mug. The Devil Dogs had been back on Fuercon almost two months. From the start, their last mission had not gone as planned. At least this time it hadn't blown up in her face. Far from it, in fact. The Devil Dogs had been dispatched with elements of First Fleet on a mission to protect the Drakkana System. They'd never made it. Instead, they had stumbled upon an attempt to invade the home system. If Second Fleet hadn't been in exactly the right place at the right time, the Callusians would have had a straight shot for Fuercon. Ash's blood ran cold at the thought of what might have happened. It hadn't, in large part to her Marines. But victory had come at a cost, both in manpower and in equipment. Which was one of several reasons why the Fuerconese Marine Corps' premier SpecOps battalion remained firmly tied to the home system.

Hopefully, that wouldn't be the case for much longer. They were Marines and this staying far behind the lines of battle didn't sit right.

As long as she didn't look at the status of her LAC units, the battalion was back to full strength. Hopefully, her LACs would be soon. If so, it wouldn't be long before the Devil Dogs received their orders to ship out. It was time they assumed their place on the front lines, taking the fight to the enemy.

But that wouldn't happen until she assured not only her division CO but the Commandant of the Marine Corps they were ready to ship out. After the enemy's attempt to invade the home system, she knew it would take more than her simply telling them the battalion was ready to return to battle. While part of her understood Fleet-Com's decision to hold her people in-system, she couldn't deny wanting to be on the front lines, doing what they'd been trained for. The war wouldn't be won sitting safely on Fuercon.

"Everyone's here, ma'am," Master Gunnery Sergeant Kevin Talbot said softly from her side. "Captain Nichols' XO is standing in for him."

She nodded. Delta Company's commanding officer's father had been in the hospital for several days and wasn't expected to live much longer. After Captain Loren Nichols responded to her message setting the time for the morning's briefing, she had ordered him not to attend. Being with his family came ahead of duty this time. She didn't want him to regret not being there for his mother and sister should his father die while he attended what looked to be another status briefing and nothing more.

"Then let's get started."

Before she could call the briefing to order, the door to the conference room slid open. Ashlyn looked up and frowned in concern as Lance Corporal Faith Connery stepped inside. The young woman had been acting as Ash's aide since their previous mission. Now she moved quickly to where Ashlyn sat and bent to whisper in her ear. Ashlyn listened, her frown deepening. Under the table, her right hand fisted. Then she nodded once before climbing to her feet.

"Excuse me, ladies and gentlemen. There's a message I need to take." She glanced around the table. "Major Laboe, get everyone started with reports on personnel and equipment needs. If I haven't returned by the time you finish with that, move on to the training schedule we discussed earlier this morning." With that, she left the conference room, the lance corporal on her heels.

"Talk to me, Lance," she said a few moments later as they moved down the corridor in the direction of her office.

"You know as much as I do, ma'am. The message has Colonel Ortega's ID attached. It is marked urgent and for your eyes only." She waited as Ashlyn placed her palm against the scanner next to the office door before continuing. A moment later, Ashlyn bent and waited as the retinal scanner did its job. "I know you said not to interrupt the briefing, but I felt you'd want to know."

Ashlyn nodded. The moment her office door opened, she stepped inside. The lance corporal followed and, before Ash could say anything, Connery activated the security screens. No one would be able to enter without the day's override code and, more importantly, no one would be able to overhear what was on Ortega's message. Trusting the lance corporal to make sure she wasn't interrupted, Ashlyn sat behind her desk and activated her comm. With privacy mode on, she waited as the wallpaper on her screen changed from that of the Warlords to her best friend's and former executive officer's face.

Ashlyn gasped softly. Then she waved Connery back as the lance corporal stepped forward in concern. Her attention riveted to the screen, Ash paused the image, taking in every detail. Ortega sat on the ground, her back against what looked like the remains of what had once been a wall of some sort. Her battle armor showed signs of having been in heavy fighting. She'd removed her helmet and looked at her video pickup with eyes bruised with exhaustion and, unless Ash missed her guess, more than a little anger. But it was the blood staining one side of her friend's face, her friend's very swollen and bruised face, that worried her.

"Ash, I'm breaking protocol with this message but I don't care. I need someone I trust to know what's happened." Ortega paused, looking to her right as the sounds of an explosion filled the air. Before she continued, she issued orders to someone out of sight. Then, as she faced the screen once again, she drew a deep breath, almost as if calming herself. "We walked into it on this mission, Ash. Not only was our intel wrong, it was totally fucked. The enemy was waiting for us when we dropped. We managed to hold them off and secure our objectives but they're pushing back now. I don't know if we're going to be able to hold them off this time."

Ortega paused again, ducking her head and shielding it with one arm as another explosion rocked the building. Dust cascaded down on her, but she ignored it as she once again continued. "Ash, it's bad. If I didn't know better, I'd swear the enemy not only knew our order of attack but who we had where and what our armaments were.

"Damn it, Ash, this shouldn't have happened. I can't deny that it feels too much like what you went through on Arterus. I'm afraid it might end even worse than your mission did." She paused once again, and Ashlyn waited, anger and fear churning in the pit of her stomach. "Status here is bad. Damn it, who am I kidding? It's critical. The battalion was already down re: personnel and equipment when MJ and I reported in. The only reinforcements we've had since our arrival are the few Devil Dogs you left with us. We've gotten nothing from Division and no explanation why. Worse, I've lost good people in this fuck up, too many of them. We needed reinforcements before this mission and I'm not sure we can hold out until they get here – if they ever do."

Anger building, Ash paused the video and quickly tapped out a series of commands on her virtual keyboard. The secondary screen on her desk came alive and she scanned the information. Her blood ran cold for a moment and then burned hot. Heads were going to roll, possibly literally, before the day was done. But that had to wait until she heard what else her friend had to say.

"Ash, if I don't make it out of here, promise you'll find out what happened and who betrayed us. I don't believe for one moment that it's dumb luck on the enemy's part. Not when they managed to ambush and kill Hammer and the others and not after what they're trying to do it to us. Someone is feeding them information about our movements out here.

"Promise me, Ash. Find the bastards responsible before they murder any more of our people." Ortega looked around, as if making sure she couldn't be overheard. "I don't know if we're going to be able to get out of this. Admiral O'Malley is doing his best topside, but the taskforce took serious damage before managing to drive off the Callusian ships. If the enemy returns with reinforcements before we get help, we're all fucked."

Another explosion rocked the area and Ortega's expression darkened with even more concern. "Do me one more favor, Ash. I know I don't have to ask it. But tell my folks I love them. If I don't make it back, let them know I don't regret one minute of being a Marine. Then locate that bastard of a division commander of mine and find out why he never sent us any reinforcements." She looked into the pick-up and a slight smile touched her lips. "Ash, you're my best friend and my sister by choice. We had some good times together. Now make these bastards pay. Ortega out."

Ashlyn leaned back, her face a stone mask of cold fury. Without a word, she replayed the message, her eyes never looking away from the screen. She didn't want to miss one detail, one nuance. As the screen faded to black, she once again activated her virtual keyboard. Her fingers flew as she typed in a new series of commands. She didn't care if the information she wanted wasn't necessarily any of her business. She had no intention of letting her friend down. If she couldn't save her, she would avenge her death and the deaths of the Marines she commanded.

But, by all that was holy, she would do everything in her power to make sure it didn't come to that.

A few moments later, she shoved to her feet. Connery looked at her in concern as she stalked around her desk and crossed the office.

"Colonel?"

Ash didn't respond. Instead, she deactivated the security system and left the office. She knew she should return to the conference room. But this was what she had an executive officer for, not to mention one of the best senior NCOs in the Corps. She'd leave the briefing to them. She had to. More, much more was at stake just then.

"Colonel?" Connery slipped inside the lift after Ashlyn, the doors barely missing her. Concern filled her voice, not that Ash appeared to notice.

"You are dismissed, Lance Corporal," Ashlyn said as the lift came to a stop and the doors opened.

"Colonel."

Ash bit back a snarl and turned to face the young woman. "Connery, return to the conference room. Inform Major Laboe he has the briefing. That's an order." She spoke softly, each word clearly enunciated.

"Where will you be, ma'am?"

"Trying to keep some good Marines from being sacrificed without reason. Dismissed, Lance Corporal."

Connery swallowed hard before bracing to attention and saluting.

Before the doors closed after Ashlyn, Connery pulled out her comm. This wasn't good, not good at all. "Master Guns, we have a problem," she said the moment her comm was answered.

———

Brigadier General Elizabeth Shaw stepped into the gym and glanced around. A frown tugged at the corners of her mouth at what she saw. More than a dozen Marines in PT gear stood around one of the sparring rings at the far end of the gym. A few called out encouragements, but most watched in undisguised concern as their CO fought. None seemed aware of her arrival and that, Elizabeth knew, spoke volumes about their worry for their CO.

Not that she blamed them.

At least Ash had chosen this way to deal with her anger instead of going after a living target. If their positions had been reversed, Elizabeth would have been hard pressed not to seek out Ortega's division commander to deal very up close and personally with him. Even so, the sight of one sparring droid sprawled on the floor of the gym, an arm separated from its body and one leg twisted in a way that, were it human, would have probably required amputation, did little to reassure her.

Squaring off against a second droid, this one showing signs of being well and truly battered, Ashlyn waited for it to make its move. She still wore her MARPATs, all save her blouse. It lay across a bench against the far wall. Sweat covered her face and rolled down her arms. It stained her tank top. So did blood from her split lip, a cut at the corner of her right eye and what looked like it could be a broken nose, not that it appeared to have slowed Ash down any.

Standing just inside the doorway, Elizabeth watched as the droid closed in on her daughter. Ashlyn bounced lightly on her toes, waiting, gauging the droid's next attack. The droid, designed to simulate the appearance of a Callusian foot soldier, narrowed the distance between them. It feinted with a right jab and followed up with a left hook that looked like it could have separated Ash's head from her shoulders if she hadn't blocked it.

Elizabeth hissed out a breath as Ash caught the droid with short but vicious backfist, striking the droid squarely across the jaw. She followed up with a quick jab to the solar plexus and a forearm to the kidney. The sound of flesh striking pseudo-flesh filled the gym, as did the occasional gasp or groan as the droid managed to land a lucky blow, staggering Ash back a step or two.

Wincing as the droid landed a quick jab that had Ashlyn's head snapping back and blood flying from her reinjured nose, Elizabeth nodded to the man standing next to her. "Sergeant Major."

The man stepped forward. For a moment, he glanced around. Elizabeth had no doubt he noted every Marine present and would have more than a few words for them given the chance. Not only because no one had called the gym to order when she entered but because no one had been on watch. They had been so focused on what their battalion CO was doing they'd left themselves open to potential danger.

"Attention on deck!"

The sergeant major's voice rang out and Elizabeth smiled slightly as every Marine instantly turned in the direction of his voice and snapped to attention. Then she winced as the droid, not programmed to respond to such orders landed a solid blow to Ashlyn's mid-section. The young woman staggered back two steps before righting herself. Even as she gasped for air, she forced herself upright, doing her best to brace to attention as the nearest Marine broke formation to deactivate the droid before it could do any more damage.

"Sergeant Major Kaplan, I'll leave you to explain to these Marines what they did wrong here today," Elizabeth said softly, but not so softly the others didn't hear. "Lt. Colonel Shaw, I'll have a word with you in private."

Trusting her daughter to follow, Elizabeth made her way across the gym to one of the two private offices attached to it. The first she checked proved to be empty. Satisfied, she stepped inside. By the time Ashlyn joined her, she sat behind the desk, looking for all the world as if she were in her own office.

Ashlyn crossed the small office and stopped in front of the desk before bracing to attention. Holding her there, Elizabeth pressed the almost hidden button on the desktop, closing and locking the door. A hum so soft it was almost imperceptible sounded as she activated security. As she did, she noted the way Ashlyn's eyes widened slightly in surprise before her daughter's expression went blank once again.

"Care to tell me why you destroyed one sparring droid and were well on the way to doing the same to a second?" Elizabeth leaned back and waited, knowing Ashlyn would understand this was senior officer to junior officer and not mother to daughter.

"It was better than the alternative, ma'am."

"And that alternative being?"

"Doing the same to a senior officer, ma'am."

Elizabeth pursed her lips and studied her daughter for a moment. She'd seen the younger woman look worse but not by much, at least not short of seeing her after battle. Worse, she saw the anger still lurking in Ashlyn's eyes and it reminded her of the near stranger Ash had been when she finally returned to Fuercon after those two long years spent in the penal colony on Tarsus.

"Would you care to explain?"

"Begging the General's pardon but no, ma'am."

The look on Ashlyn's face reminded Elizabeth of when Ash had been younger and didn't want to answer. Too bad. This wasn't a mother-daughter moment but a military one, something Ashlyn needed to remember, and sooner rather than later.

"That wasn't a request." She leaned back and crossed her legs, waiting. When Ashlyn continued to stare at a point somewhere above her head, her expression impassive but her eyes aflame with anger, Elizabeth fought the urge to sigh. Instead, climbed to her feet and moved around the desk to stand in front of her daughter. "I am not in the mood to put up with this sort of behavior, Ashlyn. The last thing I need is the CO of my Spec Ops battalion being insubordinate. What you have to understand is the proverbial shit has hit the fan and I need Lt. Colonel Shaw, not my daughter acting like a sulking, teenaged brat. Put whatever is bothering you away and start acting like the Marine I know you are."

Ash inhaled sharply. Her mouth thinned in an attempt not to respond. Elizabeth took note, relieved the younger woman hadn't let her anger take control.

"Colonel, we have ten minutes before we are to meet with the Commandant. That is why I came looking for you. Imagine my surprise when I discovered you had walked out of a briefing of your company commanders without explanation and hadn't returned. All Lance Corporal Connery would say when questioned is that you received a comm and you had dismissed her with instructions for Major Laboe to take over the briefing." She paused and checked the time. "You have exactly two minutes to tell me what upset you so much you abandoned a briefing that could be instrumental to the Devil Dogs returning to the front lines and came here to beat droids to death instead."

For a moment, Ashlyn said nothing. Then she reached into the pocket at the left thigh of her MARPATs. A moment later, she handed her datapad to her mother. "Permission to clean up before meeting with the Commandant?"

"Negative." Elizabeth checked the last message logged into the datapad and frowned. Recognizing the signature, she had all the confirmation she needed to know why her daughter acted as she had. She also knew how lucky they were Ashlyn had exercised enough restraint that she only destroyed a couple of droids instead of the real target of her anger. She glanced to where her daughter once again stood ramrod straight and sighed softly. "Take that stick out of your ass, daughter mine, and relax. You aren't in trouble and I will make sure the Commandant understands — assuming she doesn't already. But, when we meet with her, I have two orders for you. First, you are to let her see this message. I'm assuming Lucinda said something to set you off and, knowing you, it means you know she and the Warlords aren't getting the support they needed."

For a moment, Ash said nothing. Elizabeth watched the internal struggle play out across her daughter's expression. "Mom, it's more than that. She thinks they were betrayed, much as my people were on Arterus."

Elizabeth inhaled sharply as her own anger built. "All right. Then don't hedge with the Commandant. Tell her everything. Let her see this and answer her questions, all of them."

"Yes, ma'am."

"Second, you are to do nothing to clean up except put your blouse on and wipe away as much of the blood as you can with this." She tossed a mini-first aid kit to Ash, watching as the young woman caught it with one hand. "I want the Commandant to see how this impacted you and, by extension, how it will impact the rest of the Devil Dogs and the Corps."

"Understood, ma'am." Ash opened the kit and produced a packet not much larger than her thumb. A moment later, she tore it open and pulled out a medicated tissue. "May I ask a question?"

"If you can do so and get into your blouse in the next minute."

"Why do you look as angry as I feel?"

Elizabeth chuckled softly. Ashlyn always knew when something bothered her. "Because I received a message from Admiral O'Malley relaying much the same information I assume Lucinda sent you."

The fact O'Malley contacted her about his suspicions told her how serious things must be for the taskforce. Hearing how Lucinda Ortega had contacted Ashlyn with much the same information, she knew something needed to be done. It might be too late for the members of the taskforce, but they had to try.

Ashlyn tossed the tissue into the recycler and reached for her blouse. As she slid into it, Elizabeth got to her feet. A moment later, she deactivated the security shield and the door slid open. A small smile touched her lips to see the sergeant major continuing to "educate" the other Marines on what they had failed to do earlier. She had no doubt he could continue for the next half hour without pausing for a breath. However, she felt sure he had made his point and it was time to move on.

"Sergeant Major Kaplan, on me," she said as she and Ashlyn moved across the gym toward the outer corridor. "We will see this through, Ash," she continued softly once they stepped into the lift at the far end of the corridor. "I promise."

————

ASHLYN DREW a deep breath and nodded, her expression grim. She wanted to believe her mother but, after the events of the last few years, it was hard. All she knew for certain was she would do everything Lucinda asked, even if it was the last thing she did. Until then, she would make sure those responsible for betraying her friend and the others never had another good night's sleep.

The lift came to a stop and Ash winced slightly. For the first time, she felt each ache and pain from her workout. *Workout!* She almost snorted in a mixture of amusement and disgust. After apologizing to Connery, she owed her mother a thank you. From the way she hurt, she had no doubt if she'd continue trying to destroy sparring droids much longer, she would have wound up on the losing side. As it was, she knew she'd be paying Medical a visit before the end of the day.

A few minutes later, they were shown into General Helen Okafor's private office. The sergeant major peeled off at the door. As he did, he pulled his comm and Ash had a feeling he was contacting Lance

Corporal Connery. Better Connery, she knew, than Talbot. Not that it would save her from the Master Gunnery Sergeant for long.

Ash shook herself as she and her mother stopped in front of Okafor's desk and braced to attention. The Commandant of the Fuerconese Marine Corps took a moment to study them. The only indication she gave of any sort of reaction to Ashlyn's appearance was the slight narrowing of her dark eyes. Then she put them at their ease and motioned for them to be seated.

"I don't have much time," Okafor began as she leaned back in her chair. "You said it was urgent, Liz."

Ashlyn relaxed slightly at the general's use of her mother's given name. Something like this was easier done without protocol and rules. Not much but some. Better yet, her mother had the task of being the one to initiate the discussion. That gave Ash a few moments at least to gather her thoughts and try to sound like a seasoned officer and not someone out for blood. Although, just then, she'd gladly resign her commission for a few minutes alone with those responsible for the current situation.

"Ma'am, I'm afraid both Ash and I had a situation dropped in our laps earlier."

Okafor tilted her head to one side and one brow arched in question. "I take it this *situation* has nothing to do with the Warlords."

"That would be correct, ma'am." Much as Ashlyn had done earlier, Elizabeth reached into a pocket and produced her datapad. "I had a message waiting for me from Admiral O'Malley when I reported for duty this morning. What he had to say is more than a little disturbing. I later discovered Ash had received much the same information from Lt. Colonel Ortega."

As she spoke, Elizabeth leaned forward and placed her datapad on Okafor's desk. For a moment, Okafor said nothing. Then she reached for it and played the message Elizabeth had queued up.

"Liz, I am breaking more rules than I can count right now but I don't give a damn."

Admiral O'Malley's image appeared on the holo-screen behind Okafor's desk. The general swiveled in her chair to face the screen. As she did, Ashlyn focused on the image. O'Malley appeared to be seated in his ready room. He looked as tired and worn as Ortega had. More telling were the alerts coming over the ship's comms system. Requests for damage control teams followed by calls for medics filled the air. Ashlyn had no doubt each one weighed ever more heavily on O'Malley.

"Our mission has been FUBARed from the beginning. I swear the enemy knows our plans before we do. The taskforce has been hard hit since our arrival in-system. The enemy was waiting for us. Worse, they knew exactly where we'd translate in. If that wasn't bad enough, they seemed to know where our Marines would land and what their targets were." He paused and ran a hand over his face. When he looked up again, his eyes were haunted. "Liz, I've repeatedly asked for reinforcements and haven't heard anything back. I know you can't do anything about the Navy side of things but why, for the love of God, haven't the Marines sent reinforcements? Ortega's sent a good half dozen requests and each one has been denied – or ignored.

"Liz, I've lost two ships already. Others are damaged, several badly. There are more dead and wounded than uninjured. Thanks to our Marines, we currently hold the system but for how long? If the enemy manages to regroup or, worse, get reinforcements, we won't be able to hold out. We need help. I know I'm asking you to pull strings and call in favors. Please, don't let the bastards win."

O'Malley's message ended, and silence hung heavily in the office. A moment later, Okafor turned away from the holo-screen. When she did, Ash swallowed hard. The general, usually so unflappable, looked ready to go to battle. In possible, she looked angrier than Ashlyn felt.

"I take it there's more." It wasn't a question so much as an acknowledgement of something she would rather not know.

"Yes, ma'am." Ashlyn leaned forward and handed Okafor her own datapad, Lucinda's message queued up to play.

"I assume this is why you look like you just fought a Callusian regiment on your own, Ashlyn," Okafor said a few minutes later as she handed back the datapad. Ashlyn nodded. "How many droids did you destroy this time?" A faint trace of a smile touched her lips.

"One. My mother arrived before I could finish off the second."

"Not that it won't need time in maintenance before anyone else uses it," Elizabeth put in. Then she stood, serious again, and Ashlyn followed suit. "I thought you needed to know, ma'am."

For a moment, Okafor said nothing. Instead, she stared past her visitors. Then she motioned for them to resume their seats. As she did, her eyes flashed with anger. Hoping it wasn't aimed at either of them as the bearers of bad news, Ash waited for her mother to sit and then she followed suit.

"Thank you, I did need to know." Okafor paused long enough to signal her aide, asking for coffee for the three them. Then she stood and moved across her office. For a long moment, she stared out the window. When she turned, her expression was, if possible, more troubled than before. "It is also why I didn't put you off when you said we needed to meet this morning, Liz. You're not the only ones to have received messages about the Warlords." Now she looked at Ash, smiling ruefully, began to rub the knuckles of her left hand. "If you checked my gym, you'd find another droid needing a visit to Maintenance."

"And?" Elizabeth prompted. Then she winced, and Ash smiled slightly. It wasn't often her mother forgot herself, even in a supposedly informal meeting with a senior officer. "Ma'am, isn't this a discussion you should be having with SecDiv's CO?"

"Trust me, I will be." She waited until her aide placed a tray with a carafe and three mugs on her desk. A moment later the young man left the office, the door sliding closed behind him. "However, my immediate concerns about the Warlords and how best to help them include the two of you."

"Ma'am?" Ash frowned, not following Okafor's train of thought.

Okafor moved to pour coffee for each of them. As she did, Ashlyn could almost see the general's mental wheels turning. What that meant for First Division, and specifically for the Devil Dogs, she didn't know but she had a feeling in the pit of her stomach she wasn't going to like it.

Okafor leaned a hip against the edge of her desk and blew out a breath. Whatever mental battle she'd been waging with herself, she had come to a conclusion.

"For the moment, we're off the record." She waited until they both nodded. "Liz, has O'Malley voiced any of these concerns before now?"

"No. That's why I was so surprised to receive his message this morning. I hadn't heard from him in almost a year, not since he shipped out the last time." She sipped her coffee and then glanced at Ashlyn. "O'Malley and I were in the Academy together. We've kept in touch over the years. If he felt it necessary to reach out to me about what's happening, I guarantee it is worse than he's letting on."

"Just as it is with Luce." Ashlyn fought against the anger once again burning deep inside her at the thought of what might be happening to her friend and the Marines under Ortega's command.

"I might not have had a message from O'Malley, but I have had a message from Ortega and several other Marines attached to the task-force." Okafor held up a hand, stopping Ashlyn from interrupting. "None of the Marines serving with her had anything but good to say about Ortega. They also said they needed reinforcements and feel like they've been hung out to dry by SecDiv." Okafor's eyes flashed, the only indication about how angry she happened to be. "Ortega included copies of her requests back to SecDiv asking for reinforcements. Requests, I have confirmed, that were either not answered or were denied without explanation – and without passing them on to me."

"General," Ashlyn growled, her hands fisting around her mug so tightly one corner of her mind wondered at the fact the mug hadn't shattered.

"Exactly." Okafor gave a single nod. "Under most circumstances, I would have concerns about an officer jumping the chain of command the way Ortega did. But I know her, and I know the kind of Marine she is. I also know she isn't the sort to try to stab a CO in the back. The very fact she came to me with her concerns tells me all I need to know there is bad trouble with SecDiv. It is trouble I will deal with, you can rest assured on that." She pinned Ashlyn with a firm glance, waiting until the younger woman nodded. Once Ashlyn had, Okafor sent for her aide.

"Ma'am?" the lieutenant asked as he entered the office a moment later.

"Matias, locate Brigadier General Javier Hale," Okafor said as she returned to her desk.

"Yes, ma'am. Am I to tell him you wish to speak with him?"

"Not yet, Matias. In fact, I would prefer it if the general didn't know I was looking for him, at least not yet."

"Understood, ma'am."

"That will be all, Matias. Make sure we aren't interrupted."

As he left the office, Okafor leaned back and sighed. Watching her, Ash almost felt sorry for Hale. There could be no mistaking Okafor's frustration and, whether she'd admit it or not, anger over the situation in the Tenasic System. If Hale didn't have answers, and good ones, for why the requested reinforcements had been withheld, Ash knew his career as a Marine would suffer – if not come to an abrupt end. That assumed he didn't wind up being court martialed. From the look on Okafor's face, Ashlyn had no doubt the commandant wanted blood.

That made two of them.

"Now, before either of you say I should be discussing this with Hale, I will. Believe me, we are going to have a very long discussion." She sat up and Ash felt a brief flash of pity for Hale. Okafor's expression left no doubt she wasn't in the mood for excuses. "However, what I have to say to the two of you comes first."

Ashlyn's eyes narrowed, and she fought the urge to lean forward. She'd heard that tone of voice from Okafor before. The general meant business and Ash had a feeling she was going to play a role in whatever the woman had up her sleeve.

"I don't care what it takes, we are sending reinforcements to help Colonel Ortega and her Marines. I don't care if we have to hijack a ship to do it. We don't leave our people behind and we sure as hell don't hang them out to dry." Okafor might have been discussing a walk in the park. The only things giving her away was the anger flashing in her eyes and the taut set of her shoulders.

"I mean it, Ashlyn. If I have to pull strings and get you a ship, I will. You've already proven you can command one in battle. I swear to God, I'll put you on the bridge of one if necessary to get to Ortega and the rest of the taskforce in time."

Even as her stomach pitched, Ashlyn nodded. She'd had no choice on her last mission but to take command after the ship's CO had been injured. Fortunately, the rest of the taskforce – including its CO – had been nearby and she'd been able to hand off command within a matter of hours. Of course, those hours had seen more battle than she cared to remember. So much could have gone so badly wrong. She knew how lucky they had all been. Not that she would argue too much if Okafor carried out her threat. Nothing mattered as much as getting Marines in place to support the Warlords.

"I assume that means the Devil Dogs are to be prepared to deploy."

"Two companies. The rest of the battalion is to remain behind. We still have to make sure the home system is protected. I know your LAC numbers are still down, but you are to take those ready for battle with you as well."

"Understood, ma'am."

"We will meet in the morning to discuss the mission. It will take that long to get everything in place for your deployment."

And, Ash had no doubt, for her to have her "talk" with Hale.

"When you receive your orders, you will also receive notice that you are being breveted to the rank of colonel, Ashlyn, effective immediately."

Full bird colonel?

Before she could protest, the look Okafor turned on her had Ash closing her mouth with an almost audible snap.

"No arguments, Colonel. Trust me, it's necessary." Without explaining further, Okafor pushed back her chair and climbed to her feet. Before Elizabeth and Ash could follow suit, she shook her head and indicated they were to remain seated. "Liz, this means you will need to do some shuffling in FirstDiv to cover for the two companies."

"Yes, ma'am."

Okafor paced the length of her office once, twice, her hands folded behind her back. When she returned to her desk a few moments later, her expression betrayed little. "Ash, I know the Devil Dogs aren't yet back to full-strength, but you're close. I am hoping not only that you and your two companies will get to the system in time to reinforce the Warlords but that you will be enough with whatever ships I manage to convince FleetCom to send with you to hold the system until the taskforce can be relieved.

"I could send other Marines but, if Ortega and O'Malley are right, we can't wait for me to be able to free up Marines from elsewhere. Besides, you and Ortega have worked together. You will be better able to combine your people than anyone else. With that in mind, I want your recommendation on which companies should go, as well as what material and supplies you will need for the mission, by morning."

"Understood, ma'am," Ash said, her mind already turning to the task of figuring out assignments.

"That's not all."

Ashlyn looked at the Commandant, alerted by something in the woman's voice. "I also want your thoughts and recommendations concerning the SpecOps units – from the squadron level up – in the Corps right now. Specifically, their current division assignments, how they have been assigned for battle, their manpower and then I want to know how you think that can be improved. Be prepared to discuss that come morning as well."

"Ma'am?" Ashlyn looked at her in disbelief. If there was anything Okafor could have asked her she'd expected less than that, she couldn't think of it.

"Just do it." Okafor waved aside any objections or questions she might have. "I want your honest opinion and recommendations, Colonel. That's an order."

"Yes, ma'am."

"We will reconvene here at 0700 tomorrow. Liz, you're to be here as well and be prepared to answer the same questions."

"Understood, ma'am," Elizabeth said.

"Now, Colonel." Okafor smiled as she said it and Ashlyn fought the urge to groan. "You are dismissed. You have a great deal to do before morning."

"Ma'am." She braced to attention, but Okafor waved her salute off.

"One more thing, Ash. Leave Brigadier General Hale to me. I assure you, I will get to the bottom of what's going on and heads will roll if necessary."

"Thank you, ma'am."

"Dismissed."

Ashlyn didn't wait. She turned and left Okafor's office. The moment the door slid shut behind her, Connery took up her place to her right and one step behind. As she did, Ash glanced back and smiled in both appreciation and apology. She had a great deal to do before morning, but one thing came first.

"Lance, I apologize for earlier," she said as the lift doors closed behind them a few moments later. "I'll explain once we're back at the office. In the meantime, send word to Talbot and the XO that I need to meet with them in half an hour. That should give me enough time to read you in on what's going on."

Hopefully, it would also be enough time to gather her thoughts and figure out the best way to split up the battalion yet again.

3

The soft chiming of one of her father's antique clocks interrupted Ashlyn's thoughts. Looking up from Talbot's report, she leaned back and stretched until her back popped. Exhaustion dragged at her and she reached for her coffee. In the time since she left General Okafor's office the day before, she had worked almost non-stop trying to carry out the orders she'd been given. That meant grabbing what could be euphemistically called a nap instead of a good night's sleep. But it had been worth it – she hoped. She was as prepared as she could be for the morning's briefing.

Taking another sip of her now cold coffee and grimacing slightly, Ash turned her attention back to Talbot's report. Even though she hadn't explained why she wanted his recommendations for splitting the battalion once again, the master gunnery sergeant had proven as competent as always. Of course, he knew her well enough to read between the lines and understand she wasn't asking for the hell of it helped. More than that, he had obviously tapped into his sources and knew about the trouble Taskforce Liberator faced. His recommendations, based on that knowledge, matched her own thoughts almost down to the smallest detail.

Unfortunately, that did nothing to reassure her. If his sources were aware of the trouble Ortega and the rest of the taskforce faced, FleetCom should have been as well. So why hadn't they sent the reinforcements Taskforce Liberator needed?

"Well, Master Guns, let's see if you agree on one more little matter," she muttered as she opened his response to the message she sent late the previous evening.

Her one concern about splitting the battalion had little to do with their current state of readiness. The Devil Dogs, even when down on manpower and equipment, were better prepared for battle than many other battalions. This time, her concern came down to the simple fact that her executive officer was still new to the battalion. She had tapped Major Elias Laboe as her new XO on the last mission. Before her promotion to CO of the Warlords, Ortega held that position. Because they'd known one another since the Academy and had served together for years, they had the sort of relationship that made for the smooth running of the Devil Dogs. Ash trusted Ortega to do whatever might be necessary not only to carry out a mission but to get their people home safely. Laboe had served with the Devil Dogs early in his career but he was an unknown. Until the last mission, Ash had never served with him and they had yet to get to the point where she knew how he would react in any given situation.

"I have a feeling you aren't going to like my solution to the problem, Loco," she murmured a few minutes later. Talbot brought up the same concerns about Laboe she had, carefully couching them so he also let her know he felt the major was an excellent officer who only needed time to get to know the Devil Dogs. His recommendation was for her to leave a senior NCO with Laboe, one the remaining elements of the battalion would not only respect but respond to without hesitation.

She sent off her orders for the morning, reminding both Laboe and Talbot she had a meeting with the Commandant. Then she switched off her terminal and climbed to her feet. As she did, a knock sounded at the door. A moment later, it opened and her mother stepped inside. Like Ash, Elizabeth wore MARPATs and boots. In one hand, she carried a mug of coffee.

"Are you about ready?" her mother asked.

"As soon as I check on Jake."

Elizabeth nodded. One thing Ashlyn had learned after finding herself and the other survivors of the Arterus mission court-martialed on trumped-up charges was to never take anything for granted. Her young son topped that list. She made sure she tucked him in every night, even if he was already asleep. She checked on him every morning, kissing him goodbye. They had been separated by those false charges for more than two years, years they would never be able to get back. Ash meant to make sure her son understood just how much she loved him. That time apart taught her to never take a moment with her son, or any of those she cared for, for granted.

"Help yourselves to coffee and food," Okafor said an hour later when Ashlyn and Elizabeth were shown into her office.

As the door slid shut behind them, Ashlyn glanced at the conference table to her left and her mouth watered. Laid out on the near end was an assortment of fresh fruit and muffins, not to mention more traditional breakfast fare. Several carafes of coffee rested nearby. It seemed the general was prepared as always, this time making sure her subordinates had the food and caffeine they needed to face the day.

"Before we get started, are you all right, Ashlyn?" Okafor settled behind her desk and leaned forward, her expression concerned. When Ash didn't respond, she sighed softly and shook her head. "Ash, I know you. I know what's happening with the Warlords right now has to be digging up memories about what happened on Arterus. Hell, kid, they've dug up my own nightmares about what happened to you and your people."

For a moment, Ash stared into her coffee mug. When she looked up, she hoped she didn't look as angry as she felt. "Ma'am, I'd be lying if I denied everything you said was true. But I assure you I'm all right. Yes, I'm mad as hell. Yes, I want answers and, yes, I'm praying Lucinda and her people – not to mention the rest of Taskforce Liberator – aren't victims of the same sort of plot my people fell victim to."

"We all feel that way, Ash," Okafor assured her.

Now Ashlyn gave a slight smile. "Ma'am, I'll even admit I considered slipping out a couple of times last night to have a *chat* with Hale. I really, really want to know why he hasn't sent reinforcements."

"Not nearly as much as I want to know not only that but also why he didn't apprise me of the situation the Warlords found themselves in." Okafor's expression left no doubt she was not pleased with the brigadier general. But it also had Ashlyn wondering why she hadn't already discussed the matter with him.

"Ma'am?" That was the closest she'd come to asking.

"I'll explain shortly." Okafor turned her attention to Elizabeth. "Liz, were you able to find replacements for the Devil Dogs that will be joining up with Taskforce Liberator?"

"I have. I can shift a couple of companies from 3rdBatt over. I'll pull in LACs from 4thBatt. Orders are ready to be issued to that effect once I have the final timeline."

"Excellent." Okafor smiled and seemed to relax a little. "Have you decided which companies will link up with the Warlords, Ashlyn?"

"Yes, ma'am." She set her plate on the edge of Okafor's desk, her food forgotten for the moment. "Before I name them, let me explain how I came to my decision." She waited until Okafor nodded. "I've been generally aware of the makeup of the Warlords. I also assumed, and rightly so, that Hammer had been working to bring them more in line with the Devil Dogs than they had been. I know Luce will have continued doing just that.

"My guess is they are going to be short specialists and, of course, LACs. So, I'm sending two teams from Alpha Company, one team each from Beta and Delta Companies. I would like to send half our LACs as well. I would prefer taking all my LACs but don't want to strip all of them from the home system."

For a moment, her mother and Okafor considered what she said.

"Why not take all of Alpha Company?" Elizabeth asked.

"I don't think the enemy is going to try another run at the Home System, at least not so soon. But, if they do, I want to make sure we have the best chance to push them back. That means making sure at least part of Alpha Company has remained back here for command purposes."

Elizabeth shifted in her seat, turning so she looked Ashlyn in the eye. "You're trying very hard not to say something. What?" The look she gave her daughter was one Ash knew well. She wasn't going to let Ash get away with not explaining.

"It's clear the general here expects me to take the two companies to meet up with the taskforce." She nodded in Okafor's direction. "That means Laboe will be in command of the DDs remaining in-system. He's a good officer and a good Marine. I mean that. But it's been a long time since he was a member of the Devil Dogs and he's still getting to know the battalion. More than that, the DDs are still getting to know him. They will obey his orders. But, just as he and I haven't yet settled into a smooth working relationship as XO and CO, he hasn't settled into that sort of relationship with the others. Because of that, I want to make sure there are plenty of officers and senior NCOs remaining to keep things running smoothly in case I'm wrong and the shit hits the fan here."

"Are you having second thoughts about naming Laboe as your XO?" Elizabeth asked in concern.

"A few, but you know as well as I do that's because I don't know him like I know Lucinda. I've no doubt that, given time, we will settle into a smooth working relationship." It might not be as solid or as close as what she and Ortega enjoyed but it would be enough – she hoped. "But I have to look at the now, not at what the future might hold. That means making sure I leave Fuercon protected."

"Your plan?" Okafor steepled her fingers and rested her elbows on her desk as she looked at Ashlyn in curiosity.

"I haven't told him yet, but I'll be leaving Talbot behind with Laboe. The Master Guns will make sure the battalion is battle-ready, no matter what."

Both women nodded even though neither looked particularly happy with the notion. Ashlyn understood. She didn't much like it herself. Talbot had been with her since her pardon. In many ways, he had been her safety net those first few weeks and months. He'd not only kept her from doing anything foolish – like taking off to exact her own justice against those who had betrayed her and her people – he had reminded her she was a Marine, a Devil Dog, and she needed to quit doubting herself.

"Who are you taking in his place?" Elizabeth asked.

"Connery. She proved herself more than capable on the last mission. She might be young, but she's a Devil Dog through and through." Now Ash allowed herself a slight smile. "Besides, Talbot's been training her."

Neither Okafor nor Elizabeth said anything. Instead, they each reached for their datapads. As they did, Ash shook her head slightly. She had no doubt they were checking Connery's service record. Let them. They would find exactly what she already knew. The young woman had the makings of an excellent senior non-com with a little more seasoning. When Okafor glanced up a moment later, a sparkle in her eye told Ash she had something up her sleeve.

And that was not always something she liked.

"General?" she drawled.

"Would you say Connery is ready for promotion to corporal?" Okafor asked in return.

Ash opened her mouth to answer and then stopped. Her immediate response had been to say "no". Not because she felt Connery needed more time in grade but because she didn't want the brass cutting corners to make her happy or, worse, to make her feel safe. But she knew better where Okafor and her mother were concerned. Neither would put the Corps or the safety of Fuercon and its allies at risk just to make one person feel better. She had to remember that and not let her own ego stand in the young woman's way.

"I would." She leaned back and crossed her legs. Then she reached for her mug of coffee where it rested on the small table between her chair and her mother's. "Connery has proven herself, not only to my satisfaction but to Talbot's as well. He spoke with me the other day about wanting to put her up for promotion as soon as she met the time in grade requirements."

That put the ball back in her mother's and Okafor's court. If Elizabeth agreed Connery deserved promotion, Okafor could brevet her to it before she met her time in grade requirements. But it would take both of them and she waited as they considered.

"She's had consistently exemplary reviews from her senior officers and NCOs. In fact, her last two from Talbot are better than the vast majority I've seen from him," Elizabeth commented as she slid her datapad back into her pocket. "I have no doubt she'd breeze through promotion in nine months when she'd come up for it under normal circumstances."

"I know both Talbot and I would push for the promotion," Ash said.

"Consider it done then." Okafor gave a nod and then smiled. "I will make sure you have the proper paperwork by lunchtime, Ashlyn. I'll let you tell her."

"Thank you, ma'am." She had a very good idea how she wanted to do so.

"Now, how soon can your people be ready to ship out?" the Commandant asked.

"Under normal circumstances, I'd like at least a week. But these aren't normal circumstances. We have people waiting for reinforcements, men and women who will die – or worse – if we don't get there as soon as possible. There will be some grumbling, but we can be ready the ship out in forty-eight hours, sooner if necessary."

It wasn't much time, certainly not as much as she'd prefer but, if she were being honest, she'd much rather ship out immediately than wait. She knew the horror Ortega and the others faced. It went beyond the knowledge they'd been betrayed and, much as she didn't want to believe it, there seemed no other explanation. Bad as that was, the fact the enemy could return at any moment, their numbers reinforced, meant the taskforce couldn't let its guard down. That meant keeping people on watch who could have otherwise been recovering from their injuries or helping with repairs.

"FleetCom is still working out the details. Their best guess is you will be shipping out in seventy-two hours. Get everything in order and be prepared to move onboard in twenty-four to forty-eight hours.

The three of us will meet twice a day between now and when you ship out." Okafor waited until they nodded in understanding. "Ash, I won't lie. There is a good chance you will reach the Tenasic System and find that our worst fears have come true. If that's the case, make the bastards pay and bring our people home. We're Marines and we don't leave anyone behind.

"On the other hand, if you get there and the taskforce has managed to hold out, do all you can to support them until we can get more reinforcements to you. That system is vital to the war effort. Even more important is finding out who betrayed our people and why. If, as I suspect, this goes back to the Midlothians, it will be another nail in their collective coffin. The President is not going to wait much longer to reveal their betrayal to Congress."

Ash nodded. The memory of meeting with the President, as well as others of his "inner circle", after her last mission was still fresh. The mission had been simple. The taskforce commanded by Admiral Miranda Tremayne was to protect the Drakkana System, ensuring the shipping route to Ramadian remained open.

Except they never made it to the Drakkana System. Instead, before leaving the system, they had stumbled upon a Callusian task-force on an attack vector with Fuercon. The battle that followed had been fierce. Good had come out of it, however. Not only had the task-force managed to intercept the invading ships, Tremayne had forced the surviving Callusians to surrender without scrubbing their data-banks. If that wasn't enough to have the Intelligence specialists dancing with joy, Fuercon now possessed the tangible link between the Callusians and their so-called ally Midlothian. Among those taken prisoner had been Captain Bernard Hughes. The Midlothian officer had tried to deny his true identity, but Intel quickly confirmed it.

President Harper had come close to revealing the Midlothian conspiracy to Congress. Never would Ashlyn forget how, just minutes before Harper was scheduled to address Congress, she spoke out against telling them about the Midlothian connection. She, who hated politics and, if she were honest, most politicians, stepped in the middle of the game. She reminded Harper they didn't have a direct tie between Hughes and the Midlothian government. Intel hadn't had a chance to go over all the information contained in the Callusian databases. For all they knew, Hughes had been working on his own or for a shadow group of Midlothians. They needed more before they publicly accused an ally of treachery.

Harper hadn't liked it but when the others present, including his Secretary of State, agreed, he'd agreed. Ash knew it was only a matter of time before he changed his mind. Nor did she blame him. She'd prefer the direct approach as well. Let Midlothian know what they did and force them to either admit their betrayal or to reveal who was behind it.

"General, will you make sure I have access to all of Colonel Ortega's reports and communications since taking command of the Warlords?" Ashlyn tried to think what else she might need. "In fact, if I could have access to all mission pertinent comms from the Warlords as well as Admiral O'Malley, I'd appreciate it."

"Consider it done." Okafor made a quick note. "I will include Hammer's reports as well as the AARs on the mission that cost him and the others their lives."

Ash swallowed hard against the anger and sorrow that returned at the mention of her former CO's death. "Thank you."

"I know I don't have to say this to either of you, but we need to keep an open mind about what's been happening in the Tenasic System. It would be easy to assume this is another instance of betrayal by the Midlothians or, worse, that there are still some of those responsible for betraying you, Ash, still in Fleet. I've already contacted Rico Santiago to look into things for us and I've briefed SecDef and SecNav. Their orders are simple, Ash. Your Marines and the naval contingent are to do everything you can to reinforce Taskforce Liberator and hold the system until replacement forces arrive or you are to bring home our people."

"Understood, General." Ashlyn thought for a moment. "Do you have an idea about which ships will be sent?" That would tell her a great deal about how seriously FleetCom took the current situation Taskforce Liberator faced.

"Nothing has been set in stone yet, but my guess is Admiral Tremayne will send part of First Fleet, possibly supplemented by elements from Second Fleet."

It made sense. First Fleet was assigned to the home system. By using elements from it, they wouldn't have to wait for transport to arrive. However, First Fleet had suffered losses of manpower and equipment on the last mission. That was why elements of Second Fleet remained nearby. By using elements from both, home system defenses would not be impacted too heavily.

"You have a great deal to do between now and when you ship out, Colonel."

Ashlyn sat up a bit straighter at the change in the general's tone. They were back on the record and she knew it.

"I'll get it done, ma'am."

"I know you will." She glanced at her chrono. "We'll meet again at 1700 hours. Will that work for both of you?" She waited until both Elizabeth and Ashlyn nodded. "I want your preliminary departure plans at that time, Ash, as well as the other little assignment I gave you. Until then, you're dismissed. Liz, we still have a few things to discuss."

Ashlyn stood and braced to attention. Then she turned and left the office. Before the door closed behind her, her mind was racing as she considered everything that needed to be accomplished before her next meeting with Okafor.

"DAMN IT, I will not let this turn into another Arterus mission!"

Helen Okafor, as well as Secretary of Defense Linden Klingsbury and Secretary of the Navy Norton Hollingsworth watched as President Derek Harper paced the length of his office. Anger radiated off of him. The muscles of his jaw worked, and one hand fisted at his side. Throughout their reports, he had said nothing. But, with each passing moment, his expression grew harder, his eyes flatter. When he learned the requested reinforcements had not been sent, he'd all but exploded out of his chair. Now he wanted answers, answers they couldn't give him – yet.

"Which is why we're dispatching forces to reinforce the taskforce as quickly as possible, sir," Klingsbury said.

"Tell me." Harper leaned against his desk, his expression not quite as stormy as before.

Klingsbury looked to Hollingsworth and nodded.

"Mr. President, elements from both First and Second Fleets will be leaving the Home System as soon as all personnel report back to their ships and supplies have been loaded. This second taskforce has one mission: to reinforce Taskforce Liberator and hold the system until replacement forces arrive or to bring our people home if the system can't be held."

"When?" Harper pressed.

"Realistically?" Hollingsworth asked and Harper nodded. "Two days. Even though Second Fleet is in system, it will take time to move the elements around so we don't leave the Home System open to attack when the taskforce ships out."

"We also need to get the Marine contingent and its equipment in place, Mr. President," Okafor said.

"Who are you sending?"

"The equivalent of two companies of the Devil Dogs, Mr. President, as well as half their LACs. Moving that many Marines and their equipment, especially the LACs and all their maintenance crews need, takes time."

"Command?"

"Ashlyn Shaw will be leading the Devil Dogs. She's been breveted to the rank of colonel," Okafor answered.

Harper nodded. "The taskforce commander?"

"Miranda Tremayne," Klingsbury said. "With Admiral Collins remaining in-system with Second Fleet, she felt it wouldn't weaken our defenses for her to lead the taskforce."

"I want to meet with both she and Colonel Shaw before they ship out." He closed his eyes for a moment and focused on remaining calm. "Now, why were the requests for reinforcements not fulfilled?"

"We are still looking into it, Mr. President," Klingsbury said. "Sir, before you ask, there is nothing to indicate this is another betrayal like the one Colonel Shaw and her people suffered on Arterus and after."

"And the reason they needed the reinforcements?"

"We won't know for sure until Tremayne and the taskforce get on station, but there is nothing – so far – beyond suspicion that the Midlothians are involved. FleetCom made sure the details of the mission were kept under wraps and there were no Midlothians on any of the ships that comprise Taskforce Liberator."

"In other words, you're telling me to keep my temper and hold my tongue." Harper did not look or sound amused.

"Very respectfully, sir," Klingsbury said.

"For now, I will. However, if we get any information, I don't care how minor it might be, as long as it is credible, I will go public with it. I will not let those bastards do any further harm to Fuercon or our real allies."

"Mr. President, I believe I speak of all of us when I say we'd like nothing more than to deal with not only the Callusians but the traitorous Midlothians as well," Okafor said, her voice as hard as his had been. "But we must move with caution or we risk our other allies turning against us."

Harper frowned and then nodded. She was right. That didn't make it any easier to accept, however.

"Your suggestions?" He returned to his desk and took his seat behind it. Then he waited, appreciating the fact none of them rushed to answer. That meant they were considering their responses and not simply telling him what they thought he wanted to hear.

"Deontay Moore has been working with the Midlothian ambassador and has not only a good working relationship with him but an excellent insight into the man's mind," Klingsbury began. "Let me read him into the current situation and set him to sniffing out what he can find. Trust me, if he doesn't want someone to know what he's thinking, they won't know it. They won't even guess it."

Harper considered the suggestion for a moment and then agreed. "Make sure he understands how important it is the Midlothians not realize we are on to them."

Or at least some of them, he corrected mentally.

"Understood, Mr. President."

"What we need to avoid at all costs is a multi-front war," Hollingsworth said and the others agreed. "We have found no evidence anyone besides the Midlothians have been working with the Callusians. What we don't know is if our allies have been betrayed by them as we have. I believe it is time to start asking some very carefully phrased questions."

Harper drew a deep breath and held it. Part of him wanted to agree without hesitation, if for no other reason than to know, once and for all, if they were about to go to war against odds they had no chance of beating. Another part, however, hesitated. All it would take was one slip of the tongue by someone to tip off the Midlothians and, were that to happen, he had no doubt those responsible would go to ground until safe for them to resume hostilities with Fuercon.

"How do you propose we do it?" he asked. He wouldn't say no outright, not without hearing what Hollingsworth had in mind.

"We don't go the political route. Let a few trusted Navy and Marine officers and NCOs do it. If there is the least bit of scuttlebutt about Midlothian out there, they can find it."

"Helen?" He looked at the Marine Corps Commandant and waited as she considered the suggestion.

"It's a good suggestion, sir. I would add to it that we need to carefully select who we let in on the secret and ask to poke around. But, overall, I like the idea."

"The pull together a list of who you think we can call on and who they would try to speak with." He looked at the others, making sure they understood what he was asking. "We'll meet again in two days to discuss it." He leaned back and waited until they checked their schedules and nodded in confirmation. "Now, any other suggestions?"

"One." Now Klingsbury leaned forward, his expression as serious as Harper had seen in a very long time. "As Hollingsworth said, the last thing we can afford is a two front – or more – war. At the same time as we are sounding out our allies about any concerns they have about Midlothian, we start serious discussions about invading Callusian space. It will be a joint invasionary fleet meant to end this war once and for all."

A predatory smile touched Harper's lips. "Do it. Draw up your preliminary proposal and get it to me ASAP. No word about it goes beyond this room and those absolutely necessary to draw it up. Let's not tip our hand to the enemy, or to Midlothian, until everything is in place and underway."

He stood and leaned forward, palms on the desktop, his expression deadly serious. "I want this war ended but I will not sacrifice Fuercon or its allies in the process. One step at a time, starting with getting reinforcements to Taskforce Liberator. I want final plans for that operation on my desk by end of business today."

The others stood, recognizing the dismissal. Once alone, Harper sat and reached for his comm to signal his admin to send in his next appointment.

4

Midlothian Embassy
New Kilrain, Fuercon

D'anil Kalmár, Midlothians' ambassador to Fuercon, leaned back and blew out a long, worried breath. Six months. That was how long he'd held this assignment. Six months in which he'd quickly learned there was more to what was going on than his superiors were letting him know. Months in which his paranoia had grown to almost uncontrollable levels. After more than three decades in service to his homeworld, he knew a setup when he saw one and he had no doubt he was sitting smack dab in the middle of one. The problem was someone else held the trigger and could pull it at any time, leaving him to take the blame.

"Will you be needing anything else, Ambassador?"

Kalmár glanced up, careful to keep the distrust from felt for the woman standing in front of his desk from showing. Technically, Elwyn Fertig was exactly what she looked like. No one looking at the small, trim brunette would think she was anything more than his administrative assistant, and possible bed partner. He knew better. She had made her role very clear upon his arrival at the embassy that first day. She was Alexander Watchman's handpicked operative. Midlothian's Intelligence Czar put her in place not so much to spy on their allies but to make sure no one at the embassy betrayed Midlothian's best interests as defined by Watchman. Fertig was the man's blade and Kalmár had no doubt she would gladly slit the throat of anyone her boss pointed her at.

"No, that will be all." He waited until she left his office before blowing out a long breath. A thin bead of sweat ran down his spine. If she knew what he suspected, his days would be numbered. Fortunately for him, and for his continued survival, he hadn't lasted as long in politics as he had without learning a few tricks of his own. The first of which was to never, ever let a potential enemy know you had identified them as such.

He hoped it was enough.

Alone, he one again opened the latest report the embassy had received from Fuercon's Foreign Affairs Advisor. The fact the Callusians taskforce had tried to invade the system was not new. The media had been filled with reports about the attempted invasion for the last few weeks. They had hailed Admiral Tremayne and others, including Colonel Shaw, as heroes. Any opposition to the resumption of the war had been silenced. Funny how the enemy knocking on your own door tended to do that to people.

The report appeared to be straightforward as ever. But Kalmár had the nagging suspicion there was more to what happened than the report said. He could feel it in the pit of his stomach. What he didn't know for sure was what Worse, he feared he could guess. If he was right, it would explain much of what he'd seen and felt over the last few weeks. He closed his eyes for a moment and said a quick prayer he was wrong. He swallowed hard and his sense of unease turned into a stone of fear and suspicion.

Thinking about what the report said – and didn't say -- Kalmár stood. A moment later, she stared out the window behind his desk. Instead of seeing New Kilrain's skyline, a sight he usually took pleasure in, he saw distant battlefields strewn with broken bodies. Black armored Marines moved ever forward, pressing their advantage. Unit insignias flashed in the setting sun and he swallowed hard to recognized not only the insignias but the location as well. As he did, he reminded himself it was just his imagination, his own paranoia eating away at him. He needed to get hold of himself before he betrayed his doubts to anyone, especially Fertig.

But, if he was right, the information missing from the Fuerconese report only confirmed his fear there was much more to what happened during the attempted invasion and it was that *much more* that worried him.

Biting off a curse, he returned to his desk. He closed the report and ejected the 'chip containing it from his datapad. Then he slipped the chip into his pocket. Out of sight of the monitors he knew Fertig had placed in his office, he carefully slid the chip in the hidden slot in his pocket watch. Fertig had once asked him why he carried the replica of such an ancient timepiece. He'd shrugged it off, explaining it as one of his several odd habits. But the truth was that odd time piece had many times been used to carry data he didn't want anyone knowing about.

"Ambassador?" Fertig looked up from whatever she had been working on as he stepped into the outer office.

"I'll be leaving for the day, Elwyn. Please make sure you copy me the latest update of my schedule for tomorrow before you leave."

She looked at him, her hazel eyes narrowed slightly. Then she smiled and nodded. "Of course, Ambassador. Is there anything else I can do for you?"

Other than staying the hell out of my office and my comms?

"No, thank you though." She might think herself an expert at the game, but he'd been playing it much longer than she had. "Finish up the day's correspondence and then go home. I'll see you in the morning."

With that, he left. As he made his way through the embassy and outside, he made sure he did nothing out of the ordinary. He stopped and chatted with several of those he encountered along the way. He nodded to the security guards inside the embassy and paused long enough to thank the military guards at the gate. Then he stepped into his waiting car, giving the driver an address across the capital from the embassy.

"Shall I wait for you, Ambassador?" the driver asked as he parked in front of one of the many non-descript high rises in this part of the city.

"No, Anton. I'll send for you when I'm ready to leave."

With that, he climbed out of the aircar. As he made his way to the building's entrance, he listened as his driver pulled into traffic. A slight smile touched Kalmár's lips as he pressed his palm to the security plate next to the entrance. The doors swung open and he stepped inside. So far, no one, not even Fertig, had figured out the building was simply a ruse. He let the others think he had a lover, or at least a prostitute he frequented, living there. The reality was much simpler. He paid the management a nice fee to let him use the building as a cover.

A few minutes later he stepped off the service elevator and into the sub-basement. Motion activated lights came on as he moved further away from the closing doors. Some of his tension eased as he quickened his pace. This was always the tricky part – making sure he covered the distance between the building where he'd been dropped off and his next destination before Embassy Security decided to send someone in to check on what he might be doing.

Half an hour later, Kalmár dropped onto a chair with a sigh of relief. Not only was he well away from Embassy Row, he was also miles from where he'd been dropped off. For the first time in days, he felt safe, or at least as safe as he could, considering the circumstances.

"You look troubled, D'anil."

He smiled at the man who entered the room. A moment later, he accepted the snifter of brandy and sipped.

"I am." He waited for Gareth Idoya to take a seat opposite him. "The Fuerconese are playing it too close to the vest for my liking."

"About?" Idoya asked.

"The attempt by that Callusian taskforce to hit the system." He took another sip of brandy. Then he leaned forward, placing the snifter on the low table between them. "Gareth, I need your services again."

Idoya arched one brow and leaned back, crossing his legs. "I'm listening."

"I need everything you can find on that bitch Fertig. Not just what is in her file but everything Watchman has on her, and I do mean *on* her. If there is something I can use as leverage where she's concerned, I want to know."

"All right." He looked at Kalmár for a moment, his concern obvious. "What else?"

"Find out what the Fuerconese aren't telling us about the invasion attempt."

The younger man blew out a breath. "Are you sure you want to do this?"

Kalmár nodded. "I am." He stared into the distance for a moment, trying to decide how much to say. "My first loyalty is and always has been to Midlothian. But I have no desire to become the sacrificial lamb at Watchman's altar."

He all but spat out the last. Midlothian's intelligence czar might have fooled everyone else but not Kalmár. The first time he met Watchman, he recognized how power-hungry the man was. It wouldn't surprise him at all to know he was manipulating things from behind the scenes. Watchman excelled at doing just that. He excelled at something else as well – making sure others paid for his mistakes. Kalmár had no intention of being the man's next victim.

"Do you want me to deal with Fertig?" Idoya asked.

Kalmár smiled slightly and shook his head. Watchman might think he held all the cards, but he didn't. Kalmár had no doubt his friend could make easy work of Fertig. Not only could he kill the woman without batting an eye, but he would do it in such a way no one would find a trace of her. If Kalmár wanted information from her, Idoya would get it for him. But, tempting as it was, Kalmár knew he couldn't take that route yet.

Later, if there was a later, he would be more than glad to turn his friend loose against the woman and anyone else Watchman might send against him.

"Just get me what you can on her. If things go the way I suspect, we're going to need her."

Idoya dipped his chin, anticipation shining in his eyes. Kalmár lifted his snifter and raised it in a toast, feeling better. "Now, my friend, what have you heard about the attempted invasion?"

If there was more to the story than the Fuerconese had said, Idoya would know. If not, he would tap his sources to find out. It would not be long before Kalmár knew the whole story.

He hoped.

———

Government House
Caspian Bay, Midlothian

ALEXANDER WATCHMAN CROSSED his legs and folded his hands on the tabletop as he listened to the latest in a long line of speakers discussing the current war. Mild interest showed on his face as the speaker continued urging the group that they needed to do more to support their allies. Bethany Waas reminded them of their treaties with Fuercon and the other systems making up the alliance. It was a lost cause as always. Midlothian had a long history of doing its best to remain neutral when war came to the sector. It would "protect" the shipping lanes and give aid where needed but little more and that served Watchman's purposes just fine.

Waas took one last look at the dozen men and women sitting around the table and shook her head. Watchman's expression may have said little but hers spoke volumes. She did not approve of this head-in-the-sand attitude of her fellow members of Midlothian's "administrative bureau". Each member represented one branch of the government and supposedly held an equal voice. Not that it fooled any of them. Three of the twelve held the power, at least that was what they assumed. Watchman knew differently but he had no intentions of disabusing them of their beliefs.

"You speak, as always, quite eloquently, Bethany," Admiral Horace Boniface commented once the woman took her seat. "However, you know the constraints under which we operate as well as the rest of us. We simply don't have the manpower or the material to do more than we are to support our allies."

"Bullshit."

Watchman turned his attention to the newest member of the committee. Rafael Tarpinian returned his gaze without flinching. In his short time on the committee, he had proven to be more well-informed than Watchman expected. Worse, he had a flair for convincing people that his positions were right. That he now openly challenged the myth that Midlothian did not have the resources to take a more active role in the war was troublesome.

It was also something Watchman planned to deal with now. Otherwise, Tarpinian might just meet an unfortunate accident like his predecessor.

"You have something to say, Tarpinian?" Admiral Boniface arched one brow and tried to stare the younger man down. Instead, the redhead simply returned his look, smiling slightly when the admiral was the first to drop his gaze.

"I have seen the budgets for our Navy. I have also reviewed the reports we've been receiving from our allies. I would assume each of you have as well. So tell me why we don't have the resources to do as Bethany asked? Why are we, one of the oldest settled systems in this sector, relying on others to keep us safe?" He paused, pinning each of those sitting around the table with a look that spoke volumes. He wanted answers and he wasn't going to be satisfied until he got them.

"We have seen the report about how Fuercon got lucky and happened to have ships in the right place at the right time to repel the Callusian attack. I've looked at their reports and have no doubt those ships came through our own system. Why did we not know of their presence? Or did we and we simply failed to pass that information along to our allies?" This time, he looked directly at Watchman, challenging him to deny what he said.

"I will let Admiral Boniface speak to the logistics of why we can do no more than we are to support our allies at this time." Watchman sat a bit straighter in his chair. As he did, he felt more than saw how those closest to him tensed. Tarpinian might not recognize the shit-hole he had stepped into but everyone else did. Their only hope was that it didn't spread to include them. "As for your accusation the Callusians crossed our space and we either didn't know or we hid that information from our allies, I suggest you prove your allegations or retract them with an apology. Never has my office worked against Midlothian's best interest."

Of course, that "best interest" might not be what Tarpinian thought. More fool him.

"Watchman, you don't fool me, and you don't scare me."

Someone actually gasped at that and a slight smile lifted the corners of Watchman's mouth. Oh, he was going to like playing with this one. He might even let him live, at least for a bit longer, just to draw out the fun. Soon enough, however, Tarpinian would learn no one challenged him and lived for long. He would either come to heel or he would find himself suffering the same fate as so many others.

"I'm not trying to do either, Tarpinian." He inclined his head in the younger man's direction, a gesture both conciliatory and insulting at the same time. "I am suggesting that you might be a little overzeal-ous, shall we say, because you are new to this body. If you have proof of your allegations, or even evidence that would lead to a reasonable inference that what you said happened, I am more than willing to discuss it. Otherwise, I respectfully suggest you Shut. The. Fuck. Up."

Gone was the genial man who looked more like someone's loving grandfather. In his place was the man so many had learned to fear over the years. Watchman leaned forward, his expression no longer guarded. His eyes flashed and his smile. . . his smile was the sort that would turn a brave man's bowels to water. If Tarpinian wanted to play, he'd be happy to oblige in a no-holds-barred, no rules match he had never before lost.

Tarpinian swallowed hard but didn't look away. Interesting and definitely something to think about. For now, however, his point had been made and it was time to move on to other topics.

"I suggest we table this discussion until Mr. Tarpinian either presents evidence to support his accusations or withdraws them," Admiral Boniface said as if on cue. "All in favor?"

The others, all save Tarpinian, quickly agreed. Watchman smiled slightly one last time and leaned back, resuming his most non-threatening personas. As he did, he made a mental note to dig deeper into the younger man's background. There was definitely more to him than he first suspected.

————

New Kilrain, Fuercon

"Damn it!"

Evan Moreau kicked the battered coffee table, ignoring the quick flash of pain in her toes. It seemed like nothing had gone right in the last few months. It started with that bitch Shaw not only surviving her time at the Tarsus penal colony but making it back to Fuercon and being pardoned. Pardoned! After all the work she'd put in to make sure the bitch never saw another day of freedom, she was not only free but she'd been rewarded for her work in the prior war.

That had been the beginning of Moreau's problems. Those she had worked with to set up Shaw and the others had either been arrested or they had turned into liabilities she had to deal with. That meant too many bodies and too many loose ends. Never before had she found herself in such a mess. Worse, she couldn't slip off-planet and disappear into one of her other identities. Her employers were not the type to simply let her walk away. Nor did they allow for failures.

She had done the only thing she could. She walked away from the life of Evan Moreau, a comfortable life she'd grown to enjoy. As far as anyone else knew, Moreau had left the planet on business. When she would return depended on how well her negotiations went. In reality, she had traded the Moreau identity for a series of others, each one designed to distance her not only from her previous life but from those who might be looking for her.

Damn it, she should have gotten off of Fuercon and out of the system when she'd had the chance.

She tossed her jacket onto one of the two chairs at the small kitchen table and rummaged in a cabinet. A moment later, she produced a glass and a bottle of whiskey. The amber liquid caught the light as she poured several fingers into the glass. Then she tossed it back before pouring more.

Before she could pour herself a third drink, her comm beeped softly. She dug it out of her pocket and glanced at the display. Her upper lip curled back in a sneer and she programmed the incoming message for text only, blocking confirmation that she'd received the message. She didn't care if it cost her job at the docks. She wasn't in the mood to explain to her supervisor why she'd left early. Hell, even if she was in the mood, what was she supposed to say?

Hey, boss, I walked out without saying anything because I saw yet another news vid that reminded me I'm only one step ahead of the executioner?

She didn't care he threatened to fire her if she wasn't in his office half an hour before shift the next day. A slight smile touched her lips at the thought of walking into his office and dealing with him the way she did others who crossed her. The thought of how he'd piss himself in fear as she played with him. It wouldn't be the same as dealing with Shaw or a few others she could name, but it would be one irritant out of her life.

Then she could fade into the background again, biding her time until she could finally fulfill her contract. If she managed to get a little personal satisfaction along the line, that suited her just fine.

In the meantime, she needed to make sure her real employers understood she wasn't ignoring their orders. It was time to do a little surveillance and then reach out to her contact back on Midlothian.

Hopefully, that would be enough to keep Watchman off her back for a bit longer.

If not, well, she'd managed to stay alive this long. She could do it again. Then everyone who dared betray her would pay. No one played her for the fool, and that included Alexander Watchman and Ashlyn Shaw.

5

Lucinda Ortega sat up and groaned. Every muscle seemed to scream in agony. Her right shoulder felt stiff and that knee was swollen. Grimacing as she pushed to her feet, she knew she should see the medics. Not that she would. There were others, too many others, who needed treatment more than she did. But she would stop by long enough to get something to take the edge off the pain.

That had to wait, however. She had less than half an hour to dress and make her way to Admiral O'Malley's ready room. When he'd sent word just before she retired for the night of the morning's briefing, she'd had a moment of concern. It had passed but not before she'd cursed Brigadier General Hale yet again. Six times she had sent a request for reinforcements and six times he had ignored her. All she could do now was pray the enemy really had left the system with its tail tucked between its legs.

If not. . ..

She wouldn't think about that.

Exactly half an hour later, she entered the Admiral's ready room. As she did, O'Malley looked up from the report he'd been studying and motioned her to a seat. Then he told her to help herself to coffee. The others would be there shortly.

Glad to sit, she did as he said. After pouring a mug of coffee from one of the three carafes on the table, she turned her attention to O'Malley. If possible, he looked more exhausted than she felt. Worse, she saw the pain in his eyes and knew it was caused by more than his own injuries. He felt the deaths of each of those under his command, just as she did.

"Did you get any rest?" O'Malley asked as he reached for his mug.

"Probably about as much as you did, sir."

He lifted his mug in acknowledgment. Then his expression turned serious. Worried, she waited, wondering what was on his mind. Before she could ask, the hatch slid open and the others began arriving.

"Settle down," O'Malley said a few minutes later. He waited as the last arrivals found seats around the table. "Before we get to status reports, I've heard from FleetCom."

Lucinda leaned forward, praying they were finally going to get the reinforcements they so desperately needed. Even as hope flared, worry fought to drive it back down. If they were getting reinforcements, why did O'Malley look so grim? Damn it, had something else happened?

"I now know at least part of the reason why we haven't received any reinforcements from home," the admiral began. "Last month, Admiral Tremayne led a taskforce that was supposed to drive protect the Drakkana System from a Callusian invasion. It should have been a rather straight-forward mission, much like this one." A bitter smile touched O'Malley's lips and somewhere down the table someone cursed softly. "However, the mission went to Hell in the proverbial handbasket pretty damned quick."

He reached out and activated the holo screen over the table. A moment later, it displayed the home system and Lucinda watched as icons lit, indicating the taskforce as it began its journey out of the system. When a new series of icons came alive, everyone present seemed to inhale at the same moment. The silence in the room became almost oppressive as they watched the icons near one another before halting.

"As you can see, we lucked out. The taskforce really was in the right place at the right time. A Callusian taskforce tried to enter the system with obvious ill-intent. When contacted, it squawked out false IDs. Admiral Tremayne sent three ships out to challenge it. The AARs from Admiral Tremayne and Colonel Shaw will be available for your review after this briefing. I suggest you read both reports carefully."

Hearing Ashlyn's name, Lucinda didn't know whether to smile or do a quick check to make sure the woman was all right. Leave it to her former CO to be in the middle of things. Trouble seemed to find her which, as far as Lucinda was concerned, was a good thing. Ashlyn knew how to take care of herself and her people. But Lucinda also knew the chances of her friend's luck running out were high. They were Marines, after all, and long lives were the exception and not the rule during war.

"There is good news, however. Even though the taskforce suffered damage, especially the initial ships that went out to challenge the enemy as well as the LACs used as a defensive screen, they not only held but they managed to force the enemy to surrender."

"Ooh-rah!" It was out before Lucinda could stop it. Fortunately, O'Malley looked at her and grinned, obviously sharing her feelings.

"Ooh-rah, indeed." For the first time in weeks, he didn't look quite so exhausted. "As if that isn't reason enough to celebrate, Admiral Tremayne and Colonel Shaw got the enemy CO to agree to terms of surrender unlike any we've managed to get before. The enemy databases were taken intact. That means Fleet Intel is crawling through them, looking for anything that can be used to our advantage."

"But?" Captain Anson Underwood, O'Malley's chief of staff, asked.

"They also managed to confirm something FleetCom has suspected but had no solid evidence of until now." Anger and something else burned in the admiral's eyes. "Fuercon and others have been betrayed by one we thought of as an ally. Onboard one of the captured ships was a Midlothian Naval officer. He was there as an *advisor* to the Callusians."

Even though she'd known about the suspected connection between Midlothian and the Callusians, knowing they finally had proof of it turned Lucinda's stomach. "Our response?" she asked simply.

"President Harper has not yet made this information public." He held up a hand before anyone could protest. "We know Midlothian had an advisor onboard the Callusian ship and we can now trace some of their weaponry and tactics back to Midlothian. What we can't do, according to FleetCom, is tie it directly to the Midlothian government. I would remind you, as FleetCom is reminding its senior officers, that Midlothian has a long history of shadow governments. It could be this shadow government is the one pulling the strings. Before we declare war on a supposed ally and find ourselves in a multi-front war, let's make sure we know all the facts. In the meantime, every ship and every Marine detachment is to do everything possible to not only defeat the Callusians but to determine how deep the cancer runs where Midlothian is concerned."

"Are we to tell our people?" Lieutenant Sebastian Cabell-Nesmith asked from down the table.

"Not until either Colonel Ortega or I give you leave to do so." O'Malley glanced at Lucinda and she nodded in understanding. The more people who knew, the greater the chances the information could be leaked to the wrong people. The last thing any of them wanted was to give the Midlothian conspirators time to cover their tracks. "Before we move on, I have one more thing to say on this topic. This information wasn't unexpected. FleetCom has had reason for the last six months or more to suspect involvement from some element of the Midlothian government. It has played it very close to the vest where that information is concerned for obvious reasons. If I learn any of you have spoken about this without permission, you will find yourself brought up on charges so fast your head will spin. Is that understood?" Everyone answered in the affirmative and he seemed to relax.

"Next topic and a most welcome one. We are being sent reinforcements. FleetCom is dispatching a second taskforce comprised of elements from First and Second Fleets to help us hold the system until replacements can arrive to take over system command."

"Finally," someone murmured.

Lucinda couldn't help but agree.

"Colonel, you'll be relieved to know you'll be getting Marine reinforcements, complete with LACs, as well." Now O'Malley smiled at her. "The equivalent of two companies of the Devil Dogs will be part of the taskforce."

Lucinda blew out a relieved breath. Finally, some good news. She wasn't even ashamed to admit she hoped Ashlyn commanded the companies. They needed the best just then, especially when she looked at her own casualty reports and Ash and the Devil Dogs were just that – the best.

"When will they get here, sir?" Underwood asked.

"Best guess right now is ten days or so. At the time of the dispatch, they had yet to leave the home system. However, if I know Admiral Tremayne, she has instructed them to make best speed here."

Lucinda ducked her head, hiding her smile. If she knew the admiral, Tremayne was leading the taskforce herself. That meant she wouldn't waste any time getting there. It also meant she'd come ready to do battle. The Callusians wouldn't know what hit them. All Taskforce Liberator had to do was survive long enough for the reinforcements to arrive.

"Now, let's see what we can do to hold on until those reinforcements get here," O'Malley said and turned the discussion over to the taskforce's current status.

Two hours later, O'Malley dismissed everyone with instructions to let him know any changes in status. For a moment, Lucinda considered returning to her quarters for another hour or so of sack time. O'Malley even suggested it. Tempting as it was, she had too much to do. Her Marines were down by more than half. She'd suffered too many dead and even more wounded. Somehow, she had to find a way to continue doing the mission until the Devil Dogs arrived. How was the question and she didn't have a good answer.

"Well?" M. J. Anderson asked. "Please tell me there was some good news this time."

Lucinda looked up from her notes and smiled. The blonde master sergeant leaned against the doorframe, her expression serious.

"For once, there is." She motioned her senior NCO inside the office and waited as the hatch slid shut. It didn't take long to fill her in on the highlights of the briefing.

"Thank God."

Adamson scrubbed her face with her hands before looking up. In that brief moment, all her fear and uncertainty shone through. Understanding, Ortega nodded. She had a feeling she'd looked much the same when O'Malley announced reinforcements were finally coming.

"That means we have to find a way to hold out long enough for them to get here. I don't believe for one moment the enemy is going to simply leave us here without trying something. They fought too hard when we arrived to keep us out."

"Agreed." Adamson reached into a pocket for her datapad. "Has there been any intel on where they are right now?"

"Not yet. O'Malley has ordered more sensors laid throughout the system. Hopefully it will be enough to keep them from getting the jump on us."

"And dirtside?"

"We are going to have to rely more on the locals than I like." She shook her head before Adamson could say anything. "MJ, you know I'm right. We need to hold our people back as long as possible. We don't have enough to simply have them sitting at potential targets, waiting to see if we guessed right about where the enemy would strike. I don't like it any more than you do, but I don't see any other way. If you've got an idea, I'm more than open to it."

Adamson frowned and shook her head. "You're right. I just hope it doesn't bite us in the ass."

"You and me both. You and me both."

"So we do whatever we can to make sure it doesn't happen." Adamson stood. In that moment, she looked like she ought to be on a recruiting advert for the Corps. "You finish going through that stack of reports I know is waiting for you. Then let's sit down and figure out the best way to position our people so they can do the most good."

Relieved yet again that Ashlyn hadn't objected when the powers-that-be said they wanted Adamson to report to the Warlords with her, Ortega nodded. They still faced an uphill battle they very well could lose, but at least now they had a glimmer of hope. All they had to do was hold out a little longer.

6

Glenn Space Port
New Kilrain, Fuercon

"No unnecessary risks, Ash. Promise me," Elizabeth said as they watched the next to the last troop shuttle lifting off.

"Don't worry, Mom." She smiled at the woman and gave her hand a quick squeeze. "Far as I'm concerned, we're there just long enough for FleetCom to get replacements sent out. Then we're coming home."

Elizabeth smiled but that smile didn't reach her eyes. Ashlyn saw and understood. They both knew how much could go wrong. One bad mistake, one lucky shot by the enemy and any of the Devil Dogs could return in a casket. Ash had no intention of letting that happen.

"How long before the replacements will be sent?" she asked as they strolled toward the last shuttle. The rest of the Devil Dogs shipping out with her were already onboard, with the exception of Corporal Connery. Master Gunnery Sergeant Talbot stood next to the young woman, his expression showing just how unhappy he was to be left behind. "I think I'm in trouble." Ash grinned and nodded in the shuttle's direction.

"The Master Guns can be a bit of a mother hen." Elizabeth chuckled softly before turning serious. "I admit, I'd feel better if he was going with you, but I understand why you're leaving him here."

Ashlyn stopped and turned to face her mother. "Mom, if things go sour here."

"Don't worry. Your father and sister will get Jake out of the capital if the enemy makes another attempt to attack the system." She rested a hand on Ashlyn's arm. "I swear, we will keep Jake safe."

Ash closed her eyes and inhaled deeply. Then she nodded. Exhaling, she opened her eyes. It never got any easier to leave on a mission, knowing she might never see her son again. "I left a series of messages for him, Mom. Kate has a few gifts for him as well."

"Ash, don't worry. He's not going to forget you and he'll never doubt your love for him."

All she could do was give a small shrug. Perhaps she was being foolish but, after the Arterus mission her time on Tarsus, she took little for granted, especially when it came to her family.

"Any last instructions?" she asked to change the subject as they neared the shuttle.

"No. O'Malley and Lucinda know you are coming. It will be up to O'Malley and Miranda to determine if your combined forces will be enough to hold the system until relief arrives or if your best course of action is to withdraw. Officially, it would be preferred if you held the system until replacement forces arrive – which should be in less than a month. Unofficially, we'd rather go in with a stronger force to retake the system than risk losing any more people than we already have."

"Understood." She nodded to Connery and Talbot before turning back to her mother. "I'd best get onboard. Admiral Tremayne won't thank me if I delay our departure." She grinned, and Elizabeth chuckled softly. The both knew Tremayne wouldn't say anything as long as the delay wasn't too long. The admiral understood not only how but why it was still difficult for Ash to leave Fuercon.

"Good hunting, Ash." Elizabeth broke protocol long enough to give her daughter a hug. Then she stepped back and smiled as Ash braced to attention and saluted. She returned the salute and turned to leave but not before Ashlyn saw the concern in her eyes.

Doing her best to hide her own worries, Ash turned to Connery and Talbot. "Tell the pilot we'll be ready to lift in a minute," she told the corporal.

Connery acknowledged the order and disappeared inside the shuttle.

"Loco?"

"Ma'am, I understand why you have split the battalion the way you have but I don't like it." He frowned, and she knew he wanted to pace. "I'll make sure things run smoothly here. Major Laboe is starting to settle in nicely."

"I know." She motioned for him to step away from the shuttle with her. "Loco, he's a good officer. He might even make a good XO for the Devil Dogs. But I need you to be honest when we get back. If he isn't fitting in by then, I have to know. Unless I miss my guess, it isn't going to be long before we take this war directly to the Callusians. When that happens, I plan to do everything I can to make sure the Devil Dogs are leading the charge. That means I have to be able to rely on my XO and not worry about what he's going to do – or not do."

"Understood, ma'am." He looked over her shoulder in the direction of the shuttle and then looked back. "Angel, no unnecessary risks. The Devil Dogs need you and so does that little boy of yours."

She swallowed against the lump in her throat and dipped her head once. "Speaking of Jake."

"Don't worry. I'll be checking on him and I swear I will give my life if necessary to keep him safe."

"Thanks, but you know the priorities. The President, Okafor, my mother and then my son." It broke her heart to say it, but the chain of command had to be preserved.

"I know my duty, Angel."

She smiled slightly, understanding what he left unsaid. He knew his duty but that didn't mean he'd follow it exactly. Hopefully, he wouldn't find himself in the situation where he had to choose.

"Take care of my Devil Dogs, Master Guns," she said as Connery appeared in the hatch of the shuttle.

"You do the same, Colonel." He braced to attention and saluted. She returned it and then shook his hand. "Safe travels and good hunting, ma'am."

She turned and hurried across the tarmac to where the shuttle waited. Time was wasting, time she had a feeling the Warlords didn't have to waste.

———

Phoenix Rising, flagship
Taskforce Sentinel
Fuerconese System

"HAVE A SEAT."

Admiral Miranda Tremayne stood at the head of the conference table in her Ready Room. For a moment, she let her gaze wander around the room. As she did, a slight smile touched her lips. All but one of the senior officers she'd summoned to the briefing sat at the table. The exception leaned against the far bulkhead where she not only had a view of the entire room but of the room's only entrance. She might look relaxed but Tremayne knew differently. Colonel Ashlyn Shaw stood ready to meet any threat to her admiral and to their mission.

"Ladies and gentlemen, welcome to Taskforce Sentinel," Tremayne said as she took her seat. "We have one mission with two possible outcomes. We are to transit to the Tenasic System and either help Taskforce Liberator hold the system until replacement forces arrive or evacuate the survivors of Liberator. It is an either-or situation and the final decision rests with me. Is that understood?"

Once again, she looked around the table. As she did, most nodded in response. She noted the questions reflected in the eyes of a couple. But it was Shaw whose response caught her attention. Not that anyone who didn't know the younger woman very well would have caught it. However, having known Ashlyn most the young woman's life, Tremayne saw her anger and her fear. Recognizing them, as well as the reason for them, she waited until she caught Shaw's eye. Then she gave a slight nod. That was all but it was enough to let her goddaughter know she had every intention of doing whatever it took to insure they reached the Tenasic System before it was too late for Taskforce Liberator.

"FleetCom has authorized us to proceed at full military speed. We will do that and more. I will not leave our people hanging one moment longer than necessary. If you have any objections to that, I will personally sign your transfer papers and escort you to the shuttle. You have exactly five minutes to let me know and to get yourself to the bay. After that, we are pulling out and there will be no turning back until we have fulfilled our mission. Any questions?"

"No, ma'am!" Ashlyn answered in full Marine-mode.

Tremayne fought her smile. She had seen Ash do this before. It was the young woman's way of not only reinforcing her role as taskforce commander but also of reminding everyone else they were still held to military discipline, something a few of them appeared to have forgotten.

"With your permission, Admiral?"

Tremayne inclined her head even as she lifted a brow in question. Instead of explaining, Ashlyn stepped away from the wall and moved smartly around the table until she stood next to the admiral's chair. Tremayne watched as several of the others realized the import of what just happened. Ashlyn, who usually did her best to stay in the background, had claimed her position not only as the Marine contingent's commanding officer but as the second highest ranking officer in the taskforce. She had come a long way from the uncertain young officer she'd been the first time she served on one of Tremayne's ships.

"Ladies and gentlemen, the Admiral is much nicer than I am. I'm a Marine and believe in direct action. Our people have been left too long alone in the Tenasic System without reinforcements or resupply. They have taken heavy casualties as a result. If we waste time making sure everyone is all right with the Admiral's orders to get help to the taskforce as quickly as possible, we very well may be signing the death warrants of every member of Taskforce Liberator. I don't know about you, but I have enough dead haunting my dreams as it is. Because of that, I suggest you listen up. If you think the Admiral is wrong in taking this action, do not wait for her to sign your papers. Get up and haul your ass down to the shuttle bay. My Marines will make sure you get off the ship and don't delay our departure." With that, she stepped into parade rest, her expression impassive.

Tremayne fought the urge to laugh at the looks on the faces of some of the others around the table. Most simply nodded and looked as if they would help Ashlyn escort those opting out of the mission to a waiting shuttle, possibly by the scruff of the neck. The others, and she had no doubt they had never before served with her Marine CO, looked as if they didn't know whether to brace to attention and prepare for a return to boot camp or if they ought to find the nearest JAG to report her. What they were about to learn was Tremayne had her back now and always.

"For those of you who haven't taken time to review your briefing packets, two things. This is the last time you had better come to a briefing without being prepared. If you had read your packet, you would learn this is not a typical mission. FleetCom, with the full support of President Harper and his advisors, is about to institute new measures to defeat the enemy once and for all. That means there will be changes, having Colonel Shaw as second in command of this mission is only one indication of what those changes will be.

"Second, most of you have served with me long enough to understand that I will not tolerate anyone, no matter who they are, to fail to put forth their best effort. Part of that is setting the example for the rest of the crew. Some of you served on the last mission Colonel Shaw and I were one together. All of you should know what happened on that mission – and what could have happened if we hadn't been lucky enough to be in the right place at the right time and if the colonel hadn't been willing and able to think outside the box. You should know there was something different about what happened when I entered the Ready Room." She paused, waiting to see if anyone spoke up. When no one did, she looked up at Ashlyn and nodded.

"When Admiral Tremayne entered, not one of you followed military protocol and called the rest to attention," Ash said evenly. "She gave each of you plenty of time to do so before telling everyone to take a seat. That lack of discipline will not be tolerated with my Marines and it should not be tolerated by or from the taskforce's senior officers."

"With respect, Colonel Shaw, you didn't call us to attention either," Captain Aja Rocha commented from down the table.

"She didn't do so because I'd instructed her not to, Captain." The bite of Tremayne's voice caused several of those gathered to flinch slightly. Rocha, however, simply stared back at them. Frowning, the admiral knew she had a decision to make and wished it weren't so. They didn't have time to get a replacement for Rocha, but she also didn't have the time nor the inclination to deal with the woman if she was going to be a problem. "Everyone except Captain Rocha and Colonel Shaw are dismissed for five."

This time, every person present save Rocha and Shaw braced to attention and waited until Tremayne jerked her head toward the hatch. A few moments later, the hatch slid shut once again. As soon as it had, Tremayne stood and leaned forward, her palms flat on the tabletop.

"Captain Rocha, you are new to my command, so I will give you this one chance to understand that I appreciate officers who can think outside of the box – as long as doing so doesn't put our people at risk. However, I also demand my officers set the example for everyone else in the taskforce. If you cannot do so, tell me now. There will be no negative entry on your record and we will see if we can start new when the taskforce returns to Fuercon."

"Admiral." The brunette snapped her mouth shut when Tremayne arched a brow at her and gave one shake of her head.

"Colonel Shaw, is your LAC commander experienced enough to take command of not only your LACs but those assigned to the taskforce?"

Ashlyn considered for a moment before responding. "Yes, ma'am. Captain Traylor normally commands close to twice as many LAC pilots and their crews as what we brought with us. If memory serves me correctly, if we combined the Navy LACs with those of the Devil Dogs, the numbers would be approximately what the captain normally commands."

"Your choice, Captain Rocha." Tremayne waited, giving the woman time to consider her options.

"My apologies to both you and to Colonel Shaw, Admiral. If you are willing to give me a second chance, I assure you that you won't regret it." As she spoke, Rocha snapped to attention.

"Very well, Captain. Welcome aboard." Tremayne smiled and moved around the table to shake the woman's hand. "Colonel, please ask the others to rejoin us."

Ash nodded and moved to the hatch. As she did, Tremayne motioned for Rocha to sit. There was still a great deal to accomplish and even less time in which to do it.

———

"WELL?" Tremayne asked.

Ashlyn accepted the cold beer the admiral handed her and lifted it in a toast. Then she settled back on the sofa in Tremayne's day room. As she stretched her legs before her, relaxing for the first time in more than twelve hours, she waited as the redhead sat opposite her. Many would wonder what Tremayne meant by her simple question, but not Ash. She knew exactly what the admiral wanted to know. She simply wasn't sure how to answer.

"We have a week to get everyone onto the same page." She lifted one shoulder in a half-shrug. "The Marines are solid. I have no qualms where they are concerned."

Fortunately for her own peace of mind, the last mission had let her get to know many of the Marines assigned to the taskforce. They had risen to the challenges present when their ships unexpectedly stumbled upon the Callusian's attempted invasion of the home system. Each and every one of them had responded and had done everything they could to support the Devil Dogs on the mission. Ash had scored points with them upon their return home when she made sure the Marines assigned to First Fleet had received the same degree of recognition for what they'd done has had her own Devil Dogs.

"I've no concern about them, Ash." Tremayne smiled and leaned forward, helping herself to cheese and crackers from a platter on the low table in front of the sofa. "I'm more concerned about some of the Naval officers. Mixing units from both First and Second Fleets have left me working with a few senior officers I'm not familiar with."

"I'm not sure I can be of much help there, Miranda." She sighed and took another sip of her beer. "I'm still catching up after my little *vacation*." Bitterness filled her voice at the thought of the two years she'd spent at the Tarsus penal colony after the Arterus mission.

"Ash." Tremayne leaned forward and reached for her hand. "Those responsible have been caught and will pay for what they did to you and the others. You know that."

She nodded, her expression grim. The knowledge Admiral Alec Sorkowski (ret.) and others now sat in cells, either awaiting trial or awaiting transport to one of the off-planet penal colonies, helped her get through each day. It would never bring back those who died on that ill-fated mission, but it helped. Even so, she knew she needed to do one thing before Sorkowski and Thomas O'Brien, her former – and very temporary – CO, were moved off-planet. Not that she could discuss it with Tremayne. She knew the redhead well enough to know Tremayne would try to dissuade her. It was best to not mention it to her until afterwards. Not that she could do much about it until this mission was over.

"To answer your question," she said, refocusing their attention back to Tremayne's concerns. "I think the officers will shake out. I recommend you have daily briefings and you not let anything slide." Not that she'd ever known Tremayne to do so. "Consistency and setting the example will go a long way, especially for those like Rocha."

After the briefing, Ash made sure the Devil Dogs were getting their gear squared away. Then she met with her officers and senior NCOs. There had been more meetings, too many by her book, before she'd finally been able to find her office and get some real work done. Part of that had been checking out Rocha and a few of the others on Tremayne's senior staff she'd never worked with before. At least she'd seen nothing to be concerned about. Rocha's evaluations noted she tended to be prickly until getting a feel for those she served with, but she was a solid officer. Ash could handle prickly as long as Rocha got the job done.

"Are you going to get blowback from your order to open up the engines?" she asked, setting her now empty mug on the table to her left.

"A couple of ship commanders have groused, and I gave them the same option I gave the others. None were willing to risk future promotion by asking to be left behind. Once they committed to stay, I told them exactly what I told my senior staff. We will not risk our own ships, but I'm not leaving Liberator out there alone one moment longer than necessary just because I don't want to take risks."

Ash nodded, unsurprised by her response. Still, the very fact the ship commands raised the concern and brought them to Tremayne might be an indication of potential problems.

"Before you say anything, I have had a word with those who were present today and who did not deal with the questions and concerns of those captains under their command."

Ashlyn winced slightly. She recognized Tremayne's tone and knew those she'd "had a word with" would make sure they never again failed to let their subordinates know the admiral's orders and the reasons for them. At least they wouldn't if they wanted to continue in the Navy. Not that she blamed Tremayne one bit.

"Our ETA now?"

"Assuming nothing unforeseen happens, we should reach sensor range of the system in five days."

And said a quick prayer that nothing delayed them. She had a very bad feeling about what Taskforce Liberator might face between now and then. "Miranda, I know the *official* orders." She waited, hoping the woman understand what she was trying to get at. "But I also know FleetCom has given you wide discretion on what we actually do once we reach the system. If I'm not out of place, may I ask your thoughts?"

Tremayne didn't answer right away. Instead, she stood and moved to the sofa. Ashlyn watched, understanding the redhead needed time to order her thoughts. Tremayne reached for Ash's mug. She gave the younger woman a smile and then moved across the day room. Ash waited as she refilled their mugs.

"You're right." Tremayne handed Ash her beer and then returned to her seat. "I do have a lot more leeway than I told the others. Just as I'm sure you do where your Marines are concerned."

Ash nodded, confirming what she said.

"If things are as bad for Liberator as I suspect, we are going to evacuate them to safety. Then I'll make the decision about whether or not we return to try to hold the system."

Relieved, Ash leaned back. Part of her knew that's what Tremayne would say but another part, the part that knew how badly FleetCom wanted a victory, worried. Now she realized she'd worried for nothing. Tremayne would always put the lives of her people first, unless the mission demanded they make a last stand to help save Fuercon and her allies. This one did not.

"You know, I hope, that I'll back you on whatever you decide."

"I do." The redhead smiled at her in affection. "Just as I know you aren't completely comfortable being my second-in-command."

Ash shrugged. She certainly couldn't deny the truth of what Tremayne said. "I am. I'm a Marine. I fight. I lead my people into battle. I'm not a naval officer and I never, ever want to take command of a ship again." She still broke out in a cold sweat thinking about how she'd done just that on their last mission and how lucky they'd been that she hadn't gotten them all killed.

Tremayne chuckled and the gleam in her eyes did nothing to reassure Ash. "I promise I have no plans of putting us in a position where you have to take command, especially since you are assigned to this particular ship. You taking command means something would have to happen to me, my flag captain and a few others who would be in line to step into command before we ever worked our way down the chain to you."

Even though she was right, Ash still narrowed her eyes suspiciously at the woman. "You keep that in mind," was all she said. Then she yawned, belatedly covering her mouth with one hand. "Sorry. It's been a long day."

"For both of us." Tremayne stood and then leaned down to help Ash to her feet. "I know you're worried about Lucinda and the others, Ash. I'm won't tell you not to be. But you aren't going to be any good to them or to our people if you don't get some rest."

"The same goes, Admiral." Ash arched one brow and waited until Tremayne agreed. "Do you still want to meet for breakfast?"

"I do. We need to set up training schedules."

Ash pulled her datapad and made a quick note. Then she looked up at Tremayne. There was one question left to ask that night and she hoped the admiral agreed. "Connery is doing a very good job as my aide, especially considering she got thrown into the role without any real warning on the last mission. Do you think your aide would sit down with her while we have breakfast and talk with her? I know Faith has some questions that she isn't comfortable asking me and, unfortunately, neither MJ nor Loco are here to answer them for her."

"Of course. I'll have Jesse contact her tonight and arrange to have breakfast with her."

"Thanks." Ash drained her mug and carried it across the day room to the small bar. "Do get some rest tonight."

"You take your own advice," Tremayne said and walked with her to the door.

Ash smiled and gave the woman's hand a quick squeeze. Then she left, her mind already on everything she needed to accomplish to make sure her Marines were ready for whatever they found when they finally arrived at the Tenasic System.

7

J. W. Campbell, flagship
Taskforce Liberator
Tenasic System

"Admiral?"

Lucinda Ortega stepped inside Admiral O'Malley's ready room and glanced around. It didn't surprise her to see no one else there. Over the last two months, she and O'Malley had formed a working partnership, one very much like that shared by Ashlyn Shaw and Miranda Tremayne. Because of that, O'Malley often met with her before bringing in the rest of his senior staff. Of course, the number of senior staff still alive had diminished in that time and, she feared, would once again.

"The others will be here shortly." He motioned her to a seat at the table and, to her surprise, poured her a mug of coffee. "Our latest sensor readings show a group of ships incoming. General plot seems to confirm the enemy has decided to pay us a visit again."

"Shit." It was out before she could stop it. O'Malley nodded, his expression grim. "How many?"

Please don't let them have been reinforced.

"They are still too far out for a solid reading. Right now, best guess is these are the same ships we drove out last time."

Lucinda closed her eyes and prayed he was right. Then, when she once again looked at him, she nodded. "I've already ordered my Marines to their stations. For the moment, they are backing up Damage Control and the stations they have been trained on. I've also sent security details to the Bridge, Engineering, Environmental and the Med Ward. Two companies—" What a laugh. She doubted she had much more than two full companies left of mobile personnel— "are standing by in the staging area. Flight crews are prepping the battle shuttles as well as our remaining LACs."

"Excellent." Before he could say anything more, a soft beep sounded, signaling the arrival of the rest of the senior staff.

Five minutes later, O'Malley rapped his knuckles on the tabletop. Instantly, the room fell silent. Grim faces, a few showing a fear Lucinda understood, turned to him. They waited as he called up the system on the holo above the table. For what seemed an eternity but could have only been a few moments, they studied the holo and the too few friendly icons blinking green.

Fear, cold and bitter, formed a knot in Lucinda's stomach. The taskforce had lost one ship. Few of its personnel had been able to escape before the ship exploded. A second ship was little more than a limping hulk. O'Malley had made the difficult decision not to purge its databanks and scuttle the ship because he didn't want the enemy to realize just how badly it had hurt the taskforce. That was before she considered the losses to their LACs.

Taskforce Sentinel couldn't arrive soon enough.

"As you can see," O'Malley said, drawing her attention back to him. "Sensors currently show a group of ships heading in-system. They are still too far out for a solid ID. However, based on their entry trajectory, I think it safe to assume the enemy has decided to come calling again."

"Numbers?" Commander Sarah Washington asked. The *Indomitable*'s commanding officer studied the holo plot with a critical eye.

"Best guess only is they are coming in with approximately ten ships."

O'Malley's comment brought a groan from several of those present. Even though she understood, Ortega glanced at them, her expression hard. They had to believe the taskforce could hold out. If they faltered, so would those under them. If that happened, not only would the taskforce fall but so would the system. That could not and would not be allowed to happen, not if she had anything to say about it.

"If our estimate's correct," O'Malley continued, "we will be outnumbered. We have six ships that can be called anything close to battle ready. Two others are damaged but still capable of fighting on a limited basis. One, the *Reginald Perry*, is in no shape to be in a fight. Captain Ulch, you are to begin transitioning to the rear of formation immediately. All non-essential personnel are to be transported off-ship immediately. You have four hours."

O'Malley paused. His expression betrayed he knew he was asking the impossible. "Al, get as many of your people off as you can. We'll do our best to screen you from the enemy but, for now, we need your ship operational for appearances if nothing else."

"I understand, sir, and so do my people."

"We are changing our battle plans this time, ladies and gentlemen. The enemy expects us to come to them. This time, we aren't going to. We are going to let them come to us. That gives us more time to prepare. It also lets us utilize the defense platforms more to our advantage."

Ortega listened closely as the admiral laid out his plans. It galled here not to take the fight to the enemy, but O'Malley was right. They needed all the time they could get to prepare for this fight. At least they had at least twelve hours or so before the enemy was within weapons range.

"Sir." She waited until O'Malley nodded for her to continue. "Sir, I'm the suspicious sort." A few chuckles sounded, and she smiled slightly. Everyone present knew she trusted the enemy no further than she could throw them, especially when it came to the enemy sticking to known tactics. "We still have a dozen or so of the Odins. I can have the loaded onto several battle shuttles for placement." She reached for her datapad and made a couple of quick calculations. "They could be ready for launch within the hour."

O'Malley considered her suggestion for a moment. Then he glanced around the table, as if judging the reaction of the others. "Comments?"

"It's an excellent suggestion, sir," Commander Washington said. "Those missile platforms might be exactly what we need to help hold off the enemy long enough for Taskforce Sentinel to get here."

"See to it, Colonel."

Lucinda nodded and sent the order. "The shuttles will launch as soon as they have the platforms loaded and have received locations from Tactical for their placement."

"What about the civilians dirtside?" Lieutenant Brendan Wainwright asked.

O'Malley didn't answer immediately. When he did, his regret shown through. "They are on their own." He held up a hand before anyone could interrupt. "You have served with me long enough to know I would normally send at least some of our Marines dirtside to help man defensive positions there. We simply don't have the manpower to do so this time. Colonel Ortega has already ordered the Warlords to backup critical positions here on the *Campbell*, as well as on our other ships. She has to maintain her remaining LAC pilots and their crews as well as at least some of the battle shuttles."

"If I may, Admiral?" When he nodded, Lucinda continued. "The groundside defense is in far better shape now than it was when we arrived. For once, the Callusians didn't completely destroy the infrastructure as soon as they landed. Because of that, once we retook the capital, the local army was able to bring their systems back online. Repairs have been made to them and to the defense platform controls. More than that, the locals have had a taste of what it would be like to live under Callusian control. They will do all they can to prevent that from ever becoming their reality. That lets us use my Marines more to our advantage which, right now, means keeping them shipboard and ready to respond where they are most needed."

She didn't like it. The Warlords were much better trained to deal with the enemy, but she was also a reality. If the Callusians managed to defeat the taskforce, the surviving Marines would have little chance of holding them off-planet. Every one of them would die and for no reason.

Damn Hale for not sending the reinforcements she'd asked for!

"Ladies and gentlemen, we should know more about what we're facing in another few hours. Until then, let's expect the worst and plan for it. Hopefully, we will be pleasantly surprised," O'Malley said.

"Sir, I hate to say it, but shouldn't we at least consider withdrawing, even temporarily, from the system?"

Lucinda forced herself not to frown. Instead, she glanced around the table to locate the speaker. When she spotted him, she no longer fought her frown. In her time with the taskforce, she learned Commander Hunter Idell much preferred playing from a position of power. Not that she blamed him. She preferred it as well. However, she learned long ago that wasn't always possible in war. Sometimes, you simply had to meet the enemy head on.

"Commander, I appreciate you broaching the subject and the answer is no. We haven't fought this hard to protect the system just to walk away." He waited until Idell nodded before continuing. "Add to that the fact we would have to leave the *Perry* and most of its crew behind if we were to withdraw. I am not willing to do that."

For the next few minutes, the pros and cons of withdrawing the remnants of the taskforce were debated. Lucinda watched O'Malley, wondering how long he'd let the debate continue before putting an end to it. She understood why he let it continue, even after he said the taskforce would remain in-system. None of them wanted to die, which very well might happen in the upcoming hours, but they had sworn an oath to do so if necessary to protect Fuercon and her allies.

"All right, ladies and gentlemen, we have a great deal to do before the enemy is close enough for this fight to resume," O'Malley said as the debate wound down. "We will meet, not necessarily in person, every two hours until the enemy is an hour outside of weapons range. The taskforce will go to General Quarters an hour before that. In the meantime, make sure your people know what our current status is and get them ready." He stood, and they quickly followed his example. "It has been an honor and a pleasure serving with each of you and I have every confidence we will come through this upcoming battle victorious."

"Ooh-rah," Lucinda said just loud enough to be heard around the table. Then she paused, listening to the latest report coming in over the battlenet. "Sir, Tactical has probable locations for the Odins ready for your approval. Once you've given it, the shuttles will be ready to launch."

"Then let's be about it. Dismissed."

———

Callusian Warship Sobek

LUDO JURIĆ STALKED onto the bridge. As he did, he growled for someone to silence the alarms. They were still too far out for them to be sounding and they were giving him a headache. Without a word, doing their best not to bring his attention to themselves, the members of the bridge crew did as he said. They had served with the commander long enough to know not to do anything to draw his ire when he was in such a mood.

"Status?" he barked as he slouched in the command chair in the center of the bridge.

"The enemy appears to have remained in-system, Commander." As he spoke, the man activated the holo-display at the front of the bridge. "Their relative position has not changed over the last half hour."

"Are they aware of our approach?"

"They should be." The scanners operator hunched his shoulders, as if expecting a blow.

"Should be?" Jurić climbed to his feet. A moment later, he stood behind the younger man. As he rested his hands on the man's shoulders, Jurić smiled slightly to feel him flinch. Like so many others who had risen through the ranks of the Callusian military, he often resorted to assassination to do so. His crew knew it and knew, some by first-hand experience, that he did not accept anything but their complete loyalty. Failure to follow orders and to bring him the glory of victory always resulted in pain and, all too often, death.

Goran Ivanishvili swallowed hard and nodded. "Yes, sir. If their scanners are operational, they should be aware of our approach."

Jurić tightened his grip on Ivanishvili's shoulders enough to make him wince. Then he stepped back, his expression thoughtful. Inside, however, his blood boiled. The Fuerconese had surprised him time and again since the taskforce's arrival in-system. He had underestimated them and that allowed the Fuerconese to force him to flee. Even outnumbered, the enemy had managed to withstand everything he threw at them during that first encounter. Oh, he'd hurt them, but they had hurt his command worse. He had no choice that day but to withdraw and make repairs before attempting to retake the system.

Bad as that had been, the continuing interference of his Midlothian "advisor" had been worse. The late and unlamented fool kept telling him – HIM! – how to fight the battle. Worse, the fool wanted him to send for reinforcements. He didn't understand that would not only be an admission of failure but an open invitation for anyone who wanted his command to try for it. The last thing he needed was to be constantly looking over his shoulder in case someone should decide to assassinate him. He had a battle to fight and win.

During the last encounter with the Fuerconese, the Midlothian – What had his name been? Kevin Goto? – met with an unfortunate accident. At least that was what his report said. Unofficially, Goto met his fate with a fatal walk out an airlock at the point of a gun. Well, walk might not be exactly the right word. The man had been dragged, screaming and pissing himself in fear. It had been a joy to witness and something Jurić recommended each of his fellow commanders saddled with one of their new allies as "advisors" take.

Unfortunately, he hadn't acted sooner. The constraints put on him by his own senior command meant he had to listen to Goto and give him enough rope to hang himself. Those constraints cost him ships and people. But now he had a free hand and he would make the Fuerconese pay.

"What is the current estimate of the enemy force?" he asked as he returned to his seat.

"Initial estimate matches that of our last encounter, sir," Lieutenant Willem Corso answered. "We won't have a better estimate until we have closed on their position."

"Time to intercept?"

"Twelve hours at our current speed, sir," the navigator answered.

Jurić leaned forward, his brow furrowed. "The enemy's speed?"

"They appear to be holding position, sir."

Jurić turned his attention to the small plot at his right knee. As he did, he reminded himself not to react to the news the Fuerconese commander appeared to be holding his ships in their current location. Part of him hoped it meant the enemy ships had been more badly damaged in their last encounter than believed. But another part, the part that had kept him alive all these years, warned it might be a trap.

"Helm, slow our speed by one quarter," he ordered, carefully considering the plot. "Comms, send word to the bay. They are to launch a probe. Let's see exactly what the Fuerconese have in plan for us."

"Commander," the communications officer began a few moments later. "The bay reports we have no more probes. We launched the last of them as we withdrew last time."

Jurić ground his teeth together even as he pulled up the latest report. He quickly scanned it. As he did, his lips peeled back and anger spiked. Everyone on the bridge cringed when he personally sent for the boat bay officer. Silence, the silence of those who knew they just avoided the executioner's block, settled over the bridge. Jurić ignored it, turning his focus instead back to the plot and all its unanswered questions.

A few minutes later, the lift doors slid open and the boat bay officer stepped onto the bridge. Jurić glanced at him. As he did, the commander had to give it to the man. Since sending for him, the bridge crew had all but pissed themselves in an attempt to avoid coming to Jurić's attention. The BBO looked a little pale but otherwise appeared calm and confident. That meant he either felt he held the upper hand and the only way he might is if he had better political contacts than Jurić himself or he was a fool. Jurić's money was on him being a fool. Not that it mattered. Any connections the man might have were far from there and would never learn the truth of what happened to the man.

"I understand we have no probes to launch. Is that correct?" Jurić almost smiled as all but Chehallis hunched over their workstations, becoming as small of a target as possible.

"We launched the last of them as we departed from the field last time," Chehallis replied. "Sir," he added, looking but not sounding contrite for showing the proper respect.

"And you reported this when?"

"In my initial report after our withdrawal."

Jurić frowned. Chehallis seemed too sure of himself. Suspicious, the commander glanced around the bridge. Could the man have allies among the others? It wouldn't be the first time a ship's commander had been assassinated on the bridge. The gods knew, he had done it himself.

Leaning back, doing his best to look relaxed and non-threatening, Jurić slowly, carefully eased his right hand closer and closer to the pistol hidden in the arm of his command chair. As he did, a slight smile lifted one corner of his mouth. Chehallis might believe he held the upper hand but he, and any working with him, would soon learn differently.

"I see. So tell me, Mr. Chehallis, where is that report? Perhaps you wrote it but forget to send it because it is not in my comms queue."

"Perhaps the commander accidentally erased it."

Oh, he was smooth. He was also edging closer toward a quick death. Normally, Jurić wouldn't consider killing a member of his crew this close to battle but he saw no other option. He didn't dare allow insubordination fester into mutiny when his attention was on the enemy.

"Mr. Chehallis, it is clear one of us is a fool and I assure you, it isn't me." His thumb depressed the hidden button on the arm of the chair. Soundlessly, the top of the arm slid back and the pistol slipped into his grasp. "Either you failed to do your duty or you believe yourself – or someone else – would be a better commander of the *Sobek* and the taskforce. Which would it happen to be?"

Whatever Chehallis had been about to say, he fell silent at the sight of the pistol pointing at his forehead. Sweat suddenly dotted his upper lip. Jurić noted the way he glanced to his right, to the communications officer. Well, at least he had a decent back up. Besides, two bodies always made a point better than one.

"M-me, sir?"

"Very good, Mr. Chehallis." He nodded in approval. "And would you have been so foolish as to convince others to work against me on my own ship?"

"N-no, sir. I-I haven't tried to work against you, sir."

Chehallis took a step back. Before he could take another, Jurić fired. The needler ripped through the man's forehead, obliterating the top of his head. Without pausing, Jurić turned and fired into the back of the comms officer's head. Several of the others on the bridge, started nervously and left their stations momentarily. Then, eyeing their commander warily, they returned to their chairs and got back to work. Jurić smiled grimly, confident he wouldn't have to worry about them deciding to mutiny any time soon.

"Mr. Ivanishvili, contact their seconds and inform them of their promotions. Have them report to their new duty stations without delay."

"Yes, sir."

As Ivanishvili did as ordered, Jurić once again leaned back in the command chair. He looked at the plot, wondering what they would find when they were finally within weapons range. He could tell little about the enemy's formation. The fact the Fuerconese weren't coming out to meet his ships could mean several things but his gut told him it meant one thing only – he'd hurt them badly in their last encounter. It was possible, at least one ship was badly damaged. With luck, it was their flagship. He had no doubt if they managed to destroy or capture it, the other ships would fall in short order. The Fuerconese, despite all they managed to make the rest of the sector think, were nothing but cowards. They didn't understand the glory of battle, much less embrace it.

"Helm, maintain course. Make sure the damage control teams understand I expect repairs on our weapons systems to be completed before we engage the enemy," he said. "Inform section chiefs that anyone failing to complete their assignments before we enter the enemy's weapons envelop will find themselves spaced along with their crew chiefs."

The helmsman swallowed hard before acknowledging the order.

Jurić nodded in satisfaction. Soon, he would do what none of his fellow commanders had been able to accomplish since this war resumed. He would defeat an entire Fuerconese taskforce instead of just a ship or two.

Oh, the glories that would be hung on him when he returned home.

———

THE *CAMPBELL* ROCKED as an enemy torpedo made it through the ship's defenses. Lucinda Ortega cursed as the deck seemed to roll under her, throwing her against the bulkhead. Even though her battle armor absorbed the impact, it still jarred her sore muscles. The last six hours had been hell as the two taskforces exchanged fire, each trying for a kill shot that might finally turn the tide of battle.

Doing her best to tune out the almost continual requests for damage control teams and medics, Lucinda continued toward the bridge. She paused next to one of the many utility ladders and cursed again. Even though the ship still had power, she knew the dangers of being caught in a lift if the enemy managed to get in a lucky strike.

That meant using ladders between decks. For not the first time, she wished they dared turn off the artificial gravity. Moving from one deck to another would be so much better in low- to zero-grav.

"Sorceress, Agni."

The sound of her LAC commander's voice stopped Lucinda for a moment. Then she stepped to the side as yet another damage control crew slid down the last few rungs of the ladder. Once they moved out of the way, she started up, knowing she should be on the bridge just then to direct her Marines as they waited for a chance to finally take the fight to the enemy.

"Agni, Sorceress, go ahead."

"We're taking a beating out here, Sorceress," the young lieutenant said. "But we managed to break through and are proceeding to the target. Anything you can do to get us some help?"

"Doing my best, Agni." She paused and swung to the side of the ladder as two Navy ratings climbed down. Then she once again started up, calling for anyone ahead of her to make a hole. Rank had some privileges after all, even in a battle.

"Roger that, Sorceress. We'll keep at them as long as we can. Agni, out."

Ortega gritted her teeth and quickened her pace. A few minutes later, she strode onto the bridge. All around her, men and women worked to carry out Admiral O'Malley's orders. The admiral paced the bridge, his expression calm but his eyes . . . his eyes looked haunted.

"Admiral, Agni reported in. They've broken through but requesting any assistance we can give them."

O'Malley jerked his head in the direction of his ready room. Lucinda followed. A moment later, they stood in front of the hatch, their backs to the bridge.

"Lucinda, I don't have anything to send them." Regret filled the admiral's voice and she understood. He felt every death they'd suffered just as much as she did. "Unless you want to send in the battle shuttles."

She closed her eyes. He had just tacitly given his permission to send in the shuttles and she was tempted to do so. Their LAC numbers had been whittled down by enemy fire to little more than a single fighter group. That meant she had fewer than one hundred LACs still in the battle. Something had to be done to assist them before they were all lost.

But the battle shuttles. . ..

Lucinda closed her eyes and considered the option. The shuttles might help keep the battle from tipping firmly to the enemy's favor. Even so, she knew sending them in would be little short of signing their crew's death warrants. Heavily armored, the shuttles design made them perfect for boarding enemy ships. But they were slower, less maneuverable than the LACs. Perfect targets, easy targets for enemy fire.

But if it helped keep the taskforce safe even a few more hours, it might let them last long enough for Taskforce Sentinel to arrive.

"All right." She ran a hand over her face. God, she hoped she was making the right decision. "My recommendation?" She waited until O'Malley nodded. "We launch the attack shuttles from all ships except this one and the *Perry*."

"Reasoning?" he asked.

"The *Perry*'s shuttles can help protect it and pave the way if we have to withdraw. I want our shuttles available in case we finally manage to capture one of their ships. We need a way to send over boarding parties."

O'Malley considered her recommendations and then nodded. "See to it."

"May I use your ready room, sir?"

"Of course." With that, he turned and moved back to his command chair, asking for a status update as he did.

Sitting at the large table, doing her best to ignore the various reports streaming in over the battlenet, Lucinda checked her data-pad. For several long minutes, she studied not only the location and number of battle shuttles each of the taskforce's surviving ships had but also their crews. There were many things about command she loved and a few she hated. This happened to fall into the hated category. She knew, and so would her people, that she was about to send a number of good Marines to their deaths. The fact they not only knew but understood didn't make it any easier. Some would question, at least to themselves, why she chose them and not someone else. But none of them would object or refuse the duty. They were Marines and they had sworn an oath to die if necessary to protect Fuercon and her allies.

Even as she issued the orders, she wondered if she was holding enough of the shuttles back. They had another duty, one as important just then as protecting Liberator's remaining ships. They had to locate and secure as much intel as possible, especially anything that might further link – or disprove the supposed link – between the Callusians and Midlothians.

Knowing she wouldn't be seen, she dropped her head into her hands. For a moment, she let the anger and fear she'd been suppressing for so long surface. She had to let it out, at least some of it, before it became a distraction. Hale might have hung them out to dry, he and Admiral Wu, but the rest of FleetCom hadn't. Her message to Ashlyn Shaw had helped see to that. All they had to do was hang on until Taskforce Sentinel arrived.

She'd feel better about their chances if she hadn't lost so many Marines already. She felt each of their deaths down to her soul. One of the injuries hit her worse than all the others. MJ Adamson. Damned, stubborn bitch and one of the best Marines she knew. She was supposed to be confined to the Medical Ward. Instead, she'd managed to slip out. Injured as she was, she'd joined a damage control team in one of the LAC bays. Instead of retreating with the rest of her people when the bay to an almost direct hit, Adamson stayed back, making sure everyone else made it out safely. Then, as she worked to rescue one of the crew chiefs, the *Campbell* took another hit. She had been trapped in the rubble. By the time a rescue team got to her, she was almost gone. The brief message Lucinda received from the medicals was that they would do what they could but they, like everyone else onboard, were working with diminishing manpower and supplies.

Worse, she couldn't even take time to go check on Adamson and the other Marines herself. There was too much to do and too few people with which to do it. Now she was about to send even more of her people to their deaths.

Damn it, there were days she hated being a Marine.

8

"Admiral, picking up signs of battle," Lieutenant Stahl reported.

"Update the plot." Admiral Miranda Tremayne's expression hardened as the holo plot adjusted to show the fighting. Eyes narrowed, she watched the plot for a moment and then checked the incoming data. Not only were there too few ships, at least from Taskforce Liberator, but none of the planetary defense platforms registered. That meant they were either offline or destroyed. If there was any good in the situation, it was that there were no more enemy ships to deal with than there were surviving ships from Liberator. "Colonel Shaw, launch your LACs. Let's get some support out there for our people. Lieutenant Avery, signal the taskforce. Operation Freedom Force is now in effect. I repeat, OFF is now in effect. All ships to general quarters. Let's put ourselves between Liberator and the enemy and finish this fight."

"Aye, Admiral. Operation Freedom Force sent to all ships," the comms officer confirmed.

Ashlyn quickly issued orders for the first wave of Marine LACs to launch. Then she waited, watching as the sensor data updated once again. As she did, she said a silent prayer they had been in time. At least the taskforce, or part of it, survived. They were still fighting. But they were hurt, badly hurt. The question now was if they could hold out long enough for Tremayne to get her ships into place.

"LACs have been ordered to launch, Admiral. The first should be free in less than five minutes," Ashlyn reported.

"Very good." The redhead looked at her Marine commander and nodded once. Then she turned her attention back to the comms officer. Lieutenant Avery, senior staff to be ready to brief in my ready room in ten minutes. Those who can't be here in person are to report via comm-link."

"Aye, ma'am."

"Colonel." Tremayne stood and motioned toward the ready room.

Ashlyn nodded. A few moments later, they took their places at the large table in the center of the room. As they did, Tremayne instructed her aide to have the Mess send up coffee, tea and something to eat. At the same time, Ashlyn sent for Connery. A smile touched her lips as she did. She had no doubt the corporal was already on her way to the bridge to see what she could do to help her colonel.

"Comms, any word from Liberator?" Tremayne asked once everyone had arrived or checked in via comm-link.

"Negative, Admiral."

Ashlyn had no doubt her expression matched Tremayne's. Since arriving in-system, the *Phoenix Rising* had been trying to hail the *Campbell* and the other surviving ships of Taskforce Liberator. So far, there had been no answer to their hails, no challenges, nothing. The only thing that reassured any of them was the fact the Campbell and the other ships still fought. Unfortunately, Taskforce Sentinel was still too far out to get solid readings on what was going on or on how badly Liberator's surviving ships had been damaged. Worse, it would be at least another hour before Sentinel could rendezvous and place itself between the enemy and Liberator.

"Number of enemy ships?" Tremayne asked.

"CIC reports preliminary count of half a dozen, ma'am," Lieutenant Gideon answered. "Most of them appear to be badly damaged but they show no signs of retreating."

"Any other signs of enemy activity in the system?"

"Negative, ma'am. Without the defense platforms, however, we don't have a clear picture of the entire system," Gideon said.

"Suggestions?" the admiral asked. "The last thing we need is to walk into a trap."

"We could play it the way you did on the last mission, ma'am," Captain Lars Vilhjalmsson said.

Even though she nodded, Ash could tell Tremayne didn't like the idea. Not that she blamed her. They didn't know if the enemy had managed to get a comm off, detailing how they'd responded to the attempted invasion of Fuercon's home system. It would be a risk, a potentially fatal one, to attempt the same tactic without knowing more about the current situation.

"Colonel?"

Ashlyn stepped forward. "We've already launched one flight group of LACs. They are making best speed toward the enemy's rear. Once they are within range, that should take some of the pressure off of Liberator."

Tremayne and several others at the table nodded.

"I recommend launching another squadron with the Helios mini-platforms. Their sensor buoys will give us a better idea of what we're facing."

"Any arguments or counter-suggestions?" Tremayne waited and, when no one said anything, signaled in her approval. "What else?" she asked as Ashlyn instructed Connery to issue the order.

"Captain Vilhjamsson's suggestion?" Ashlyn prompted, not at all liking the idea for several reasons.

Instead of commenting, Tremayne stood and moved to stare at the holo display that currently showed the Tenasic System. Green icons indicated the location for the ships from Taskforce Liberator they had on sensors. As she did, a frown tugged at the corners of her mouth. She stood there, her hands clasped behind her back. Ash and the others waited, watching as the redhead listened to the reports coming in, weighing them against what they knew and what she suspected.

"All right." Tremayne straightened her shoulders. "Comms, get me Commander Akachi."

Ashlyn frowned slightly at the admiral's last comment. Akachi commanded the Navy LACs assigned to the flagship. She hadn't worked with him before this mission but had studied his record. He was a solid commander and an excellent pilot. Even so, without knowing what the admiral had in mind, she preferred using the Devil Dog's LACs. If this was a trap, her Marines were best able to handle it.

"Colonel, when Commander Akachi arrives, I want the two of you to figure out the best use of our LACs. They need to screen not only our approach but keep the pressure on the Callusians until we are able to relieve Liberator and give them some breathing room.," Tremayne said, as if reading her mind. "You are also to have your battle shuttles prepped and ready to launch on my command."

"Yes, ma'am." She stepped away and signaled her own LAC commander, asking for his input on possible attack plans.

Tremayne returned to her chair. As she looked around the ready room, Ash marveled at her control. Only someone who knew the admiral as well as she did would realize Tremayne wasn't as calm as she appeared. Ashlyn saw the quick flash of anger in the woman's eyes. She felt Tremayne's concern. But, like the best officers Ash had ever served with, Tremayne didn't let her worry show. Instead, her calm presence seemed to reassure the others in the ready room.

Me included.

"If I may, Admiral?" Ash waited until Tremayne nodded. "I recommend preparing at least one battle shuttle to take a squad of Marines to the *Campbell*. That gives us eyes onboard as well as the ability to link comms through the shuttle. We need to know what they have faced and what support, besides weapons, they need.

"As for the captain's suggestion, my vote is against it. Liberator is already down a number of ships and we have no idea how badly the surviving ships have been damaged. The last thing we need is to risk any of our ships without knowing more. In this situation, the power rests in our greater number of hulls."

"Agreed on both counts." Tremayne glanced up at her. "Go brief your people, Colonel. Be back in thirty. We should receive the preliminary reports from our LACs by then."

Ash braced to attention and, as soon as Tremayne dismissed her, she left the bridge, Connery on her heels.

"Ten-hut!"

The order rang out across the Marines' staging area as Ashlyn stepped off the lift a short time later. Instantly, every Marine present stopped what they were doing and braced to attention. Ashlyn paused and took a moment to glance around the area. Then she nodded, pleased to see the Devil Dogs had wasted no time once GQ sounded. They were armored up, their gear and weapons ready for whatever their orders might be.

Ooh-rah!

"Listen up!" she said after putting them at their ease. "We have Taskforce Liberator on sensors. That's the good news. The bad news is they aren't responding to our hails. The worst news is there are Callusian ships in-system and they are engaging what remains of Liberator. Sensor readings also make it clear Liberator is down even more ships than when we left the home system. We have already launched one flight group of LACs to engage the enemy from the rear. Hopefully, that will buy Liberator time until the admiral gets Sentinel's ships into place to not only protect them but engage the enemy. Another squad of LACs will launch Helios mini-platforms to give us a better picture of what is happening. The last thing the admiral wants is for us to fly into a trap."

There were a few grumblings and she gave them a moment to die down before continuing. "The remainder of our LACs are to stand ready to launch. Raptor, get your people and their crews ready." She watched as her own LAC commander gave a quick salute and hurried off, his comm in one hand as he issued his own orders.

"Captain Nichols, get four battle shuttles manned and ready to launch. I'll leave troop assignment to you. My squad has the fifth shuttle." As she spoke, she felt Connery stiffen at her side. "Hot bunk on the shuttles until further notice. My shuttle is to be ready for launch in thirty. Any questions?"

"Negative, Colonel." Nichols waited until she dismissed him. Then he started calling out assignments.

"All right, Corporal. Let's get armored up and then see what else the admiral has to say."

And what arguments she'd have to try to keep Ashlyn onboard instead of on the battle shuttle.

Half an hour later, Tremayne entered her ready room. Before Ash could call those gathered to attention, the admiral shook her head. Expression grim, she moved to her place at the head of the table. The moment she sat, she motioned for the others to do the same. As she did, Ashlyn frowned, worried. A quick spike of fear ran through her as she thought of her friends with Taskforce Liberator. Had they been too late after all?

"Initial report from the LACs confirm they will be within weapons range in another half an hour," Tremayne began. "They have intercepted a message from the *Campbell*, however. The task-force has been hit hard three times by the enemy. Each time it has managed to hold the system but not without taking heavy casualties. They are now down to half strength and their arsenal is basically depleted. Their power plants and environmental controls are straining to keep up with the demands of the remaining ships because they have taken on the survivors from the other ships. Admiral O'Malley followed FleetCom orders and wiped the data-banks of the one ship he had to scuttle before this last attack. Since then, another ship has been lost and two are barely functional. The Campbell and two others are doing their best to screen the badly damaged ships."

"And the enemy, ma'am?" Ashlyn asked grimly.

"The *Campbell*'s CIC identified a pattern to the enemy's attacks. Unfortunately, they have deviated from that pattern this time. My guess is the enemy commander feels he has enough firepower to either defeat Liberator outright or force its surrender. Otherwise, had he held to pattern, the enemy would have withdrawn by now."

"Which means it may try to do so once it realizes we are on-station," Vilhjamsson commented.

"Agreed." Tremayne tapped in a series of commands using her virtual keyboard and the holo display split, one half showing the current data from the system and the second half showing Tremayne's proposed battle plan.

For several long minutes, the group studied the plan. Ash frowned as she did. Tremayne was splitting their forces, sending most of the taskforce to assist Liberator's ships. The remainder would follow the LACs in to attack the rear and, hopefully, cut off the enemy's escape.

"Admiral, I hate to be the one to ask, but is the information from the *Campbell* confirmed?" Captain Justin Montgomery, Tremayne's XO, asked.

"As best as it can be at the moment." Tremayne leaned back and they waited. Ash closely watched the redhead, reading the conflicting emotions on her face. "The message the LACs intercepted said the *Campbell*'s long-range comms, as well as those of the other ships, have been damaged in the fighting. A visual of the ships confirms all have sustained heavy damage, damage that would appear to confirm the claim. However, contact was audio only."

"Admiral, I believe this is now a job for the Devil Dogs," Ashlyn said after a moment's thought. "My recommendation is to launch another three squads of LACs. Set up patrol patterns to make sure the enemy doesn't try to slip in behind us. As much as I want to believe the only enemy ships in the area are those currently engaging Liberator, I don't want to bet their lives or ours on it. Something has caused the enemy commander to change his attack pattern and we need to keep that in mind.

"My next recommendation is to go ahead and launch the battle shuttle we designated to rendezvous with the *Campbell*. It can transport some naval personnel who can assist the *Campbell*'s crew as well as Marines."

"Agreed." Tremayne didn't like. Her tone of voice, not to mention her expression, made it clear. But she wasn't going to turn down their best bet for discovering exactly what happened. "How soon can your people be ready to launch?"

"You just have to give the order, ma'am." Now came the sticky part. Ashlyn knew without saying anything how the admiral would respond to her next comment. "Admiral, I will be accompanying the shuttle." She waited, placing a mental bet on how the redhead would respond.

"Under normal circumstances, I'd tell you no." Tremayne smiled grimly and Ashlyn nodded, relieved. "But we don't know what you'll find and that means I need not only a senior officer onboard but also someone who won't be afraid to make the difficult decisions. You have, time and again, proven to be that person, Colonel. I know I don't have to tell you not to take unnecessary risks."

"Understood, ma'am."

"Make sure to sync your comms through the LACs so we have a running record of everything."

Another nod.

"Go get your people ready to launch, Colonel. Let me know when you're set."

Fifteen minutes later, Ashlyn looked up as those around her fell silent. Seeing Tremayne striding across the staging area, she stood from her where she'd knelt next to her footlocker. Before she could do anything else, Tremayne motioned toward her office. Ashlyn nodded and then turned to Connery. The corporal quickly assured her she'd finish loading her equipment onto the shuttle.

"Close the door," Tremayne said as Ashlyn entered the office. The redhead waited as she complied. Then she leaned against the desk and blew out a breath.

"What's wrong?"

"I don't know that anything is, at least not anything more than we already knew, Ash. But I don't like the lack of communication. The LACs intercepted the one message and nothing else. Now, it could be because of damage to their comms system or it could be something else."

Ashlyn understood. It worried her as well.

"If I didn't have to send you over, Ash, I wouldn't. I'm not going to lie to you."

Even though she didn't like it, Ashlyn appreciated the fact Tremayne was honest about how she felt.

"I know." She managed a smile. "And I promise to remember that I'm the CO and no longer the one to be the first through a hatch. But you know I'm right. I need to be with my people to judge the best way to proceed."

"Just be careful."

"I will." She stepped forward and reached for Tremayne's hand. "Miranda, I promise you aren't going to have to tell my mother something happened to me."

"Good." The redhead smiled and gave her hand a squeeze. "I do have one last order, Ash. If you start suspecting this is a trap, you are to abort the mission and get back here. Understand?"

"Yes, ma'am." She hoped it didn't come to that. They needed to know what happened. More than that, Liberator's survivors deserved to know they hadn't been abandoned by FleetCom or by the Corps.

"Keep your comms open, Ash."

"I will." She followed Tremayne to the door. "We'll be ready to launch in five."

"Very good, Colonel." The admiral looked around, pausing when she spotted Connery at the shuttle hatch. "Corporal, a moment, please."

Ashlyn fought the urge to roll her eyes. She had no doubt why Tremayne wanted to speak with Connery. Nor did she doubt it was unnecessary. The corporal had been told by Talbot, by her mother and by General Okafor to stick close to Ash during the mission. She didn't need Tremayne telling her the same thing. Not that it seemed to be stopping the redhead.

Instead of standing there, watching them, Ashlyn entered the battle shuttle. She glanced around, nodding in satisfaction. Those accompanying her were ready for launch. Gear had been carefully stowed. The Marines waited, taking advantage of the last few minutes before launch to check their weapons once again.

"Talon, be ready to lift as soon as Brigid has boarded and we receive clearance," she said as she moved to her place immediately behind the shuttle cockpit.

"Roger that, Angel."

Knowing all she could do was wait, Ashlyn settled into her jump seat. It wouldn't be long now.

———

"SIR, CIC reports point defenses down to twenty-five percent," Tactical said.

Jurić snarled in frustration. Damn the Fuerconese! They shouldn't be this difficult to defeat. He had them outgunned. But their commanding officer had to be Satan's spawn. Nothing he did, nothing he threw at them seemed to be enough. Even with their ships damaged and bleeding atmosphere, the Fuerconese continued to withstand him. It was as if they didn't fear death.

He could almost admire this Admiral O'Malley who stood, along with his remaining ships, between the *Sobek* and the Tenasic System.

"Concentrate fire on the *Campbell*. Those fools will surrender once their commander is destroyed."

The comms officer turned to relay his order. Before he could, an alarm tore through the ship. Stunned, Jurić pushed out of the command chair and crossed to the holo plot. Bile bubbled up from his stomach and he gritted his teeth to keep from cursing. Suddenly, without warning, the plot showed close to one hundred blue dots, each one representing an enemy LAC. Worse, hundreds of red dots closed the distance between the LACs and his ships.

"Time to impact?" he snapped.

Where had they come from? Had this O'Malley willingly sacrificed so many of his men and women, so many of his ships, just to lure him into a trap? No, he couldn't have. He wouldn't have. That was what a Callusian would do, not a soft Fuerconese. This had to be a ruse of some sort.

He repeated it over and over like a mantra, trying to convince himself so he could convince his crew they weren't about to meet their deaths.

"Six minutes," Tactical announced.

"Has CIC confirmed?"

"Yes, sir."

"Evasive maneuvers, Helm." He returned to his chair, "Tactical, release countermeasures." Hopefully, that would be enough to cause at least some of the incoming missiles to misfire or deviate from their current course.

"Sir, CIC reports sensor hits on a number of ships coming in behind the LACs. Preliminary estimates are a minimum of twelve hulls."

Jurić couldn't hold back his curse this time. The gods were truly against him. After everything he had done, victory was being snatched away from him. He'd been so close to triumph. He'd been so sure the Fuerconese would fail to send reinforcements in time. That confidence caused him to take risks he wouldn't under most circumstances. Now those reinforcements had arrived. He had only one decision to make – stay and try to destroy as many ships as he could before his own command was destroyed or retreat.

"Order our ships to withdraw," he said as he slumped in his seat.

Even as he issued the order, he knew it was too late. The enemy missiles continued to close the distance. Before the course change could be implemented, they would reach their targets. All of this, all he worked for, had been for naught.

———

"COLONEL, you aren't going to believe this." The shuttle pilot looked back at her, his expression stunned.

Worried, she released the locks that attached her armor to the bulkhead and moved toward the small cockpit. "What is it, Vic?"

"Look." He nodded first to the small plot before them and then to the viewscreen.

For a moment, Lucinda thought she had to be dreaming. Maybe

she had been injured in the fighting and this was all a hallucination. If so, she didn't want to wake from it. Finally, her prayers had been answered. There was no other explanation for it. The tide of battle had turned and they might just survive after all.

She watched as missile after missile closed in on the enemy ships. Their trajectory made it impossible for any of Liberator's ships to have fired them. That meant one thing. FleetCom had come through. Taskforce Sentinel was on-station and doing all it could to end the battle as quickly as possible.

"Vic, I think our luck just changed." She grinned and thought for a moment. "Signal not only the *Campbell* but the incoming ships. Send this under my code. Enemy flagship disabled. Sorceress and company boarding. We'd appreciate some cover."

"Roger that, Sorceress."

Relieved, mentally adjusting the mission plans, Lucinda returned to the shuttle's crew bay. As she did, she felt the eyes of every one of the Marines accompanying her. When they'd left the *Campbell*, they'd known it was most likely a one-way mission. Now, finally, they had a chance and she was damned if they'd blow it.

"Listen up," she said. "Our mission parameters just changed. No longer is this a mission to disrupt the *Sobek*. This is now a mission to grab the contents of her databanks and anything else we can find." She activated the screen so they could see what she had in the cockpit. When several of the Marines cheered as a volley of missiles cut through the *Sobek*'s defenses, she smiled slightly. Part of her wanted to join their cheers. Another part knew she needed to stay focused. There was still a great deal that could go wrong. "We haven't received confirmation, but it would appear our reinforcements have arrived."

And not a moment too soon.

"Sorceress, with this change, shouldn't we get you back to the *Campbell*?" Sergeant Frey asked.

She shook her head. Normally, she would never lead a mission like the one they'd planned before leaving the *Campbell*. Hell, she wouldn't have sent her people over. But she, as well as O'Malley, knew the taskforce was losing. They had to do something to keep the system safe a little longer. More than that, they needed to get as much information about not only the mission but the Callusian taskforce for FleetCom. Maybe now, however, they had the chance to not only survive and keep the system safe but to get the information FleetCom so badly needed.

"Negative. We've come this far. Now we need to trust Angel and the rest of Taskforce Sentinel to keep the rest of the Callusian ships busy and off our asses until we land." She turned back to the cockpit. "Vic, status of the *Sobek*?"

"She's been hit hard, Sorceress. Bleeding atmosphere all over the place. If I had to guess, we won't have much time before the power plants go critical."

"What does CIC say?" Even as she asked, she prayed the *Campbell* had managed to survive the latest round of enemy fire.

"Not much more than that, I'm afraid. They are trying to patch through to the *Phoenix Rising* but you know the state our coms were in. Until Admiral Tremayne's closed the distance between our forces, we are going to have to make some educated guesses about what we're going to face."

She didn't like it. This was too much like going in blind. But they had no other choice. They'd go in, weapons armed and ready, make their way to the bridge and, if luck was still on their side, be in and out without incident.

"Get a view of the *Sobek*," she ordered and turned back to the cabin. "All right, Marines, that's our target," she said as the image of the *Sobek* appeared on the screen. For a moment, she studied it. The ship looked like a derelict. As the shuttle pilot said, she leaked atmosphere like a sieve. There might be some survivors onboard, but she doubted there would be many. A few escape capsules launched from the ship but the visible damage to the hull told her most of the crew had been trapped or killed in the battle. Hopefully, they'd be able to get to the bridge without much problem and then be off before it was too late.

"Take us in, Vic," she ordered. "We're going in hot. Heavy armor off first. Secure the bay and hold it. The rest of us have one target: the bridge. We need to secure and download the databanks and then get the hell out. Questions?"

"Sorceress," Frey said over a private link. "You need to stay with the shuttle. I'll lead the team."

"Negative, Grinder." Her time working with Rico Santiago had taught her a great deal, including how to break the security on the data banks quicker than anyone else in the squad could.

Before he could argue, the pilot announced they were making their approach to the bay. Lucinda held her breath. This was where it became even more dangerous. This close in, they could be hit by any remaining ship's weapons or by heavy weapons from the bay. She turned to warn Vic only to have him assure her he was on the lookout for trouble.

"Heavy armor, go!" she ordered the moment the shuttle touched down. As she did, she slammed her fist against the hatch control.

She waited as the lead elements moved to clear the bay. As they did, she listened to their reports. They confirmed what the pilot reported. The bay had sustained heavy damage in the fighting. Airlocks leading deeper into the ship had been blown. Radiation readings were climbing and soon their armor would not be able to protect them.

"Hold position." Lucinda thought hard for a moment. "Is there a working terminal out there?" she asked, holding the rest of the squad onboard the shuttle.

She waited as the half dozen Marines searched the bay. After what seemed an eternity, one of them reported in.

"Sorceress, Hunter. I found you a terminal."

Praying they'd just gotten lucky, she turned to Frey. "Grinder, hold the rest of the squad on the shuttle. I'm going to see if I can hack the system from here."

"On one condition, Sorceress. If our readings worsen, you get your ass back onboard without argument so we can get the hell out of here, all of us."

"Agreed."

Trusting him to keep an eye on her six, she left the shuttle.

Instantly, two of the heavy armor Marines took up positions on either side of her. They escorted her across the bay to a terminal. As she studied the readout, activated the virtual keyboard. Her heart skipped a beat and her breath hitched. She forced the uncertainty down. She could do this. She had to do this. She would do it and then she'd get back to the *Campbell*.

A bead of sweat ran down her spine as her gloved fingers flew across the virtual keyboard. The lack of atmosphere in the bay combined with the lack of resistance reassured her. Even so, she knew so much could go wrong. But she couldn't think about that. She needed to concentrate. The sooner she got into the system, the sooner they could get off this floating coffin and back to safety.

"Sorceress, Lir." O'Malley's voice cracked over the battlenet. "You need to get out there. The power plants are going critical."

"Just a few more minutes, Lir, then we'll be clear." She cut the transmission before he could protest. If he wanted to bring her up on insubordination when she returned to the ship, so be it. But for now, she needed to concentrate on the task at hand. "Grinder," she radioed.

"Go, Sorceress."

"Tell Vic to have the shuttle ready to take off. I'm sending the others back. As soon as I'm done, we're out of here."

She breathed a sigh of relief as the system accepted her last line of code. Soon the data would be downloaded. Turning, she ordered the others back to the shuttle. All but the two acting as her escorts complied. At the same time, the shuttle's engines powered up. Good. That was good. That meant as soon as the hatch shut behind them, they could take off.

Suddenly, the decksole vibrated beneath her boots. She cursed softly and checked the download. Almost there. She only needed a few more seconds. A low rumbling sounded from somewhere deep inside the ship. At least one of the power plants had gone critical. Time was up.

"Sorceress, move your ass!" Frey yelled from the shuttle's hatch.

The emergency lights flickered. The terminal readout seemed to stutter and then the terminal went dark. Cursing again, Lucinda turned and started running. She had to get this information back to the *Campbell*. If she'd done all this for nothing. . ..

"ADMIRAL?" Connery braced to attention in front of Tremayne, her expression betraying none of her concern.

"Stand easy, Corporal." Tremayne glanced around, as if making sure no one could overhear them. "We don't know what you're going to find when you rendezvous with the *Campbell*. There's a very real chance this is a trap."

"Yes, ma'am."

"I have one order for you, Connery. I'm trusting you to carry it out."

"Ma'am?" She narrowed her eyes in suspicion.

"If you see anything that makes you think this is a trap or that the condition of the *Campbell* is such it is no longer safe, you are to get Colonel Shaw away from there. I don't care what she says."

Connery drew a deep breath, her mind racing as she tried to figure out how to answer without seeming to be insubordinate. "Admiral, you are putting me in a difficult situation."

"Corporal, I understand that. I also know I'm not the only one to give you that particular order. Consider mine a final confirmation of it." Tremayne paused, as if waiting to see what the young woman would say.

"Admiral, you are asking me to potentially disobey orders from my CO, lawful orders I would have no legal reason to disobey."

Tremayne frowned and then nodded. As she did, her expression softened. "Connery, I assure you that you will face no discipline for following these orders. Your colonel might bitch about it, but she has also received the same orders."

Connery nodded, not feeling any better about what the admiral asked.

"There is something else, something your colonel isn't letting herself consider. We know Taskforce Liberator, the *Campbell* included, has taken heavy damage. You've been a Marine long enough to know that means people have been injured and killed. There is the very real possibility that you will find Colonel Ortega or Master Sergeant Anderson among the wounded or dead. I shouldn't have to tell you how that will impact Colonel Shaw if that's the case."

Connery swallowed hard and nodded.

"Stick with her, corporal. Make sure she doesn't do anything foolish. If you have to hit her over the head and drag her back here, do so. You'll be covered. I promise."

"Yes, ma'am."

"Dismissed, Connery, and take good care of your colonel."

Connery nodded and executed a parade ground about face. As she crossed the staging area to the shuttle, she wondered just how in the hell she was supposed to explain to her colonel what the admiral had said. Now she understood what Talbot had meant when he told her she might find herself with conflicting orders and loyalties if the proverbial shit should hit the fan. All she had to do was figure out a way to not only keep her colonel happy but to keep her safe.

9

J. W. Campbell, flagship
Taskforce Liberator
Tenasic System

Ashlyn sat in the rubble that had been Admiral O'Malley's ready room and closed her eyes. Exhaustion and sorrow so strong it became physical pain washed over her. Tears burned her eyes and tightened her throat. She couldn't give in to them, not yet. Not for a long time. Too many other lives depended on her keeping a clear head and convincing Tremayne that they needed to withdraw before more of the enemy arrived in-system.

Connery almost silently entered the ready room and placed a mug of coffee and a plate with a sandwich on it on the table in front of her. Then, in a break of military protocol, she placed a gentle hand on Ashlyn's shoulder. It wasn't much but, just then, it helped keep Ashlyn focused. They would mourn their dead soon enough. For now, they had to focus on the living.

"Comms has managed to set up a secure link to the *Campbell*, Angel."

"Thank you. Make sure Admiral O'Malley's last report is transmitted as well as the latest damage control reports for not only the *Campbell* but the other ships as well." Her voice sounded harsh, even to her own ears.

"Already done, ma'am." When Ashlyn didn't do or say anything else, Connery knelt next to her chair and waited until she looked at her. "Angel – Ashlyn, I'm making you a promise right now that I will find those responsible and they will pay. I swear it as a Marine, as a Devil Dog and as your friend."

Ashlyn nodded, her expression hard. Then she reached out and, much as Connery had done earlier, rested a hand on the young woman's shoulder. "*We* will make them pay," she corrected. Then she sat up and scrubbed her hands over her face. She needed to pull herself together. "Status?"

"The Devil Dogs are doing all they can to help the crew keep systems operational. I've put Tank to assessing the status of the Marines stationed onboard. It appears they, especially the Warlords, have taken the highest number of casualties."

Ash nodded. That didn't surprise her. "Have him get me a report as soon as he can." She sighed as her comm beeped. "I'd best report to Admiral Tremayne."

Connery stood and stepped back. Ash smiled slightly to realize the corporal wasn't leaving. The young woman was going to be there for her if she needed her. When they returned to Fuercon, she planned on making sure Talbot knew how well his protégé had done. Then she would have a long talk with Connery about what her plans in the Corps happened to be.

"Ash, what's the status over there?" Tremayne asked as her image appeared on the small holo screen on the table.

"Bad would be an understatement, ma'am." She paused and cleared her throat. She had to get through this. "Ship's company is officially down by half. Realistically, it is down by more. Most of the crew is wounded to some degree." She entered a command on the virtual keyboard and watched as the latest damage reports began to scroll down one side of the holo screen where both she and Tremayne could see. "The attempt by the *Inquisitor* to ram the *Camp-*

bell caused major damage. Admiral O'Malley was seriously injured at that time."

She leaned back and ran a hand over her face. "Ship's systems are held together with prayer and not much more. It is still bleeding atmosphere in more areas than I'm comfortable with. Most weapons are off-line. I doubt the *Campbell* has more than a dozen torpedoes left. Not that they can be launched right now. Defensive screens are down to single digit levels. To say the *Campbell* is a mess is putting it mildly."

"The other ships?"

"As bad or worse, ma'am. There is no way any of them can stand up to another attack."

For a moment, Tremayne said nothing. "Your recommendation?"

"Admiral, I don't see we have any choice. The ships need to withdraw. Our taskforce needs to act as escort to make sure they don't run into any further trouble. Then, once safely away from the system, the wounded need to be transferred to other ships for treatment. At that point, a decision can be made if it is even feasible to return the remaining ships home or if it would be best to strip their databanks and then scuttle their hulls."

"Are the ships capable of leaving the system?"

Ash blew out a breath and shook her head, one corner of her mouth quirking up. "The engineers say they can, as long as they don't have to push their systems. That's the best I can tell you."

"And O'Malley?"

"Critical." To give herself a moment, Ash reached for her mug and sipped. "Right now, Lt. Commander Yaris is the acting senior officer for the entire taskforce. The NCOs have been hit even harder. The survivors are doing the best they can, but it won't be enough if the enemy returns."

"Ash." Tremayne looked out from the holo screen, fear reflected in her eyes. "Who did we lose?"

That was it. She didn't ask anything more. Ashlyn closed her eyes and inhaled. She held the breath for a long moment before exhaling. At least Tremayne would understand.

"MJ's critical and the doctors won't say if she's going to make it. She lost her right leg below the knee. That arm was seriously damaged. She took shrapnel in her left eye. Hell, Miranda, the list of her injuries is too long to recite right now."

"Regen?"

"They can't do anything along that line here. The tanks were damaged in the last attack."

Tremayne turned and said something to someone off-screen. When she turned back, gone was the concerned friend.

"Ashlyn, answer me. Who else did we lose?"

"Lucinda." She barely got it out. Pain and anger filled her. They'd been too late. She had been too late. "Three hours, Miranda. We were three fucking hours too late." She reached up and dashed away her tears before they could roll down her cheeks.

"Colonel, do I need to transfer to the *Campbell*?"

"No, ma'am!" She shook herself and sat a bit straighter. Then she motioned for Connery to leave the room. The moment the hatch shut behind the corporal, Ashlyn leaned forward, elbows on the table, her expression serious. "Go to privacy mode."

"Ash?"

"Miranda, I swear to God if you try to leave the *Phoenix* for any reason other than abandoning ship, I will order the Marines to place you under guard." She shook her head, her eyes flashing, before Tremayne could protest. "These ships are flying death traps, Miranda. If we had time, I'd recommend transferring everyone over to our ships. But I can't help worrying that we're on the clock and losing the race. If the Callusian commander managed to send for help, reinforcements could arrive at any time."

"I'll agree with your recommendations with two changes. The critically injured will be transferred to our ships now. That includes both O'Malley and Anderson. I've already dispatched shuttles with medical teams to see to it. The second is that you and Connery will return to the *Phoenix* on the first medical shuttle. I'm sending a command team, as well as engineers, to replace you. Before they get there, gather whatever data you feel I need to review immediately and bring it with you. Understood?"

She didn't like it, but she understood. "Yes, ma'am."

"Then get the injured ready to transfer. Shuttles will be there in half an hour. Tremayne out."

Ash leaned back and blew out a breath. She should have known she couldn't hide her feelings from the woman. But now she had a great deal to do and not much time in which to do it. Connery could deal with downloading the records she knew Tremayne needed to see. That left one duty to her, one very important duty. She wanted to make sure Lucinda's personal belongings were secured and taken back to the *Phoenix*. Once home, she'd make sure they found their way to her best friend's parents.

But first things first. She needed to let the medical team know to prepare the critically injured for transfer.

I swear I will make every person responsible for what happened pay, Luce. I promise.

CONNERY STOOD SILENTLY, her expression carefully neutral. Across the room, a medical team prepared Master Sergeant Adamson for transfer to the *Phoenix Rising*. The blonde looked so small and fragile as she lay on the narrow bed. Pain etched deep lines in her face. Heavy bandages covered her forehead and left eye. Her left hand fisted at her side, bunching the sheet. Her mouth pulled tight. But not once, not one single time did she complain or so much as moan in pain.

"We'll be back when the shuttle's here, Master Sergeant. Rest until then," one of the medics said. Then he turned his attention to Connery. "Corporal, she needs to rest."

"Understood. I'm just here to make sure she is on the shuttle." She waited as the team left the room. Then she moved to stand next to the bed. "They're gone." She laid her hand over Anderson's.

"Status?" the blonde rasped. She looked up at Connery, her one blue eye feverish.

"Admiral Tremayne agreed with Colonel Shaw that we need to withdraw from the system. As soon as you and the other critically injured have been transferred to either the *Phoenix* or one of the other ships that came with her, we'll get underway."

"Lucinda?"

Connery's mouth firmed. "I'm sorry, Master Sergeant. The *Sobek*'s power plants started going critical while she and a squad were still onboard. Sorceress was trapped in one of the blasts. The others managed to get her and the two Warlords with her free from the rubble. They did everything they could, but she didn't make it."

Adamson didn't say anything. She closed her eye and turned her head away. Seeing the tears escaping from beneath her eyelid, Connery gently wiped them away. Then she waited, giving the blonde as much time as she needed. As she did, she remembered her promise to Ashlyn to do all she could to help the master sergeant. The colonel had known how hard the news of their friend's death would be on her.

"Her body?"

"Is being transported to the *Phoenix* to be taken home. Colonel Shaw isn't leaving her, or any of the rest of our people, behind."

Painfully, Adamson shifted positions. As she did, she held onto Connery's hand as if her life depended on it. "Is she all right?" She cursed as she moved wrong, jarring her injured leg. "Damn it, is Angel all right?"

"She's hanging on, Reaper." Connery bent and helped her get settled again. Then she glanced over her shoulder, giving the medic waiting just outside the room a signal to be ready. "And she will be returning to the *Phoenix* on the same shuttle you'll be on."

"You take care of her, Brigid. Swear to me, you'll take care of her."

"I will." She stepped back as the medic moved to the bed. He checked Adamson's vitals and then administered a painkiller. "Looks like your transport team is here, Sarge. Lie back and let us get you out of here."

"I'll be all right. Go find Angel. Stay with her. That's an order." The last three words slurred as her eyes closed. Before the transport team moved into place, Adamson was asleep. Connery blew out a breath. Then she turned her attention to the medic. "Take her on. Colonel Shaw and I will meet you at the shuttle."

With that, she left the Medical Ward. She had a pretty good idea where to find the colonel and she did not plan on breaking her word to Adamson. The two of them would be on the shuttle, even if she had to knock the colonel over her head and drag her onboard.

———

Miranda Tremayne waited, her concern building, for Ashlyn to join her. The shuttles carrying the injured had reached the *Phoenix* and other ships in Taskforce Sentinel almost an hour earlier. She'd sent word for Ashlyn to join her in her day room as soon as she could. Now, realizing how much time had passed, she wondered if she needed to comm Connery and see what was keeping the colonel.

A knock sounded a moment before the hatch slid open. A Marine private stepped inside and braced to attention. At Tremayne's nod, he relaxed slightly. "Colonel Shaw to see you, Admiral."

"Show her in, Private."

Standing before the viewport, she waited. From the moment she learned of Ortega's death, she'd worried about Ashlyn. The younger woman had been more than best friends with Ortega. They had been as close as sisters. Ortega had been one of the driving forces behind the move to not only find out what really happened on the Arterus mission but who had been responsible for setting up Ashlyn and her squad.

When the hatch slid open again, Tremayne turned. She watched as Ashlyn stepped inside. Before the private could say anything, Tremayne dismissed him. Then, as the hatch closed behind him, she hurried across the room to where Ashlyn stood. Her heart broke as she looked at her goddaughter. Anger and pain shadowed her expression. She moved as if exhausted. Without a word, Tremayne led her to one of the chairs in front of the viewport. As Ashlyn settled, the admiral hurried to pour her a drink.

"We should be out of the system in the next six hours," she said as she handed the younger woman a whiskey.

Ash thanked her and took a careful sip. "Good. There is no way Liberator's ships can survive another battle. Honestly, if you don't put O'Malley and his people up for recognition for what they did, I will. The fact they survived long enough for us to get here is a miracle."

Tremayne nodded. She had reviewed Ashlyn's initial reports concerning Taskforce Liberator and its status. To have withstood three enemy attacks and not have lost more people than they had spoke volumes about not only O'Malley but Ortega as well. The bodies of every Marine lost, with the exception of those stationed aboard the *Carrington* that had been lost when a lucky shot from the Callusians hit its power plant, had been recovered. It was almost the same story with the Naval personnel. At least their families would be able to lay them to rest.

"Ash, it's just us and there's no rank tonight." Tremayne sat next to her and turned so she could look at her. "Are you all right?"

For a moment, Ashlyn said nothing. Then she took another sip of her whiskey. When she looked at the redhead, her eyes burned with an anger the woman understood.

"No," she said simply, honestly. "I'm far from all right." She shoved to her feet. After draining her glass, she crossed to the bar and poured herself another whiskey. "Three hours, Miranda. We were three hours too late. She didn't have to die. She wouldn't have died if that son of a bitch Hale had sent reinforcements when she asked for them." She tossed back the second whiskey and poured a third.

Understanding, Tremayne waited. If Ashlyn needed to get drunk that evening, she'd let her. But she needed her to focus for a bit longer first.

"What happened? I assume you found out."

Ashlyn nodded. Then she reached into a pocket and, a moment later, produced a datachip. "If I may?" She waited until Tremayne nodded in response. Then she plugged the chip into her datapad before handing it over to the admiral. "If you don't mind, I've seen it already and don't want to watch it again."

Tremayne glanced at her, worried. Then, seeing the pain in Ashlyn's eyes, she stood and moved to her side. She lifted her hand and gently cupped the younger woman's cheek. With her thumb, she wiped away the single tear that escaped Ashlyn's right eye. "Wait in my bedroom. I'll let you know when I'm done."

"Thanks." She reached up and rested her hand on Tremayne's and then left the room. Tremayne didn't object when, as Ash passed the bar, she reached for the bottle of whiskey. She had a feeling this was the first time Ash had really let herself feel since learning of her friend's death.

Sipping her own whiskey, Tremayne watched as the first images appeared on the datapad. Her mouth drew tight at the scene. It was one she had seen too many times before. Ortega and her Marines landed in the badly damaged bay onboard the *Sobek*. Ortega issued orders, not only taking into account the ship's status but the fact fighting still went on around them. Then, with two Marines in heavy armor escorting her, she'd made her way to the nearest terminal. Despite the danger she knew existed, Ortega had done her duty. She'd been a Marine to the end.

Ortega had done nothing wrong. If she had opted to withdraw after learning the power plants were going critical, Ortega very well might still be alive. Instead, she had done what she should have. She tried to secure the ship's databanks. The download had just finished when a second explosion rocked the ship. Ortega and her escorts had been caught as the rear of the bay collapsed. Risking their own lives, the other Marines worked quickly to free them, doing everything they could to save their fellow Warlords. The fact they managed to retrieve the three and get off the ship before it blew was a miracle.

Tremayne ended the recording and set the datapad to one side. If she had anything to say about it, Hale would have to watch the recording every day for the rest of his miserable life. Ashlyn was right about one thing. Had the taskforce received the requested reinforcements it was not only possible but probable Ortega would still be alive. With more ships to force the Callusians surrender, Ortega wouldn't have felt compelled to board a badly damaged ship.

Damn Hale and everyone else who ignored those requests.

But that had to wait. She wanted to make sure Ashlyn was all right. Then it would be time to begin preparing their reports back to not only FleetCom but Okafor. By the time they returned home, Tremayne wanted everything in place to not only lay their dead to rest but to make sure this sort of disaster never happened again.

10

Glenn Spaceport
New Kilrain, Fuercon

"Escort parties are ready, ma'am."

Corporal Connery spoke softly, yet her words seemed to echo throughout the stripped-down battle shuttle. Gone were the armor racks and jump seats. Gone were the weapons lockers and supply bins. Instead, more than a dozen flag-draped coffins rested in the "passenger area", each guarded by six Marines in mess dress uniforms. Many of them bore the scars of recent battle. Expressions grim, they waited for the order, an order Ashlyn prayed she never had to give again.

It didn't help that she knew this was only one of a number of such shuttles that would be making landfall that morning. Some would be carrying wounded to the Medical Center. Too many others would, like this one, carry their dead, Naval and Marine. The mission had been costly, but it could have been worse. Ash reminded herself of that even as her hand rested on the coffin next to her. The personal cost of this mission had been much too high, and she swore to make those responsible pay.

The shuttle gave a slight lurch as it settled on the tarmac. At the same time, each escort team moved into position. Ashlyn, from her place near the hatch, turned. Her eyes burned, her tears unshed. She had no doubt her expression was as grim as those of her Marines. This duty was both an honor and a burden and she needed to make sure each of them were all right in the coming days. It was too easy to feel the failure of the mission even though the failure had not been theirs.

As the shuttle hatch slid open, Ashlyn drew a deep breath and took her place next to the first casket. A touch of her fingertips and the casket was freed from the locks holding it in place. At the same time, she gave the order for the first escort team to assume their positions. It was time to bring their fallen comrades home.

"On my command," she said softly, "lift and shoulder the caskets. We will do this right and we will honor our fallen brothers and sisters."

A soft "ooh-rah" was the only response.

"Atten-hut!" Her voice rang in the confines of the shuttle. She took two steps forward and executed a perfect about face. For a moment, she studied the Marines, her eyes missing not the smallest detail of their appearance. Satisfied, she returned to her place near the head of the first casket and ordered her team to lift and shoulder it. "Forward march."

Tears once again blurred her vision when a lone drummer began his slow cadence. As one, her team moved down the ramp and across the tarmac toward a waiting hearse. Standing near the dark vehicle, one of many there to accept the fallen, were Lucinda Ortega's parents, her brother and sister and their families. Also present were General Okafor and Brigadier General Elizabeth Shaw, as well as members of the Devil Dogs who had not been part of this latest mission, all in Mess Dress uniforms. But it was the sight of President Harper and Secretary Klingsbury standing with Lucinda's parents that resonated with Ashlyn. Their presence didn't surprise her. Since her pardon, she had learned one thing about the two, and especially about

Harper. He not only respected the military, but he felt every one of its losses as if it were his own.

At the hearse, they carefully loaded the casket into the back. The others stepped back, giving their CO one last moment with her best friend, Academy roommate and former XO. Ashlyn stood there, head bowed, one hand resting on the cool metal of the casket lid. She had lost other friends in battle before, but none had hurt like this. It went beyond their friendship and the fact they had been sisters in all but blood. It was the senselessness of it all. If only the Warlords had gotten reinforcements when Lucinda first requested them . . . .

Ash drew a deep, bracing breath and turned. The rest of the escort team fell in behind her as she moved to where Lucinda's family waited. As one, they braced to attention and saluted, their hands slowly coming down in unison on Ashlyn's order. Ash reached inside a pocket. Her fingers closed around the dog tags she had carried for the last several weeks. Swallowing hard, she extended them to her best friend's mother.

"There are no words." Her throat tightened, and she paused, blinking back her tears. "Lucinda died a hero. She was my friend, my sister, and I'm going to miss her. My life and the lives of every Marine who served with her are better for having known her." She pressed the dog tags into Mrs. Ortega's hand, closing her own hand over the woman's as she did. "She asked me not long ago to tell you she loved you. I hope you know how much she cared for each of you and how badly she wanted to come home."

"Thank you."

Alejandro Ortega slipped an arm around his wife's waist and held her close as they looked down at the dog tags resting on her upraised palm. Then, when Maria Ortega looked up at him, he nodded once. Ash watched, her brow furrowed, as Lucinda's mother carefully removed one of the two tags from the chain. When she pressed the newly freed tag into Ashlyn's hand, tears burned Ash's eyes and she no longer tried to hold them back.

"You were her friend, the sister of her heart. Through her, you became our daughter in all but blood. We would be honored if you'd take this, Ashlyn," Mrs. Ortega said softly. "Please."

"I will wear it proudly." She pulled her own dog tags from beneath her uniform and carefully fitted Lucinda's tag onto the chain. "May I come see you?" There was so much she wanted to say, that she needed to say, but this was not the time.

"Please. You're as much ours as you were hers," Mr. Ortega said. He reached out and rested a hand on her arm. "We will mourn our Lucia together and we will celebrate her life."

"Thank you."

"Ashlyn, we know you have other duties to see to now. But will you and your family sit with us at the funeral?" Mrs. Ortega asked.

"It would be our honor." She bent and hugged the woman before doing the same to her husband. "I will speak with you later today, I promise. Please, if you need me before then for anything, anything at all, comm me."

They promised to do so. Ash hugged them one last time and then nodded to the rest of the escort team. With the exception of Connery who would remain behind with Ashlyn, the team would escort the Ortegas as they followed the hearse to the funeral home. Members of both the Devil Dogs and the Warlords would be with the family until Lucinda's funeral. After that, Ash meant to make sure the Devil Dogs would always be there for their fallen comrade's family.

For the next hour, Ashlyn spoke with the families of each of the fallen who had been brought home on the shuttle. It didn't matter that they had belonged to the Warlords and not the Devil Dogs. They were Marines and, as far as she was concerned, that made them hers. Until the Warlords had a new CO, she would do everything possible to help them recover, physically and emotionally from the loss of their last two commanders. She also planned to make those responsible for not only Lucinda's death but Colonel Pawlak's as well paid and paid dearly.

"My office in fifteen, Colonel," General Okafor said softly as she stepped up to Ashlyn's side as the last of the hearses drove off. "I won't keep you long, but I need your AAR."

"Yes, ma'am."

"Corporal Connery, you are to accompany your colonel," Okafor added before walking off, Elizabeth following her.

"Ma'am?" Connery waited until Ashlyn turned to face her.

"Once we've finished reporting to the Commandant, you're free until day after tomorrow. Spread the word to the rest of the combined battalion. The Warlords especially need the time to mourn their dead now that we're home." Ashlyn heard how flat her voice sounded but that was nothing compared to how she felt.

"Are you taking the time, ma'am?" Connery asked.

Ashlyn almost smiled. In the corporal's short time as her aide, she'd come to know her CO very well. This time, however, Connery had nothing to worry about. As soon as she finished briefing Okafor, Ashlyn planned to go home and see her son. Once Jake had gone to bed, she planned on drinking herself blind. Maybe then she wouldn't hurt so much.

"I do. I want to spend time with my family and I want to be there for Lucinda's family should they need me."

Then she planned on having a *chat* with Brigadier General Hale. SecDiv's commanding officer was going to become very well acquainted with how he had failed his people and cost their lives, even if it was the last thing Ashlyn did as a Marine. She owed that much to Lucinda and the other Marines who died in the Tenasic System.

"Sit, both of you," Okafor said the moment Ashlyn and Connery were shown into her office.

Before they could respond, Elizabeth was there, handing them each a glass of whiskey. Then she nodded to the two chairs in front of the Commandant's desk. Ashlyn gave Connery a shrug and a nod before doing as they were told. As Connery followed suit, Elizabeth moved to stand next to Okafor's chair behind the woman's desk.

Sipping her whiskey, Ashlyn waited. This was not how she expected her debrief to begin. Then, seeing the compassion reflected in both Okafor's and Elizabeth's eyes, she understood. They understood how badly the mission had hit her. More than that, they knew what Lucinda's death meant to her. Then, as she looked at the two, she saw the toll it had taken on them. Not that she'd doubted they would feel the loss any less than she. This was the first time since hostilities officially resumed with the Callusians that Fuercon and its allies had been forced to withdraw from the battlefield. That hurt, especially in light of the reasons why.

"Let me begin by saying how sorry I am, Ash. I know you and Colonel Ortega were as close as your mother and I are." Okafor spoke softly, her expression filled with compassion.

"Thank you, ma'am."

"I've reviewed your reports, as well as the reports from Admiral O'Malley before his injury. I have several things to tell you before I let you go. First, neither Colonel Ortega nor Admiral O'Malley did anything wrong. Given the circumstances, we're lucky our losses weren't much worse. In fact, your recognition of how serious the situation was with the remainder of Taskforce Liberator and your recommendation – the only reasonable recommendation in my opinion – that we withdraw from the system prevented it from potentially turning into a complete disaster."

"Thank you, ma'am." Even though she knew she'd made the right recommendation, it had galled her to know they were giving up the system, even if only temporarily. "I wish we could have gotten there sooner."

And that was something she would have to live with for the rest of her life. She had not been there for Lucinda and the others, not when they most needed her and her Devil Dogs. Three hours. Three fucking hours too late. By the time Taskforce Sentinel arrived, Lucinda was dead, or close to it, and MJ Anderson seriously wounded. Most of the Warlords were dead or injured. At least Taskforce Sentinel had been there in time to finish the fight and defeat the Callusians. Even so, with Taskforce Liberator's remaining ships badly damaged, they'd had no choice but to leave the system.

Not that she was going to complain. That withdrawal had saved Fuerconese lives.

"As do we all, Ashlyn, but wishes don't help at this point. We need to learn from what happened and make sure it is never again repeated." Okafor held her gaze until Ash nodded.

"The second thing I want the two of you to know is that you, as well as the rest of the Marines returning home, are on leave until after you lay our people to rest. There may be a few briefings for you to attend but, other than that, you are to take time to heal. Is that understood?"

"Yes, ma'am," Ash and Connery answered in unison.

"The last point is simple. I have reviewed all the reports that have come in, as has Liz here and Rico Santiago, among others. It would be easy to say Taskforce Liberator had been betrayed but there is no evidence of it. FleetCom kept the taskforce's orders under wraps until it was well on its way to its destination. No Midlothians or anyone with ties to Midlothian were involved in the formulation of the battle-plan. Our best guess is the enemy simply happened to be in the right place at the right time."

She held up a hand to forestall any interruptions. "Think about it for a moment. The taskforce apparently had the misfortune of running up against one of the Callusians' more innovative commanders who happened to have equipment and training that, given time, we will trace back to the Midlothians. I promise you that.

"As for our having to withdraw from the Tenasic System, you know as well as I that there are times you leave the field of battle to save your people. You do so in order to be able to fight again in the future. I assure you, FleetCom is already preparing to send enough ships back in to retake the system. We will avenge the deaths of our people.

"In the meantime, we will go over the data Colonel Ortega secured before her death. I know Colonel Santiago is already putting people on it and I will be as well. If there's anything there to help make the connection between the Callusians and the Midlothians, we will find it and we will act on it. Lucinda's death, and the deaths of all the others, will not be in vain."

Ashlyn took another sip of her whiskey. "If I may?" She waited until Okafor inclined her head slightly before she continued. "We will all eventually accept what you say is true, ma'am. However, there's no denying the fact the taskforce would never have been in that situation had it received the reinforcements requested not only by Admiral O'Malley but also by Lucinda. The delay in supporting the taskforce because those requests were ignored caused the deaths of our people just as surely as the Callusians did." She made no attempt to keep the anger from her voice. "Please tell me something is going to be done about that failure."

For a moment, Okafor didn't respond. Then, when she started to say something, Elizabeth reached out and lightly touched the Commandant's arm. Okafor glanced up and Elizabeth simply shook her head. Surprised, even worried, Ashlyn waited, not sure what to make of her mother stopping Okafor from speaking.

"Ash, you'll be fully briefed on that after we lay our people to rest. Just know those responsible will never be in the position of causing this sort of harm again," Elizabeth said.

"Not good enough, Mom." She shook her head and tossed back the rest of her whiskey. Then she stood. As she paced the office, she didn't think about how she might be breaking military protocol. Nor did she think about how her actions could be seen as a sign of weakness. All that mattered was getting her temper under control to the degree she could speak rationally about what happened.

She stopped before one of the windows and looked outside. Without turning back to the others, she continued. "I need to be able to tell the Warlords their sacrifices weren't in vain. The Devil Dogs need to know why they were held back as long as they were and why our fellow Marines were basically sacrificed by their division CO. The Corps deserves to know officers willing to sacrifice our own for no good reason will not be tolerated."

For a long moment, no one said a word. Silence, broken only by the sound of someone pouring another drink, filled the office. Then Okafor stood next to her. The general pressed a glass into her hand before gently urging her back to her chair.

"Your mother and I agree completely, Ashlyn." Okafor dropped to one knee and waited until Ash looked at her. "And steps are being taken even as we speak. It's not happening as quickly as any of us would like because we are doing everything we can to make sure those responsible aren't left with loopholes that can allow them back into command positions in the future. But I assure you this will be dealt with, if not before Lucinda and the others are laid to rest then soon after. You have my word on that not only as the Commandant of the Corps but as your friend."

Ashlyn wanted to believe her. But her own history of being betrayed by those in command made it difficult. Perhaps that was why Okafor had Elizabeth present. The Commandant knew them well enough to understand Ash would trust her mother not to lie, especially not about something like this. Still, it would be nice to hear what steps had been taken to deal with Hale and any others involved in withholding reinforcements for the taskforce.

"Ma'am, I do trust you." She did. She might not trust some of the others involved, but she did trust Okafor.

"Good." The general lightly patted Ashlyn's knee and then stood. "We will have an official debrief tomorrow. I wish it could wait, but it can't. But that, both of you, is the only time you are on duty tomorrow except for the first of the funerals. If I have to make it an official order, I will." She looked from Ashlyn to Connery and back. Both young women shook their heads.

"Tonight, the bar at the Memorial Club has been reserved for your people. The first round is on me. Spread the word. Remember your friends, celebrate their lives. I promise that soon you will have the chance to avenge their deaths."

Ashlyn knocked back her whiskey, wincing slightly as it burned going down. Then she stood. The moment she did, Connery climbed to her feet. They braced to attention and waited.

"Dismissed, Corporal. Let the others know about tonight," Okafor said. She waited as the young woman left the office. Then she turned her attention to Ashlyn. "I have one favor to ask of you, Ash. Will you let me know if Lucinda's family needs anything?"

She swallowed hard against the lump in her throat. "Yes, ma'am."

"Are you going there now?" Elizabeth asked.

She shook her head. "I'm going home. I need to see Jake." She needed to hold her son close and remember life still went on. Then, somehow, she had to find a way to tell him "Aunt Lucinda" would never come home again.

How the hell was she supposed to tell him that and not leave him scared that every time she left on a mission she might not return?

———

ASHLYN STEPPED out of the aircar and told the driver he could leave. For a long moment, she stood there, looking around. The sun had set more than an hour earlier. Most offices in this part of the capital had closed hours ago. Elsewhere, families gathered together for an evening meal. Life continued, no matter how badly she hurt or how fiercely the need for revenge burned deep within her.

Before her was the Memorial Club. Marines gathered there as they had for the last century and more. No one knew exactly when or how the club became the unofficial *sending off* point for the Marines. All Ashlyn knew was she had spent too many evenings at the club in the special room set aside for such send offs over the course of her career and none of them hurt as much as this one did.

A short time later, she paused outside the old wooden doors deep inside the building and drew a deep breath. She had delayed her arrival until most of those coming would be there. Unlike the other occasions, she wouldn't stay the evening. Her Marines didn't need "the Old Lady" there, putting a damper on the night. She didn't want to burden them with her own sorrow. But she had to make an appearance. She owed it to them and to their fallen.

She blew out a breath and pushed open the doors. As she did, those gathered turned in her direction. Before anyone could fall back on protocol, she shook her head. Not tonight. Tonight wasn't about her or even about them. Tonight was about their fallen comrades.

She stepped up to the bar and ordered a beer. One drink. She'd promised herself one drink with the men and women of the Warlords and the Devil Dogs and then she'd leave. They needed time together and she needed time with her family.

"Mr. Yasui." She nodded to the bar manager as he brought her beer. "Tonight's on me. You should have my information on file."

Yasui, a small, pale man who had managed the bar for as long as Ashlyn remembered, shook his head. "Tonight's tab has already been taken care of, Colonel."

She looked at him in question. "Okafor?"

"No, ma'am, although she did send word the first round was on her. President Harper is taking care of the tab. He said to tell you it is the least he can do for Marines willing to pay the ultimate sacrifice for Fuercon."

She nodded, unsurprised. Harper continued to prove how different he was from his predecessors.

"He also left instructions not to spread the word."

Again, that was so like the man. "I understand." She sipped her beer and glanced around the private barroom. "Mr. Yasui, we're all hurting, and you know that means some of us will over-indulge." She left the rest unsaid, knowing he would understand.

"No worries, Colonel. Arrangements are already in place to make sure your Marines are well cared for."

She smiled and thanked him. Then she watched as he moved down the bar, making sure the other bartenders were keeping up with their orders.

A few minutes later, she tapped the top of her mug, indicating she was ready for the second drink she hadn't planned on having. When Yasui delivered it to her at her place at the near end of the bar, she thanked him. Then, mug in hand, she moved to the center of the room. It was time.

"Listen up!" Conversations stopped, and all eyes turned to her. She waited, making sure everyone had a drink. "We're here tonight to remember our fallen. This last mission cost not only the Warlords but all of us. We're Marines one and all. When one of us falls, we all feel it. When they are our brothers-in-arms as these brave men and women were, it hurts even more.

"Warlords, each of you represent the best of the Corps. You have faced the enemy and have bled in the defense of Fuercon and her allies. You have paid a price higher than any other battalion in this war. In too short of a time, you lost not one but two COs. This loss was not through any action they took nor by actions taken by your battalion. That blame falls directly at the feet of the enemy. But, even in the face of those losses, you carried on. You did not only Colonel Pawlak proud but Colonel Ortega as well.

"Our Marines – yes, *ours*, because every Devil Dog here stands with you as brothers- and sisters-in-arms – bleed with you tonight. But I want you to remember something. None of our fallen, none of our brothers and sisters, would want us to mourn. They would want us to celebrate their lives and their service. Then they would want us to put on our battle armor, pick up our guns and make those responsible pay.

"And that is exactly what we're going to do. General Okafor has personally promised those responsible for leaving Taskforce Liberator exposed will pay. She, as well as President Harper and Secretary Klingsbury, have promised that the Callusians will pay for each and every life lost and injury inflicted. I promise you here and now that I will do everything I can to make sure you are there when that vengeance is exacted.

"So, here's the first toast of the night, to my friend, my sister and the best damned Marine I've ever had the honor of serving with. To Lucinda Ortega. May we each carry her memory into battle and may we shout her name as the last of those responsible for her death and the deaths of the rest of our people fall to our vengeance."

She lifted her mug and waited as, one by one, each of the other fallen were named.

"To the fallen!"

She slammed back her beer and then pounded the mug down on the nearest table. For a few moments, silence held the barroom. Then conversations started back up. A slight smile touched Ashlyn's lips as the stories began. It wouldn't be long before humor replaced the sorrow and the healing would begin.

"Mr. Yasui, I'm going to slip out now. Comm me if things start getting out of hand and I'll come deal with it," she said softly as she took one last glance around the barroom.

"They'll be fine, Colonel." He looked at her, his expression concerned. "But will you?"

"I will," she hedged. "Close it down at midnight, please."

"Yes, ma'am."

Satisfied she had done all she could do for the Marines, Ashlyn left the barroom. Now if she only knew what to do for herself, not to mention for Lucinda's parents. This was one price of command she'd happily never have to pay again.

––––––

TALBOT WATCHED as his colonel had one last word with Yasui before she slipped out of the bar. She had done their dead proud. More than that, she said what the Marines needed to hear. But he'd seen the pain in her eyes and his heart ached for her. He knew, probably better than anyone present, how much Ortega meant to Ashlyn and how deeply she felt the woman's loss. Worse, he had no doubt the last mission had resurrected her own demons and memories of the Arterus mission.

He prayed those memories did not send her back to the mental hell she'd been in when she first returned to Fuercon from the Tarsus penal colony.

But she wasn't who interested him just then. He glanced around the bar, finally spotting the Marine he'd been looking for. Standing near the doorway, Connery watched as Ashlyn left. Before she could slip out after the colonel, Talbot caught her eye. He gave a quick shake of his head. Then, before she could protest, he crossed to where she stood. Without a word, he led her to a table where they could talk with at least a modicum of privacy.

"No rank tonight, Faith," he said as Yasui brought them another round of drinks.

"All right."

From her expression, he knew she didn't understand why he'd stopped her. More than that, she didn't appreciate it. She had a duty to perform, one he'd given her before they shipped out the last time, and he wasn't letting her do it.

"I need you to be honest, kid. How is she?"

He didn't have to explain who "she" was.

"God, Loco, it was bad, so fucking bad." She stared at her mug as she moved it around the tabletop. "When we reached the system, we went immediately to General Quarters. Sensors had picked up signs of battle and we were about to fly right into the middle of it." She went on to describe what happened leading up to transferring to the *Campbell* with Ashlyn and the rest of the company. "When we finally docked, it was clear things were worse than we expected. A lieutenant commander was in command of the taskforce. An LC who had never been in a major battle before and there wasn't a senior NCO, naval or Marine, with as much battle experience as me onboard the *Campbell*." She fell silent and he gave her the time she needed to gather her thoughts and get her emotions under control.

"Admiral O'Malley was seriously injured. Colonel Ortega was dead. She died as we were transferring to the *Campbell* onboard a battle shuttle and Admiral Tremayne was still moving the rest of the taskforce into place to protect what was left of Liberator. Making matters worse, the medics weren't sure if Master Sergeant Adamson was going to make it or not." Connery lifted her mug and took a long drink. "I've never seen Angel like she was those first few days. It was as if she'd shut down emotionally. She functioned but it was as if she were an AI in a very human body."

Talbot nodded. He'd seen Ashlyn like that before and had hoped never to do so again.

"And now?"

"To say she's pissed is putting it mildly." Connery shook her head. "We all expected to find evidence those who can't be named–" She all but ground it out. – "Had a hand in what happened. But, unless there is something in the data Colonel Ortega managed to get from the enemy databanks, there's nothing to confirm the taskforce was betrayed, at least not in that manner. Now, that doesn't mean the Callusians didn't benefit from better equipment and training they've from those bastards. Hell, we know that's what had a hand in what happened. But that's not something we can lay directly at their feet – yet."

Talbot leaned back and frowned. "There's something you aren't telling me."

Connery didn't answer right away. Instead, she pushed her mug to one side and leaned forward, forearms resting on the table. As she leaned in, he saw the anger smoldering in her eyes. Worried, he matched her, leaning in so their heads were close together and the chance of being overheard lessened.

"Angel's hurting for more reasons than you know." She glanced over her shoulder, as if making sure Ashlyn nor anyone else was near. "The real reason the taskforce was hurt as bad as it was? Both Admiral O'Malley and Colonel Ortega had requested reinforcements. Worse, they'd done so more than once. None were sent. Not a single ship, not a single living body and not one bit of supplies. By the time we were dispatched, it was too late. All we could do was pray enemy reinforcements didn't arrive until we could transfer the critically wounded to our ships and then escort the surviving ships out of the system. Once the admiral put some distance between us and the system, we finished transferring the survivors of two of the remaining Liberator ships to our own. Then we scrubbed their databanks and scuttled those ships. Once that was done, we escorted the remaining ships home. That took time and that time did nothing to help Angel's temper."

Talbot closed his eyes and swore softly. No wonder Ashlyn looked like death warmed over. No, that wasn't right. She didn't look like death warmed over. She looked like Death come to render judgment on those who harmed or betrayed those she cared for. She was ready to fully embrace the call sign he and Anisimova had given her so long ago – the Angel of Death. What would the Gunny think now if she could see the young second lieutenant fresh out of the Academy they both knew held so much promise?

She'd tell him to get off his ass and make sure that now colonel didn't do anything foolish. Then she'd tell him to make those responsible for what happened pay. No one, abso-fucking-no one got away with betraying their beloved Corps.

"What did Okafor have to say?" he wanted to know.

Connery shook her head. "I can't give you the details, Loco, you know that."

He didn't like it, but she was right. In fact, he had drilled into her that there would be times she'd be forced to keep things from him and from the rest of the Devil Dogs simply because not everything Ashlyn knew could be shared immediately.

"But I will say that other than a briefing in the morning, we are all on leave until our dead have been buried."

That made sense. They needed time to grieve and they needed to be able to be with the families of the fallen.

"And you?"

"Angel's told me I'm not to worry about her and to take time for myself."

"But?" He had a feeling there was more.

"Let's just say her mother overruled her. Whether the general's told her that or not, I'll find out in the morning." A rueful smile touched Connery's lips.

"I'll deal with Angel, Faith."

She shook her head before he could continue. "Negative, Kevin. You trained me for this and, to be honest, she needs you right where you are. I don't think she can take much more right now and knowing you are looking out for the battalion helps."

He didn't like it, not one bit. But he understood. Laboe was still learning the ropes as the battalion's XO but he wasn't there yet. The best he could do for the Devil Dogs, and most especially for Ashlyn just then, was continue helping the major settle in.

"All right." He leaned back, relieved she seemed to have settled into her role as Ashlyn's aide and protector as quickly and easily as she had. "Faith, I know I don't have to say it, but you have one duty right now and that is to take care of Angel. If you need me, comm."

"Understood." She finished her beer and stood. "I'd best find my rack and get some sleep. The next few days are going to be long and hard."

He nodded and watched as she made her way out of the barroom. A slight smile touched his lips as he did. Connery stopped along the way, talking with one group of Marines or simply having a hand or fist bump for another. Whether she realized what she was doing or not, he did. She was gauging the mental state of those she might one day have to command. She was learning, from him and from Ashlyn. Hopefully, she'd learned enough already to help keep their colonel from going off the deep end.

11

Ashlyn stood on the balcony outside her bedroom and stared out into the night. She'd made it home again from yet another mission but too many hadn't. Pain tore at her at the thought of never again being able to talk with Lucinda. They had been through so much together since they first met at the Academy. She'd known she could always count on her friend, no matter what. That's why, when she learned Okafor's plans for Lucinda, she'd been tempted to try to block her friend's promotion and transfer out of the Devil Dogs. Now she wished she'd given in to that temptation. If she had, her dearest friend might still be alive.

And, in all likelihood, many more Marines would have died.

Their deaths would have been on Ashlyn's head. Knowing that didn't make Lucinda's death any easier, however.

A gentle breeze came in from the ocean beyond the capital. The night seemed so peaceful and yet she couldn't enjoy it. She doubted she would know peace again until those responsible for her friend's death, as well as the deaths of all the others in the taskforce, paid. The Callusians who attacked Taskforce Liberator already paid with their lives. But there were others, including General Hale and Admiral Wu, who still needed to. Whatever it took, Ash swore to make sure they never again left another member of the Navy or Marines looking death in the face because they failed to send the necessary reinforcements.

At least they'd managed to bring almost all their people home so they could be laid to rest with the honors they deserved. Not that it helped ease the pain the Ortegas or any of the other families felt.

She reached up and pulled her dog tags out from under her shirt. Her fingers closed around the third tag, the one Lucinda's parents had given her several days ago. It was her reminder of not only what could go wrong but what she fought for. Now it was time to get back to the fight, assuming she could convince General Okafor, not to mention her own mother, of it.

No more sitting on the sidelines. No more waiting because not all of those accused of conspiring against her and her people had gone to trial. Fuercon was at war and she commanded the system's best Marines. Somehow, she had to convince the powers that be to turn them loose against the enemy once and for all.

"You need to get some rest, Ash."

She turned. It didn't surprise her to see Elizabeth standing in the doorway. Unlike her, the woman had changed out of her uniform after the day's last memorial service. Now she wore loosely woven pants and a silky top. Even though her face was in the shadows, Ash knew her mother frowned in concern.

"I'm not sure I remember how, Mom."

She tried to smile but failed. Then she shrugged. Her mother would understand. One thing they had done over the last few days was talk. For the first time, Ash learned her mother had lost one of her best friends early into her Marine career. The circumstances might have been different but there was an understanding for much of what Ashlyn felt. More than that, knowing her mother had suffered as she did now let Ash talk more openly about her feelings and that, in turn, helped her deal with her own pain at losing Lucinda.

"You're being too hard on yourself, Ash." Elizabeth moved silently across the balcony to stand next to her. "You did all you could. You made sure Okafor knew what was happening. You pushed your Marines to be ready to depart as quickly as possible. Then you helped Miranda push the taskforce, probably more than either of you should, in an attempt to get to the Tenasic System on time. No one could have done any more than you did. Lucinda wouldn't thank you for beating yourself up like you have been and you know it."

Even though she wanted to deny what her mother said, she couldn't. Elizabeth was right. She could almost hear Lucinda telling her to quit feeling sorry for herself and to make that bastard Hale pay for not sending reinforcements. Then she was to make sure Lucinda's Marines were all right. Most of all, she was to take the fight back to the Callusians and finally beat them, once and for all.

"Perhaps." She wasn't quite ready to let herself off the hook. "Mom, I've got to know. What is the commandant going to do about Hale?"

For a moment, Elizabeth said nothing. Then she slid an arm around Ashlyn's waist and gave her a quick hug. "All I know for sure is she wants to meet with us tomorrow. We aren't the only ones either. Hale is to be there as are several others, including Admiral O'Malley if he's physically able. You're to bring Connery."

Ashlyn nodded. Maybe, just maybe, there would be at least a little justice for the fallen.

"She also told me she spoke with the Medical Center and they approved setting up a video feed of the meeting so MJ can take part."

Ash inhaled sharply at that. Adamson was still confined to the medical center and would be for some time yet. Even after her discharge, it would be months – or even longer – before she could return to full duty. The fact Okafor wanted her to take part in the meeting the next day could mean much or nothing at all beyond keeping the Warlords' senior NCO in the loop.

"Have her doctors cleared it?" she asked.

"They have. They weren't happy, but they understand how important this is, not just for Okafor to get her input but for MJ to see action is being taken."

Ash nodded slightly. "Mom, when she's released from the medical center, she's going to need to stay close."

"Her family's still on Novo Crimea, aren't they?" Elizabeth asked in return.

"They are. They're part of a farming consortium there."

"Why don't you suggest she stay here?" She smiled at Ashlyn in understanding. "We have more than enough room and that way, whenever you're home, you can keep an eye on her. When you aren't, we'll take good care of her for you."

"Thanks." She rested her head on her mother's shoulder and stared into the night. "I'm going to miss Luce so much, Mom."

"I know, love. We all are." Her lips brushed the top of Ash's head. "But we will keep her alive in our memories."

It wasn't enough. It would never be enough, but it was the best she could do – at least for now.

"Why don't you try to get some sleep? You promised Jake you'd take him to school in the morning before reporting to duty."

At the mention of her son, Ash smiled, some of her sadness lifting. "What time does Okafor want us to report?"

"Nine." She began leading Ash inside. "I'd appreciate it if you stopped by my office first."

"Will do." Ash closed the door behind them. "Uniform?"

"MARPATs."

Good. She'd be perfectly happy if she didn't have to wear her dress uniform or mess dress uniform for the next decade or two.

"Mom, you can quit worrying about me. I'm all right."

She switched on a light and glanced around her room. As she did, she winced slightly. It showed just how depressed and angry she'd been since returning home. Clothes tossed over furniture, empty beer bottles – most from that day – and more. The fact Mrs. Dumont had not been in to clean spoke volumes. She knew Ash needed her space and understood. But now Ash needed to figure out a way to carry on, not just for herself but for those who cared for her as well as for those who relied upon her.

"You're on your way to being all right," Elizabeth corrected. Then she reached for Ash's hands and looked her daughter in the eye. "Ashlyn, I know how much Lucinda meant to you. She was more than your friend and fellow Marine. She was your sister in all but blood. In some ways, you were closer to her than you are to Kate. Let yourself mourn, but don't let it paralyze you."

"I won't." As long as there was justice for Lucinda and soon. If not, well, she'd damn well see to it herself.

"Get some rest. I'll check on Jake on my way to bed."

Ashlyn smiled and lightly kissed her mother's cheek. "Thanks. I'll see you in the morning."

Hopefully, it would be a better day than the last month or so had been.

————

AT PRECISELY FIVE 'til nine the next morning, Ashlyn followed one of Okafor's aides into a conference room down the corridor from the commandant's office. Connery followed close behind. As they entered, the aide told them to help themselves to coffee and then find seats. The commandant would be with them shortly. Ashlyn thanked the young woman and then made her way to the table, carefully choosing her seat so her back was to the wall and she had a clear view of the rest of the room.

When the door slid open a few moments later, Ash instantly climbed to her feet as Admirals Tremayne and O'Malley, leaning heavily on a cane, entered. Tremayne looked as serious as Ash felt. O'Malley looked as if he should still in bed which, considering the severity of his injuries, he probably should have been. Before Ashlyn could move around the table, Connery was on her feet and hurrying to help O'Malley to a chair. Once he was seated, she poured him a mug of coffee before offering one to Tremayne.

Colonel Rico Santiago, FleetCom's intel chief, arrived next. He greeted everyone. Then he moved around the table to where Ashlyn sat. For a moment, he simply looked at her, as if judging how she was.

Then he smiled slightly and gave a nod. Whatever he'd seen, it apparently satisfied him.

"You okay?" he asked softly as he took the seat to her left.

"Better." That much was true, as long as he didn't ask how much better.

Before he could say anything else, the door once again slid open. Connery instantly popped to her feet and called everyone to attention. General Okafor entered the room, followed closely by Elizabeth. Okafor put them at their ease and then took her seat at the head of the table. Elizabeth sat to her right and leaned forward to pour each of them a mug of coffee.

Ashlyn frowned slightly as the women settled back. All the players were present save one. Well, two, but Adamson was joining them via 'link, assuming the doctors permitted it. So where was Hale?

"Brigadier General Hale will be joining us shortly." Okafor took a sip of coffee before continuing. "I wanted the chance to discuss what I hope to accomplish this morning before his arrival. I also wanted to let you know what FleetCom has decided about Admiral Wu. But, before we get started, Corporal Connery, will you contact the Medical Center and set up the 'link with Master Sergeant Adamson?"

"Yes, ma'am," Connery replied. The young woman got to her feet and moved to the main comms board at the rear of the room and went to work.

"Let's begin with the Navy end. Admiral O'Malley?"

Ash turned her attention to O'Malley. As she did, her anger of the debacle that had led to the mission's failure returned. Even though the admiral had been in the Medical Center until a few days earlier, his injuries were still easy to see. The brace on his left leg spoke volumes about how badly broken the leg had been. The way his left arm was strapped across his abdomen was much the same. This was a man who had come close to losing his life and, judging from the look in his eyes, that was the least of the demons haunting him just then.

"FleetCom has reviewed each of my requests for reinforcements, as well as those sent by Colonel Ortega. I've been assured Admiral

Wu will be disciplined for her failure to act. While her reasons for not sending the reinforcements were understandable, at least on the surface, the fact she didn't take my requests and accompanying reports to FleetCom or SecNav are enough to cause them to look closer into her motivation as well as her actions as fleet CO over the last few years."

"I actually have the latest information," Tremayne said. "I met with SecNav and senior members of FleetCom this morning before breakfast. Admiral Wu is being reassigned. She will be taking over command of the system defense for the Daedalus System. They aren't dropping her in rank, but this reassignment makes it clear to her and to anyone else with an ounce of sense that her career is over. My guess is that she will choose to retire instead of accepting the transfer. It's not the punishment she deserves or the satisfaction your dead and injured deserve, but it is the best that can be done under the regs since she didn't violate the rule of law, only the spirit of it." She gave everyone a moment to digest what she said. "I don't know who will be taking her place yet. However, unless you object, Admiral, you and your ships will be transferring to First Fleet."

For a moment, O'Malley simply looked at her. Then a smile, the first Ashlyn had seen from him since they'd been forced to withdraw from the Tenasic System, touched his lips. "I would be honored."

The redhead smiled and shook his hand. Then everyone turned their attention back to Okafor. Before she could say anything, Connery cleared her throat.

"I have the Master Sergeant, ma'am."

Okafor activated the virtual keyboard in front of her and input a quick command sequence. A moment later, the holo screen over the conference table came to life. The image showed M. J. Anderson sitting up in bed. Pain etched deep lines in the blonde's face. Someone had settled a black patch over her injured left eye, covering the bandage that protected the eye as its nerves regenerated. Ash knew that beneath the sheet, her right leg was missing below the knee. At least the regen treatments were working. Her injured right arm, much like O'Malley's injured arm, was strapped across her abdomen. It would be months before they knew for sure if Adamson could return to duty, but Ashlyn's money was on her friend. In the meantime, Ash meant to do all she could to keep her friend occupied so she didn't brood too much about what happened.

"Master Sergeant, I hope you're feeling better," Okafor said.

"I am, ma'am, thank you."

"Your doctors have made it clear we aren't to keep you long today and I have no intention of disobeying them. Because of that, I have an order for you. If you start to tire, you are to let me know and we will recess until you feel able to continue. Will you promise to be honest and do that for me?"

"Yes, ma'am."

"One last question, Master Sergeant. Are you up to making your report in front of Brigadier General Hale?"

For a moment, the blonde didn't reply. A flash of anger crossed her expression followed by a look that sent a cold chill down Ashlyn's spine. Her friend might not be physically able to confront Hale, but she looked forward to doing it via the holo-link. Not that Ash blamed her. Hale had a great deal to answer for.

"I am, General."

"Good." Okafor smiled at her in encouragement and approval. "Hale will be here in a few minutes. We'll let you rest until he is." She turned to Connery and instructed her to switch the holo image over to her personal wallpaper. Connery did as ordered and Okafor signaled her aide to escort Hale in as soon as he arrived.

The next ten minutes seemed to crawl by. Ash listened with half an ear as the others talked. No one mentioned the reason they'd been called together. No one spoke Hale's name. Frustrated, insulted because the man kept them waiting, Ash fought the urge to stand and pace. Instead, she pulled out her datapad and checked her email. At least the morning reports from Talbot and Laboe gave her something to concentrate on.

When Okafor's aide finally signaled Hale's arrival, Okafor rapped her knuckles against the tabletop. Everyone fell silent. Most sat a bit straighter in their chairs as they waited. As they did, Connery softly told Adamson to stand by. Ashlyn blew out a breath and waited, reminding herself she couldn't physically attack Hale for being an incompetent ass., no matter how tempting it might be.

"Brigadier General Hale, Commandant," the lieutenant announced a few moments later as she escorted Hale into the conference room.

"That will be all, Lt. Ulloa."

Ulloa slipped out of the room, closing the door behind her. As she did, Hale glanced around the table, as if looking for a place to sit. Then, without much more than a passing nod at Okafor, he made his way to the empty chair next to Tremayne. Even though she was the most junior officer present, Ashlyn railed internally at the slight. Hale's resentment at being called before Okafor seemed to radiate from him. Ash glanced at the commandant. Seeing Okafor's slight frown, she had no doubt the commandant would soon disabuse him of that idea.

At least she hoped so.

Okafor waited, watching as Hale pulled out his chair. Then, as he began to sit, she arched one eyebrow. Without a word, she glanced at Ashlyn and gave a single nod. Mouth twitching in amusement, Ashlyn climbed to her feet. As she did, she called the room to attention. Even as Hale dropped onto his chair, the others stood and did as ordered. Even O'Malley, who needed help from Tremayne to stand, braced to attention. Ashlyn waited, watching as Hale sat there for a moment before complying. It would be interesting indeed to see how Okafor handled his insubordination.

"Thank you, Colonel Shaw," Okafor said as she climbed to her feet. "Please get those present ready for inspection."

"At once, ma'am." She glanced around the table and then the room. "You heard the commandant, ma'ams, sirs. Fall in at the far end of the room. You have thirty seconds."

Instantly, everyone hurried to do as she instructed, even O'Malley who leaned heavily on his cane as Tremayne helped him to where Ashlyn indicated. Everyone except Hale. Resentment burned in his eyes and his jaw worked. The others had fallen in at the far end of the room before he managed to step away from the table. Ashlyn glanced at Okafor and the general nodded once more. Taking entirely too much pleasure from what she was about to do, Ashlyn moved to where the man slowly walked toward the others.

Doing her best to channel Adamson on the parade ground, she fought back her smile and barked, "Sir, when the commandant says we are to fall in, that means we fall in NOW!" She leaned forward, her mouth not far from his ear as she all but yelled the last word. "I respectfully suggest you get your ass in gear and do as instructed, sir."

"Back off, Shaw!" He turned shoved her back.

He opened his mouth to say something else but, before he could, Okafor spoke. "Brigadier General Hale, you will never again place your hands on another officer under my command, do you hear me?"

Ashlyn swallowed hard at the cold anger in the woman's voice. Instead of answering, Hale simply stared at Okafor, disbelief reflected on his expression.

"I suggest you do as Colonel Shaw instructed and you will do it NOW!" The commandant's voice rang with both command and condemnation. "Colonel, take your place," she added.

"Yes, ma'am." Ash hurried to her place between Santiago and Connery. Once there, she braced to attention.

At the same time, Okafor moved purposefully around the table, her eyes never leaving Hale as he finally followed orders. Resentment once again hovered around him like a dark cloud as he took his place next to Elizabeth. Ashlyn wished she dared turn her head to look but this wasn't the time. She had no doubt Okafor was about to make a point, one of many the woman had planned for the day.

"Corporal Connery, you'll assist me."

"Yes, ma'am." Connery hurried to stand behind and to the left of Okafor, her datapad out and ready to take notes.

Okafor began her inspection with Ashlyn. At her command, Ash took two steps forward and once again braced to attention. She remained there, motionless, her expression never changing, as the general checked every aspect of her appearance. After what seemed like an eternity, Okafor motioned for her to step back.

"Excellent, Colonel Shaw, not that I expected anything less from you." She glanced at Connery and said, "Nothing to note," before moving to Santiago.

A few minutes later, she stopped in front of Hale. As with Ashlyn and Santiago, she ordered him to take two steps forward. She moved slowly around him, pointing out fault after fault with his MARPATs, everything from dangling threads to ill-fit to wearing the wrong boots. Connery listed each issue, reading them back as she did.

When Okafor finally stepped back, Ash wondered if Hale felt like he'd just gone through his first inspection back in boot camp. Then, to her surprise, Okafor kept Hale where he was and asked Connery to step forward.

"Corporal, do you see anything I missed?"

Ashlyn fought her smile when she heard Connery swallow hard. The corporal didn't disappoint her, however. Where some junior non-coms would have stuttered or instantly answered in the negative, Connery didn't. Instead, she glanced at her notes and then looked up.

"Begging the general's pardon, ma'am, but I do see several things."

Okafor smiled slightly and nodded for her to continue.

Only someone who knew Connery well would have caught the hint of uncertainty about her as she listed an additional half dozen things Okafor "missed". Ashlyn had no doubt the woman had seen them but had left them as a test for Connery, one the young woman passed with flying colors. Not that Hale seemed to appreciate it. Even though Ashlyn couldn't see his face, the way he held himself combined with the audible grinding of his teeth spoke volumes.

"Very good, Corporal." Okafor reached for Connery's datapad. "Let's start the inspection over and this time you take the lead."

Fifteen minutes later, Okafor put everyone at their ease. She paced up and then down the line. As she did, Ashlyn fought the urge to fidget. Memories of when she served under Okafor early in her own career returned. With them came the realization the general was anything but happy. Whether it was simply because of Hale and his actions, or lack of action, or something else, she didn't know. She wasn't sure she wanted to.

"I want to congratulate most of you for how well you presented for inspection," she began. "As senior officers, it is all too easy to forget that we are supposed to set the example for those who serve under us. Unfortunately, it is also clear one of you made that mistake. That stops now. Starting today, every officer, no matter what their rank, will be subject to inspections on a regular basis, including myself. Is that understood?"

"Ma'am, yes, ma'am!" they answered, even those who weren't Marines.

"Find your seats and let's get started. Corporal, re-establish the link with Master Sergeant Adamson please."

12

Kevin Talbot paused at the doorway and glanced around. He'd promised the medic on duty that he wouldn't disturb his patient if she happened to be sleeping. But that didn't keep him from hoping Anderson was awake. He needed to talk with her, find out what happened to Taskforce Liberator. His normal channels of information had dried up. It was as if the powers-that-be had locked down all information about Liberator's mission. That reminded him too much about what happened after Colonel Shaw's ill-fated mission on Arterus. If history was about to repeat itself, he wanted to be ready because the fallout this time would be worse, much worse.

Fortunately, Adamson lay propped up in bed. Talbot schooled his features not to react as he studied her. He knew she'd been badly injured but this. . . this was more than he expected. A black patch covered her left eye, white bandages visible beneath it. Her right arm was strapped across her abdomen, immobilizing it. That leg. . .. He swallowed hard, finally accepting the fact she had lost her right leg below the knee. Then, as she glanced at him, the worry he'd felt eased. Anger and determination reflected in her good eye and she lifted her left arm, motioning him inside.

"Damn it, MJ." He grasped her hand and closed his eyes, once again striving for calm. "What can I do for you?" Nothing else mattered just then. He would find another way to get the information he wanted. The last thing he wanted was to add to her pain, emotional or physical.

She didn't say anything for a moment. Instead, she shifted painfully on the bed. He waited, watching as the bed automatically adjusted to her new position. Part of him wanted to help her but another part, the part that recognized she needed to do it on her own, waited. They knew one another well enough she'd ask for help if she needed it. At least he hoped she would.

"It's not as bad as it could have been." She spoke softly, slowly. Worried, he waited, giving her the chance to say more if she wanted. "What do you know?"

"About the mission?"

Adamson nodded.

His mouth firmed and anger flared. He didn't know much but it was enough to tell him someone had royally fucked up. No, they had fucked those with the taskforce, costing too many good men and women their lives.

"Not much." He didn't try to hide his frustration, knowing she would understand. "Angel has said little more than she's needed to. Connery has been as closed-mouthed as we trained her to be. There have been several closed-door meetings with General Shaw and the commandant. Other than hearing both Admiral O'Malley and Sorceress requested reinforcements more than once, that's about it."

Adamson's good eye darkened and she nodded. "That is pretty much it, Kevin." For a moment, she fell silent. He waited. If she needed time to decide how much to tell him, he'd give it to her. "It was a clusterfuck and not because of anything Lucinda or the admiral did. I can't tell you anything else, not yet."

He looked at her, his eyes narrowed. That one statement said a great deal. Unless he was mistaken, that was exactly what she wanted. Still, he needed at least one more question answered.

"Tell me this at least, are the rumors that reinforcements weren't sent when requested true?"

She nodded.

He closed his eyes. Anger welled up and pushed it down. He couldn't jump to conclusions. As much as this seemed like a repeat of what happened to Colonel Shaw, he didn't know that for certain. The fact she hadn't gone after those she held responsible for Lucinda Ortega's death reassured him. Either she knew those responsible would pay for what they'd done – or not done – or she already had something in place to deal with them. He prayed it was the former and not the latter.

"I have to ask. Was this a repeat of Arterus?"

She shook her head. "No, I don't think so." She winced as she changed positions again. "Kevin, I can't say anything more than this. General Okafor is dealing with it, at least where the Marines are concerned."

He didn't like being left in the dark, but he'd been in the Corps long enough to understand how things worked. At least under Okafor they really did work. "All right, MJ. Just remember I'm here if you see something that needs to be done."

She looked at him and nodded. "Angel? Is she all right?"

"She's hurting but pushing through it. You know Angel. She attended every funeral or memorial service she could for the Marines who died on the mission. She is also pushing the Devil Dogs, trying to keep us busy so we don't have too much time to think about what happened and get mad."

A slight smile touched Anderson's lips. Then it was gone, and worry clouded her expression. "Kevin, stay close to her." She reached for his hand and held it tightly, her concern for their friend clear. "Has she said anything about Lucinda's death?"

He shook his head. The colonel hadn't said anything, and he hadn't asked. He hadn't wanted to cause her any more pain.

Adamson didn't say anything for a moment. Then, as if making up her mind, she nodded once. "I can't go into details yet. But you need to know this much at least. Lucinda died when one of the power plants on the *Sobek* blew. The explosion had enough power that it caused the part of the landing bay Lucinda and two others were in to collapse. They were trapped in the rubble. The rest of the squad managed to get them out. They were on the shuttle and away from the ship before it blew. Lucinda died before the shuttle got back to the *Campbell*." She looked away but not before he saw the tears pooling in her good eye. "Kevin, if Tremayne had been able to get her ships there three hours sooner, Lucinda would still be alive."

It hit him like a sledgehammer. Three hours? God, no wonder the colonel looked like she wanted to kill someone. She pushed as hard as she could to get the taskforce to leave the home system sooner than it had. That delay had cost how many lives? Did FleetCom understand how lucky it was she hadn't gone public with that information or that she hadn't gone on the warpath? The fact she hadn't proved she trusted Okafor to make sure Lucinda Ortega and all the other fallen were avenged.

He wasn't sure he could do that.

"Connery told me it had been a matter of hours." He cursed himself for not taking the younger woman at her word. He owed her an apology. "And you? When were you injured?"

"Most of this happened in the last battle."

He knew there was more to the story but, before he could ask, he heard someone approaching. A quick glance over his shoulder confirmed his guess. Anderson's doctor approached and that meant their conversation was over.

"MJ, get some rest and don't worry about Angel. I promise I'll keep an eye on her." He rested his hand on her shoulder and gave it a reassuring squeeze. "I'll be back later. Comm me if you need anything."

"One thing," she said, stopping him before he could leave. "Tell Connery I want to see her."

He promised to pass on her message. Then, as he made his way to the nearest lift to take him to the ground floor, he began putting together his arguments to present to the colonel to convince her to finally let go the burden of guilt he knew she carried. It wouldn't be easy. It never was. But it had to be done, not just for her but for the

Devil Dogs. The battalion functioned better when their CO wasn't beating herself up for something she had no control over.

———

"Ma'am, would you mind telling me what in the hell is going on?" Connery asked softly as they made their way back to the conference room.

An hour earlier, Okafor's aide entered and apologized for the interruption. Then she hurried to Okafor's side. Bending, she whispered something in the general's ear. Okafor listened, her expression betraying nothing. Then she nodded once, telling the lieutenant that she would take care of it, whatever "it" might be, before dismissing the young woman. A few moments later, she excused everyone except Elizabeth, telling them to be back in an hour.

Taking advantage of the break, Ash returned to her office. She spent a few minutes on the comm with Lucinda's sister, making sure the family was all right. When she ended the call, she asked Connery to make sure O'Rourke's, Lucinda's favorite restaurant in the capital, sent dinner to the family that evening. With that much accomplished, she turned her attention to the first of almost a dozen reports that had come in since she last checked her email.

Now, hearing the corporal's question, she wished she had an answer.

"Your guess is as good as mine." She paused before the door and pressed her palm against the lock plate. A moment later the hatch slid open. "But, knowing the commandant, we will learn soon enough."

As the hatch slid shut behind them, Ash glanced around. With the exception of Okafor's aide and several Marine privates laying out food and drink, no one else was present. The lieutenant prepared to call the others to attention and Ash waved her off. Thanking her, the young woman suggested they help themselves to food and drink before the meeting reconvened.

Five minutes later, Okafor entered the conference room, Elizabeth just behind her. This time, before Connery could call them to attention, the general shook her head and told them to remain where they were. Then she glanced around and Ash guessed she was taking a mental roll call. Nor did she have any doubt what caused her to frown. Once again, Hale had not appeared when he was supposed to. The question became what Okafor would do about it.

"Lieutenant, has there been any word from Brigadier General Hale?" Okafor asked her aide.

"Negative, ma'am."

Okafor leaned back, her expression thoughtful. She seemed almost too calm and Ashlyn knew that was not good, at least not where Hale was concerned. "Colonel Santiago, would you be so good as to use your resources to locate him? Once he's done that, Colonel Shaw, I think it would be more than appropriate for you to dispatch a three-man squad of Devil Dogs to escort the brigadier general here? Let's make sure he hasn't lost his way by any chance."

Ashlyn fought her smile. Before responding, she thought of a slight twist on the general's "request" and decided to suggest it. "Ma'am, it would be my pleasure. However, if I may, I would recommend one member of the team come from the Warlords. I do believe that might help get your message across." Besides, they needed to know the commandant was not going to let what happened to them go unpunished.

Okafor's grin told Ash all she needed to know. "An excellent suggestion, Colonel, and I will add one of my own. Corporal Connery, I would like you and Master Gunnery Sergeant Talbot to represent the Devil Dogs. I will leave it to you to choose someone from the Warlords. My only recommendation is it be a senior NCO who won't be intimidated by the brigadier general."

Connery stood and braced to attention, and Ashlyn saw her doing her best not to smile. "Yes, ma'am. Permission to step out to contact the Master Guns?"

"Before you do, Corporal, I'm sending you General Hale's current location," Santiago said. "I will update you if there are any changes."

"Thank you, sir." She turned her attention back to Okafor.

"Commandant?"

"Dismissed, Corporal." She waited until Connery disappeared through the hatch. "All right, Rico, where is our errant Marine?"

"In his quarters, ma'am." He glanced down at his comm and then turned his attention back to Okafor. "It appears he took a walk, ma'am, and then returned to his quarters. He's been there for the past half hour."

"Interesting. We'll leave him to his escorts. In the meantime, there are several matters I'd like to deal with before he arrives."

Worried, Ashlyn set her coffee mug on the table and leaned forward. As she did, she noted her mother was the only one who didn't look concerned by what Okafor said. In fact, if anything, her mother looked slightly shell-shocked. But that didn't make any sense. When she tried to catch Elizabeth's eye, the woman gave a slight shake of her head. Whatever it was, she either couldn't or wasn't ready to discuss it now.

And that did nothing to reassure Ash.

"Admiral O'Malley, Admiral Tremayne, we won't keep you much longer," Okafor began. "I do appreciate your input, but I don't want to risk setting your recovery back, Kieran. If you trust me to discipline Hale and make sure he is never in the position to cause harm to another of our missions, I promise I will do justice for your people."

"I more than trust you, Helen." Anger and pain reflected in his eyes. "I would appreciate knowing what sort of punishment you hand down."

"How about a full recording of the meeting?" she asked in return.

"Even better." Now he grinned, a predatory grin that sent a chill down Ash's spine, especially when it was matched by Tremayne.

"Miranda?" Okafor asked.

Ash leaned back and glanced at her comm when it vibrated in her hand. A slight smile touched her lips to read Connery's brief text. The corporal, Talbot and Sergeant Gregori Kuznetsov were on their way to "help" Hale find his way to the conference room. Satisfied, she waited, listening as the others spoke. Tremayne agreed with O'Malley. As long as she knew what action Okafor took against Hale, she was more than happy to leave it to the commandant. Okafor asked a few more questions of them. Then she glanced at her own comm and a slight smile touched her lips. Then she promised she would do right by all those injured or killed from Taskforce Liberator. Apparently satisfied, Tremayne helped O'Malley to his feet and they left the room. Now it was only Marines which, as far as Ashlyn was concerned, was how it should be when Okafor dealt with Hale.

"While we wait, let's take care of a couple of housekeeping matters," Okafor said. "Rico, I know it will take time for your people to go through the data Colonel Ortega managed to secure before her death. I want daily updates, more often if you feel you have something of import. We need to know not only why the enemy's tactics were so different this time but also if there is anything solid tying them to Midlothian. If, by any chance, you come across future battle plans, that would be icing on the cake."

"Understood, ma'am."

"As for you, Ashlyn, you are to quit beating yourself up. You did nothing wrong. Nothing. In fact, you and your mother probably prevented the complete destruction of the taskforce and its personnel. The two of you, along with Lucinda and O'Malley, are the only reason we managed to save as many of our people as we did." Okafor pinned her with a firm look, waiting until she nodded. "When he gets here and we are on the record, I want you to tell Hale exactly what you know and how you, as a Marine and as a senior officer, feel about his lack of action. Don't step over the line, but also don't hold back. Let's see how he reacts."

"Gladly, ma'am." Her only regret was she couldn't step over that line. Hale owed her, not to mention the rest of the Corps and the families of the fallen, a price he wouldn't be forced to pay because he had managed to stay just within the bounds of the regs. Damn him.

"Once you have, we will see if he has anything of value to say. Then he'll learn what happens when officers under my command fail to do their duty. Worse, who fail to support their fellow Marines." Her eyes flashed, and Ash relaxed a little. That was enough to reassure her Okafor wasn't going to let Hale off.

It didn't take long for Connery and the others to arrive with Hale. From the moment they entered the conference room, it was obvious Hale wanted to be anywhere but there. At least he was smart enough not to voice his objections to being brought back under what was essentially armed guard. Ashlyn knew her people well enough to know that, even though no weapons were visible, they were there. Apparently, Hale did as well. Part of her regretted the fact he hadn't tried to make a run for it. Both Connery and Talbott, and probably Sergeant Kuznetsov, would have made certain he didn't get far.

If he suffered a few bumps and bruises along the way, too bad. Ash wouldn't mind treating him to a few herself.

This time, as Hale looked around for his seat, he found none. When Tremayne and O'Malley left, Okafor had instructed her aide to remove all unoccupied chairs. Ash hadn't been the only one to smile when she did. The general was making it very clear Hale was not there as anything but someone about to be give a report and possibly receive discipline.

Who said Marines weren't good a psychological warfare?

"Corporal Connery, if you would be so good as to man the comms panel again."

"Yes, ma'am."

"Master Guns, Sergeant, I'd appreciate it if you'd hold outside the hatch until I send for you."

The two left the conference room and the hatch slid silently closed behind them.

"Before we begin, please re-establish the link with Master Sergeant Adamson, Corporal," Okafor said. She waited until the blonde's image appeared on the holo screens in front of each of them. "Master Sergeant, do you feel well enough to continue?"

"I do, General."

"Very well. Before we get started, there is one matter I need to deal with." Okafor smiled and looked directly into the pickup. "Master Sergeant Adamson, as senior NCO for the Warlords, I wanted you to be the first to know that I have signed off on a post-humous promotion for Lieutenant Colonel Ortega to full colonel.

Her family will be informed come morning and will receive benefits commiserate with the colonel's new rank."

For a moment, Anderson's mouth worked as she fought her grief. "Thank you, ma'am. The only reason any of us made it back is because of actions she and Admiral O'Malley took."

"As well as actions you took," Okafor corrected gently. "Before her death, Colonel Ortega recommended a battlefield promotion for you to the rank of Sergeant Major. I have signed off on that as well. Congratulations, Sergeant Major Anderson. You have done your battalion and your CO proud."

Anderson's good eye filled with tears and she reached up to dash at them before they fell down her cheek. "Ma'am," she began in protest.

"It's already done, Sergeant Major." Okafor smiled again and then sobered. "Now for more serious business." She turned her attention to Hale, "Brigadier General Hale, for the record, you are currently assigned as the commanding officer for Second Division, Fuerconese Marine Corps. Is that correct?"

"It is."

"The Warlords are under your direct command?"

"They are."

"And, until her death, Colonel Lucinda Ortega was CO for the Warlords."

"Correct."

"Colonel Shaw?"

Ashlyn looked up. In that moment, Hale suddenly represented not only the tragedy that had befallen Taskforce Liberator but the conspiracy against herself. She hadn't been able to defend herself or her people against the false charges leveled against them. This time, however, she would do everything she could to get justice for Lucinda and her people. She would be their champion just as Lucinda had been hers.

"General Shaw." She considered standing and then decided it was more of an insult to him to remain seated while he was forced to stand like a prisoner in the dock. "I've got a simple question for you.

Did Colonel Ortega request reinforcements once Taskforce Liberator arrived in the Tenasic System and engaged the enemy?"

For a moment, Hale didn't respond. His mouth worked, and he glanced around the table at the openly hostile faces watching him. "I exercised my judgment as a Marine and as Second Division's commanding officer, knowing the requirements of the rest of the division, in making my decision."

"Which answers my questions. She did request reinforcements." She paused, considering her next question. "Did you or did you not deny her request? Or did you just ignore it and hope it would go away?"

Hale's eyes flashed, and he looked from Ashlyn to Okafor. "I object to being treated this way, Commandant, and especially by a junior officer. I was told this would be a debriefing about the mission. It suddenly feels as if I am on trial. Perhaps I ought to ask for counsel."

"That is your right, Hale." Okafor sounded as if they were discussing nothing more serious than the weather. "However, if you do, I will adjourn this meeting and will ask not only Colonel Shaw, as the commanding officer of the Marine contingent sent to reinforce Colonel Ortega, but Admiral Tremayne as well as Admiral O'Malley to meet with JAG to determine exactly what charges should be drawn up against you for your actions regarding Colonel Ortega's requests. I have no doubt that, at the minimum, you will be forced to defend yourself against charges that you failed to do your duty to fully support troops under your command."

Ash waited, watching the emotional battle play out over the man's face. "Ask your questions," he all but spat a few moments later.

"Do I need to repeat my question, General?" she asked in return.

He shook his head. "I did not send the requested reinforcements because, at the time, I did not feel they were necessary. I believed Ortega was overreacting to her first command situation."

Anger flared, burning deep inside of Ashlyn. She forced it down. She knew he was trying to bait her and she wouldn't give him the satisfaction. But she would use his own admission to hang him, figuratively if nothing else.

"And her second request? Or how about requests three through six?" She punched in a series of commands using her virtual keyboard. When she did, each of Lucinda's requests appeared on the holo screens before them. "Were they overreactions, even in light of the losses the taskforce had taken?" Now she brought up the casualty reports attached to each request as well as the lists of equipment lost in the fighting.

This time, Hale didn't answer. Not that she blamed him. What could he say that wouldn't dig an even deeper hole for him?

"Sergeant Major Anderson, since the general doesn't seem to have an answer, I'll ask you. Were Colonel Ortega's requests for reinforcements unreasonable or the actions of an officer panicking in the face of the enemy?"

Adamson's face looked out at them from the main holo screen, her expression hard. "Negative, Colonel. They were the results of a seasoned Marine officer who took into account not only the actions of the enemy and their consequences but also our own orders from FleetCom."

"Another question, if you're up to it, Sergeant Major." She waited until Adamson nodded. Ash had a feeling there was little, if anything, that would keep the blonde from having her say about what happened. "Were you aware of the colonel's requests at the time she made them?"

"I was, and I was in full agreement with them."

"Thank you, Sergeant Major." Ash turned her attention back to Hale. "I assume you aren't going to insult any of the rest of us, much less the sergeant major, by suggesting she panicked and made unnecessary requests." She didn't wait for Hale's response. Now she stood, leaning forward, her palms on the tabletop. For the first time, she let her anger and distaste for Hale show. "You are a Marine. General. You took the same oaths as each of us sitting at this table. How could you ignore not one, not two, but six requests for reinforcements? Why did you not forward those requests to Commandant Okafor if you felt your division was unable fulfill them? More importantly, why did you leave your people to die?" The pain of Lucinda's death tore through her and she inhaled sharply. "My God, General, how in the hell do you expect any Marine to trust you to have their back and their best interests at heart after what you did to the Warlords?" She returned to her seat, her point made.

"All very good questions and some I suggest you confer with legal counsel about," Okafor said. "Until I decide whether or not to bring you up on charges of dereliction of duty, Brigadier General Hale, you are removed from command of Second Division. You will receive your new orders by end of day."

"You can't!"

"I not only can but I have," Okafor countered. She stood and moved to the hatch. When it slid open, she signaled to someone. A moment later, Talbot and Sergeant Kuznetsov stepped inside. "Escort the brigadier general to his office. He may remove any personal items there. However, he is allowed to take nothing pertaining to the Corps or Fleet that is not personal. You are then escort him to his quarters. Once you have left him there, you are dismissed to return to your regular assignments."

The two crossed the room to stand on either side of Hale. Talbot gestured for him to lead the way. As Hale left the conference room, Talbot glanced at Ashlyn, a thousand questions in his eyes. Understanding, she inclined her head slightly. Hopefully, he understood she not only agreed with what happened but would fill him in soon.

"Now," Okafor said as the hatch once again slid shut. "Sergeant Major, I assure you your injured and dead will have justice. For now, get some rest and do everything the doctors tell you. I want you back to duty as soon as possible."

"Yes, ma'am. Thank you, ma'am."

Okafor gave her a smile and ended the transmission. Then she turned to where Connery stood. "Corporal, you are dismissed as well."

Frowning, Ash looked down the table to where her mother sat. Elizabeth shook her head, her expression concerned. Wondering what other bombshells the general had to drop on them, Ashlyn leaned back and waited. She had a feeling she would soon wish she'd been dismissed with the others.

"Rico, you're dismissed as well."

The intelligence officer stood and quickly left. As he did, Ashlyn's stomach did a slow roll. She most definitely did not like where this was going. Not one bit.

"Ash, I want a full report from you, detailing not only what you found when Taskforce Sentinel arrived on-station but also the information you received from Lucinda that started all this. Include what you learned when you investigated her concerns." Now Okafor smiled and Ash felt herself chuckling. "I know you, Ashlyn Shaw. I know the moment you received Lucinda's message, you started looking into the situation. I also know you looked at it from the viewpoint of a battalion commander and a Marine on the line. I need that information and your conclusions. Have it on my desk by morning."

"Understood." Fortunately for her, she had already prepared much of what Okafor asked for.

"That leaves SecDiv without a CO and the Warlords down most of their senior officers and senior non-coms," Elizabeth commented.

"And it brings up something I'd asked the two of you to consider and report on before Ash left on this last mission." Okafor poured herself a fresh mug of coffee. "The Corps hasn't had a major realignment in more than a century. It has operated under the rule of *if it ain't broke, don't fix it*. However, while it might not be broken, it can be made stronger."

"Ma'am?" Elizabeth looked at her in surprise.

"With the changes in technology, not to mention the fact we apparently have been betrayed by someone we thought an ally, it is past time for us to adapt. Ashlyn, you have been part of that already."

Ash narrowed her eyes, wondering what Okafor meant.

"When Miranda Tremayne left you in command of the *Nagato*, she broke with a long tradition of Marines never commanding anything more than an attack shuttle. You proved a Marine is more than capable of doing more."

"General," she began, her mouth going dry as the possible implications hit her.

Okafor laughed before continuing. "Don't worry, Ash. I'm not going to try to make you into a space jockey. I have other plans for you."

Oh, she did not like the sound of that one bit.

"To cut to the chase, I am going to be realigning the Corps. I have already discussed this with FleetCom and with the President and they all agree with what I have in mind." Okafor waited, giving them time to accept that much of what she said. "The first change, and it goes into effect immediately, is that all SpecOps personnel will now be under one command. I've been aware for some time now that having the different companies and battalions assigned to different divisions wasn't working as well as it should. There was a time when that was the optimal way of doing things but no more. With us once again at war, I plan to correct that mistake."

Ash glanced at her mother, worried how she might react to the news. Then she swallowed hard at the thought of someone besides Elizabeth being Division CO for the Devil Dogs.

"The SpecOps forces will now become part of the newly designated 7th Marine Division. Liz, you will be the division CO. Your division will be comprised of three regiments: the 10th, the 14th and the 15th. The 10th Marine Regiment will include the HQ company as well as three battalions. Those battalions will be the Devil Dogs, the Warlords and the Panzers. Regimental CO will be you, Ash."

"W-what?" Not the most intelligent of responses but it was the best she could do, especially in light of the fact Okafor had just taken the command of the Devil Dogs away from her.

"Don't look so worried, kid." The general smiled and leaned back, crossing her legs. "That gives you two battalions that will be very good fits to one another and a ground pounder. And, before you run out of here to resign your commission, you will still be in command of the DDs, at least until you have someone you feel capable of taking your place."

"But a regiment?" She still couldn't believe it.

"Yes, a regiment," Okafor confirmed. "We'll get into the details later. Right now, you have two priorities. The first is finding replacements for those in the Warlords chain-of-command who either died or were seriously injured on this last mission. I won't lie. It's not going to be easy because you have to take into account not only the officers but the senior NCOs. However, you have resources you can look to for help, including MJ Anderson. It's going to be months before she is able to return to duty but that doesn't mean you can't pick her brain.

"The second priority is to evaluate each battalion under your command and determine what is needed where. I'd like the information tomorrow, but you have an even more pressing assignment from me already and I know it will take time for you to get up to speed on the rest of it. You have until the end of the week to get me your report. Sooner would be better."

"Yes, ma'am." She still felt shell shocked.

"Liz, you will have a full briefing packet on the 7th in your inbox by the time you return to your office. Review it and let me know if you have any questions. I'll have information on the other regiments to you by the end of the week."

"Yes, ma'am."

At least Elizabeth looked as stunned as Ash felt.

"Ladies, this next is for your ears only." Okafor waited until they assured her they understood. "The President and FleetCom have decided it is time to quit playing a defensive war. That is another reason for the realignment of our forces. The Navy will be doing much the same thing. For one, it ensures we have the best possible people in command of our special forces and tactical units. For another, it gives us a reason not to include certain of our allies who have never had much to do with the actual fighting end of the war."

Ash nodded. That much, at least, made sense. The realignment would require time for the Fuerconese forces to get used to things. You wouldn't want to muddy the waters, so to speak, with others from outside taking part and confusing things.

"That said, as soon as possible, we are taking this fight straight to the enemy. No more following after them and forcing them out of systems they have already taken. No more waiting around, protecting systems they may or may not try to attack. The President has authorized the drawing up of plans to attack the major Callusian strongholds. We are going to take this war to them and end it, once and for all."

"And the Midlothians?" Ash asked, voice hard.

"The President is only waiting for solid proof their government is involved. The moment he gets it, he will go public. Then, if they are lucky, they will find themselves facing the end of a number of trade agreements, not only with us but with our other allies. If, however, the treachery goes as deep as we fear, it may be war. That is why President Harper wants to end the current conflict as quickly as possible."

"And if we don't get that confirmation?" Elizabeth asked.

"He will have a message delivered to the Midlothian government detailing the dangers of continuing to harbor those who have actively worked for our destruction." Okafor grinned but there was no humor in it. "Our president is tired of being played the fool. Soon, the enemy will find the sides have changed and they are the ones fighting for survival."

"Good." That said it all. Ash knew she spoke for every Marine. This was what they had wanted for as long as she could remember.

"The two of you will be busy over the next several weeks, possibly even months, as this comes together. Once you know what your regiment needs to come up to full strength, let me know, Ash. Liz, the same goes for you and the division. I'd like the two of you to confer on the rest of the division and its command structure. Present it to me for final approval. I'll handle SecDef and FleetCom."

Even as one part of Ashlyn's mind rebelled at the idea of being regimental CO, another part recognized the challenge it presented and reveled in it. She also had a few ideas about how to keep from being tied to a desk, now or in the future. She'd have to discuss it with her mother, but she had a feeling Elizabeth would understand. The challenge would be in convincing Okafor and FleetCom. She'd cross that bridge when she came to it. Hopefully, she'd do so with a plan they couldn't help but approve.

13

"Ash, I didn't imagine it all, did I?"

M. J. Adamson carefully sat up and waited for the bed to adjust to her new position. As she did, Ashlyn pulled a chair next to the bed. Before sitting, she placed an old-fashioned folder on the bedside table. Then, with a smile of understanding, she sat and reached for her friend's hand.

"You didn't imagine it."

Ashlyn grinned, her first real grin in too long, at the memory of the meeting. Helen Okafor proved yet again why she was one of the best, if not the best, commandant the Corps had ever had.

"Then I didn't hallucinate Okafor, not to mention you, ripping Hale a new one?"

Ash tried not to laugh. She'd bet herself that would be the first thing Adamson asked when they saw one another. Not that she blamed the blonde. Between the drugs the doctors still had her on and the very fact it wasn't often a senior officer, much less one of Okafor's rank, took another senior officer to task in front of anyone, Ash had asked herself that very same question more than once over the last few hours. If she hadn't been there to witness it, she'd have a hard time believing it. But it had happened and it had been a glorious thing to see.

"You didn't hallucinate that or the fact you've been promoted to sergeant major." She watched as Adamson once again carefully shifted positions. There was an almost imperceptible *hum* as the bed adjusted to her new position. Once it had, the blonde sighed softly and leaned back. As she did, Ash reached for her hand, giving it a reassuring squeeze. It would take time, but she had no doubt her friend would make a full recovery, at least physically. It was the emotional scars Adamson would bear that worried her. She knew that sense of anger and guilt all too well. "Not only did she rip Hale a new one, and more than once but, before she brought you in on things this morning, she put us through a full inspection, all of us, including Hale. Let's say the brigadier general would never pass one of your inspections. You would have loved it, MJ. After Okafor conducted her inspection, she asked Connery if she'd missed anything."

For a moment, Adamson looked at her in disbelief. Then an almost evil grin lit her expression. "Please tell me the kid didn't freeze up."

"Not only did she not freeze up, but she pointed out half a dozen problems Okafor didn't note." Ash chuckled at the memory. "I thought Hale was going to stroke out then, especially after Okafor had Connelly repeat the inspection on the rest of us before telling everyone that no one was safe from inspections and she was putting through orders that even the most senior officers were to stand for inspection on a regular basis."

"Damn, Ash, I'd give almost anything to have seen his reaction to that."

"Well," she drawled and produced her datapad. "General Okafor thought it might do your recovery good to see the entire meeting, including the inspection."

"After you tell me what happened after the doctor came in and said I needed to rest." Her frustration at not being able to take part in all of the meeting was obvious.

"MJ, I know you wanted to take part. Okafor did as well. But you have to understand the most important thing right now is making sure you do everything you can to recover from your injuries." She covered her friend's hand with hers, waiting until the blonde nodded. "And, before you say anything, I know the most important thing as far as you're concerned is making sure everyone responsible for what happens pay. So, I'll remind you what you and so many others told me after the President pardoned me and those sent to Tarsus with me. Trust us to make sure those responsible for what happened to the taskforce pay. You know I'm not going to let this go. I can't. I have to follow through for you, for Lucinda and for all the others."

Adamson swallowed hard and tears glistened in her good eye. Then she nodded, her expression hard. Ashlyn understood. Hurt as she was, the blonde couldn't be part of the hunt. At least she didn't think she could. But Ash, as well as her mother and Okafor, thought otherwise and that was part of why Ash had come that afternoon.

"Before I tell you what Okafor is going to do with Hale, let me tell you what's going to happen with the Warlords as well as the Corps; other SpecOps units."

Adamson looked at her in surprise. When she did, Ash knew she had taken the right approach. Now she had the blonde's attention and the sergeant major was thinking as a Marine and not as an angry friend who wanted nothing more than vengeance.

"Very simply put, Okafor is making a major realignment of the Corps. It won't be done overnight, with the exception of the SpecOps units. But, as she pointed out, the Corps is operating under the same basic command structure it has for more than a century. It is past time to realize that just because something worked before, it doesn't necessarily follow that it will now. What happened with the Warlords is only one indication of the problem. Add to that the fact certain people know how we operate and she feels it is time to shake things up.

"So, effective immediately, all SpecOps units are now part of 7th Marine Division. The units will keep their individual specializations, pending review by the commandant and the division CO. The

Seventh will be split into three regiments to start. The one we are interested in, the 10th, will be comprised of the Devil Dogs, the Warlords and the Panzers as well as the HQ company. The other SpecOps units will comprise the remaining two regiments."

For a moment, Adamson didn't say anything. Then she smiled, her good eye gleaming. "Damn, I like it, but I bet there have been some howls of protest."

"I'm sure there will be once the plan is made public. But, as Okafor said, it takes a special sort of Marine to be a SpecOps CO, especially on the division and regimental level. Some of the problems we've faced during the last war, not to mention this one, have been the results of division COs not really knowing how best to utilize their SpecOps units because they were never a Devil Dog or Warlord, etc... This takes that potential problem away."

"What about staging? By having the different units assigned to different fleets, we were able to respond fairly quickly when needed."

"That isn't going to change, at least not right away." The potential future changes had Ashlyn's mouth going dry. She remembered the gleam in Okafor's eye when the commandant mentioned how she had taken command of *Nagato* during the last mission. Even though Okafor swore she wasn't going to try to turn Ash into a space jockey, that didn't mean she wasn't considering giving SpecOps its own ships – assuming FleetCom agreed. It was best not to consider how that might come together. "What changes is we will have a centralized command structure now. That means the right unit will be sent instead of having to worry about inter-divisional competition, etc."

Adamson let out a soft whistle. "But a regiment?"

"More of the realignment Okafor has in mind and, before you ask, not only has FleetCom signed off on it, so has the President."

"I can't help wishing she'd done this a few months earlier." Pain once again filled Adamson's eye and this time Ash knew it was for the friends and fellow Marines she had lost on the last mission.

"I know, MJ. I wish the same. Hopefully, this move will prevent another such situation from happening."

For a long moment, Adamson stared off into space. Then she

inhaled deeply and nodded. "Who are the division and regimental COs?" she asked. "Please don't tell me it's that bastard Hale." Bitter anger roughened her voice.

"Nope, far from it, in fact." Ashlyn grinned, knowing her friend would approve of Okafor's choice as much as she did. "Seventh's commanding officer is Brigadier General Elizabeth Shaw."

Adamson's lopsided grin was all Ash needed to know her friend agreed with the choice. Then the blonde cocked her head to one side and looked at Ash in open question. "If your mother's commanding the division, who has command of the three regiments?"

"So far, Okafor and my mother have named only one regimental CO, the one for the 10th."

"You're avoiding the question, Ash. Who is 10thReg's CO?"

"Me." Even as Adamson laughed, Ash rolled her eyes. She was still getting used to commanding a battalion. How the hell was she supposed to command a regiment? "Keep laughing, Sergeant Major, because I have plans for you."

Adamson fell silent and the look she gave Ash spoke volumes. It also confirmed what she'd been afraid of. Her friend had yet to accept that she would heal and be able to return to duty. Well, she planned to put an end to that now, if at all possible.

"Ash."

"MJ, you're going to listen to me for a change." She pinned the blonde with a firm look. "I get that you're scared. I would be too. But I've talked with your doctors. So have my mother and Okafor. We have all been assured that you are going to make a full recovery. It's going to take time, but you will recover. The regen therapy is already starting to work, not only on your eye but on your leg as well." She waited, hoping her words got through to her friend. When Adamson said nothing, she decided to push the point. "Tell me one thing. Are you ready to cashier out of the Corps and become a civilian or are you going to fight to recover as quickly as you can?"

"Fight."

Ashlyn had a feeling she didn't necessarily mean fight to recover, or at least not just fight to recover. But that was all right. She could work with that.

"Good." Now she stood and reached for the folder she'd brought with her. "Before we get to the official part of this, not to mention telling you about what happened with Hale, you can do me a favor unofficially."

Adamson frowned and waited for Ashlyn to explain.

"Connery has done an excellent job in the time she's been acting as my aide. But she still needs some seasoning. Loco has done what he can but, I'll be honest, his time is limited right now."

"Is everything all right?" Adamson interrupted.

Ash nodded. "I've had him working with Laboe, helping the major come up to speed with the Devil Dogs. That's even more important with the reorganization." More than Ash even wanted to think about at the moment. "I'd like you to take Connery under your wing, teach her what she needs to know, as long as we're still dirtside. She's going to make an excellent NCO given time and seasoning. Unfortunately, I can't wait for either."

"Tell her to stop by and I'll see what I can do."

"Thanks." Not only would it help Connery develop into a top-notch NCO, Ashlyn knew it would give Adamson something to look forward to and to be a part of. That would be important during these first few weeks of her recovery. "You can start with finding her a new call sign. She needs something to match not only her new assignment but her ability as a Marine."

Adamson's lopsided grin told Ashlyn all she needed to know. The sergeant major agreed and already had something in mind. Good.

"Next, are you going home to your folks' when you're discharged?" Even as she asked, she had a hard time imagining her friend on a farming consortium.

"Hell no!" Adamson laughed. "I love my parents but, even if I didn't need to stay close to the medical center, I wouldn't go back. I'd go crazy there and, if the boredom didn't get to me, my mother smothering me would."

"Then I'd like you to consider something." She shook her head before Adamson could interrupt. "Like you said, you're going to need to be close to the center here and you're going to need to be somewhere you can have help until you are up and about. Will you consider staying at my place?"

Adamson closed her eye. Ash waited, understanding she wrestled as much with needing help as she did with the rest of it. Finally, the blonde looked at her. When she did, she reached for Ashlyn's hand and held it as if it were her lifeline.

"Your parents?"

"Are expecting you and said they won't take no for an answer."

"Are you sure?"

"I am."

"All right, at least to start."

Relieved, Ash smiled and opened the folder. "One more thing before I tell you about Hale." She glanced at the folder's contents and then pulled out a sheet of paper. "If you accept, you're going to be transferred to the HQ Company for 7thDiv. It is only a temporary assignment because, once you're back on your feet and cleared for active duty, I want you back with the Devil Dogs."

"The Warlords?"

"My mother and I are trying to find the right CO to replace Lucinda." She paused and swallowed against the lump in her throat. "We also need to set up a solid NCO presence for them. I have no doubt we'll be consulting with you before making our final decisions. Of course, that assumes you want to return to the Devil Dogs – which I plan to see to as soon as you're released to active duty – and not stay with the Warlords."

Adamson nodded, tears shining in her good eye. "Devil Dog forever, remember?"

"Good." Ash smiled and rested a hand on her friend's shoulder. "Then, are you ready to see what Okafor did about Hale?"

"More than." Before Ashlyn could bring up the video on her datapad, a knock sounded at the door and one of Adamson's doctors looked inside. Adamson sighed and motioned him inside. "Just tell me the high points."

"Let's just say our beloved commandant has once again lived up to her reputation for not suffering fools gladly. He's been reassigned to the capital where he will be part of the Public Information Office. I believe she said something about him being in the Research Department."

Anderson barked out a laugh and Ashlyn grinned in response. There were few assignments worse for a combat Marine than being a PIO. Being a researcher for the PIO was one of them. The fact Okafor had muttered something about finding the deepest, darkest basement to bury him in only proved just how little faith she still had in his abilities.

"There's something else, MJ." She glanced at the doctor and gave a quick shake of her head before he could interrupt. "The commandant has instructed several people with knowledge of what happened to Taskforce Liberator to prepare full reports. Once she has reviewed them, she will decide whether to recommend charges be leveled against him."

Anderson drew a deep, shuddering breath. Then she exhaled. "Tell her I will be more than glad to give her a report."

"I will." In fact, she already had.

"Colonel, I'm sorry, but she needs to get some rest," the doctor said before she could say anything else.

She nodded. "I'll be back tomorrow, MJ." She bent and gently hugged her friend. "Can I bring you anything?"

"The video?"

Ashlyn looked at the doctor. "Would it be all right if I returned in the morning, around 0700?"

"As long as she's awake. She has an appointment with the regen tank at 0900."

"I'll bring the video and maybe something else then, MJ. You get some rest and comm me if you need anything."

"I will."

Ash smiled and slid her datapad into her thigh pocket. Then she left the small room. As she did, she felt better than she had since reaching the Tenasic System. Adamson might still look like hell, and who wouldn't after all she'd been through, but she was recovering. Knowing she'd ask about the other wounded, Ash made a note to check their status before returning the next morning. For now, however, she had done all she could.

———

EVAN MOREAU WATCHED the latest newscast in growing frustration. For close to a week, the media had covered little besides the return of Fuercon's ships from the Tenasic System. According to the media and the politicians, Fuercon had routed the Callusians that had invaded the system. Their own dead were hailed as heroes who gave their lives to prevent Fuercon's enemies from enslaving anyone else. It didn't seem to matter that the Callusians had been kicking Fuercon's ass until that bitch Tremayne arrived with reinforcements.

Worse, despite all the media coverage, nothing gave Moreau any clue about what Fuercon planned next. Experience told her they would be sending another taskforce, this one more heavily armed than the previous one, to help secure the system should the Callusians decide to try to retake it. In one way, that served the needs of her employers by further depleting the ships available to protect the home system. However, her gut told her there was more at play than either she or those she answered to knew and that worried her.

As the newsreader moved on to a report about an appearance President Harper made earlier in the day to one of the local schools, she switched off the screen. A thoughtful look on her face, she sipped her whiskey. As she did, she glanced around. She had changed her appearance, as well as her ID, again and this time she was making use of some of the money she'd set aside for emergencies. Four days earlier, she had moved into her current rooms and they were definitely a step up from where she'd been living. They might not close to what she had enjoyed as Moreau but Lessa Reager enjoyed a comfortable life.

Unfortunately, she knew it wouldn't last. That bitch Fertig would find her sooner or later. Until she figured out how to satisfy

Watchman so he called off his dogs, Moreau had to play along with the woman. That mean reaching out to the few sources she still trusted and hoping they knew enough to help her finish her mission.

"Bastards," she murmured before splashing more whiskey into her glass.

She did know one thing her employers did not. When the Fuerconese thwarted the attack on the home system, the Callusian ships hadn't all been destroyed. For the first time, at least that she knew of, at least some of the ships had been captured. Moreau knew that could spell disaster for not only her employers but for herself if the Callusians hadn't managed to wipe their databanks before the ships were captured. She wanted to believe the fact the Fuerconese hadn't discussed the possibility the Callusians might not be working alone meant they were still in the dark about what her employers were up to. But she had a nagging feeling in the pit of her stomach that they knew and were planning something in response. Still, she had to admit her own judgment might be compromised by the knowledge her life could end any moment. All she could do was hope Harper's government didn't realize what was going on until she was far from this damned planet.

"Get hold of yourself," she said softly, pushing her glass away before she gave into the temptation to pour another drink. She needed to keep a clear head if she was going to stay one step ahead of Fertig.

Five minutes later, she stepped outside into the fading evening sun. As she did, she knew no one from her past life would recognize her. Her blonde hair was now a brassy red. Her skin lightly tanned. Her blue eyes now hazel. The shape of her jaw might be the same but her nose had a slight crook. The disguise was good, very good, but she knew it wouldn't hold up if the authorities looked too closely. But it would do, especially since she knew her ID papers were as close to perfect as possible.

"Hey, Lessa," a man said as she entered the bar.

She nodded and forced herself to smile. "Evening, Alain," she said as she stepped behind the bar and reached for one of the folded aprons under the counter. "Let me log in and then I've got it here."

The young man nodded and stepped closer. "How about we grab a bite after your shift?" he asked.

"Sorry, Alain. I've got plans."

Hopefully those plans would include going home with some talkative member of the government or the military who had drunk too much. She needed something to feed Fertig before the woman decided to carry through with her threat to permanently end their "business relationship". In the meantime, she'd play the barmaid who didn't mind being glad-handed by the patrons, male and female, as she kept her mouth shut and her eyes and ears open.

Who knows, maybe one day she'd get really lucky and that bitch Ashlyn Shaw would walk through the doors and she could finally deal with her, once and for all.

———

ASHLYN STOOD at the edge of the terrace at the rear of her parents' house and inhaled deeply. She had put Jake to bed a few minutes earlier after reading him several of his favorite stories. Her sister had gone into town to meet friends for dinner and a play. Her parents were inside. She could have joined them, but she needed some time alone.

Damn it, Luce, I'm sorry. I couldn't get to you in time, but I promise I'll take care of your family.

Tears stung her eyes. She hadn't let herself truly mourn her friend yet. She'd been afraid to. Lucinda had been part of her life, her best friend and confidante, since their Academy days. They hadn't always been assigned together but their friendship had grown over the years. Even during those dark days on Tarsus, she knew Lucinda was out there somewhere, doing everything she could to not only free her but clear her name. They had always had one another's back and, when Lucinda needed her the most, she'd failed her.

Except she hadn't. She knew it intellectually. But it would take time to accept it emotionally. The only ones to blame were Hale, Admiral Wu and the Callusians. Hale and Wu had been dealt with, their careers effectively over and their reputations ruined. As for the Callusians, she planned to make sure they paid for Lucinda and every other Marine who died on that last mission.

Then there was Okafor's little surprise. She still hadn't wrapped her mind around that yet. Nor had she finished her report for the commandant. Sleep would be in small supply tonight and probably the next several nights, unless she missed her guess. Not that she minded. The nightmares were too close and the last thing she wanted to see her dead, Lucinda included.

"Ash, are you all right?"

She turned and smiled slightly. She'd been so deep in thought, she hadn't heard her mother's approach. "Just thinking."

"Anything I can help you with?"

She started to shake her head and then stopped. Instead, she motioned for them to take seats at the edge of the terrace. "I was thinking about Lucinda and that led to thinking about today's meeting and all that entailed."

Elizabeth smiled in understanding. Then, instead of sitting, she disappeared inside the house. Frowning, wondering what her mother was up to, Ash leaned against the stone wall surrounding the terrace. This time, instead of looking out over the yard below, she watched the house. Through the open door, she saw Elizabeth cross the den. When she returned a few minutes later, she carried two glasses and a bottle of whiskey. She placed the glasses on the low table between the chairs Ash had indicated earlier and poured generous drinks. Then, setting the bottle down, she took her seat, waiting for Ash to do the same.

"Mom, I'm not sure I'm ready for this new assignment."

There, she'd said it. She hoped her mother didn't think less of her for it.

For a moment, Elizabeth didn't say anything. Then she reached for her daughter's hand and waited until Ash looked at her. "You are. You just have to believe it. Remember, Helen wouldn't have given it to you if she had any doubts you could do it." She sipped her whiskey, giving Ashlyn time to consider what she said. "What you need to understand is that this isn't going to be that much different from what you've already been doing. It will just be on a slightly larger scale."

Ash closed her eyes and blew out a breath. "I don't want to give up the Devil Dogs, Mom." And that was it. For as long as she could remember, she wanted to command the Devil Dogs. She'd never really considered doing anything other than that. It had been her goal, even before she joined the Marines.

"You aren't giving up the Devil Dogs. If you need to, consider the entire regiment Devil Dogs because, in a very real way, that's what they will become." Elizabeth took another sip of her whiskey. "Ashlyn, think about the history of the Devil Dogs. Initially, they were a single platoon. Then they grew to a company and from there to a battalion. This is the next logical step."

"I don't know, Mom. The Warlords and the Panzers, especially the Panzers, are two very different types of units."

"Not really, especially not where the Warlords are concerned." She motioned for Ash to drink her whiskey. "I know Helen dropped this on you without warning. Hell, child, she did the same to me. But I want you to think about this for a minute. First, Pawlak and then Lucinda worked hard to bring the Warlords up to Devil Dog standards. Second, as badly decimated at the Warlords were on this last mission, you have the chance to rebuild them exactly the way you want which, unless I miss my guess, is into the equivalent of the Devil Dogs. Do that and then worry about how to deal with the Panzers."

"Except I have a real problem with the Devil Dogs right now and, by being regimental CO, I will have even less time with them than I did before Okafor dropped this on me." She stared into her glass, wondering how in the world she was supposed to deal with everything now on her plate.

Elizabeth turned her chair to look more closely at her daughter. "Ash, what's going on?" Concern roughened her voice.

Ashlyn blew out a breath and placed her glass on the table between them. "Mom, you know the reservations I've had about

Laboe." She waited until Elizabeth nodded. "Don't get me wrong. He really is a good officer and I think he will make a good member of the battalion – sorry, the regiment – given time. But, from what Okafor told us today, we don't have time to wait for that to happen. I need someone as my XO I can count on to handle the day-to-day command of the Devil Dogs until I find someone to take command of them." And she still didn't want to think about that. "Now I have to worry about that and integrating the Warlords and Panzers, not to mention bringing all three battalions up to strength. Then there's the HQ Company. How the hell am I supposed to do all that?"

For a moment, Elizabeth stared out over the yard. "Ash, tell me this. Would Laboe be a good fit for the Warlords or the Panzers?"

"Are you asking as my mother or as division CO?"

"Maybe as both?"

Ash reached for her glass and considered. "He was excellent as Miranda's Marine CO. I think the only reason she didn't fight me when I asked for him as my XO was she recognized the situation we were about to go into and knew he could fulfill both roles at the time. She has also said she would kill to have him back."

"And?"

"I'm not going to let him go back." She smiled slightly. "He was excellent as a shipboard Marine CO because he understands not only how to get our people working seamlessly with their Naval counterparts but also the LACs. The Warlords lost their LAC CO as well as a number of their pilots. I don't think he's ready to take command of a SpecOps battalion, but he could do a lot of good with the Warlords as XO. But we need to find him the right CO." And that would leave her, again, without an XO.

"How about Major Andrea Raptis as CO?"

Ashlyn thought for a moment. She knew Raptis by reputation but had never served with her. A little older than Ash, instead of aiming for the Devil Dogs, she had set her sights on one of the other SpecOps units. If Ash remembered correctly, her specialties had been recon and explosives. She also had a reputation for being innovative and not afraid to think outside the box in order to accomplish a mission. Everything, as far as Ash was concerned, a good SpecOps CO needed to be.

"What's her current assignment?"

"She's been on restricted duty after being injured four months ago on a mission. She just cleared medical waivers and is waiting for orders. Her last assignment was as Marine CO for Fourth Fleet, but she's been in line to return to SpecOps for more than a year."

"Is she on-planet?"

"She is."

"Then let me meet with her." She chewed her lower lip as she considered her options. "If she agrees, and if I think she'll be a good fit, she will need a promotion. I will not knock Laboe down in rank."

"Agreed. I'll make it happen."

Ashlyn smiled and finished her whiskey. "And that leaves me without an XO again, not to mention the other areas where I'm light on officers."

They sat silently for a few minutes, both lost in their thoughts.

"Ash, have you considered going a bit unconventional to fill those slots?"

"What do you mean?"

"You have some excellent senior non-coms you could recommend to be mustangs. Do that and you can move some of your senior officers around."

Ash shook her head. No way did she want to lose Talbot as Master Guns. She needed him exactly where he was. Her officers, as well as the enlisted members of the Devil Dogs, all trusted him. She needed someone the new officers could lean on and who the others knew would keep their asses safe in case a butterbar decided to do something exceedingly stupid on the battlefield.

Then she smiled. "I know just the person – but you have to promise not to poach her from me."

Elizabeth looked at her in question and then laughed gaily. "MJ?"

"MJ." Ashlyn nodded in confirmation. "She can start learning her new role while she's on limited duty. I can live without an XO while she does." At least she hoped she could. She would certainly rely on Talbot and even Connery to help fill the gap.

"Write up the request. I'll approve it and send it to Okafor. I'll do everything I can do to make sure it goes through."

"Thanks." For the first time since getting Lucinda's message, she felt good. "But I mean it, Mom. No poaching."

"Now, would I do something like that?"

"In a heartbeat." Ashlyn grinned and then laughed as her mother acted as if she'd been hurt by the comment. "And I had better get inside and get back to work. I want – no, I need – to do everything I can to make sure Hale never has the chance to cost another Marine her life." Tears filled her eyes and she blinked them back. "I wish to God there was some way for him to pay for what happened to Lucinda and the others. I'm not naïve enough to expect it to happen. But I trust Okafor to make sure he never again commands combat troops. For her to do that, I need to give her everything I have and everything I discovered after receiving Lucinda's message."

"I need to do the same." Elizabeth finished her drink and climbed to her feet. Then she held out her hand, smiling as Ashlyn took it and let her help her stand. "You need to mourn Lucinda, Ash, but you also need to honor her and all she meant to you and to the Devil Dogs. You do that by being the Marine she knew you could be, the Marine we all know you can be. You do that also by taking this fight to the enemy, exactly as Okafor plans."

And then, to the Midlothians. They would pay for their betrayal as well. Even if it was the last thing she did.

Contingency Plans

14

Rico Santiago stood before the non-descript apartment building and glanced around. Nothing seemed out of the ordinary. Security feeds showed no unauthorized entry attempts in the week since he had last visited. Even so, he wasn't going to risk becoming careless now. So far, they had managed to keep the Midlothians in the dark about their "guest" and he preferred it that way. The problems that would arise, political and otherwise, if their so-called allies learned one of their Naval officers had been captured were something he didn't want to consider.

Not that he didn't have even bigger concerns just then. Ashlyn Shaw worried him. Lucinda Ortega's death would have been hard on her under the best of circumstances. Knowing her friend and former XO died because her battalion had basically been betrayed by their division CO, Shaw had to be remembering how she and her people had been betrayed. She'd lost good men and women on that mission and the survivors, Shaw included, had been court martialed. They spent two years in a brutal military prison before being released and then pardoned. He knew her well enough to know she would do whatever she could to make sure Hale never again betrayed another member of their beloved Corps. He worried she didn't give in to the desire to try for vengeance. So he needed to give her something else to focus on.

And that was why he'd returned to the apartment building.

He continued down the block to the next building. At the door, he entered the security code assigned to the apartment rented by Michael Shepherd, one of his many aliases. Once inside, he crossed the lobby to the lift. A few minutes later, he walked through the utility corridor connecting the two buildings. At the other end, he entered another security code. Then it was a quick ride in the service lift and he would be at his destination.

"Anything I should know?" he asked the Marine guard on duty as he stepped off the lift. The entire floor had been turned into housing for special "guests" of FleetCom. Usually, those guests were there to help FleetCom. This one was supposed to but, so far, he had done nothing to earn the relative freedom they had given him and Santiago was tired of playing games.

"No, sir. It's been routine as usual."

"All right, Corporal. I shouldn't be long."

He crossed to the door to Bradford Hughes' quarters and knocked once. Without waiting for a response, he unlocked the door and stepped inside. As he did, Hughes appeared from the bedroom. The Midlothian wore a pair of dark trousers and a loose overshirt. Irritation flashed across his face followed quickly by resignation as he recognized Santiago. Without a word, he crossed to sit in one of the chairs in front of the viewscreen, the closest thing to a window he had seen since his capture.

"I didn't think I'd be seeing you so soon." Hughes leaned back and crossed his legs. He might be a prisoner, but he still possessed the confidence that had made him a formidable naval officer.

Santiago had done nothing before now to shake that confidence. That was about to end. He would do so gladly and without hesitation if it meant keeping Shaw from doing something foolish. Even more importantly, it was past time to find out just how deep the betrayal ran in Midlothian and find out if any of Fuercon's other allies were involved.

"We've played the game long enough, Hughes." Santiago leaned against the wall, arms crossed, and waited as his words sank in. "Fuercon has done everything it promised when you were taken prisoner. But there was a price, one you haven't begun to pay. It is time to answer our questions or I promise your presence on the planet will be revealed to the Midlothian ambassador."

For the first time, Hughes' calm façade broke. It wasn't much but it was enough. He inhaled sharply and one hand fisted on the arm of his chair. Then, as if realizing he might have betrayed himself, Hughes relaxed. He returned Santiago's stare with a cold one of his own.

"No."

That was all. A simple "no". One corner of Santiago's mouth lifted into a sneer. Hughes obviously thought he held all the cards. He was about to learn just how wrong he was.

"I think you are under the mistaken belief that I'm bluffing." Santiago shook his head, a smile touching his lips. "I'll make this very simple, Hughes. A very good friend of mine, as well as a number of other good men and women, died not long ago. The Callusians used weaponry and tactics they did not use during the previous war. Tactics we have traced back to your homeworld. The same is true of the weaponry. Because of that, I'm not in the mood to play games with you any longer and neither are those higher up the chain of command." He pushed away from the wall to stand a few feet in front of Hughes.

"You have a simple decision to make. You either fulfill your part of the bargain you made with Colonel Shaw or I'm hauling you out of here and making sure the media soon learns not only that you are in the capital but how you managed to get here."

"You wouldn't dare."

"I most certainly would." Santiago closed the distance between them. "Colonel Lucinda Ortega wasn't just my friend, Hughes, she was Colonel Shaw's best friend, her former XO and her roommate at the Academy. They were as close as sisters and considered themselves as such. Shaw gave you a free pass when she agreed to bring you here under terms where your own government would not know you'd been captured. You violated the trust she put in you. You know her reputation. How do you think she will react if she learns you haven't done as promised?"

This time, Hughes paled a little.

"Your choice. Start talking or choose to either face Shaw or your own people." Another smile. "I'd say you are in a no-win situation unless you talk to me."

"You're as much of a cold-hearted bastard as Watchman," Hughes snarled.

"You have no idea." He stepped back, thinking quickly. "I'll give you until tomorrow to make up your mind." He turned and started toward the door. "Just so you don't decide to do anything foolish, you'll be having company until I return."

With that, he left the room. He quickly informed the guard two Marines were to remain with Hughes until he returned. At no time was the man to be left alone. The corporal assured him he understood. With a nod, Santiago made his way to the life. He had a lot to take care of before he returned to speak with Hughes. Hopefully, he hadn't just overplayed his hand.

———

"Master Guns."

Faith Connery stood in the doorway to her quarters, her expression neutral but her heart pounding in concern. Never before had Talbot been there. That he'd come without warning was enough to tell her something was wrong. His serious expression only confirmed it. Something had happened, but what? Colonel Shaw was all right. She would have been notified right away otherwise. Not that the knowledge eased her concern much just then.

"Corporal, may I come in?"

She nodded and stepped aside. As she did, she glanced around the small living area. A frown touched her lips as she saw the empty coffee mug and the beer she'd been drinking just before he arrived.

Her datapad lay open on the sofa. It might not be enough to fail an inspection, but it wasn't how she wanted a senior NCO to see her living quarters.

Talbot stood in the center of the room and glanced around. As he did, Connery realized he felt as uncomfortable as she did. Instead of reassuring her, it only increased her worry. Pushing that down, she motioned him to sit and then moved to the small cold box and grabbed a beer.

"Here you go." She handed it to him and then took a seat opposite him.

"Thanks." He took a drink and sat back. They sat in silence for a few moments. Then he blew out a breath. "I hope I'm not interrupting anything."

"No." She shook her head. "I had just finished making some adjustments to Angel's schedule tomorrow."

Talbot placed his beer on the floor next to his right foot. Then he leaned forward, elbows on knees. "Faith, what the hell happened today?" The moment he said it, he seemed to relax.

She looked at him, surprised. That was the last thing she expected him to ask. Thinking about it, though, she understood. She'd probably be asking the same thing if their positions were reversed. The only thing she needed to figure out was how much she could tell him without getting into trouble.

"About?" Stupid question, she knew, but it gave her a few more moments to decide what she should say.

Talbot closed his eyes for a moment and she waited. When he looked at her again, he smiled slightly, almost apologetically. A moment later, he reached for his beer and took a long pull on it.

"Faith, I'm not asking you to betray confidences or orders."

She nodded. She knew him well enough to understand that, but it helped to hear him say it.

"And I'll admit I'm more than a little overprotective where Angel's concerned. You weren't with the Devil Dogs when those bastards Sorkowski and O'Brien set her and our other people up. You can't know how angry we were, how close some of us came to mutiny, when they were brought up on charges and then convicted. But you know what happened then. You know how some left the Corps or the Navy to work to find out what happened to free Angel and the others. Others of us remained in the Service, doing what we could from there. The way they were betrayed was something we all felt and we all wanted to right."

She gave another nod. She remembered those days. Very few in the Corps hadn't want to know the truth about what happened. More than that, they wanted justice for Colonel Shaw and her people, living and dead. The fact it had taken more than two years was still something the Corps was dealing with. Fortunately, the colonel had returned to the Devil Dogs and had helped bring down those behind what happened to her and her people.

"I've been with her almost every day since her pardon. I know how hard it was for her those first few weeks and months to believe she wasn't being set up again. I have always respected her as a Marine and as an officer." A small smile lifted the corners of his mouth and he chuckled softly. "Do you know the first time I saw the colonel?"

Connery shook her head.

"I was a corporal back then. On my way back to my ship after leave, I came across a wet behind the ears butterbar who had just been shoved to the side by a couple of enlisted personnel who, unfortunately, were assigned to the same ship as I was."

Imagining the scene, Connery groaned softly. It was bad enough for enlisted personnel to lay hands on an officer, even by accident. You never knew how the officer would take it. But for a butterbar to get shoved, that could be the recipe for disaster.

"Yeah." Talbot chuckled. "But, to my surprise, instead of ripping them a new one, the butterbar asked me to stand them off to the side, out of the way of everyone else. Then she introduced herself to all of us. After making sure the two were simply idiots and not under orders to report back to the ship ASAP, she suggested they exercise better judgment in the future. As far as she was concerned, that was the end of the matter. Then she left them to me to deal with them."

"Damn." Connery shook her head. She knew seasoned officers

who would have ripped the two Marines a new one for being so foolish. To hear a butterbar, a second lieutenant fresh out of the Academy, not only reacted with restraint but had been wise enough to leave any discipline to a non-com, amazed her.

"That young butterbar was one Second Lieutenant Ashlyn Shaw on her way to her first assignment after graduating."

"I knew you'd known one another for a long time." It also explained a great deal about their relationship. Talbot had watched that second lieutenant mature and grow into the officer she was today. For her part, the colonel had learned to trust the man, as a Marine and as a friend.

He nodded. "So, you understand my concern and curiosity about today's events."

Connery leaned back and made up her mind. At least most of what she knew would be made public by morning. The real question was how much did she not know? The colonel had remained shut away with General Okafor and Brigadier General Shaw for several more hours after she had been dismissed.

"Basically, the commandant removed General Hale from command of SecDiv. There's no question he ignored six requests for reinforcements and resupply from Colonel Ortega. The only question is whether or not the commandant will recommend JAG bring him up on charges. Admiral Wu has also been removed from her command and reassigned, pending review of her actions and the possible filing of charges.

"The colonel is preparing a report for the commandant based on what she knows of the situation. General Okafor made it clear she wanted Angel's report to include not only the information from Sorceress' message to her that got all this started but also what Angel found when she looked into Hale's command. She also wants Angel's report on what we learned after we joined up with Taskforce Liberator."

"How is she?"

"Honestly?"

Talbot nodded.

"I'm not sure." She lifted a hand before he could interrupt. "Loco, I'm not trying to avoid your question. I honestly don't know." She needed to explain better. "You've seen Angel when she's preparing to face the enemy."

He nodded.

"That was her this morning, before the meeting began. She did what she needed to do, just like she always does. It culminated with Okafor removing Hale from command of SecDiv. That's when you and Sergeant Kuznetsov were sent for. I was dismissed shortly after that and, other than a few comms from the colonel, I haven't seen or spoken with her since then."

Talbot finished his beer and climbed to his feet. Connery watched as he walked into the small kitchen and placed the bottle on the drainboard next to the sink. When he turned, she arched a brow in surprise to see the mix of concern and approval reflected in his eyes.

"Faith, thank you." Now he lifted a hand to keep her from interrupting. "Angel needs people she can trust and you're proving to be one. It happens I trust you as well and consider it an honor to serve with you. You're a good Marine and a damned fine Devil Dog. I've told you this before but I'm going to repeat it. You keep an eye on her. Let me know if you think she needs me – or if you need me. Angel's special. She's hurting right now and that means she might not always think things through."

"Understood, Kevin. So far, however, she isn't taking chances with herself or with the Devil Dogs." And she planned to keep it that way. "You can do something for me."

He looked at her in question.

"You need to be honest with her. We both know she has concerns about Major Laboe. We also know she is discounting them, or trying to, because he isn't Sorceress and they don't have the kind of relationship she and Sorceress have – had. But I have been hearing some grumblings from the ranks. You know as well as I do that if I'm hearing rumblings so is Angel."

Talbot frowned. "I'll have a talk with him tomorrow." From the sound of his voice, it wasn't a conversation he looked forward to.

"Faith, one more thing. If you need to talk with anyone and I'm not around, tag Master Sergeant Anderson. Reaper knows Angel as well as I do."

"Thanks. I will."

Talbot nodded, apparently satisfied. "Sorry to have barged in."

"Any time, Loco." She meant it. They were Devil Dogs and the good of the battalion, including the good of their CO, trumped all.

———

ASHLYN LOOKED up and frowned as her desk unit signaled an incoming e-mail. Before reaching for it where it rested on the desk-top, she frowned and checked the time. Then, seeing who it was from, she frowned a second time. Nothing good came from messages received close to midnight, especially not when they came from FleetCom's chief intel officer.

For a moment, she considered ignoring the message. After all, he hadn't marked it urgent. Besides, she still hadn't finished her report for Okafor, a report due in a matter of hours. As it was, she would be lucky to get any sleep. Tempting as it was to act as if the message hadn't come in, she couldn't. Even if her curiosity didn't tell her to see what the man had to say, duty did.

But that didn't mean she couldn't get a fresh mug of coffee first.

Nor did it stop her from going upstairs to check on her son. Jake lay in bed, his favorite stuffed animal next to him. He had grown so much since her return from Tarsus. But that was nothing compared to how much he'd grown during the months leading up to her court martial and then her two years at the penal colony. Sorkowski and the others had cost her so much and they had yet to pay for it. They would. She knew it intellectually but, at times like this, it was hard to believe emotionally.

"Are you all right?"

She started nervously at the soft voice behind her. Before answering, she closed Jake's door. Then she turned and, smiling wryly, shook her head to see her sister standing a short distance away. Kate was the youngest of her siblings and the only one not to go into either the Navy or Marines. Instead, she was a geologist. Her work often took her away from Fuercon. But when the call home came, she complied and Ashlyn was glad. She had a feeling things were going to get much worse before the war ended and she wanted her sister as far from the fighting as possible.

"Just checking on him." Ashlyn smiled and led her sister away from the little boy's room. "Are you just getting in?"

"Yeah. Don't tell Mom or Dad. They still act like I'm sixteen and under curfew."

Exasperation and affection filled Kate's voice and Ash chuckled softly. She knew exactly what her sister meant. She might be a battle-hardened veteran but, once home, she was their parents' little girl and nothing would ever change that.

"Tell me about it." She linked arms with her sister and they walked slowly down the corridor in the direction of Kate's suite of rooms. "We haven't had much time to talk since you got home. How about we take a few hours away this weekend and have some sister time?"

For a moment, Kate narrowed her eyes. Then, apparently seeing nothing in Ashlyn's expression to worry her, she nodded, a smile on her lips. Ash grinned and gave her shoulders a squeeze. There were things for them to discuss but they could wait. She did want time to relax and simply enjoy being with her sister. They didn't get time alone with just the two of them often and she planned on enjoying it.

"I'd best get back to work. Okafor wants a report in the morning and I'm nowhere near done with it."

Kate reached out and stopped her. "Ash, is everything all right? You and Mom both were a bit off this evening before I left for dinner."

Ashlyn mentally kicked herself and made a note to talk with their mother. They both needed to be more careful around Kate. She had always been able to tell if they were worried or upset about something. Considering how she was still trying to wrap her mind around everything that happened to Taskforce Liberator, not to mention

Okafor's *little* change in the Corps, it was no wonder Kate wondered if she was all right.

"Everything's fine, Katie." She gave her sister's shoulders another quick squeeze. "Okafor is just making some changes. They will be very good for the Corps and for Fuercon but, for a while at least, it means more work for a lot of us, Mom and me included."

"Ash." She reached out and grasped Ashlyn's hand before Ash could walk away. "Talk to me. I know you're hurting right now. We all are. Lucinda was part of our family. You can't keep your emotions bottled up inside of you. You need to talk them out, if not to me, to someone."

Ash closed her eyes. Then she nodded. Kate was right, but she was also wrong. The question was how to convince her of that.

"Katie, you're right. I am hurting. I miss Lucinda. Even when we weren't stationed together, I always knew she was there, that she had my back. She was my best friend, my sister by choice. But I can't let my emotions out right now and I can't explain all the whys about it to you. Part of that is because of what the Corps may or may not do after what happened to the taskforce.

"Part of it is also because what happened to Luce strikes too close to home. It reminds me too much of the Arterus mission and what happened afterwards. The only thing keeping me from doing something foolish is the knowledge that Okafor and others won't let this be a repeat in any way, shape or form. Beyond that, I made a promise to Luce to look after her family and I can't do that if I do something foolish and wind up back on Tarsus."

"I understand, I think. But I am here if you ever need to talk."

Ash smiled and reached for her sister's hands. "I know, kid, and I promise I'll take you up on it." She gave Kate one more hug and stepped back. "Now, I really do need to get back to work."

And see what Santiago had to say.

Mug of freshly brewed coffee in hand, Ashlyn once again settled behind her desk a few minutes later. She stared at the notice of Santiago's email. Then, hoping she wouldn't soon regret it, she opened the message. For a long moment, she stared at it, not quite believing her eyes. Then an almost feral expression settled on her face. He most definitely wouldn't like her response. She didn't care. If he wanted her help, he was going to have to do something for her.

Maybe, just maybe, she would finally be able to put some of her personal ghosts to rest and, in doing so, she might be able to help get the information FleetCom needed to finally get to the bottom of the Midlothian's connection with the Callusians.

Still smiling like a cat about to pounce on its prey, she sent her response, outlining exactly what she wanted in return for helping him the next morning.

Satisfied, she leaned back and closed her eyes. She needed to put Santiago's request out of her mind and worry about his response to her demands later. She had other things to worry about, like finishing her report for Okafor. Then she needed to turn her attention to the new regiment, her regiment.

Just the thought of all she had to do to bring the Seventh up to battle-ready status made her head hurt. She had to fill the vacancies left in the Warlords after the last mission. She had to replace equipment. She needed to review officer and senior non-com assignments. Most of all, she had to talk with MJ Anderson, not to mention Talbot and Connery, about her plans for the three of them.

Somehow, she had to make it all work before the division shipped out and that, she had a feeling, would be happening sooner than anyone expected.

15

"Ashlyn, what are you up to?"

Elizabeth stepped inside her daughter's bedroom and closed the door behind her. Hearing her mother's voice, Ash inhaled deeply and held it for a moment before exhaling. She should have known Elizabeth would realize something was going on. For the past week, they had ridden into the city together. The fact she had changed their plans without explanation, and on a day when they were both supposed to start with a briefing with Okafor, had set off all her mother's warning bells.

Ashlyn didn't answer right away. Instead, she checked her appearance once last time in her mirror. She wore MARPAT, as she did most mornings. Her dark hair was pulled back into a short braid. She wore just a hint of makeup, more to hide the shadows under her eyes than anything else. But it was the look in her eyes, a look she knew would send Elizabeth into full mother-mode, that was different. She looked ready for battle.

"Ash?" Elizabeth's tone was all mother and Ashlyn fought the urge to roll her eyes.

"There's something I need to do before reporting to duty this morning, Mom. That's all." She did her best to smile. From the way Elizabeth's eyes narrowed, she knew she'd failed.

"Ash, don't make me pull rank."

This time she did roll her eyes. "Mom." She turned and, seeing Elizabeth's concern, relented. "I had a message from Rico Santiago last night. He wants me to have a word with our guest." She didn't explain further, trusting Elizabeth to understand who she meant. "I told him I would be glad to if he did something for me in return."

Now Elizabeth inhaled sharply. As she exhaled, she once again narrowed her eyes and then she crossed her arms. Gone was the concerned mother. In her place was the concerned and not very happy senior officer. "And why does he want you to speak with our guest?"

"I don't know." But she could make a fairly good guess.

"You said you wanted him to do something in return. What?"

"Are you asking as my mother or as my CO?"

"Both."

Ashlyn couldn't help it. She shook her head and laughed. For a moment, Elizabeth looked at her, anger flashing in her eyes, then she chuckled. It wasn't often their dual roles intersected like that. They worked hard to keep the personal out of the professional. But recent events had made it harder on them both to separate the two aspects of their relationship.

"My guess is he wants to use me as leverage with our guest. I offered him safe passage and made sure his presence on-planet wasn't made public. In return, he was supposed to give us what intel he had. From what we've learned in our earlier briefings and from what Rico's said privately, that hasn't happened. And, after what happened to Taskforce Liberator, you know as well as I do that Rico's not going to wait any longer. It's put up or get out time for our guest."

Elizabeth nodded.

"As for what I asked in return, it's simple. I need to lay my demons to rest and he can help me do it without breaking regs or risking going back to Tarsus."

"Just don't do anything foolish." Elizabeth began to turn to leave and stopped. "Will you be back in time for the briefing with Okafor?"

"I will."

"Do I need to take Jake to school?"

"No." A smile softened Ashlyn's expression as she thought about her son. "I'll drop him on my way."

Elizabeth nodded once and left the room. As she did, Ashlyn dropped onto the edge of her bed. That wasn't how she'd planned on starting her morning and it had put her behind schedule. At least Elizabeth hadn't tried to stop her. She needed to think about that later but, for the moment, she put it aside.

As she stepped outside a few minutes later, Jake skipping ahead of her, Ashlyn bit back her smile. Corporal Connery leaned against the side of a waiting aircar. Seeing Ash approaching, Connery stepped forward and reached for her briefcase. Then she smiled at Jake. Ash grinned as her son gave Connery a quick hug before running back to grab her hand.

"Are you going to be able to pick me up today, Mom?" Jake asked as they climbed into the aircar.

"I don't know." She pulled him close before telling the private piloting the aircar to stop first at Jake's school. "Do you want me to?"

"Uh-huh." When he looked up at her with a sly smile, she chuckled softly. "We could go to the park if you do."

"I'll have to see, sweetie. If I can't make it, your Aunt Katie will pick you up. I bet if you ask her really nicely, she'd take you to the park."

"Aunt Katie's fun, but not as much fun as you."

Laughing, Ash hugged her son close and promised to do her best to be there when he got out of school. Hopefully, he'd understand if she couldn't make it. At least he knew she was there whenever she could be. She had so many bedtimes, birthdays, and other occasions to make up for. At least he didn't seem to blame her for all those long months and years they were apart.

"Ma'am, the Master Guns is not going to be happy," Connery said an hour later as they stepped out of the aircar several blocks from their ultimate destination.

Ash frowned and nodded. She had no doubt once he found out what she planned for the morning, Talbot would be in her office with more than a little to say about it.

"Let me guess, he's still got you on a short leash where I'm concerned."

Connery chuckled softly and then shook her head. "Not too short of one, ma'am." When Ashlyn looked at her in question, the corporal sighed. "He worries about you, ma'am. He knows how hard this last mission was on you."

"And he's only doing his job," Ashlyn completed for her. "What did you tell him?"

"That you were doing what you needed to and I would let him know if I thought you needed him."

Ashlyn waited as Connery opened the door to one of the many non-descript apartment buildings on the street. After stepping inside, she motioned for the younger woman to follow her to one side. "Thank you." When Connery looked at her in surprise, she continued. "We don't have time to go into it all right now. But I do trust you to have my back and part of that is letting Loco know if you are worried about anything. I do expect you to talk with me about it first." She waited until Connery nodded. "What else did you tell him?"

"That you needed him to be honest with you about the state of the Devil Dogs and especially about Major Laboe." Connery looked a little uncomfortable with the admission.

"Thank you." She meant it. "Faith, you said exactly what you should have. Loco is my senior NCO and I am going to rely on him even more over the next few weeks and months for reasons you'll be read in on later today, reasons he doesn't know yet. You are my aide, assuming you still want the assignment."

Connery straightened. "I do, ma'am."

"Good." Ash smiled and started off. "Let's deal with the next hour or so and then we'll get down to the real work."

It took almost fifteen minutes to move through the various utility tunnels between the buildings to reach their final destination. Waiting for them by the service lift, Rico Santiago looked relieved when he finally saw them. Before he could ask, Ashlyn assured him they hadn't been seen and certainly had not been followed.

"Before we go up, are you going to do as I asked?" Ash waited, not about to get onto the lift until he answered.

He didn't respond immediately. Instead, he looked uncomfortable, as if he didn't want to answer. Ashlyn arched one brow. Then, frustration building, she turned on her heel, signaling for Connery to follow. If Santiago wasn't going to hold up his part of their bargain, she had other things to do that morning.

"Wait!"

She turned back.

"It's set up, but I want you to think for a moment, Ash. What good will it do to see them?"

"It will help bring me closure, something I thought you'd understand."

"I do." He blew out a breath. "I'm not doing this well. I do understand, Ash, but I can't and won't let you do anything foolish either."

"Don't worry, Rico, Connery here is going to make sure I don't do what I want to." She glanced at her wrist unit. "I have one hour to get this done, all of it, before I'm due at the Commandant's office."

He gave her one last, long look and then nodded. She knew he wasn't convinced but he didn't have any choice. "Let's go."

Five minutes later, Ashlyn stood in front of Bradford Hughes. Like her, he had recovered from the injuries he sustained before his capture. There were other changes as well. He had been defiant then, but they both knew it had been bravado. In space, with him captured helping the enemy, she could have treated him as an enemy combatant. She had every right to. But she had offered him an out, one he had taken without hesitation, at least not much. Now that defiance was back, and she knew it was real this time. He thought he held the upper hand. What he didn't know was she was about to prove to him just how wrong he was.

And she would start with an attitude adjustment. He might be a member of another system's military, but she was still a senior officer since their systems were supposedly allies.

"On your feet, Captain!" she snapped. Her lips twitched in an attempt to smile as he popped out of his chair and started to brace to attention before he could stop himself. "I'm not going to waste either of our time with platitudes or pleas. This situation is quite simple. When you were taken into custody, you were acting as an advisor to enemies of my homeworld and our proven allies. You were under no duress do to so. Furthermore, you had been assisting the Callusians under orders from someone in your government. I offered you only safe passage to Fuercon and I promised to keep your presence here secret from your government. In exchange, you were to tell us everything you knew about how and why the Midlothians were working with the Callusians. I made that offer in good faith and I carried through with my end of the bargain."

She paused, giving him time to think about what she might say next.

"You, however, have proven to be a man without honor. You are a disgrace to the uniform you wore and to those men and women who have died protecting not just Fuercon but your own homeworld in the fight against the Callusians."

He stiffened and his mouth tightened into a thin line.

"You have continued to refuse to cooperate with Colonel Santiago and other members of my government. Because of that, I am giving you one chance to redeem yourself. If I am not satisfied by the time I walk out the door that you're going to do as you promised, I will revoke my assurances to you. I will make sure the Midlothian embassy immediately learns of your presence here. I will also contact certain members of the media and let them know we've had a mole in the enemy camp, one who has presented us with all the confirmation we need to know our so-called Midlothian allies have been selling us out to the enemy. Then I will give them your address so they can interview you themselves. To ensure you won't be *harmed*, I will make sure you have a Marine guard on duty during the interviews. Of course, once the interviews are over, you will be on your own. I figure by then the Midlothians will have figured out where you are and will be quite anxious to have a *chat* with you."

Hughes looked at her in disbelief. Sweat pricked out on his brow and his pupils dilated as the import of what she said registered. One hand fisted at his side. His chest rose and fell in quick, shallow breaths. She saw it and sneered. He should have known better than to try to play them.

"You can't," he rasped. "They'll kill me. They'll kill my family."

"You should have thought about that before you decided not to do as you promised." She turned to where Connery leaned against the wall next to the door. "Corporal, signal the car. Tell the driver we're ready to leave."

"Yes, ma'am." She pulled her comm from her pocket.

"Wait!" Hughes started to reach out and then stopped when Santiago stepped between them. "You don't understand. If I say anything, my family is dead."

"And I told you we would do all we could to get them to safety. But you had to show good faith first," Santiago countered.

"Well?"

Ashlyn crossed her arms and waited. For one long moment, no one said anything. Then Hughes nodded. He took a step back, almost stumbling, before he dropped onto the chair he'd been sitting in when she first arrived. She watched as he buried his head in his hands. Part of her wanted to feel pity for the man but she couldn't. The Callusians had caused too many deaths and he, along with at least some in his government, had helped.

"All right."

"Good. Don't make me return here, Hughes. The next time I do, it will be to paint you as a hero of Fuercon and an enemy to Midlothian."

With that, Ashlyn turned and left the apartment, Connery on her heels. By the time they reached the lift, Santiago caught up.

"He'll be kept under close guard. I don't want to risk him doing anything foolish. I told him to start writing his statement."

Ash nodded. One down, two to go. She had a feeling the next two would be a great deal more difficult for her than this had been. Once those two interviews were over, she could finally close the door on that chapter of her life. At least she hoped so. She needed to put it behind her so she could focus on what she knew was coming.

Later, she and Connery followed Santiago through the corridors of the highest security section of the cells where Alec Sorkowski and Thomas O'Brien were being held. They had been moved there several days earlier in preparation for transport to one of the military penal colonies. Ashlyn didn't know which one but part of her hoped they would soon find themselves housed on Tarsus. That would be justice. Let them try to survive the hell she and her people had been forced to. All she knew for certain was that by this time the next day, they would be off of Fuercon and any chance she'd had of seeing them one last time would be gone.

As the heavy security door at the end of the corridor closed behind them, Ashlyn fought down a brief moment of panic. The sound of the locks engaging, the smell of the corridor brought back memories of when she had been housed in this wing awaiting transfer to Tarsus. Then came the memory of her return to the capital without explanation until Miranda Tremayne told her about her pardon. She'd been on-planet several days by then, still confined and still without a clue about why she'd been removed from the penal colony but those sent there with her had not been. Almost a year had passed since then and the nightmares still woke her on occasion. Hopefully, what happened in the next few minutes would end them.

"Ma'am, are you all right?" Connery asked softly as Santiago went ahead of them to the guards' monitoring station.

Ashlyn nodded, swallowing against the lump in her throat. "Yeah." Then she shook her head. She needed to be honest with Connery if they were to have a chance of developing the sort of relationship she shared with Talbot. "No, I'm not. But I will maintain. However, if you feel I am about to do anything foolish, if you think I am about to lose control, you are to get me out of here. I don't care if you have to knock me over the head and drag me out."

"Understood, ma'am." Connery waited and when Ashlyn looked

at her, she reached out and placed a hand on the colonel's upper arm. "Angel, you can do this. Otherwise, I'd have found a way to keep you away from here. I also know you need to do this. But I have a favor to ask of you. If you see me about to lose control – and I may because I want a piece of those bastards for what they did to you and the others – don't stop me."

Ashlyn looked at the corporal in surprise. Then she grinned. Before she knew it, she was laughing. Connery smiled in satisfaction. As she did, Ashlyn lightly punched her shoulder. The young woman might not be Talbot, but she was quickly learning how to handle her colonel.

"Colonel?" Santiago said from the entrance to the small office where the monitors were.

She nodded and moved down the corridor to join him. At the same time, Santiago dismissed the guards. Then he motioned for Ash to take a seat before the monitors. With Connery guarding the door, she took a seat and waited as Santiago took the seat next to her. A moment later, he adjusted the monitor feeds to show two cells only. Before she could question him, he assured her the guards were monitoring the others from the secondary station.

She nodded and focused on the monitors. Seeing the two men confined as she had been helped more than she dared hope. Knowing they would never again see a day's freedom helped even more. But it wasn't enough. Not by itself. There was one more thing she needed to do and then, maybe, her dead wouldn't haunt her every time she closed her eyes to sleep.

"Are you ready?"

Ashlyn nodded and stood. When she turned, she caught Connery's eye. The corporal gave a miniscule nod but that was enough to reassure Ash. Connery would give her the time she needed but she wouldn't let her do anything foolish.

The sounds of their boots as they walked echoed down the long corridor. At the fourth door, Santiago stopped. Ashlyn waited as he input a code in the security panel. The heavy cell door slid back. The security field hummed softly. Inside the cell, Thomas O'Brien, formerly Major O'Brien of the Fuerconese Marine Corps and currently busted down to private until he served out his sentence and received his dishonorable discharge, sat on the edge of his cot. Head bent, hands hanging loosely between his knees, he gave no indication he realized the door had opened and all that stood between him and possible freedom was the security field.

"On your feet, O'Brien."

At the sound of Santiago's voice, he looked up. When he did, Ash forced herself not to react. The man staring at her in open hatred bore little resemblance to the Marine she had the misfortune to serve with. Gone was the cocky major who listened to no one save Sorkowski. No longer did he look as if he spent more time on his personal appearance than almost anything else. Now he looked old and beaten. New scars, scars she knew he had gotten while incarcerated, marked his face and arms. His once thick hair had thinned and grayed. Hatred burned dully in his eyes. She had no doubt given the chance he would gladly slit her throat.

Well, that went both ways.

"What the fuck are you looking at, Shaw?"

Santiago started to respond but she shook her head. Then she took a step closer to the security field, a slight smile pulling at her mouth.

"I'm looking at someone who never really understood what it means to be a Marine."

"Go to Hell."

"After you, O'Brien." The band of tension across her chest loosened and, for the first time in more than three years, she could breathe easily.

"What do you want?"

He tried for another sneer but failed. In that moment, Ash knew he was as broken as she'd feared becoming while on Tarsus.

"What do I want?" she repeated. "Just this. I wanted to see the right person sitting in a cell for what happened on Arterus. I wanted to know the person responsible for my people's deaths was going to pay for his crimes. I hope you enjoy your new life, O'Brien. I promise your worst nightmares are nothing compared to what life in a penal colony is like."

She looked at Santiago and nodded. He didn't hesitate. He input a series of commands into the security terminal. Ashlyn's last sight of O'Brien as the outer door slid into place was of him dropping his head back into his hands, a man defeated by his own crimes.

"Ash?" Santiago asked.

"I'm fine." Much better, in fact, than she had expected. "Let's finish this."

For a long moment, Santiago looked at her, as if making sure she told the truth. Then he started down the corridor, pausing only long enough to rest his hand reassuringly on her shoulder for a moment. As he moved off, Connery stepped up. Instead of saying anything, she gave her CO a nod. That was all but it was enough. Ashlyn returned it and then followed Santiago to the last cell in the bloc.

Ashlyn studied the viewscreen outside the cell. Every muscle in her body seemed to stiffen. Even though the prisoner had no way of knowing anyone waited outside the security door, he looked up. Memories of everything he had done, every order he'd given that led to the debacle on Arterus, washed over Ash. Marines under her command died because of him. The survivors had been court-martialed and sentenced to the penal colony where they would have died had it not been for people like Lucinda Ortega, Miranda Tremayne and others who fought to clear their names.

Ash's hands fisted at her sides and she gritted her teeth so tightly it was a wonder they didn't shatter. For the first time since telling Santiago she'd talk with Hughes only if he let her see Sorkowski, she doubted the wisdom of her decision. Seeing him in the cell simply made her realize how easy it would be to kill him. But that was too easy. He needed to suffer for what he'd done.

"Colonel?" Connery spoke softly. But it was the gentle touch of the young woman's hand on her arm that broke through to Ashlyn.

Instead of answering, Ash forced herself to relax. As she did, she felt Connery watching her. When she glanced away from the display, she saw not only Connery looking at her but Santiago as well.

"I'm all right."

For a moment, neither responded. Then Connery gave a nod. "Open the security door, sir," she told Santiago.

The intel officer didn't look happy, but he did as Connery said.

"Alec Sorkowski," Ash began as the outer door to the cell slid open.

Once again, the man looked up. As their eyes met, Ash felt her lips twist into a sneer. Alec Sorkowski flinched under her gaze. Then his expression turned neutral, but not before she saw his fear. A laugh fought for release. If he was scared now, wait until he was processed into the penal colony. He'd learn what real fear was then.

"Here to gloat, Shaw?"

He pushed to his feet. As he did, she had to give it to him. He still tried to act as if he held the power when they both knew the truth. That was more than O'Brien had done.

"Not exactly." Her head tilted to one side and she studied him, wondering how long it would take that bravado to disappear once the guards came to prepare him for transport. "Look at me, Sorkowski. My face is going to be one of the last ones you saw before your transport to the penal colony. Look at it and remember that I'm the one who brought you down, thanks to the loyalty and assistance of a number of good Marines and naval personnel.

"You betrayed your oaths as a naval officer to protect Fuercon's best interests. You betrayed people under your command for personal gain. Your greed and dishonor cost who knows how many of those who looked to you their lives. I hope each of their faces haunt you for the rest of your miserable existence." She paused, waiting to see if he would say anything. When he didn't, she continued. "To make sure of it, I've arranged – well, the JAG arranged at my request – for the images of those whose deaths we have been able to link to you be displayed in your cell all day, every day so you don't forget. May you rot in Hell for what you've done."

With that, she turned on her heel and walked off, Connery following close behind. She'd had her say and now, hopefully, her own dead could rest in peace.

16

Elwyn Fertig paused outside the ambassador's office and frowned slightly. Throughout the day, she kept wondering if he might be up to something. Something about his attitude seemed off. It wasn't anything she could easily put her finger on but she learned long ago not to ignore her instincts. For him to send for her at the end of the business day without giving her a clue about why did not bode well.

She smoothed her hands over her suit. If he happened to be watching her via the hidden security feed, she knew he'd set up weeks ago, he'd see only a vain woman making sure her clothing looked the best it could after a long day behind her desk. He wouldn't know she was actually making sure her weapons, weapons she wasn't supposed to have, were within easy reach. If he tried anything foolish, she'd deal with it and figure out later how to explain to Alexander Watchman that she'd had to terminate their government's ambassador to Fuercon.

"You wanted to see me, ambassador?" she asked as she stepped inside D'anil Kalmár's office a few moments earlier.

"Have a seat, Elwyn."

He motioned to one of the two chairs before his desk. Then he waited as she complied before taking his own seat, the desk between them. For several long moments, he said nothing. For the first time since taking the assignment as his "secretary", the security operative fought the urge to squirm. Had he finally realized exactly who and what she was? If so, how would he react?

Kalmár leaned back and rested his hands on the desktop. "Let's get something clear right now. I know you are Watchman's eyes and ears here. Don't bother denying it. I have enough proof to send you packing back to Midlothian. I doubt I need tell you how your boss will react to learning your cover's blown."

She inclined her head. The first point went to the ambassador, but the match was far from over.

"Before I do that, I'm going to give you a chance to save yourself. I'll let you remain here and I will make sure no one else in the embassy learns you have been spying on them and reporting back to the Intelligence Czar. But I want something in return."

"And that would be?" She crossed her legs and relaxed. This was the sort of cat-and-mouse game she played so well.

"We form our own partnership and share information."

Fertig let one brow arch as she inclined her head, indicating he should continue.

"Our flow of information from the Fuerconese has all but come to a halt. The slowdown began approximately six months ago and has continued to lessen with each passing month. It became very obvious after the Callusians made their ill-fated attempt to invade the system three months ago. We get the same information packets the other allies do but nothing more. Not even unofficially. Comments?"

She considered what he said. "It would appear the Fuerconese are holding their cards close. The question is why."

"And would you have any idea why?"

She had a very good idea, one she didn't like.

"Before I answer, let me ask you something, ambassador." The fingers of her right hand drummed a quick rhythm against her thigh. "Have the Fuerconese cut the flow of information to their other allies?"

"Not that I can tell."

Ah, that told her a great deal. Members of the diplomatic community in New Kilrain spent a great deal of time socializing with one another. That was part of their job. Much could be learned and deals were often made over drinks or in bed. The fact Fuercon kept their other allies in the information loop meant they suspected Midlothian, or at least members of the embassy, of acting against its interests.

"None of your sources have explained why?"

"That's two questions," the ambassador pointed out. "But no."

Fertig thought for a moment, not liking the possible explanations. "Mr. Kalmár, I believe we need to start working together. As a show of good faith, I will admit I am here because Mr. Watchman sent me to keep an eye on things. You've been in government service long enough to know he has people in each of our off-world facilities. We are his eyes and ears in his effort to make sure Midlothian's best interests are served."

Kalmár inclined his head.

"I will also tell you he isn't happy about some events that have taken place here. Several of his operatives, ones not assigned to the embassy, have either turned up dead or have gone missing. He has asked me to look into what's happened and find out who is responsible and what their motivation is."

"I see." Kalmár took a moment to consider what she'd said before continuing. "Are there other of his operatives on staff that I don't know about?"

She shook her head. That had been the one requirement she'd had before accepting the assignment. Even though Watchman assured her there were no other undercover agents on staff, she checked out everyone herself once she arrived on-planet. The only other members of his department were those officially listed as security personnel.

"And those others Watchman sent?"

This was where it got sticky. She didn't know for sure what the Intelligence Czar was up to, but she had her suspicions. But suspicions weren't enough to risk her life on, not yet at any rate.

"He hasn't read me in on what their missions were, only that they were here on his behalf." She let a hint of frustration creep into her voice.

"What have you discovered?"

"Nothing of any help so far." He did not need to know about Moreau, not yet at any rate. She didn't trust the woman and had no doubt Moreau would turn on her in a heartbeat given the opportunity. Even so, if she had plans for the woman and the ambassador might play a role in them later.

"You are to inform me when you do learn something. You are also to keep me informed about your communications with Watchman. In the meantime, I have an assignment for you." His smile sent a chill down her spine. Never before had she seen this side of him. Gone was the almost invisible diplomat. In his place sat a man who might possible be able to give Watchman a run for his money. She'd been a fool for not realizing Kalmár played a role, one that helped make him a successful diplomat for more than the obvious reasons.

"Sir?" She'd play along, at least until she figured out what her options were.

"Use your contacts, put pressure on where you need to, but find out what is going on with the Fuerconese." He waited and she nodded once. "Just in case you don't understand how serious this situation is for both of us, if the Fuerconese take action that is against the best interest of our homeworld, my head will be the one in the figurative noose. If that happens, I won't have to take you down with me. Watchman will sign your execution order without hesitation because you will have failed him. You're smart enough to know that."

Like it or not, he was right. "Agreed." She stood and leaned across the desk, extending her hand. "Mr. Ambassador, I believe it is in both our best interests to work together. I'll get the information you want but you have to do something for me in return."

"And that is?"

"There is someone in the embassy feeding information to an independent contractor, one Watchman initially hired and who has been showing signs of going rogue. I have reason to believe the leak knows my real role here and they have done a very good job covering their tracks. Locate that person and let me have their name. I will deal with them and then with the local contractor." And, depending on the situation at the time, she'd deal with Kalmár as well.

Without waiting for him to respond, she left his office. He might think he held the upper hand and, in some ways, he did. But she wanted him to think about why Watchman put her in place in the embassy. If he was as smart as she believed, Kalmár would quickly realize any attempt to betray her would lead quickly and inexorably to his death.

17

"Are you sure about this?" General Okafor asked as she settled behind her desk.

Six weeks had passed since Taskforce Sentinel and the surviving ships of Taskforce Liberator returned to Fuerconese space. In that time, Ash often found herself praying there were more hours in the day. No matter how much she managed to do, there was always more on her desk to deal with. The only thing that kept her going at times was the knowledge that soon they would be shipping out to finally take the fight to the enemy. Finally, after too many years of simply reacting, Fuercon and its allies – its true allies – were going to show the Callusians they no longer had the upper hand. Not that they ever really had. But the allies had listened to the Midlothians. They'd let themselves be manipulated by them into a war of attrition, one meant to weaken the allies.

"Yes, ma'am, I am."

Even though she had initially agreed with her mother's suggestion to "mustang" MJ Anderson out of the senior NCO ranks, she'd hesitated to make the actual recommendation. Part of it had been because she knew Anderson would refuse. Ashlyn even understood. Anderson needed time to accept there was nothing she could have done to save Lucinda Ortega. Their friend had died doing her duty, exactly as they were prepared to do each time their strapped on their armor or picked up a weapon.

Then there had been the blonde's own injuries. The emotional wounds cut as deeply as the physical ones. Adamson needed time to heal. It would still be months before she could return to full duty. But, a week after they had released her to finish her recovery, they had agreed she could return to very limited duty.

"And Laboe?"

"Settling in nicely as the XO for the Warlords."

Okafor glanced at Elizabeth who nodded in agreement.

"Very well. Let's bring them in and get started."

A few minutes later, Okafor sat behind her desk. Elizabeth stood to her right. Ashlyn watched as Connery helped Anderson to a chair. The blonde leaned heavily on a pair of crutches. Even though the regen treatments were working, it would take time for her leg to regenerate below the knee. At least the nerves in her eye hadn't required as much time to heal.

The last member of their party was Talbot. The master gunnery sergeant glanced at Ash and lifted one brow in question. She gave a minute shake of her head. This was the commandant's show, at least for the moment.

"Sergeant Major, it is good to see you back in uniform," Okafor said once everyone had found seats.

"Thank you, ma'am. It is good to be back in one."

"Are you doing everything the doctors say?"

"Yes, ma'am." She cast a quick look at Ash and flashed a quick grin before turning her attention back to Okafor. "Colonel Shaw made it very clear she would kick my ass if I didn't do exactly as the docs said."

"Which is what I will do as well," Okafor said. Then she sat back and studied the four sitting in front of her desk. "Before we get started, there are a couple of housekeeping matters to be taken care of. Sergeant Major Adamson, have you made a decision about whether you are going to stay in the Corps once you are released to full duty or if you are going to take your retirement?"

The blonde blinked in surprise. As she did, Ashe fought the smile that fought to lift the corners of her mouth. If Anderson was surprised by that question, just wait.

"I'm a Marine, ma'am, a Devil Dog. I'll retire when I'm dead."

"I'm glad to hear that." Okafor's expression didn't change but the twinkle in her eyes was something Ashlyn had learned to suspect. It usually meant the general had something in mind for her. This time, however, she wasn't going to be the one on the end of one of the woman's surprises.

"Ma'am?"

"Colonel Shaw?"

Ashlyn nodded and climbed to her feet. As she moved to stand in front of Adamson, she reached inside the thigh pocket of her pants. A slight smile touched her lips as her fingers closed around the jeweler's box. As she pulled it out, she chuckled to herself. She knew the only thing saving her from the blonde chasing her down and beating her for springing something like this was the fact the blonde couldn't run. Not that it would save her once Adamson finished rehabbing. But it would be worth it. She only hoped her friend thought so as well.

"Here you go, ma'am." She handed Okafor the small box once the general joined her.

Adamson looked at the two of them in undisguised suspicion. Then, as if she suddenly realized two senior officers stood before her, she reached for her crutches and slowly climbed to her feet. Ashlyn caught her grimace of pain and fought the urge to reach out to help her. Adamson wouldn't appreciate it, especially when she realized what they were about to do.

"Ten-hut!" Elizabeth's voice rang out and instantly everyone braced to attention.

Ashlyn waited as her mother joined them. Then she took two steps back before assuming her place next to Elizabeth.

"Sergeant Major Adamson, you have served the Corps with

distinction," Okafor began as she took a single step forward, closing the distance between the two of them. "If Colonel Shaw hadn't threatened to resign her commission if anyone tried to poach you from her command, I would have transferred you to my staff long ago. You proved your loyalty to her and to the Corps when you left active duty status after she and others of the Devil Dogs were betrayed. I know how instrumental you were in finding the proof that helped clear their names and reinstate them to our beloved Corps."

Anderson flicked a quick glance in Ashlyn's direction and then nodded once.

"You have never hesitated to do what the Corps, what Fuercon asked of you," Okafor continued. "Colonel Shaw, I believe you should have the honor." She handed the small box back to Ashlyn.

"Thank you, ma'am." She looked down at the box and then stepped forward. It didn't surprise her when her mother stepped up next to her. Ashlyn opened the box and removed the silver bars resting inside. After handing the box to her mother, she smiled a little sadly. "I find myself in need of an XO I can trust to have my back, who can step in and command the Devil Dogs and the regiment in my absence. I need someone I know the regiment respects, someone who understands what it means to not only be a Marine but to be a Devil Dog.

"Five years ago, I pinned these bar on the collar of a friend of ours, of our sister and of one of the best damned Marines I've had the honor of serving with. I know she would approve you being the next to wear them."

"Ma'am." Anderson looked at her, disbelief reflected in her eyes. "I-I don't understand."

"This is a time of war," Okafor said before Ash could reply. "That means extraordinary steps are often taken to make sure the best people are in command positions. Colonel Shaw reviewed all her options and recommended we take one of those steps. Both General Shaw and I agreed it was the perfect solution for the situation the regiment finds itself in. Captain Adamson, you are our first mustang in 7thDiv."

Ashlyn fought to keep from laughing as Anderson's eyes went wide and the blood drained from her face. She knew the only thing keeping the blonde from fleeing was the same strict discipline she demanded of every Marine served with. She also knew she was going to get an earful the moment the two of them were alone.

"General, I'm not officer material." She shook her head, her hands gripping her crutches so tightly her knuckles turned white.

"You are exactly that, Captain." Okafor smiled gaily for a moment before sobering. "Captain Adamson, the Corps needs you in this role. Fuercon needs you in this role."

The blonde closed her eyes for a moment. When she opened them, she straightened as much as she could while continuing to lean on her crutches. "Thank you, ma'am." Then she turned her attention to Ashlyn. "Colonel, I will remind you what you of something you once told me: it isn't nice to spring surprises like this on someone fresh out of medical." Balancing on her good leg, she reached up and touched the silver bars on her collar. "Lucinda's?" she asked softly.

"Yes." Before she could protest, Ashly continued. "I asked her parents for them, explaining who I'd be pinning them on. They said to tell you she'd be proud of you and that it was only right that you wore the same bars I pinned on their daughter, bars my mother pinned on me."

Adamson swallowed hard and braced to attention. "I'll wear them proudly – even if I haven't a clue what I'm supposed to do now or why you tagged me for this." She smiled and shook her head. "Me, an officer."

"Master Gunnery Sergeant Talbot," Okafor said before anyone else could speak.

Ashlyn couldn't hold back her laugh as the man looked at the general as if he were facing a firing squad. He took a giant step back, mimicking the old adage of never being the one to volunteer until you knew what you were being asked to do.

"Stand easy, Master Guns." Okafor chuckled gaily and waited until she returned to his place next to the new captain. "You are now the senior NCO for the regiment. I expect you to do everything you can to assist Captain Adamson as well as your colonel."

"Gladly, ma'am." The relief in his voice almost set Ashlyn to laughing again. Even Adamson laughed softly.

"Corporal Connery, step forward," Elizabeth ordered.

Surprised because neither her mother nor Okafor had said anything about Connery beforehand, Ashlyn glanced at the brigadier general. Her expression carefully neutral, the only indication Elizabeth gave that everything was all right was a slow wink in her daughter's direction. Then, as Connery obeyed her order, Elizabeth turned her attention to the young woman.

"Corporal, what are your goals in the Corps?" she asked.

"I plan on making it my career, ma'am."

Elizabeth nodded. "If you could emulate anyone in the Corps, who would it be?"

Connery didn't answer right away. When she flicked a glance at Ashlyn, Ash lifted one shoulder in a shrug. She had no idea what her mother was up to.

"Ma'am, I come from a long line of Marines. Each of them chose to enlist rather than go the officer track. The reasons vary but it always came down to one thing: they wanted to be on the front lines, doing everything they could to protect Fuercon and her allies. That is why I enlisted. It is why I did everything possible to qualify for SpecOps and to earn my place with the Devil Dogs. If I had to pick one person, and not family, I'd have to choose Sergeant Major – sorry, Captain Adamson. I heard about her before I arrived at Basic. Every good senior NCO I've served with save Master Gunnery Sergeant Talbot came up through the ranks under her. She has the respect of every Marine and, to be honest, she scares the hell out of most of them as well."

Elizabeth threw her head back and laughed. A moment later, she sobered and, with a nod from Okafor, reached into her pocket. "Well said, Connery." Now she looked at Ashlyn. "Colonel Shaw, you are regimental commander and you are in need of a lieutenant to act as your aide. Would Lieutenant Connery be acceptable?"

For a moment, Ash stared at her mother, not sure she heard right. Then a slow smile spread across her face. "Lieutenant Connery would be very acceptable, ma'am."

"Buck up, LT," Talbot said before Connery could protest. "I've a lot of experience handling wet behind the ears lieutenants. Don't I, Colonel?"

"You most certainly do, Master Guns," Ashlyn said and watched as her mother pinned lieutenant bars onto Connery's uniform.

"Captain Adamson," Ash said as her mother shook Connery's hand before stepping back. "I asked you earlier to find another call sign for the new LT, something that fit her role in the regiment better."

Adamson took a firm grip on her crutches and carefully stepped forward and then turned, placing herself to Ashlyn's right. "Lieutenant Connery, your new call sign is Artemis."

"Protector and hunter," Ash commented, liking the choice. "Is that suitable, LT?"

"Y-yes, ma'am."

"Excellent. Everyone, find a seat," Okafor said as she returned to her desk. "We have a great deal to discuss, starting with the news that most of 7thDiv, including the 10thReg, will be shipping out next week as part of a joint force that will be delivering a message to the Callusian home system. . .."

————

"Would someone please tell me what the fuck just happened?"

Anderson dropped onto a chair in the small sitting room connected to her bedroom at the Shaw's home. As her crutches clattered to the floor, Connery and Talbot found seats. As they did, Adamson realized they looked as stunned as she felt. At least that answered one question. They'd been as surprised by the events of the day as had she.

"And you, Master Guns, can quit grinning in relief. You might have avoided becoming an officer this time, but Angel just proved she isn't above offering any of us up as mustangs," she said as she leaned back.

An officer! How the hell had that happened?

"Ma'am, what the hell am I supposed to do now?" Connery looked as stunned now as she had back in Okafor's office.

"Start by dropping the ma'am except when we're on duty." That was something else she'd have to get used to. Damn Ash for doing this to her. "Sorry, Faith, I didn't mean to snap. I'm not one to like being on the receiving end of surprises."

"Tell me about it," the younger woman muttered.

"You two done pissing and moaning?" Ash asked from the doorway. Before entering, she lifted her hands to show she brought whiskey and glasses. "If you are, we can get down to business."

For a moment, three sets of eyes settled on her. Then Adamson jerked her head, motioning the others to leave the room. Seeing it, Ashlyn shook her head. Adamson narrowed her eyes and then huffed out a breath. She'd known Ash long enough to recognize the signs. The woman wanted to talk and nothing the rest of them said was going to stop her.

"You have no idea how much pissing and moaning I am going to do if you don't tell me why in the hell you saddled me with officer's bars?" Adamson said as she watched Ash cross the room and drop onto the far end of the sofa.

Ashlyn inhaled, her expression darkening. Then she relaxed and Adamson had an idea it wasn't easy for her to do. Well, too bad. After the little bombshell she, not to mention Okafor and Elizabeth, had dropped on her, Ash had a lot of explaining to do.

"All of you, shut your mouths and listen up." The bite in Ashlyn's voice had them all sitting a bit straighter. She might have come as a friend but now she was their commanding officer. "The actions taken today were not done so lightly and without a great deal of thought, especially where you're concerned, MJ. One of the things that made stepping into Hammer's place as CO of the Devil Dogs was having you as the senior NCO. You are one of the best damned NCOs I've served with. But everything that makes you an excellent senior non-com will also make you an excellent XO and that is what I need right now. I need someone who knows the Devil Dogs, someone who can motivate them if I'm not around."

"Ash, how can I be your XO when I'm tied here? You know as well as I do the DDs, not to mention the rest of the regiment, will ship out before long."

"Sooner than any of you know," she muttered. "You will do it, MJ, by working with the commandant while we are gone. Kevin and Faith here will fill in for you. While we are gone, you will also be working to find replacements for those slots in the regiment that haven't been filled yet, especially in the Warlords. If that isn't enough to keep you busy in between your appointments at the medical center, I want you working closely with Rico Santiago. We still need to know how badly the Midlothians have betrayed our interests and I want to know why I seem to have been targeted."

"Why mustang me and not Kevin?"

"God, you sound like you'll start whining at any moment," Ash laughed. "For the simple reason that you had been acting as Lucinda's XO." She held up a hand to ward off the blonde's protests. "MJ, Luce told me how it was with the Warlords. Her XO was good, but he didn't have the experience she felt he needed and she knew the rest of the battalion didn't trust him the way they did the two of you. Think about it. You were doing much of what he should have been.

"But, more to the point, at least where I'm concerned, I needed someone who didn't need to be told what to do next. Laboe is a good officer. Miranda would never have had him as her Marine CO if he wasn't. But he wasn't settling into the role of the Devil Dogs' XO as quickly as I needed. Before we shipped out as part of Taskforce Sentinel, I had to decide how to split the DD's. Kevin and Faith here can tell you how difficult that decision was. It went beyond the fact we were still trying to get back up to full-strength after the prior mission. It was because I couldn't trust Laboe to lead the elements sent with Sentinel because he wasn't a Devil Dog in mentality yet. Do you really think my mother and Okafor would have agreed to me leading the mission, especially after we knew the Callusians had tried to invade such a short time before, if there had been any other option?"

"She's right," Talbot said softly. "I've talked with others who have served with Laboe. They all said he's a good officer, one they'd follow into battle without a second thought. But he's been out of SpecOps for years. You know as well as I do that it takes time to get back into our sort of mindset. Time's something the regiment doesn't have."

"But—"

"MJ, I know we sprang this on you without warning. But it isn't as if you are being thrown right into the fire." Ash waited until she nodded. "I wouldn't have asked my mother, much less Okafor, to consider taking you mustang if I didn't think it necessary. I need you as my XO. I need someone I trust not only at my back but able to take over the Devil Dogs and the regiment if something happens to me. Besides, the only real change is that you can go to the officers' club now. You'll still be the biggest bad ass in the regiment and I'll still rely on you to put together obstacle courses that will turn the insides of our Marines to water." Ashly grinned and Adamson chuckled softly.

"What would you have done if I'd turned down the commission?"

Ash smiled, a wicked twinkle in her eye. "I'd have asked the commandant to contact the medical center with her concerns for your mental health."

"Bitch," she laughed. "And Faith here?" She nodded to where Connery sat across from her. The young woman still looked shell-shocked, not that Adamson blamed her.

"That I didn't know about, not that I would have objected." Before Connery could say anything, Ashlyn continued. "Faith, they were right. I need an officer as my aide with the way Okafor realigned the division. More than that, I don't want anyone but you in that role. We've made a good team and Kevin here knows he can trust you to make sure I don't do anything too foolish."

"She's right," Talbot confirmed when Connery looked at him in question.

"I know the three of you need to bitch and moan a bit more, so I'll leave you to it. MJ, you have therapy in the morning, don't forget.

Faith, if you'll make sure everything is set for it, I'd appreciate it. Tomorrow, you can pull together recommendations from within the DDs for an aide for the good captain." She threw a cocky smile in Anderson's direction.

"Yes, ma'am," the newly promoted lieutenant said.

"Then I will leave you to it. Loco, meet with the senior NCOs for the other battalions in the regiment tomorrow morning. Full report on the enlisted ranks tomorrow afternoon."

"I'll see to it, Angel."

"Then I'll take my leave." She stood and then dropped a hand to Anderson's shoulder. "I'll check on you before I head to bed."

When the door slid shut behind her, Anderson turned to the others. To say the day had been full of surprises was putting it mildly. She knew one thing for certain, however. She was going to do whatever it took to keep their CO safe. She'd already lost Ortega. She was damned if she'd lose Ash as well and the sooner her companions realized it, the better.

"Faith, we both got blindsided today but we're Marines. We not only cope, we overcome."

"Yes, ma'am." Connery grinned as Adamson groaned.

"Not a word, Loco, not one word or I swear I will tell Angel you should be mustanged as well." She glared at Talbot, daring him to see if she'd do it. "If I know our dear colonel, she will have already made arrangements to have our uniforms updated to reflect our new ranks, Faith. However, if you'd check to be sure, I'd appreciate it."

"Consider it done."

She smiled and began to relax some. "I also want you to copy me on Angel's schedule each day. I might not be on duty yet, but I need to be kept in the loop."

Connery nodded.

"Kevin, we're going to be having some long talks about what happened with the DDs after Lucinda and I transferred out."

"After you get some rest," he said. As he spoke, he subtly motioned to Connery it was time for them to leave.

"Not yet." Adamson smiled as Talbot sighed slightly before

nodding. "Like it or not, I'm tied dirtside until the docs release me. That means the two of you are going to have to be my eyes and ears. It also means I will have your asses if you left anything happen to Angel. I am not going to lose another friend, another CO to those bastard Callusians. Understand?" She pinned both of them with a firm look.

"We understand," Talbot assured her. "But you have to understand something. We are going to make sure you do as you are supposed to as well. We need you back to duty as soon as possible. More than that, Angel needs you."

"Which means I will be doing everything I can to find you an aide who you'll be able to work well with but who will also have enough of a spine to keep you from doing anything foolish," Connery told her.

Adamson narrowed her eyes and then chuckled. Ash had been right. She'd chosen well when she picked "Artemis" as the young woman's new call sign.

"We'll discuss it tomorrow." She yawned, suddenly tired. "Go on. The next few days are going to be busy for all of us, especially for the two of you."

"Go on, Loco," Connery said as she got to her feet. "C'mon, Captain, you need to get some rest." She handed Adamson her crutches and watched, ready to help, as the blonde got to her feet.

Later, lying in bed, Adamson blew out a long, exhausted breath. She'd done more that day than she had since being injured. Exhausted physically, her mind refused to relax. It was going to take time for her to wrap her mind around the fact she was now an officer. And officer, damn it! But it was more than that. In very short order, her Marines, her friends and family, were shipping out and she should be with them. She couldn't be so she would, by God, do all she could from there to help make their mission a success.

Battle Stations

18

Phoenix Rising, Flagship
First Fleet
Fuerconese Navy

"Ten-hut!"

Connery's order cut through the conversations taking place. Instantly, chairs were shoved back and boots scraped across the decksole as the men and women gathered climbed to their feet. By the time the hatch slid shut behind Admiral Tremayne and Brigadier General Shaw, everyone had braced to attention. Though silence now filled the room, Ashlyn felt the sense of expectation as the others waited, wondering if they were finally going to learn what their orders were.

"Be seated," Tremayne said once she and Elizabeth had taken their places at the head of the table.

As they did, enlisted personnel poured coffee and tea for those gathered. Once everyone was served, they left the admiral's ready room. The hatch slid shut behind them and Elizabeth engaged full security. No one would be able to get in or out without her permission. That, by itself, was enough to put everyone on edge.

From her place at the opposite end of the table, Ashlyn took a moment to study the others. Each unit of their improvised fleet as represented. It would be up to them to make sure those under them knew their orders as well as the need to maintain OPSEC. Hopefully, the steps they had taken so far had kept their mission parameters secret not only from the Callusians but from the Midlothians as well. If not. . . she didn't want to think of the potential problems that could happen if the Midlothians knew their plans and decided to take advantage of them.

"Ladies and gentlemen, it is time to read you in on our mission," Tremayne said as she activated the holo screen over the table. "In ten days, we will rendezvous with fleets from the Drakkana, Cassius, Nystrom, Bennington and Braxis systems. From there, we will transit to the Alpha Rhogana System where we will deliver a message to the Callusians. Our orders are simple. We are to destroy system defenses and all military and military-related installations in the system. We will then deliver our final message to them. They are to immediately cease hostilities or we will move on to the Callusian home system with an even larger force and end this war once and for all."

"Admiral, a question?" Rear Admiral Korin Atsma said.

"Go ahead."

"Why aren't the Callusians taking part in the mission?"

"If I may?" Captain Jocelyn Farnham said before Tremayne could answer. Ash frowned and glanced at her mother. Farnham, CO of one of the non-SpecOps units to take part in the mission, fell under her mother's command. "Why are there no Midlothians assigned to our own ships, for that matter."

Elizabeth's jaw firmed and Ash winced slightly to see the anger flash in her mother's eyes. Before she could respond, Tremayne did.

"To answer Admiral Atsma's question, the Midlothians are not involved in this mission because we have received and confirmed intel that there are members of their government working against the best interests of not only Fuercon but of our true allies as well. Colonel Shaw?" She looked to where Ash sat and nodded, giving her permission to tell the others what she knew.

"During an earlier mission, the Devil Dogs helped secure intel that began explaining not only how the Callusians suddenly came to possess ships and weaponry that came close to the level of our own but also why their tactics changed so dramatically. While Fleet Intel worked to confirm the information we obtained, we stumbled across irrefutable evidence of a Midlothian conspiracy. What we don't know yet is whether we have been betrayed by the Midlothian government or only by certain people within it. So, FleetCom, along with President Harper and his closest advisors, decided that the Midlothian government would not learn of this mission until after the fact. How they respond should say a great deal about how deep the cancer runs."

For a moment, no one spoke. Then a low murmur of anger began. It quickly rose in volume. Tremayne allowed it to continue and Ashlyn waited. She'd known the admiral long enough to recognize what she was doing. Tremayne understood the others needed time to accept what she'd said. Unfortunately, that time was limited and, accept it or not, they needed to move on.

"Are you sure?" Farnham asked.

Instead of answering immediately, Ash glanced first to her mother and then to Tremayne. Both women gave quick nods. That was enough. She'd answer Farnham's question but she would almost make sure the captain understood this was not the time to question a senior officer with more knowledge of the situation than she.

"Lieutenant Connery, display File 114-799A," she said.

A moment later, the contents of the file appeared on the holo screen. Even though the name of the interviewee had been blacked out, the import of his statement was obvious. He was a member of the Midlothian Navy, one of many who had been assigned to work with the Callusians, advising them on tactics and helping train them on the new equipment their Midlothian benefactors provided.

"That is the small portion of the information provided to us by the man. He was captured several months ago during the Callusians' failed attempt to invade our home system. So, to answer your question, Captain, we are most definitely sure of the information." The scathing tone of her voice was enough to cause several of those present, Farnham included, to wince. "Ma'am?" She inclined her head to both her mother and Tremayne as she returned to her seat.

"You are cleared to inform your crews of our mission goal. The information about the Midlothians is need-to-know only and they do not need to know. If you feel differently, you will bring the matter up with either General Shaw or myself in private. Understood?"

"Ma'am, yes, ma'am!"

"If someone does ask why the Callusians aren't sending ships," Elizabeth said, "simply remind them that they were not active combatants in the last war nor are they ones in this war. Because of the urgency of this mission and the need for seasoned troops, it was decided not to include them."

At least that explanation had the benefit of being the truth. Hopefully, no one would try to press the issue. Although, if they did, it would be of interest to know why. With that thought in mind, Ashlyn made a mental note to discuss it with her mother and Tremayne later.

"Over the next week, we will be conducting a number of training exercises. Some will involve the entire fleet and others only parts of it. The training schedule has been sent to your comms. You will note when you review it there are several that are not to be announced to your staff and crews. Others you will see don't have more than basic parameters set out. That is because General Shaw and I have some twists up our sleeves and we want to see how you and your people respond."

Ashlyn didn't – quite – groan at that one. She knew all too well what those "twists" could be like and didn't look forward to them.

"Admiral Tremayne is correct. There is something else you will find noted in the information the Admiral sent. Our Marines are to be working with their naval counterparts whenever they are on duty. The only exceptions are if they are taking part in a training exercise or if they have other duties assigned them by Colonel Shaw or myself. Understood?"

"Ma'am, yes, ma'am!" the Marines responded.

"Good. Then let's review the day's schedule and get to work." Tremayne entered a command using her virtual keyboard and the holo display once again changed, this time showing the fleet's current position relative to the Fuercon System. "We'll begin with status reports."

Two hours later, Tremayne ended the briefing. As the others began filing out of the room, Ash glanced at her mother. Without seeming to see her daughter looking in her direction, Elizabeth reached up and tapped two fingers against her left temple. Then she repeated the motion. The left side of her mouth quirked up briefly before Ash schooled her features back to neutral. She knew that signal. Her mother had used it since she was a child. It was Elizabeth's way of telling her they needed to talk in private. Two fingers meant two hours. Ash coughed softly, covering her mouth with her hand. When she did, Elizabeth nodded once. Trusting her mother to get word to her later about where and exactly when to meet, Ash stood and gathered her things. Then she motioned for Connery to come with her. They had a great deal to do and not much time in which to do it.

———

New Kilrain, Fuercon

"What do you mean they've moved a number of ships and Marines out-system?"

D'anil Kalmár stared at Elwyn Fertig in disbelief. In the weeks since their new *understanding*, they had settled into a working relationship that utilized their strongest talents. He worked other members of the diplomatic corps in the capital. She worked in the shadows, milking her sources for any information they could give her. Unfortunately, there had been a dearth of any real information and now they might know why.

"My source at the space port told me today that First Fleet, supplemented with elements from several of the other fleets, left on training maneuvers a week ago," Fertig said as she dropped onto one of the two chairs in front of his desk.

"And?" he prompted. There had to be more to it or she wouldn't have bothered him with the information.

"It doesn't make sense. After the attempted invasion, they wouldn't have pulled First Fleet out, especially not after reinforcing it with additional elements."

"Did your source say which ships replaced First Fleet?"

She nodded. "Second Fleet."

He cursed softly. First Fleet was formidable. Second Fleet, with its new general warships, was doubly so. Whatever the Fuerconese were up to, it wasn't playing war games. But what?

"And the Marines?"

She huffed out a breath and frowned. "My contact didn't know for sure but he swore he saw Ashlyn Shaw and members of the Devil Dogs, as well as at least three other Marine units, shuttling up to the ships that pulled out."

He clamped his mouth shut to keep from cursing. Then he moved around his desk. He needed to think. The Fuerconese were up to something, no doubt about it. He'd heard nothing about it from other diplomats. That might not mean anything or it might mean everything. His task was to figure out which.

"Do you have a current location on the ships?"

"No. All I know for sure is they are no longer in the system."

He leaned against the desk and closed his eyes. What was Harper up to?

"I assume you've heard nothing from Watchman that might give a clue about what's going on."

Fertig shook her head. "Nor has his contractor here said anything."

Something about the way she said it caused Kalmár to look at her closely. She didn't meet his gaze for a moment. Seeing it, he knew there was more to this so-called contractor than Fertig said.

Curious, more than a little suspicious, he decided to make a side trip on his way home that evening. It was time to put eyes on Fertig, eyes who would report back to him and not try to withhold information.

"I suggest you keep looking," he said. "And I will do the same. The Fuerconese are up to something and you know as well as I do that Watchman will blame us if they do anything to upset his plans."

Whatever those plans might be.

———

ONE HOUR after leaving the embassy, Elwyn Fertig strolled into a café far from Embassy Row. As she did, a smile touched her lips. No one glancing in her direction would recognize the always fashionable ambassador's "secretary". Instead of her favored expensive suits and well made up hair and face, she appeared so ordinary she all but blended into the background. Like most everyone there, she wore coveralls, dotted here and there with grease and grime. Her facial features appeared broader, her skin pock-marked with scars. Even her gait and posture were different. She knew her attempt to hide her identity was successful when Moreau's gaze slipped past her without a single hint of recognition. That changed to surprised frustration when she slid onto a chair at Moreau's side. Before Moreau could react, Fertig pressed the muzzle of her gun to the woman's ribs, smiling slightly to feel her stiffen in fear. Moreau thought herself so accomplished when, compared to Fertig, she was little more than an amateur.

Fertig shifted pocketed her pistol, keeping her hand wrapped around the butt and her finger on the trigger. Then she motioned for Moreau to pick up her drink. She'd need it when she realized just how little there was about her Fertig didn't know. In fact, the assassin would absolutely shit a proverbial brick to know Fertig had uncovered her biggest secret – her true identity. That was one card Fertig didn't plan on playing unless she had to. It was her ace and she was a very good poker player.

"Who are you?" Moreau hissed, her left hand slowly inching its way under the table.

"I wouldn't do that, Evan," Fertig said softly. "In fact, I suggest you take care and let me see both your hands."

Moreau's lips pulled back, baring her teeth briefly. Then she nodded. A moment later, she wrapped both hands around her glass. Fertig arched one brow and gave a quick shake of her head. The glass, like the silverware on the table, could easily be used as a weapon, not that she had any intention of letting Moreau do so. Still, it would be better for them both if the woman didn't decide to try any foolish.

"Palms on the table might be safer, Evan dear." She waited until Moreau complied. "As for who I am, you should be able to figure that out. After all, we've had several conversations and I have been to your apartment on more than one occasions." Moreau's eyes widened and she nodded in confirmation. "You've been trying to avoid me and that is very foolish."

"What do you want?"

"Let's begin with the obvious." Fertig waved off a waiter approaching the table. "I won't miss from this distance. If move wrong, look at me wrong or try to call for help, you're dead. When we leave here, if you try to leave the capital or flee the planet, you're dead. Try to hide and I will find you. You are good at your job but I'm better. Nod if you understand."

Moreau nodded, her eyes blazing with anger.

"See, that wasn't so difficult." Fertig leaned back, allowing herself to relax slightly. She'd made her point and she doubted Moreau was foolish enough to try anything, at least not just then. "And I have a way that will let you live a little longer, especially if you are successful. If you are, I will help you get off-planet. Then you can disappear and use the resources you've been gathering the last ten years in preparation for the day when you finally cut all ties with Watchman."

"I'm listening."

"I need two pieces of information. The first should be easy enough for you to ascertain. Ambassador Kalmár has someone not associated with the embassy gathering information for him. I want a name and location on his source. He isn't to know what you are doing, and you are not to contact him. Kalmár is much more intelligent, not to mention cagey, than he appears." Something she wished she'd been aware of when she first arrived at the embassy. If she had, she would never have been forced into her current position. Hopefully, Moreau would find information that would once again put her in control of her relationship with the man.

"What else?"

"Here." She shoved a data chip across the tabletop in Moreau's direction. "Find out everything you can about why this happened and what is being planned. I want a report in forty-eight hours."

Moreau's nostrils flared as she palmed the chip. "I can't guarantee I'll find anything by then."

"You will. Your life depends on it." Fertig let her words sink in. Then she jerked her head in the direction of the front entrance. "Get out of here. You have a great deal to do and very little time in which to do it. I'll cover the tab."

"One day you will get too cocky for your own good," Moreau murmured.

"Perhaps, but not where you're concerned." She waited until Moreau looked at her. "Constance."

All color drained from the woman's face. Her hand, as she reached for her bag, shook. Fertig couldn't have planned it better if she'd wanted to. Moreau knew her darkest secret was no longer secret.

"How?" she whispered.

"As I said, I am very good at my job. Now get on your way. I expect results in forty-eight hours. Don't fail me."

She watched as Evan Moreau, once Constance Mumby, left the café. Once outside, the woman headed north. Not that it fooled Fertig. She had no doubt Moreau would try find someplace close by to watch the café. It is what Fertig would do if their positions were reversed. But she'd planned for the woman to try just that. When she left, a cab would be waiting for her. She'd take it several miles away from the café. Then she would get out at one of the capital's most popular shopping areas. There she would disappear into the crowd. Moreau would never find her.

Now if it could only be that simple keeping Watchman out of the loop until she knew what her next move should be

19

Phoenix Rising
Combined Allied Attack Force
Alpha Rhogana System

"Connery, get to the staging area."

Ashlyn ripped open the locker she'd had installed in her quarters onboard the *Phoenix Rising*. Inside was a duplicate set of battle armor, an identical match to that in her locker inside her office near the staging area. It had cost a small fortune to not only have the second set of armor made but to duplicate most of her weapons, but it was worth it. She'd learned years earlier that the enemy didn't wait until the crew could suit up. This way, at least, she had a better chance of being prepared when the shit hit the fan and, judging by the sounding of General Quarters, that possibility was far off. She struggled into the body suit with its infernal "plumbing" connections and then looked up. Connery waited, seemingly unfazed by the alarm claxon.

"Tell Loco to check on each of the company commanders. This is not a drill. If anyone needs encouragement, he is to give it to them, preferably with a boot up their asses. Attack shuttle crews are to hot bunk onboard their shuttles. LACs are to be prepared to launch. Everyone else to their battle stations after they have armored up. All Marines, not just those with the 10th, are to be weaponed up as well. Let's not run the risk of the enemy boarding and our people not being prepared to repel them."

"Aye, ma'am." Connery paused, her head tilted to one side. When her right hand lifted to cup that ear, Ash knew she was listening to a message coming in over her comm. "Admiral Tremayne wants you and General Shaw to report to her ready room ASAP."

"Inform her I will be there shortly." Ashlyn checked the weapons laid out on her bed and began strapping them in place on her armor. "Once you've confirmed everything is under control in the staging area, turn it over to the Master Guns and find me. It looks like things are about to get interesting."

"Colonel, you have a very strange definition of that word." Connery gave her a cocky grin and then left Ash's quarters.

"Loco, Angel," she commed as the hatch slid shut behind Connery. "Artemis is on her way to you. Anything I need to know?" she asked as she slid her battle rifle into its place in the double tactical rifle scabbard strapped across her back. Her sniper rifle followed.

"Roger that, Angel. Everything under control here. What's our status?"

"On my way to find out." She paused, listening to a report coming in over the battlenet. "Looks like we're about to deliver our message to the enemy, Loco. Get everyone ready. I'll be down as soon as I finish with the Admiral."

When she stepped off the lift onto the bridge a few minutes later, she looked around. Each station was manned with back-ups sitting next to them. Reports flowed back and forth as information was coordinated and exchanged. The main holo plot showed the Alpha Rhogana System. Green icons indicated the combined allied attack force. Each icon represented a taskforce. Each taskforce represented at least six battle cruisers and four destroyers. The count varied depending on which navy the taskforce belonged to. That meant close to seventy-five ships, almost a thousand LACs and enough Marines to give nightmares to the enemy for years would soon enter the system and rain down hell on the enemy.

"The admiral is in her ready room, Colonel," Captain Montgomery said.

She thanked him and crossed the bridge to the ready room. As the hatch slid shut behind her, she nodded to find Tremayne, Elizabeth, Captain Vilhjalmsson and several others there. They were gathered around the plot, their expressions concerned. Worried, Ashlyn moved to stand next to her mother.

"It seems as if we are in the right place at the right time once again," Tremayne said with a grim smile.

As she spoke, she highlighted a group of red icons on a course out of the system. Ash studied them, frowning, as she calculated their trajectory. If she was right, and she didn't know if she wanted to be or not, they would intersect the attack force's course all too soon.

"CIC reports with confidence that in the ships are on a preliminary trajectory to the Tenasic System," Tremayne continued. "Also, they do not appear to be aware of our presence yet."

For a moment, no one spoke. Finally, Tremayne told them to be seated. "Recommendations?" she asked.

"We can't risk them making it to the system, Admiral," Montgomery said from his place at the far end of the table.

"I agree." Ashlyn fisted one hand at her side, waiting for her temper to cool a bit. "Even though reinforcements are in place there, system defenses are not ready to take another hit from the enemy." She tried not to think of the sacrifices their people had made, that Lucinda had made, to protect the system. Sacrifices that would be for naught if they simply let the enemy ships fly by and once again attack the Tenasic System.

"Admiral Tremayne, I agree with Colonel Shaw."

Ashlyn turned her attention to the secondary holo screen. On it, images of each of the allied fleet commanders appeared. One of them, Rear Admiral Yuri Xing, looked as grim as she felt. Not that she blamed him. If the Callusians managed to take the Tenasic System and hold it, their next logical target would be the Braxis System. In the previous war, the system had seen more than its fair share of the fighting. Ash knew it was still rebuilding its infrastructure and it would be years yet before it returned to normal.

"I have to agree as well," Elizabeth said. She waited until Tremayne nodded before continuing. "We're here to make a statement. The best way we can do so is to destroy those ships. Not only will it prevent them from attacking another of our allies, it will plant the seed of doubt in their minds as they wonder how we knew to attack at precisely this moment, striking when we could not only hurt the system but destroy one of their battle groups."

Over the next few minutes, tactics were debated. Only one of Tremayne's commanders suggested letting the enemy ships fly by. The others offered various approaches on how to deal with them. Each suggestion had merits, even the one to do nothing. Ashlyn waited, praying Tremayne didn't consider that particular option. She wanted blood. She wanted to avenge the deaths of all those who fell in the Tenasic System. More than that, she refused to let Lucinda and all the others have died in vain.

"All right." Tremayne studied the plot once again before continuing. "Admiral Xing, you will have the honors. Your ships are to transit to the head of the formation. Commodore Marcello, your ships will assist."

"Thank you, Admiral. It would be our pleasure," Xing said.

"The rest of the attack force will continue toward our designated targets. General Shaw, Marine LACs will launch as soon as we are within range. Once they have dealt with the enemy forces, rejoin the attack force, supporting the Navy LACs that will remain in closer formation to protect our leading elements. Until we are within weapons range, we will continue running under stealth conditions." She glanced around the table, making eye contact not only with those present but those taking part via link. "Any questions?" When there were none, she dismissed everyone, saying they would meet again in an hour.

As the hatch closed behind the last to leave, Tremayne leaned back and smiled grimly at the two who remained. Elizabeth leaned forward and poured the admiral a mug of coffee. When she looked at Ash and lifted the carafe, Ashlyn shook her head. There would be time for coffee later.

"Well?" Tremayne asked, setting her mug on the tabletop.

"This is what we came for, Miranda," Elizabeth said. "Not exactly the way we planned it but then what battle ever follows the initial plans?"

"Ash?"

"Mom's right, Miranda. I still wish we were hitting the Callusian home system, but this will do for a start. It's past time for us to take the fight to them." Even if she didn't think their mission parameters went far enough.

"Ash." Understanding shone in Tremayne's blue eyes. "I think I speak for your mother when I say neither of us thinks the mission plans go far enough."

Ashlyn had to agree. The element of surprise would disappear as soon as the first shot was fired. But that was nothing new. The fact they weren't going to play by their own rules was. The attack force was under orders to hit the sector with everything it had. The only targets off-limits were civilian installations. However, for once, their senior officers were not being limited by rules of engagement that allowed for no unintended casualties. No longer would the enemy be allowed to hide behind the civilian population. Where bombing raids from the LACs and attack shuttles couldn't be used, the Marines would be. They would hit hard, destroy as many military and industrial facilities as possible and then withdraw – after delivering President Harper's message that the Callusian government had one chance to surrender with prejudice of they would bring the battle straight to the Callusian home system.

"How long until your people are ready, Ashlyn?"

She glanced at her wrist unit and then smiled. "They are by now, ma'am. They're just waiting for their orders."

"Then go get them ready. Things should get interesting in another couple of hours."

Ashlyn stood and saluted. A moment later, she left the ready room. As the hatch slid shut behind her, she heard her mother and Tremayne beginning to discuss how best to handle the different ways the enemy might respond to the attack.

———

Hammer of God, Flagship
Callusian Naval Attack Force Infidel's Woe
Alpha Rhogana System

"WHAT IS GOING ON?"

Commander Jan Kacper tossed back the sheet and sat up. The signal for battle stations blared over the comms system, each repetition seeming to sync with the pounding in his head. Cursing, he called for lights and climbed to his feet.

If this was someone's idea of a joke. . ..

"Sir, scanners picked up readings you need to see," his first officer said.

"Erycsson," he growled.

"Sir, you're needed on the bridge now," Simon Erycsson said.

Without another word, Kacper reached for his uniform where he'd tossed it over a chair mere hours before. As he pulled on his boots, he began thinking of ever more inventive ways of dealing with whoever was responsible for misreading the sensor hits. The defense platforms would have warned them of any ships attempting to enter the system without permission. Beyond that, the Fuerconese and their allies were too cowardly to bring the battle to him.

"Turn off that damned alarm," he ordered as he stepped onto the bridge ten minutes later.

Because he was so sure someone had made a mistake, he hadn't hurried. He didn't want his crew to see him worried for no reason. That would be a weakness and he had no desire for someone to decide now was the time to slide a knife between his ribs so they could move up the promotions chain.

Erycsson, a small, wiry man in his middle years, motioned to the holo plot. A moment later, Kacper's mouth went dry. His heart seemed to skip a beat and his stomach did a slow roll. For a moment, he studied the plot, trying to make sense of it. But he couldn't. What he saw went against everything he knew of the enemy. Worse, it meant they had managed to find a way past his preliminary defenses and were now within weapons range.

"Order all ships to battle stations. Weapons and shields are to go hot. Form up the battle group. LACs are to launch as soon as they are ready," he ordered. "How the hell did they manage to get this far in-system without you noticing?" He pinned Erycsson with a gaze that had the older man flinching.

"No explanation, Commander," his first officer said. "We were monitoring the taskforce's departure from the system. It was there and then, without warning, it was gone, destroyed. By the time our scanners cleared and reset, the enemy ships were here. My best guess is they came in cloaked and managed to avoid our sensor arrays."

Kacper ground his teeth before moving to the command chair. He had to think. No matter what he did, he was going to lose ships. At least he knew his men would die in glory, taking as many of the enemy with them as they could. But it wasn't enough to atone for this insult. Who had the audacity to bring the fight straight to them? It was an insult. But it was also a stroke of genius. None of their leaders expected Fuercon or its allies to do anything like this. Worse, he hadn't expected it and he'd not kept his ships at battle ready. Because of that, they were about to be torn apart by an enemy he had under-estimated.

"Comms, send a message to groundside command. We will hold the enemy as long as we can. Gods be with us, we may be able to turn them back. But we need groundside to take control of system defense platforms."

And that would take time, time he feared they didn't have. But he would make them pay. The Fuerconese would learn how foolish it had been to come against a Callusian stronghold. If he died that day, he would do so with honor and glory, taking as many of the enemy with him as possible.

———

"STATUS?" Tremayne asked as she watched the holo plot update once again.

Icons flashed and disappeared. This was the part of battle she hated. The leading elements of the attack force had met the enemy. While the ships, along with their LAC support, appeared to be making short work of the enemy force, it wasn't without cost. Admiral Xing had lost one ship from his taskforce. Another was damaged badly enough it had fallen back to be screened by the following battle element. Their LACs had dealt the enemy a great deal of damage but their lighter shielding resulted in more than two dozen had been destroyed in the initial confrontation. That number had risen but their pilots continued to harass the enemy, giving the battle group time to get into position.

"Admiral Xing sends his respects and reports the departing task-force has been destroyed. He has one squad of LACs flying SAR patterns in case there are any survivors. His taskforce continues to push forward. Commodore Marcello recommends we activate Attack Plan Medusa," Captain Montgomery reported.

"Our Marines?" Tremayne looked to where Elizabeth stood next to her command chair.

"Ready for the order to move out," she answered. "Colonel Shaw has the 10th standing by. The rest of the Marines are backing up naval personnel until they are needed elsewhere."

Tremayne nodded. She saw the slight strain around her friend's eyes and understood. It was caused by more than the battle. This was the first time mother and daughter had been on the same ship and it was the first time Elizabeth had faced the possibility of neither of them returning home. Not that Elizabeth feared for herself. She worried for her daughter, as any mother would.

"Very good. Send the colonel my regards and tell her to have her

Marines standing by. I have a feeling they're going to get into the fight soon."

"Admiral, we are receiving a message from dirtside," the comms officer said.

Tremayne looked at Elizabeth and arched one brow. Interesting. She hadn't expected them to attempt to make contact quite so soon. Not only was it unexpected, she had no doubt it was meant to distract her. If that was the case, they were about to learn how foolish that maneuver had been.

"Justin, send a message to Admiral Xing. Let him know what's happening and tell him to be prepared. My gut tells me this is a trap." She thought for a moment. Then she nodded once. "Then contact Commander Paulus. The rear elements are to form up. I want his LACs patrolling to the rear. Have them drop sensor arrays. I want to make sure the enemy doesn't have the chance to slip in behind us. Once you have, spread the word that we are going to follow Commodore Marcello's suggestion. On my command, we will go to Attack Plan Medusa."

"Aye, ma'am."

"Comms, once he's done that, put the dirtside message through."

"Admiral, whenever you're ready," Comms said a few minutes later.

"CIC, keep an eye on their defense platforms," she ordered as she leaned back in her chair and did her best to look relaxed. Once she was ready, she nodded to the communications officer. Then she turned her attention to the holo screen to her right. A moment later, the ship's wallpaper faded away and a man's pale face appeared.

"This is Anselm Harris, Occupational Governor for the Alpha Rhogana System. You have violated our space and attacked our ships without provocation. Ceasefire now and we will let you withdraw without further incident."

Tremayne glanced up at Elizabeth and grinned. Did he really think he held the upper hand?

"Governor Harris, I have a counter-offer for you," Tremayne said. "My name is Admiral Miranda Tremayne, commanding officer of the

Combined Allied Attack Force. We have already destroyed the task-force you were sending to the Tenasic System. We have destroyed most of the ships you had in place for system defense. You will order the remaining ships to stand down and take their shields and weapons off-line. The crews will abandon those ships without scrubbing the databases or setting the ships to self-destruct. You have ten minutes to issue those orders. If you fail to do so, we will finish the task we began and destroy them as easily as we destroyed your departing taskforce."

She paused, presenting a relaxed and confident exterior in direct contracts to the fear she saw in his eyes. "You will also abandon your weapons platforms, industrial platforms and all military installations both in space and on the ground. You have three hours to do so. At the end of that time, I will order my ships to open fire. Any deaths occurring after that will be on your head."

"You have no right!"

"I have every right," she countered firmly. "I am giving you the chance to save your people. Frankly, I don't give a damn if you do or not. I will destroy every military target in this system. Every industrial target capable of creating military tech or machinery will be destroyed as well. Do not make the mistake of thinking I am bluffing."

"Admiral, incoming missiles!"

"Governor Harris, I wish I could say you disappoint me, but I can't. I anticipated this." She looked at Montgomery and nodded. Her aide quickly issued the order to the attack group's leading elements to launch countermeasures. Then they were to focus their fire on the remaining Callusian ships. "Fuercon and its allies will no longer sit back and wait for your government to decide what system to target next. We are bringing the battle to you. Surrender the system defenses now or face our wrath. You have ten minutes to decide."

She signaled for the feed to be cut. Then she leaned forward, her eyes on the plot. "General, I believe it is time for the Devil Dogs to get into the action. Inform Colonel Shaw that I want her Marines ready to launch in ten minutes. I don't want to waste any time if Harris is foolish enough to try to call my bluff."

"Yes, ma'am."

"Signal all ships. Be prepared to execute Attack Plan Medusa in ten minutes. They are to wait on my command."

With that, she leaned back and glanced at the chrono. Nine minutes.

Nine minutes until either sanity or all-out war.

That is a job for the Devil Dogs. They send for Ash, along with the senior NCOs. Depending on what they had to say, they'd know whether the mission risks were acceptable or not.

20

Ashlyn steadied herself as the attack shuttle rocked. In the cabin behind her, came the sounds of grumbling from the vets and a few concerned comments from the newer members of the company. She listened as Connery assured the newest Devil Dogs not to worry, the Old Lady knew what she was doing. Besides, they had the enemy on the ropes. This was going to be a walk in the park compared to some of the battles she'd seen.

Smiling, proud of the young woman, Ash ducked inside the small cockpit. As she rested a hand on the pilot's shoulder, he glanced up. Then he nodded toward the plot. She watched, her expression grim, as icons light up and then disappeared all around them. At least the LACs were doing their jobs. They were keeping the shuttles safe.

"Shields holding, Angel," he said as the shuttle rocked once again. "Their targeting is getting a little better." As he spoke, several LACs raced ahead, their lasers effectively dealing with several enemy missiles headed in their direction. "The boots doing okay?"

She chuckled and shook her head. "They aren't boots, Talon."

Not technically at least. Each of the newest members of the regiment had been in the Corps at least three years. That had been one thing she'd insisted on. She wanted the 10th manned by experienced

Marines, even if they weren't necessarily experienced SpecOps members.

"Close enough," he said as the sounds of someone puking as the shuttle lurched once more reached them. "ETA in three, Angel," he added a moment later.

"Very good. Inform the flag." Leaving him to do so, she returned to the cabin. As she did, she nodded in satisfaction. Talbot and Connery moved through the cabin, checking on each of their people. Trusting them to let her know if there was anything she should be aware of, she activated her helmet and opened a private comm channel to her mother.

"We're three minutes from target," she reported. "Any update to our orders?"

"Negative. Download the information in the databanks on the platform and then set the destruct sequence. Do not take time to search for anyone left onboard."

"Understood. Download data, set charges and get the hell out of there," she confirmed.

"Ash, don't take unnecessary chances," Elizabeth said. "I know they've been putting up a fight but it still feels like this has been too easy."

Even though she knew her mother couldn't see, Ash nodded. She'd been worrying about the same thing. The fact her mother had the same concerns didn't reassure her. it did, however, confirm she'd been right to make sure several heavy armored Devil Dogs were on the shuttle.

"Understood. You and the admiral keep that in mind as well," she said. She did not want to risk losing either her mother or her godmother, not have losing Lucinda not that long ago. "We'll send heavy armor in first."

"Keep your link open, Ash."

"Understood." She paused and nodded to Talbot as the pilot announced they were beginning their approach to the defense plat-form. "Got to go, Mom. We're about to hit the target."

"Ash." That was all.

"I know, Mom. See you soon." She closed her eyes for a moment and said a quick prayer that nothing went wrong and she managed to bring all her people home after this mission. Then, as she opened them, she moved to stand next to the main hatch. "Listen up! We have one minute. Heavy armor out first. Secure the bay. Then we get to work. Questions?"

"Ma'am, no, ma'am!"

"Then let's get to it."

"Angel, Red Witch."

"Go, Red." She waited for the LAC commander to respond. "Enemy is trying to seal the bay."

Ash shook her head. She would never understand the enemy. Instead of surrendering and living, and possibly fighting another day, they would rather die. Well, if they were that determined to die, who was she to stop them?

"Blast us a whole, Red," she ordered.

"Roger that, Angel. Blasting a hole."

Ashlyn turned to the cockpit and watched their approach. The LACs flew ahead, weapons firing. The large defense platform shuddered as they hammered at the bay doors. Debris filled the space around the bay, a testament to the success of the LACs. One challenge met. How many more to go?

"Weapons hot, Ace," she said.

"Already done, Angel," he assured her. "Platform is venting atmosphere, ma'am."

Once again, she stepped into the cockpit. As she studied the readings from the platform, her mouth firmed. They needed to move fast, before the enemy managed to get reinforcements to the bay or the platform blew.

"Tell the other shuttles to hang back," she ordered. "It's clear the enemy is still onboard the platform. Let's not risk any more of our people than we have to."

"Roger that."

"Then take us in, Ace."

———

CONNERY LOOKED at the scene before her and smiled slightly. Ashlyn warned her to be ready for anything. She knew the colonel hadn't been happy that she couldn't send Talbot with her. A few of the new members of the 10th didn't know her or her history. All they saw was a brand new lieutenant, one they didn't know had seen more battle than most of them. At least Talbot had backed her when she suggested she lead the third group of Marines securing the defense platform's databanks. As the master gunnery sergeant noted, three teams increased their chances for success.

But this. . . this was not what she'd expected.

"Tank." She looked at the heavily armored Marine and his four prisoners. "Would you mind telling me where you found the strays?"

"Didn't find them, Artemis," he said, humor in his deep voice. "Then walked right up to Hound and me and said they wanted to make all friendly like."

"Really?"

She turned her attention to the four men. Then youngest she guessed to be about the colonel's age. The oldest, complete with thinning hair and, unless she missed her guess, more wrinkles than he'd had twelve hours ago, looked to be older than Admiral Tremayne by at least a decade. Each of them wore dark trousers and tunics. To the untrained eye, they looked like civilians. But she recognized the discipline in the way they stood and the wariness in their gazes. Unless she missed her guess, her squad had just found something even more valuable than the contents of the enemy database.

"Just how friendly did they try to be?" she asked, noting the scorching on Hound's armor.

"Well, one of them did have a bit of an itchy finger, Artemis," Hound answered.

"I see." She took a step forward, eyeing the prisoners closely. "Secure them. Then strip them and search them." When one of the four, the oldest and, unless she missed her guess, the one with the rank, opened his mouth to protest, she cut him off. "You opened fire on my men. You will stand down and do was instructed or I will order you spaced right now."

"Y-you can't!"

Now she smiled, a predatory smile that would have done Ashlyn proud. "I can and I will. And thank you for confirming my suspicions. That accent comes from only one system and it proves you have been conspiring with our enemies. Tank, Hound, you have your orders. Make our Midlothian guests a bit more uncomfortable."

"With pleasure, Artemis," Tank said and nodded to the rest of the squad to do as she ordered.

Leaving them to follow orders, she stepped away and signaled Ashlyn. As she waited for Ash to respond, she watched as Tank and Hound cuffed the man before letting the others begin stripping them. It didn't surprise her to see dog tags hanging around each man's neck or the various weapons her Marines located on them.

"Go ahead, Artemis," Ashlyn said a few moments later.

"Angel, we're about to head back to the shuttle with a gift for you. Four of them, in fact," she reported.

Silence met her announcement. She could picture Ashlyn as she processed what she'd said. Then, she heard her colonel chuckle almost evilly.

"Do you have confirmation, Artemis?"

Just to be sure, Connery stepped up to where one of the four stood. Her gloved fist closed around his dog tags and she pulled them from his neck. As she studied them, anger ran through her. She'd known what she would find, at least in general, but actually holding it in her hand was something else. It also meant she would need to keep an eye on Angel and make sure she didn't do anything foolish.

"It is confirmed, Angel." She held the dog tags up so Ashlyn could see them through her video pickup.

"Have you secured the data?"

"That's a roger."

"Then report back to the shuttle on the bounce, Artemis. I'm sure the admiral will be more than interested in having a chat with your new friends."

"On our way." She switched to a private channel. "Angel, are you all right?" she asked.

"Don't worry about me, kid. Just get your ass back to the shuttle."

"Roger that," she said and ended the transmission. Then she turned her attention to the prisoners. They stood, hands secured behind their backs, dressed only in their underwear. It meant the trip back to the landing bay would be a bit uncomfortable for them but she didn't care. Traitors and enemies of her homeworld didn't deserve to have it easy. "Angel wants us back to the shuttle on the bounce," she said. "Hound, you have point. Tank, Boomer, you are in charge of the prisoners. Whisper, you have the rear. Let's move out."

"You can't make us go like this!" the youngest prisoner protested. "We'll never make it."

Without hesitation, she closed the space between them in two quick strides. The man gasped and backed up until he found his escape blocked by the very solid figure of Tank. Connery didn't realize she'd pulled one of the several knives she carried into battle until she pressed it against the man's throat. Her free hand rested on the grip of her pistol.

"I can and I will," she snarled and pressed the edge of her blade harder against the soft tissue of his throat. He whimpered as the skin broke and blood welled up around the blade. "We surrendered. There are rules."

"Rules!" she spat. "Like the rules you broke by working with the enemy?" She forced herself to lower her blade and take a step back. "I'm going to put this to you in simple terms. You will shut the fuck up and keep your mouth shut or I will have you gagged. Each of you will do as my Marines say, when they say it. Failure to do so will be viewed as an attempt to not only escape but harm us and I will space you. You are worse than enemy combatants. You are in civilian clothing yet you are members of the military. That makes you spies or pirates and either allow me, under the laws of my home system, to execute you without benefit of a trial." She gave them a moment to consider what she said. "Please, one of you, test me to see if I will do as I say."

When none of them did, she motioned for the Marines to move out.

"Very good, Artemis. Who knew you could be such a bad ass?" Ashlyn chuckled over a secure link. "Now get back to the shuttle before anything else happens."

———

"Admiral, incoming from the planet's surface," the comms officer reported.

"Governor Harris?" she asked as she returned to her command chair.

"Unknown, ma'am. Message is, at the moment, voice only."

Tremayne frowned. For a moment, she studied the plot. The only icons indicating battle-worthy ships belonged to the allied attack force. The enemy ships had been captured or destroyed. The defense platforms had met the same fate. The remaining platforms would be destroyed as soon as the attack shuttles were clear. Even though groundside defenses had not been completely destroyed yet, their effectiveness had been greatly diminished. Could the so-called occupational governor finally be ready to surrender?

Not in the mood to play games, Tremayne considered her options. "Lieutenant, inform whoever is on the other end of that message to show themselves. If they haven't done so in the next two minutes, we will open fire on their location." Without her having to ask, Tactical plotted the coordinates of the strike and sent them to the LACs with orders to standby.

"You have Toliver Ooster, Admiral."

"Put him through." She leaned back, her right ankle resting on her left knee. A few moments later, the image on her holo screen changed from her official wallpaper to the face of a dark-skinned man. Everything about him oozed and screamed politician. Wary, she waited, wondering what he had to say.

"Admiral, I have taken over for Occupational Governor Harris. He's met with an, er, unfortunate accident."

One corner of Tremayne's mouth quirked up. She doubted Harris had met with an accident. Maybe an "accidental" assassination.

"That changes nothing, Mr. Ooster. Your time to surrender is past. I will give you one last chance to comply with my demands or we will begin our bombardment of the surface."

"Admiral," he began.

"Sixty seconds... thirty... ten... nine...."

"All right!" he all but screamed, sweat running down his cheeks.

"Evacuate your people from the groundside facilities. You have one hour. At the end of that time, we will begin eliminating those targets."

She nodded, signaling the comms officer to cut the link. Then she blew out a breath. Part of her wanted to celebrate. The entire battle had been easier and taken less time than she'd expected. But another part warned her not to relax. It had all seemed too easy. Until they destroyed their targets and were on their way home, she couldn't drop her guard. Too much could still happen.

"Signal our LACs and gunnery crews. They are to confirm their targets. We will open fire on my command in one hour."

Then, hopefully, they could head home. She wasn't foolish enough to think the Callusians would let this attack go unanswered. The only question was which of the cooperating systems would be targeted.

21

Glenn Spaceport
New Kilrain, Fuercon

President Harper watched as the shuttle came in for a landing. As they waited for the newcomers to disembark, his guards stepped a bit closer. Until they knew for sure the shuttle occupants presented no danger to the man, they would not let him get any closer.

A few moment later, the hatch slid open. Harper watched as a Marine, a Devil Dog if his eyes hadn't failed him, stepped outside. Armored, as much on alert as his own guards, the Marine checked the area. Then she turned back to the shuttle and nodded. Another armored Marine stepped out, followed closely by Admiral Tremayne, Brigadier General Shaw and two more armored Marines. Concerned, Harper waited. This once, he would do as his guards said and let the newcomers approach him instead of the other way around.

"Stand easy," he said as the six stopped before him and snapped to attention. As he did, his brow creased in concern to realize Ashlyn Shaw was one of the armored Marines. "Admiral, General, I assume there's a reason for the show of force."

Neither answered right away. Instead, they glanced around, as if making sure no one could overhear. Then Tremayne nodded, her expression a mix of resignation, frustration and humor. "There were a few developments during the mission we didn't report, Mr. President," she said. "Developments that caused Colonel Shaw to insist on taking a few extra precautions upon arrival."

"I see." Except he didn't. "Do we need to discuss them before we head out?"

"We can brief you on the salient points on the ride to the security complex, sir," Tremayne told him. "But it boils down to one thing: Lieutenant Connery and her squad got the confirmation we've been looking for in the form of four Midlothian *advisors*."

For a moment, Harper felt rooted in place. He stared at Tremayne, not sure he wanted to believe her or not. In spite of all the evidence implicating Midlothian before then, he had held out hope an ally had not betrayed them. It was one thing to consider certain elements of the Midlothian government had been working against them. it was another thing entirely to know the government itself had been. Yet, that wasn't exactly what Tremayne had said. He needed to hear what they'd learned from the prisoners before jumping to conclusions.

"We will discuss this in the aircar." He glanced at the six and made up his mind. "Admiral, you, General Shaw and Colonel Shaw will accompany me. The rest can follow in the next car." He heard his head bodyguard start to protest and simply shook his head. He needed to know what the three had to say before they arrived at the security complex.

"If I may have a moment, Mr. President?" When he dipped his chin in agreement, Ashlyn turned to the three Marines who had spread out in a protective formation around her mother and Tremayne. A slight smile touched his lips as she used hand signals to give them their instructions. A moment later, she turned back. "Thank you, sir."

"Now, you said you got proof," he said as the aircar pulled away from the spaceport a short time later. "I assume you meant proof of Midlothian involvement."

"Yes, sir," Tremayne said. "Proof in the form of four captured Midlothian officers. Two naval and two army. They surrendered when Colonel Shaw and members of the Devil Dogs boarded a defense platform. Their mission had been to download the contents of the platform's database. Lieutenant Connery and her squad hit the jackpot when the four surrendered."

"Have they been more cooperative than Hughes?"

Tremayne's smile answered his question. But, instead of explaining, she looked at Ashlyn and nodded. Curious, Harper settled back and waited, wondering what the colonel had to say.

"Lieutenant Connery put the fear of God in them, Mr. President," Ashlyn said proudly. "She pointed out they had presented themselves while dressed in civilian clothing. They had not identified themselves as military even though they clearly were. Then she pointed out that, under our laws, she would be well within her rights to space them then and there as either spies or pirates. They decided it was in their best interests to cooperate."

"Now be honest, Colonel. The fact she marched them through corridors of the defense platform in nothing but their underwear might have help loosen their tongues. They didn't know if the next corner they turned would lead to an area without an atmosphere," Elizabeth Shaw said with a smile.

"True."

Harper looked between mother and daughter and then shook his head. A smile lifted the corners of his mouth and, a moment later, he chuckled almost evilly. Then he sobered. "What did they have to say?"

"Like Hughes, they want assurances that their cooperation won't be disclosed and, no, I did not give it to them. Instead, I promised to personally deliver them to their embassy here, stopping only long enough to make sure the ambassador knows how helpful they've been."

Harper looked at her in surprise. He'd known she would do whatever was necessary to protect Fuercon. What he had never seen before was this streak of ruthlessness. It didn't bother him. Far from it. If he were honest, he approved.

"And?" he prompted.

Tremayne handed him her datapad. The moment the first of the data scrolled across it, he knew the mission had been a bigger success than he'd dared hope.

———

EVAN MOREAU MOVED INTO POSITION. As she did, she smiled slightly, confidently. She still couldn't believe her luck. Harper's press secretary had announced earlier that day he would be holding a press conference to announce the results of a "joint exercise" between the Fuerconese Navy and the navies of several of its allies. A few calls and she had the information she needed. Not only did she know the time but the location of the press conference. Better yet, it was one where security would look tight but would be anything but. Now she could fulfill her contract with Watchman and, hopefully, take care of a little personal business as well.

The only possible snag was gaining access to the best observation point. She'd had to move quickly. A few changes to her appearance and then she presented herself at the embassy gates as a courier with a delivery for the ambassador from the Braxian ambassador. A low-level clerk cleared her for entry. Once inside, she stepped into a powder room on the second floor where she was supposed to be making her delivery. When she emerged a few minutes later, she bore a striking resemblance to that bitch Fertig. If everything went according to plan, Watchman's pet would soon find herself answering some very difficult questions.

Then came the wait. She moved almost silently across the embassy roof, carefully choosing her position. It took less than three minutes to get everything set up. Bipod for the rifle, scope in place. Jammers to prevent anyone on the lower levels from calling for help. Explosives just in case she needed a diversion to get away. Even the building itself became her weapon of sorts. Anyone looking up from street level would see nothing out of the ordinary. The muzzle of the sniper rifle disappeared in the shadow cast by the ornamental cutouts of parapet surrounding the roof. It also served to hide her from view. By the time the authorities figured out where the shot came from, she'd be gone and the damage would be done.

It had to work. This was her only chance to get it right and get away before embassy security or Fertig decided to put a slug between her eyes. Nerves higher than usual, she took a moment to calm them. She breathed deeply in and then out, reminding herself of her training. How ironic it was that Fuercon had trained her for this sort of mission. Too bad it hadn't recognized her talents and put them to use.

She checked her rifle one last time and then got into position. As she did, movement below and almost half a mile away caught her eye. She adjusted the scope and smiled. Soon, very soon, her wait would be over. Coming down the street were three aircars, the second one flying the colors of the president.

A few moments later, the aircars parked down the road from the embassy. Harper's guards as well as armored Marines climbed out of the front and rear aircars. At the same time, the front doors of the security building opened and more security appeared. They assumed positions around the aircars. Some pulled weapons while others scanned the area. In most situations, their actions would be enough to keep Harper safe. But this wasn't most situations and she was not an ordinary assassin.

Finally, one of the guards approached the president's car and nodded. A moment later, the doors closest to the security building opened. As they did, Moreau snugged the rifle stock against her shoulder. As she looked through the scope, her ocular implant synced with it. There was a moment's disorientation. Then she smiled. She was the cat and Harper was about to learn what it was like to be the mouse.

She waited, wanting him to move away from the aircar and the safety it represented. Good as she was, she knew her angle wasn't the best. There was the slight possibility of her missing her shot. If that happened, she wanted to insure he couldn't get away.

"That's it," she murmured. "Just a little bit farther."

Then the world slammed to a halt. Unable to believe her luck, she scanned the faces of the others who'd exited the aircar behind the man. She knew each of them, recognized them from media and her own briefing materials. Then she saw the one face that had haunted her so much of her adult life. Now it was personal. She'd take the shot and then she'd deal with Harper. Two targets and she would finally get her life back.

One breath. Two. A third and then she squeezed the trigger. Joy unlike any she'd known in years raced through her as the target dropped. Then she made a quick adjustment. There was still one more target to hit. Once she had, she could get the hell out of there and never look back.

22

Elizabeth glanced around, eyes narrowed, missing no detail. She had liked the president's plan to hold a press conference outside the security complex no more than had Ashlyn. It went beyond the fact she preferred staying behind the scenes. There hadn't been enough time to set up proper security. More importantly, there was still a great deal they needed to brief him on. She understood why he wanted to finally let the public know how Midlothian had betrayed them but the Marine in her did not like it. There were still too many unanswered questions and too many things that could go wrong.

"Ash, stay close to him," she said softly.

Ashlyn nodded and took a step toward the president. As she did, one of his guards looked at her in surprise. Then he stepped back, letting her take the lead. She glanced around, catching Connery's eye. Elizabeth caught the way she signaled the young lieutenant to close in even as she sent Talbot and Private Crowley to watch the perimeter.

Satisfied she had done all she could, Elizabeth turned to see where Tremayne had gone. As she did, a flash from above and down the block caught her eye. It happened so fast, she almost ignored it.

Then every instinct called for her to take action. Her subconscious recognized the flash.

"Gun!" she yelled as she spun in the direction she'd last seen the president.

The sound of a shot echoed against the buildings lining both sides of the street. Harper's security team closed in on the president, but not before Ashlyn acted. She didn't hesitate. She leapt at the man, her arms wrapping around him as she tackled him to the ground. Members of his security leapt on top of them, adding their bodies to hers as layers of protection.

"Loco, Zed, get a trajectory!" Connery ordered as she pulled her comm. Then she turned and saw both Elizabeth and Tremayne standing there. Cursing, she raced across the plaza in their direction. She grabbed them both and all but dragged them inside the building, shoving them at a couple of Marines responding to the call for help. "Keep them inside. It's your head if anything happens to them." With that, she ran back outside.

"Liz?" Tremayne looked at the pandemonium beyond the clear doors.

"Corporal, send for Colonel Santiago and contact General Okafor," she said, cursing silently even as she issued her orders. "I want the block cordoned off. Capital security will want to take point but, until further orders, we will be in charge of security." She watched as he stepped back to do as she said. Then she turned to Tremayne. "Stay here. Brief Okafor when she gets down here. I need to take control out there."

Grimly, Tremayne gave a quick nod. Then she pulled her own comm. Elizabeth didn't wait to see who she was contacting. There was too much to do and, if they didn't act quickly, the shooter would get away.

Her breath caught as members Harper's security team helped knelt on the ground near where she'd seen the president and her daughter go down. The president told them to get back as he rolled to his hands and knees. Before he could stand, several of his guards grabbed him and all but dragged him into the aircar. Moments later, it sped away, leaving the rest of them to figure out what happened and who was responsible.

"Loco, anything?" Connery called as she hurried to Elizabeth's side. "Ma'am, you need to get inside. I have this," she added, taking the woman's arm and turning her away from where others knelt near where she'd last seen the president.

"Angel?" she asked softly, barely daring to breathe.

"I'll find out. I promise. But I need you to get out of the line of fire." When Elizabeth didn't move, Connery stepped in front of her. "Ma'am, please. I promise, I will do everything I can to make sure Angel's all right. But I can't do that if I'm having to worry about you." She swore softly when Elizabeth remained rooted where she stood. "General Shaw, with all due respect, you are not in armor and you aren't armed. You are a distraction and a danger right now. Please get your butt inside and wait there until I come to you." Not waiting for Elizabeth to respond, she motioned to one of the Marines exiting the building and ordered him to take her inside.

"Artemis, we have a preliminary trajectory," Talbot said as he hurried in their direction.

Elizabeth jerked out of her escort's grasp and took a step forward. "Where?" she demanded as Okafor joined them.

"The Midlothian embassy."

"Lieutenant Connery, take what Marines you need from here and set up a perimeter around the embassy. Call in the Devil Dogs. Once they are in position, move in. I don't give a damn if the ambassador tries to prevent you from entering. Someone shot at the president and, in the process, injured Angel. We will find the shooter and they will face justice.," Okafor said. coldly. "Understood?"

"Understood, ma'am. Loco, call it in. I'll get things organized here."

Elizabeth swallowed hard and looked to where her daughter lay. Blood pooled under her. Seeing it, she fought the panic rising in her. Ash wore her armor. That would have protected her from the worst the projectile could have done. The armor would also be working to stabilize her conditions. All they had to do was make sure the medics got there quickly, before she lost too much blood.

God, who had done this to her?

More importantly, why?

———

MOREAU ROLLED to her knees and began breaking down her rifle. Quickly, carefully, she placed the pieces in its carrying case. All she had to do now was get out of the embassy. Once she had, she would disappear into the panic on the streets below. In a day or two, she'd send confirmation of the hit to Watchman. Then her life would be her own again. She'd get off Fuercon and recharge. She'd return. There were loose ends to be tied up. But they could wait. The rest of it was done and she felt better than she had in years.

She snapped the case lid shut and smiled. Her smile froze and her relief at having completed her mission flowed away as the unmistakable feel of a muzzle pressed against her temple registered. Icy fear lay heavy in the pit of her stomach. Before she could react, a hand reached around her and relieved her of her rifle case. Another hand shoved her to the rooftop. A knee was painfully planted in the small of her back. Panic set in and she tried to fight. Except she couldn't. There were too many of them, too many hands holding her. Forcing her arms behind her back. Her wrists were secured, and she was roughly hauled to her feet.

She found herself face-to-face with both the ambassador and Fertig. It didn't make any sense. Then it did. They had decided, for whatever reason, to work together. That put her at a disadvantage. All she could do, for now at least, was wait and pray they didn't kill her outright. She didn't think they would. They would still have Watchman to answer to – unless he'd authorized this action. No, he wouldn't have. She still had value to him.

Damn it, she should have fled long ago.

"Search her," Fertig told one of the guards. "She'll have at least three weapons hidden on her somewhere."

"You bitch!" Moreau spat.

Fertig's hand flashed out, catching the woman across the chin. Moreau cried out and staggered back a step before the guard stopped her, holding her upright. She tried to lash out with her right foot, but he sidestepped her. A moment later, he wrapped his hand in her hair and pulled her head back, painfully exposing her throat.

"You shouldn't have tried to get clever," Fertig said. "This attempt to discredit those of us at the embassy will be your last mistake. But don't worry, we aren't going to kill you. The ambassador has a much better plan for you." She smiled and lightly patted the woman's cheek.

"W-what are you going to do?"

"You not only tried to implicate us in the plan to assassinate Harper, but you failed to kill him," Kalmár said. "You also let your personal agenda take precedence over your orders. She you are going to be sacrificed. But, as Ms. Fertig said, not by us. We'll leave that to the Fuerconese. We'll turn you over to them. You will serve as an excellent example as to what happens to those who betray Midlothian."

"You can't." She struggled against the hands holding her. "I know too much."

Fertig glanced at Kalmár and gave him a nod. He inclined his head once and reached into his jacket pocket. Moreau's eyes widened in fear. She struggled frantically as she recognized the vial he held. The hand wrapped in her hair once again pulled her head back. Other hands held her head in a steel-like vise. Fertig smiled as she reached over and covered Moreau's mouth and nose, cutting off her air. Tears ran down her cheeks and soon her lungs burned from lack of oxygen.

Suddenly, Fertig removed her hand and she could breathe again. Instinct took over. Moreau opened her mouth and drew a deep breath. When she did, the ambassador broke the vial and held it in front of her mouth. Almost instantly, her mind numbed as the drug spread through her. Her struggles lessened to nothing in a matter of a minute or two.

The hands, all but the one twined in her hair released her. Her heart pounded and her brain screamed for her body to respond. But it didn't. It wouldn't. She knew it. She'd used this same drug many times before. She had seen its effects as her victims watched helplessly as she killed them. Or left them to die. Never had she thought it would be used against her. Damn them all. Did they think she wouldn't have safeguards in place? She'd take them all down, even if they killed her.

"You really are doing one last service for Midlothian, my dear," Fertig said as she motioned for the guards to lift Moreau to her feet. "You are proving to the Fuerconese that we aren't the enemy. I'll be sure to let Mr. Watchman know how well you performed this last mission for him."

A moan of protest was all she could manage as Fertig reached for her face with one hand. In the other, she held a white capsule. As if she could hear the screams of denial, of terror, in Moreau's mind, the woman smiled and lightly caressed her cheek with her thumb. "Don't worry. This is just to throw the Fuerconese off the track. It won't harm you – much." She gently opened Moreau's mouth and inserted the capsule. Her gloved hand firmly closes the woman's mouth, crushing the capsule between her teeth.

"You'd best return to your office, Mr. Ambassador. You can monitor what happens from there," Fertig said as she bent and retrieved the rifle case. "I'll report to you as soon as this trash has been dealt with."

"Make sure the Fuerconese understand we will do everything we can to assist in their investigation," he said. He looked down at Moreau and smiled slightly. "I'll begin drafting our report to Watchman about what happened."

Fertig nodded and motioned for the two security guards to take Moreau on. Unable to move her head to look around, all Moreau can see is the floor as she is dragged off the roof and inside the embassy. They continue down the corridor toward the life. No one spoke. No one made any attempt to ease her fears. Instead, once inside the lift, Fertig secured the doors and snapped her fingers. The guards held

Moreau between them as the woman struck her first in the face and then the ribs. Time and again she struck. Unable to defend herself, Moreau wondered if the talk of turning her over to the Fuerconese had been a ruse. Then Fertig stopped and once again reached out, this time lifting her prisoner's face.

"We couldn't let them think you surrendered without a fight, could we?" the woman asked with a smile.

The elevator gave a slight lurch and started on its way down. All too soon, Moreau realized she had been dragged outside. Afternoon sun beat down on her. She watched as the marble entry hall turned to stone pavers. The guards' boots sounded loudly against the pavers as they moved further from the building. Finally, they stopped and she saw the base of the fence that surrounded the embassy. A low moan escaped her lips, the best she could do. Someone, she assumed it was Fertig, cuffed her behind the ear and told her to shut up.

"Lieutenant, here is your shooter. We discovered her on the roof of the embassy after finding the body of one of our secretaries," Fertig said as the gate opened. The guards dragged her out and off of embassy grounds.

"What happened to her?" a woman asked as she lifted Moreau's head and looked in her eyes.

"My best guess is she tried to poison herself when she realized she couldn't escape. It wouldn't be the first time that's happened."

"Very well. The Fuerconese Marine Corps appreciates your assistance. It is my understanding that President Harper wishes to have a word with the ambassador in the next day or two."

"Please tell the president that the ambassador looks forward to speaking with him."

"I will make sure to pass on the message. Please let me know if there is anything else we can do to assist Fuercon."

Moreau's mind screamed in denial, in anger, as she was dragged off. All her careful plans, all her contingencies and they'd been for naught. How?

Damn it, how had it all gone so wrong?

23

The door slid open with a muted whoosh. As it did, Elizabeth drew a deep breath and braced herself. She didn't worry about anyone getting inside in an attempt to hurt Ashlyn again. Short of bringing a full company of armed and armored Marines with them, no one without the proper authorization could get near the younger woman. The Devil Dogs, along with the Warlords, had taken it upon themselves to set up security for their injured CO. Not only were guards posted outside Ashlyn's room, but others stood posts throughout the medical center. Unlike the hospital's standard security, the Marines were not only armed but armored – and they were ready to do whatever it took to keep Ashlyn safe. Elizabeth knew she should tell them to go home but she couldn't. Not until she was confident those responsible for injuring Ash had been captured. Besides, she had a feeling even a direct order wouldn't be enough to send most of them away. They were as devoted to her daughter as she was to them.

Turning, hoping this time the doctors had good news, she braced herself for the bad. Even though they had assured her Ashlyn would eventually recover, Elizabeth had her doubts. How could she not when her daughter looked so pale and almost fragile as she lay on the hospital bed? From the moment Ash first said she wanted to be a Marine, Elizabeth had prepared herself for the possibility she'd lose her eldest child in battle. Military service meant sacrifice, often the ultimate sacrifice. But this...this she hadn't been ready for. How could she be? Ashlyn had made it home safely once again, only to be struck down by a sniper.

Instead of seeing one of the many doctors treating Ashlyn, Elizabeth found herself face-to-face with Helen Okafor. Before she could brace to attention, Okafor shook her head. The expression on her face said it all. This wasn't an official visit.

Without a word, the general moved almost soundlessly across the room to stand next to Ashlyn's bed. A slight smile touched her lips, easing some of her worry, to see Jake curled up at his mother's side. Then, in a very ungeneral-like manner, the woman rested a light hand first on Ashlyn's forehead and then her cheek. When she looked up at Elizabeth, worry once again clouded her dark eyes.

"How is she?"

"I'll live." Ashlyn's voice was soft and filled with pain. But her eyes no longer looked unfocused and, when she glanced down at Jake sleeping next to her, a slight smile lifted the corners of her mouth. "Thirsty."

Elizabeth poured a cup of water from the waiting pitcher. Carefully, she helped Ashlyn lift her head enough to sip from the cup. A moment later, her daughter lay back. Pain etched deep lines in her face, but she had a little more color. Reassured, Elizabeth set the cup on the bedside table and signaled the nursing station that Ashlyn was awake.

"W-what happened?" Ash asked.

"You were shot trying to protect the President," Okafor said.

Ash's brow furrowed and she shook her head. "Don't remember."

"It's all right, love. The doctor said that might be the case." Elizabeth grasped her hand.

"Your mother's right." Okafor smiled reassuringly. "When you get out of here, you can remind me to never question when you suggest it might be a good idea to be armored. The fact you were wearing your light armor probably saved your life. It slowed the projectile and then kept you stable until medical help arrived."

"Corporal Connery also proved she's going to be every bit as good as Adamson or Talbot, Ash. Even as she called out orders to find the shooter, she was working to make sure your armor was stabilizing you. Her quick action probably saved you." Elizabeth's voice hitched and she cleared her throat. Ashlyn didn't need to know how close it had been, not yet at any rate.

"W-was anyone else hurt?"

"No. The shooter only managed to get off a single shot. We'll tell you everything after you've gotten some more rest." Elizabeth glanced over her shoulder as the door once again opened. This time Ashlyn's lead doctor stepped inside.

"Colonel, your mother and General Okafor are going to give us a few minutes alone so I can check you," Dr. Ahern said as he stopped at the foot of the bed. "Your son can stay." Now he grinned. "I'm not sure we could get him to leave you. He's been very adamant about needing to stay and make sure you're all right."

Ashlyn smiled and ran a hand over her sleeping son's head. When she looked up at Elizabeth, her mother saw her concern.

"You're going to be all right, Ash. I promise." She bent and brushed her lips against her daughter's cheek. "I'll be right outside. Dr. Ahern will send for me as soon as he's done here." The look she gave the doctor left no doubt what she'd do should he fail to comply.

She waited until Ash nodded and then she followed Okafor out of the room. The moment the door closed behind them, Elizabeth leaned against the wall. Without realizing it, she slowly slid down until she sat on the floor. Knees drawn up, head bent, she fought for control. Since arriving at the hospital, she'd refused to let her fear surface. She'd done everything she could to reassure the rest of the family, the Marines who arrived to check on Ashlyn and then all the others. She'd been strong so Jake wouldn't know how badly injured his mother was. She had maintained, but she didn't know how much longer she could continue doing so.

For hours she had stood watch outside the operating room as the doctors worked to save Ashlyn. Then she had followed as her daughter was moved to a room. In the hours that followed, she hadn't moved from her daughter's side. Even when Abe and Kate tried to get her to go to the cafeteria with them, she'd refused. She'd wanted to be there when Ashlyn woke.

"It's all right, Liz."

Okafor sat next to her. A laugh, slightly hysterical, bubbled up and Elizabeth shook her head. What would the staff, much less the two Devil Dogs standing guard on either side of the door, think to see a brigadier general and the Commandant of the Marine Corps sitting on the floor like a couple of kids?

"She's going to be all right."

She said it more to convince herself than Okafor. It was the mantra she'd repeated over and over again for the last twenty-four hours. She might finally be to the point of accepting it. Maybe if she told herself that often enough, she would finally believe it.

"I know she is." Okafor rested a reassuring hand on her arm for a moment. Then she leaned back and stared down the corridor. "She's going to want answers. We might be able to put them off for a little while, but it won't last."

"She's not the only one who wants answers." Anger laced Elizabeth's voice. She wanted more than answers. She wanted time alone with those responsible for hurting her daughter. It wouldn't take her long to get the answers they all wanted. Of course, she'd then have to turn herself in to face a court martial, but it would be worth it if it meant an end to the conspiracy against not only Ashlyn but their home system. "Have you heard anything?"

Okafor shook her head. "No. Rico promised to brief us as soon as possible. My sources tell me he hasn't gone off-duty since the shooting."

Elizabeth sighed and closed her eyes. She trusted Santiago to find the answers, but it couldn't happen soon enough. Before she could say so, the sounds of someone approaching from down the corridor reached them. She opened her eyes in time to see Okafor climb to her feet. Elizabeth pressed the palm of her right hand to the floor and prepared to stand. Before she could, Okafor told her to stay where she was. She would handle this.

Too tired emotionally and physically to argue, Elizabeth obeyed. She watched as Corporal Connery, along with Adamson and Talbot, approached. Connery and Talbot wore light armor. Adamson, leaning heavily on a pair of crutches, wore MARPAT. All were armed. Seeing the case Connery carried, Elizabeth frowned slightly. As they neared, the brigadier general wondered what had happened now.

"Report." Okafor spoke softly but the command was clear.

"Teams of Devil Dogs and Warlords are alternating guard shifts here at the hospital and the Shaw's home. They will continue to do so until the colonel is released or until we are sure everyone responsible for her being injured have been taken into custody. So far, all shifts are being covered by volunteers and I have received messages from not only the other Marine units on-planet but from naval personnel as well saying they wish to assist," Talbot answered.

"We have increased security around HQ and the space port, ma'am," Anderson said as she shifted a bit uncomfortably on her crutches. "I've also been coordinating with President Harper's security force. We will be informed if additional assistance is needed there."

"Excellent." Okafor paused for a moment and, even though she couldn't see the general's expression, Elizabeth had a feeling she was thinking hard. "Inform your people that they are to tighten surveillance on their targets. We will proceed with the next phase of the op as soon as we receive the go-ahead. You may tell them I expect that to happen soonest."

"Ooh-rah, ma'am." There could be no mistaking the newly minted captain's desire for vengeance. "With your permission, Ma'am, how's the colonel?" Adamson looked past Okafor to where Elizabeth sat against the wall.

"She's conscious. The doctor's with her." She wanted to be able to say more, to reassure two of her daughter's closest friends and the young woman she knew was fast becoming a friend, but she couldn't, not until she knew more.

"Ma'am, if she needs anything, you're to let us know," Talbot told her.

"I will, Loco." She smiled at the Master Guns' surprise at her use of his call sign.

Before anything else could be said, the door opened and Dr. Ahern stepped outside. Seeing him, Elizabeth climbed to her feet. With Okafor at her side, the others just behind them, she waited, her mother's fear overriding everything else. Then, when Ahern smiled and reached out to lightly rest a hand on her shoulder, her knees felt as if they'd buckle under the weight of her relief.

"Ash?"

"She is going to be fine," he assured her. "I'm not going to lie. It will take time. She's got at least a month, possibly more, of recovery time ahead of her, but she will be all right." He paused, making eye contact with each of them. Then, as the sounds of others approaching reached them, he looked down the corridor. He waited until Abe and Kate joined them, their expressions as worried as Elizabeth's had been, before continuing. "As I was saying, Colonel Shaw should make a full recovery. She is responding well to treatment, but she still has a long road ahead of her. I anticipate she will be off duty at least a month and on limited duty for at least as long afterwards. As I told you when she came in, her injuries were serious. We were lucky she wore her armor and that Corporal Connery acted as quickly as she did."

Relieved, Elizabeth looked at Connery and nodded once. Later, she'd make sure the young woman knew just how much she appreciated all she'd done for Ashlyn. Then, reaching for Abe's hand, she turned her attention back to the doctor. "When can she start having visitors?"

"In a day or two." Ahern pinned them all with a firm look. "I understand you need to give her the outline of what happened. If you don't, she's only going to worry and that isn't good for her. But that is the only thing close to dealing with her duties she is to have anything to do with until I say otherwise. She needs to focus on getting well and nothing else right now."

"We understand," Okafor assured him.

"I also want you to go home and get some rest, General Shaw. Your husband or daughter can spell you for a few hours."

"But," Elizabeth started to protest.

"I understand, truly." Ahern's expression softened. "But you haven't slept in more than a day. Just as she doesn't need to worry about the regiment, she also doesn't need to worry about you."

"Mom, you and Dad can take Jake home. I'll sit with her until you get back," Kate said softly.

"We will be glad to take turns sitting with her as well, ma'am," Adamson said. Talbot and Connery nodded in agreement.

"We'll set something up," Okafor said before Elizabeth could respond. "You three go check on her now. Let her know everything is all right."

Elizabeth nodded and motioned for her husband and daughter to go ahead. Then she turned to Connery. "Corporal, might I ask what you're up to?" As she spoke, she motioned to the case the young woman held in one hand.

"I thought the colonel might feel a bit better with some of her own clothes, ma'am."

Elizabeth nodded and did her best not to smile. She had no doubt there was more than clothes in the case. It wouldn't surprise her one bit to discover Connery had packed a few "toys" that would help keep Ashlyn safe should an assassin somehow manage to get past the guards outside.

"Very good." She nodded in appreciation and started back to Ash's room. She paused at the door and turned back. "MJ, I'll take you home. I promise I won't be long. Loco, I'm trusting you and Freya to keep my daughter safe."

With that, she opened the door and stepped inside. Ashlyn was going to be all right. She had to believe that. Nothing else was acceptable.

———

ASHLYN CAREFULLY CHANGED POSITIONS. As she did, she clenched her jaw against the pain. She'd been injured worse before. That was the cost of being a Marine in wartime. But she didn't remember it hurting so badly. Nor had her mother been around those first few days afterwards, worried and hovering. That was bad enough. Worse were the grim faces of the Marines standing guard inside, and she suspected outside, her room.

When she first regained consciousness, their presence sent her pulse racing fast enough a nurse had come running into her room. Before she even realized why fear shot through her like a wildfire, Elizabeth had sent everyone from the room. Understanding, guilt, even anger darkened her mother's eyes. Then, carefully helping her change positions, the woman had apologized. None of them had considered what Ash might think to wake and find herself under armed guard.

At least now she knew the guards were there to protect her. The Tarsus penal colony was behind her and those responsible for sending her there had met their justice. At least most of them had. She had no doubt some had managed to escape but, if she had anything to say about it, that wouldn't last long. However, for the moment at least, she needed to focus on recovering.

"Do you need more pain meds?" Elizabeth asked in concern.

"No."

She did, but she wasn't going to tell her mother. She had spent much of the last three days sleeping because the doctors had kept her pumped full of drugs. Part of her understood. Her body needed time to heal. Even with the nanites doing their magic, it was going to take time to recover and it was going to hurt – a lot. Everyone seemed so worried and so determined to make sure she didn't suffer any more pain than absolutely necessary. While she appreciated it, she also needed answers and she wouldn't get them if the doctors put her under again.

"Ashlyn."

She closed her eyes and prayed for patience. It was bad enough her mother, not to mention her father and sister, had been hovering since she first regained consciousness. Now Okafor stood next to her bed, looking as concerned as Elizabeth. The commandant had arrived a few minutes earlier along with Rico Santiago. His presence was the real reason she did not want another painkiller yet. She wanted – no, she needed – to know what he could tell her about what happened.

"I promise I'll let you know if I start hurting too badly." That was all she'd give them. Now it was their turn, whether they liked it or not. "What about the shooter?"

Instead of answering, Santiago looked first to Okafor and then to Elizabeth. Seeing it, Ashlyn all but growled in frustration. If she could have done so without hurting badly enough she'd possibly lose consciousness, she would have crossed her arms. Of course, the effect wouldn't be as dramatic as if she could do so while on her feet. But she knew better than to even try that. If she did, assuming she managed to stand before her mother forced her back onto the mattress, she'd fall on her face.

To her embarrassment, both Elizabeth and Okafor looked at her and chuckled. As they did, she narrowed her eyes, glaring.

"You were right, Liz. She does look exactly like Jake when he doesn't want to do as he's told," the commandant said, a twinkle in her eyes.

"I'd remind you the doctors said I wasn't to stress about anything but that might be considered insubordinate," Ashlyn muttered. "I might even be tempted to remind you that, after being the target of a conspiracy for so long, holding information back from me might trigger my paranoia."

For a moment, no one said anything. They didn't need to. Their expressions said it all. Each of them looked surprised by her comment and then angry. She had a feeling they weren't angry with her but with themselves. Elizabeth cursed softly. Then she bent and carefully helped Ashlyn as she tried to sit up some. The bed adjusted to her new position and Elizabeth tucked the sheet around her waist before lightly kissing her cheek.

"We didn't mean to upset you, Ash. It's just that we've been so worried."

"I know, Mom. But you have to understand that the not knowing is harder on me than knowing the truth." She waited, watching her mother until Elizabeth nodded slowly. Once she had, Ash turned her attention to the others. "Rico?"

"When you're stronger, you can review the full report, Ash." When she opened her mouth to protest, he gave her a look that had her snapping it closed. "But I will give you the high points, such as they are."

"What do you mean?" she asked with more than a trace of suspicion.

"Quite simply, we have more questions now than we did before."

She cursed softly. How long would it take to finally get the answers they needed? How many more were going to have to die before then?

"Just tell me." She nodded in thanks as her mother handed her a mug of coffee.

"We have the shooter. Thanks to Lieutenant Connery's fast think-ing, a team of Devil Dogs traced the shot's trajectory to the Midlothian Embassy. When they arrived, they didn't have to storm the gates as they were prepared to do. In fact, the ambassador and members of the embassy's security team were waiting for them. They had the shooter in custody and were ready, even willing, to hand her over."

Ashlyn frowned. Had they been wrong about the Midlothians or was the ambassador playing some kind of game to throw them off the scent?

"Who?" she asked.

"Evan Moreau."

Ashlyn hissed in pain as she sat up straighter. Instantly, Elizabeth was there, easing her back against the mattress. Before she could ask if Ash was all right, Ash waved her off. Moreau? Maybe now she'd get answers to some of the questions that had been plaguing her for so long.

"And?" She drawled out the word.

"Like I said, we have more questions than answers – again." Santiago ran a hand over his short-cropped hair, his expression frustrated. "As we'd suspected, the Moreau identity is fake. It is also the best I've ever encountered. It's no wonder she managed to live and work under it as a successful businesswoman here in the capital for years. Nothing about it sent up any red flags."

He turned and paced across the small room. Ashlyn watched, worried, as he stopped before the window and looked outside. When he turned back, he looked as if he might start punching holes in the wall any moment. That wasn't good, not from him. One of the things that made him so good at his job was the fact he never let his emotions get the better of him.

"Ash, I promise, I will find out who she is. No fake ID is beyond breaking, and I will break hers." He shoved his hands into his pockets and stared at the floor for a moment. When he looked up, he blew out a breath before continuing. "As I've told General Okafor and FleetCom, what you have to understand is this goes beyond fake papers. Moreau changed her appearance with more than mere enhancements. She's had extensive surgery. The specialists we've called in are still trying to determine just how much and to what extent. Right now, they are confident it includes facial and body sculpting, not just a change in hair color but in hair itself. That takes time and a great deal of money and hurts like hell from what they've told me. There's more and it is in the report when you're strong enough to go through it. Let's leave it with the opinion that she looks nothing like she did before the surgery."

Ashlyn listened in growing concern as he continued describing what they knew and what they had inferred. Moreau somehow had the connections to remove her DNA tags from not only the computer records on Fuercon but from those records held by its allies. Of course, that assumed she had been off of Fuercon before her capture and Santiago would bet good money she had. Some of the treatments she'd received weren't available on their homeworld or even in the system. That meant she had money and connections, both of which they had to find.

"Right now, my people are working to track Moreau's every movement for the last six months. We're looking for her bolt-holes, other aliases she used and where she might have worked. I also have people, inside and out, keeping an eye on the Midlothian embassy and its employees. Despite what the ambassador has said, someone inside the embassy was involved in your shooting. They had to be. There is no way Moreau could have gained access to the grounds, much less the embassy roof, otherwise. The ambassador and his people are being *helpful* even though they have given us nothing to work with."

Ashlyn didn't need to see the suspicion in his eyes to know they were being anything but. "What has she said?"

When Santiago didn't respond, she looked first to Okafor and then to her mother. Neither woman would meet her eyes. Frustrated, worried, she fisted one hand on top of the sheet. Then she turned her attention back to Santiago. "Rico?"

"She hasn't told us anything. She can't."

For a moment, she looked at him, not sure she had heard right. "What do you mean she can't? You said you had her in custody."

"We do." He blew out a long breath and then gently sat on the edge of her bed. "Ash, we don't know what happened. When the Midlothians turned her over to us, she was conscious but unresponsive. They denied doing anything to her. In fact, they suggested she must have taken some sort of poison or other drug just before they arrested her. The doctors who examined her once your Devil Dogs got her back to the security building found the remnants of a capsule in her mouth."

"But?" She had a feeling she wasn't going to like what he had to say.

"Test results confirm the capsule's contents wouldn't explain her current condition." He nodded when she looked at him in surprise. "Unfortunately, we have proof of no other explanation. Not that it fools any of us. However it was done, Moreau's alive but locked in a waking coma of sorts. Until the medicals could figure out what happened and how to counteract it, she isn't going to tell us anything."

Ashlyn nodded, frustrated she was stuck in bed. She couldn't even get up to pace. Damn it, the woman who had targeted her, who had been part of the conspiracy that led to her people dying and to others, herself including, being sent to the penal colony, was in their hands finally. But it did them no good. Worse, they now had a connection between the woman and the Midlothians. Santiago had been right when he said all they had were even more questions now than before Ash was shot. Unfortunately, it was a connection they couldn't explore as long as Moreau remained non-responsive.

"Ash, look at me." Santiago waited until she did. "You aren't going to be released to desk duty for some time. But that doesn't mean you can't use your mind. I plan to put you to work, starting right now. Here's an image of Moreau. Do you recognize her?"

Ashlyn looked at the image displayed on his datapad. To the best of her recollection, she'd never crossed paths with the woman. Still, there was something about her eyes, something familiar. She couldn't place it. Nor did she mention it, for fear it was nothing more than an artifact of the drugs she had been on.

"No." She shook her head.

Before she could say anything else, a single knock sounded at the door. It slid open. Instantly, everyone in the room snapped to attention. Where she lay on the bed, Ash tried to sit up straighter, only to be held down by a firm hand on her shoulder. Elizabeth hissed at her to stay put. That was followed by a direct order from President Harper to do as her mother said.

"I can't stay long," he said as he moved to stand next to the bed. "But I wanted to thank you, Colonel. Your actions saved my life."

Ash shook the hand he extended. She had seen the video of the shooting. Even though she didn't remember more than bits and pieces yet, the video told the tale. Something had warned her. She didn't know what. But it had been enough. She had reached out and pulled the President back behind a quickly formed wall of armored

Marines. A moment later, a split-second really, she'd been struck in the chest. Fortunately, Moreau – if she had been the real would-be assassin – wasn't a long-distance shooter. If she had been, and if she'd taken a head shot, Ash wouldn't have survived.

"I was simply doing my duty, Mr. President."

"A duty you shouldn't have had to do." He frowned and then shook it off. "If I had followed my gut and announced our suspicions about Midlothian --"

"Mr. President, no," Ashlyn interrupted. "Moreau targeted me for whatever reason long ago. We also know she had her hand in the conspiracy surrounding what happened on Arterus. Whether that traces back to the Midlothians or not, we may never know. One thing is for certain. She's been working against not just me but Fuercon. If she hadn't taken her shot the other day, she would have later. Fortunately for Fuercon, she shot me instead of you, sir.

"But, just because we know she has a grudge against me, we can't ignore the fact she was at the Midlothian embassy when she took the shot. As Colonel Santiago said before your arrival, it is obvious someone at the embassy helped her. Otherwise, she'd never have been able to get to the embassy roof. The question remains, has the Midlothian government been working against Fuercon or its shadow government or someone we don't yet suspect?"

She closed her eyes and silently cursed. Her injuries were working against her again. Her pain level had increased and, when she'd tried to sit up the last time, she'd moved wrong and aggravated her injuries. Sweat pricked out on her forehead and she reached up to wipe it away. As she did, she saw her mother watching her in concern.

"Ash?" Elizabeth didn't say anything else. She didn't need to.

"I'm all right." She prayed her mother understood she needed another few minutes to finish this before agreeing to another round of pain meds. "What are you going to do now, Mr. President?"

For a moment, Harper didn't answer. He didn't need to. His expression said it all. He wanted blood. Ashlyn understood, just as she understood what happened to her was only a small part of it.

Their world, their system and their allies had been betrayed by a government they had trusted. Harper wasn't going to let that go unchallenged.

"I'll be addressing the press when I leave here, Ashlyn," he said. "It is time for everyone to understand Fuercon isn't going to stand idly by while her best interests are attacked or betrayed."

She expected him to explain, but he didn't. Instead, he smiled down at her, pride reflected in his eyes. "Ash, I am giving you an order as your president. Get well. We need you back on the line, not in a bed and not behind a desk. If we are to win this war once and for all, we need you and your Marines. Will you do that for me?"

"Ooh-rah, sir."

"Ooh-rah, indeed, Colonel." He patted her shoulder and nodded in approval. "General Okafor, I do believe you have eyes on the Midlothian embassy."

"I have, sir."

"Instruct them they no longer have to be hidden. When you do, send reinforcements. I want a very clear statement made that we will protect those on Fuerconese soil. I also want the Midlothians to understand that they are, in reality, prisoners in their own embassy."

"Understood, Mr. President."

"Very well." He looked back at Ashlyn. "Colonel Shaw – Ashlyn, you have once again given much to Fuercon. I offer you not only my thanks but the thanks of your homeworld. Now get some rest and do as the doctors say."

Before she could respond, he turned and left the room, the door sliding closed behind him.

"We'll let you rest now, Ash," Okafor said and motioned Santiago to the door. "Elizabeth, briefing at 1600."

"Yes, ma'am." She waited until only she and Ash remained. "Now, young lady, you are going to lie back and rest."

Hurting too badly to argue, Ash nodded. As she closed her eyes, she listened to her mother as she told the nurse she needed her pain meds. "Mom, I want to see the president's statement," she said softly.

"After you get some rest. I promise."

24

Caspian Bay, Midlothian

Alexander Watchman sat in the study of his home. On the wall in front of him, the holo screen replayed Harper's press conference. In the upper right corner of the screen four smaller images were displayed. Seeing them, Watchman's anger ratcheted up. The fools! They'd failed him just as Moreau had. The woman's image was displayed in the upper left corner of the screen. Damn them. Damn them all.

"Ladies and gentlemen, to say I hope the cooperation we have received from Ambassador Kalmár and his staff reflects the true sentiment of the Midlothian government toward Fuercon and her allies, we will be proceeding with caution. The four men whose images are currently displayed were captured by members of the Combined Allied Attack Force in the Alpha Rhogana System. They have been confirmed to be members of the Midlothian Navy and Army. We are currently conducting an in-depth investigation to determine whether or not their government was aware of their actions or not.

"But that is not the important news I wish to tell you," Harper said and, as if on cue, the images disappeared from the screen. "The Combined Allied Attack Force struck deep inside Callusian territory and delivered a decisive message to the enemy . . .."

Watchman silenced the audio. He had already listened to it twice. Repetition didn't make the message any easier to take. Damn Moreau. She managed to screw this assignment up every way she could. If he didn't know better, he'd swear she had done it on purpose, even knowing what he would do to her for failing. He also knew he had to move and move quickly or he would become his government's sacrificial lamb. It wouldn't matter that everything he did, he did for Midlothian. The cowards in power would hand him over to Fuercon to keep Harper from declaring war against them.

Well, he was no one's patsy. He had planned for this eventuality and would be gone before they acted. He'd learned one important lesson where they were concerned. They took no action without debating it to death. By the time they decided they needed to talk to him, much less do anything more serious, he would be off-planet. It would take time, but he would finish this mission he'd set for himself. Now he simply had to deal with it himself.

The war might not be over, but the first battle went to Fuercon. He planned on making sure the next one went to Midlothian, even if the government didn't know it. Then, when the time was right, he'd return and take his rightful place on the ruling council and Midlothian would finally wield the power it deserved.

REQUEST FROM THE AUTHOR

It has long been said that the best form of advertising is word of mouth. That is especially true when it comes to books. Friends and family members trust reviews and suggestions for books that come from people they know.

That word of mouth goes even further in this digital age. If you enjoyed this book, do me a favor. Spread the word. Tell people on your various social media accounts. Leave a review on Amazon. If you're a blogger, write a post about it. All that does help. Besides, it is the one way we, as authors, know you really enjoyed our work.

Thanks!

AUTHOR'S NOTE

When I started *Vengeance from Ashes*, the first book in the *Honor and Duty* series, I had envisioned the series consisting of three books. By the time I got to the second book, *Duty from Ashes*, I realized Ashlyn Shaw's story arc could not be finished in just three books. Well, it could but the last book would turn out to be at least 200,000 words. That doesn't seem like much in an e-book, but in print it could be used as part of your weight training.

Fire from Ashes is nearing the end of the current story arc. That doesn't mean there won't be more stories in the *Honor and Duty* universe. There will be. I love these characters too much to say goodbye to them just yet

www.ingramcontent.com/pod-product-compliance
Lightning Source LLC
Chambersburg PA
CBHW031132210626
46816CB00014B/233